JUDITH GOULD

TIME TO SAY GOODBYE

WARNER BOOKS

A *Warner* Book

First published in the United States of America by Dutton in 2000
First published in Great Britain in 2000 by
Little, Brown and Company (UK)
This edition published by Warner Books in 2001

Copyright © Judith Gould 2000

The moral right of the author has been asserted.

A CIP catalogue record for this book
is available from the British Library.

ISBN 0 7515 2963 X

Typeset by Palimpsest Book Production Limited,
Polmont, Stirlingshire
Printed and bound in Great Britain by
Clays Ltd, St Ives plc

Warner Books
A Division of
Little, Brown and Company (UK)
Brettenham House
Lancaster Place
London WC2E 7EN

www.littlebrown.co.uk

FT
Pbk

This book is dedicated with love to three of the Gallaher musketeers:

Joyce Rucker
Suzie Bissell
and
Robert W. Gallaher

A thing of beauty is a joy forever:
Its loveliness increases; it will never
Pass into nothingness; but still will keep
A bower quiet for us, and a sleep
Full of sweet dreams, and health, and
    quiet breathing.

—JOHN KEATS, *Endymion*, Bk. I

ACKNOWLEDGMENTS

The author gratefully acknowledges the kind help of Terry Root, proprietor of The Orchid Zone in Moss Landing, California, for the personal tour of his extraordinary facility and the tidbits he passed along to me from his vast store-house of knowledge about orchids. Any mistakes regarding orchids are my own. And, as always, thanks are due to Nancy Austin and Bill Cawley for their countless kindnesses, not least of which was introducing me to the wonders of Santa Cruz County, California.

TIME TO SAY GOODBYE

The End as the Beginning
Early Fall 2000

The weather was peculiar for this time of year. Perhaps, the man thought, it was in deference to the occasion. The sun was virtually obscured in the overcast autumn sky, only the palest milky specter breaking through the cloud cover. The fog shrouded the landscape amid its moist swirls, making even the majestic redwoods appear to be ghostly apparitions.

A small shell-encrusted vase had been made especially for the occasion. Filled with the remains.

A whole lifetime reduced to a handful of ashes, he thought.

The man turned to his companion. His handsome features did not conceal the unbearable loss and pain that he felt, hard as he tried to mask them, but he straightened his shoulders and they began the short walk to their car. He opened the door for her, then walked around and slid in on the driver's side, carefully placing the vase on the seat next to him. He started the car, backed out, and began the drive over to the coast, then south, down to Big Sur.

The drive was silent but for the occasional sigh or a choked sob from the passenger seat, a sound that barely registered on the man's consciousness, absorbed as he was with his loss and the task at hand. As if to cloak his sorrow, the fog obscured the beauty of the wildly dramatic coastline, offering only an occasional view of the precipitous headlands and narrow canyons, the rocky outcrops and marine terraces. It wreathed the pines and cypresses, enveloped the heights of the gnarled live oaks and ancient redwoods, and congealed the coast's special light into a pearlescent gray.

Nearing their destination, he slowed the car, searching for the turnoff. It was not well marked and all but invisible in the fog. Then, suddenly, there it was to the right. Sycamore Canyon Road. He hit the brakes and swerved onto the road, jogging her out of her reverie, but she swallowed her fright, maintaining the silence.

He pressed the button to roll down his window, and the car was filled with the relentless roar of the surf crashing on the rocky shore. *This is a place that begs for tragedy*, he thought, *despite its great beauty or perhaps because of it*. He slowed to a snail's pace, suddenly reluctant to do what he had come here to do. He parked, turned the ignition off, then stared straight ahead into the swirling fog. After a few moments he turned to her.

'I won't be long,' he said. Without waiting for a response, he got out of the car and reached back in to retrieve the shell-encrusted vase. Then he began the lonely walk to the beach, his precious cargo in the crook of his arm.

His long strides brought him to the edge of a granite and sandstone outcrop. He stopped and looked around to get his bearings. Through the vaporous tendrils of fog, he could make out the familiar path down through the rocks, and in the distance the deep indigo of the sea.

This is a truly magical place, he thought, *all crashing waves, sea caves, and arches. A place of grandeur and mystery and aching beauty.*

And now it is to be her final resting place.

With that thought, he took a deep breath, the salty sea air filling his lungs. The path, he knew, was narrow and steep, dangerous in places. With his lips set in a line of grim determination and the vase clutched securely against his chest, he began his descent, carefully picking his way over the barren rocks, down to the sea. His muscular body was constrained by the suit he'd worn to the memorial service, but he didn't think of it. The numbness that had carried him through the last few days saw him down the path toward the sea and his inevitable duty.

When he finally reached the shore, he saw that no one else was about. He was alone with her. He planted his feet in the sand and glanced out at an invisible horizon, then north, south, and back up at the rocky outcrop down which he had just climbed. Shifting his gaze back to the south, he began walking. It was only about fifty yards or so to the spot she had chosen, the spot that he knew so well in his mind's eye, as she had. The wind whipped against his jacket and tie, blew salty spume in his eyes, and danced madly in his hair, but he ignored it, concentrating on his destination.

Reaching the place, he looked about him again, then nodded with satisfaction.

This is it, he thought.

He waded out into the water, not caring about the shock of its icy chill. He shifted the vase from the crook of his arm to his hands and looked down at it.

How do you say good-bye to someone who was so full of life? Who found life endlessly curious and amusing, sometimes mysterious, but always interesting? Someone who had never tired of taking chances with him, of risking her all for him? Someone with whom he had shared so much passion? So much love?

Her life had been stolen away and now she was but ashes. Tears began to form in his eyes, and as he removed the lid from the vase, they slid unchecked down his cheeks.

He lifted the vase up, up to the heavens, letting the wind pick up the ashes – *her ashes* – and scatter them hither and yon.

'Good-bye, my love,' he whispered. 'Good-bye.'

At that moment the sun broke through the clouds

and shone down, bathing him and the sea in an ethereal light, and he imagined that he saw her ashes swirl heavenward, toward that golden light above this magical place. Suddenly blinded, he lowered the vase to his waist. Then he took it in one powerful bronzed hand, and drawing his arm back, heaved it in an arch to the sea, where it splashed in the water, bobbing only a moment before disappearing. It would disintegrate along with her ashes.

He walked back onto the sandy shore, looking up at the rocky outcrop. The climb back up would be a chore, not the joyous trip that it had always been with her, but he strode toward it on soaked feet.

How do I go on living? he wondered.

When he reached the top of the rocky outcrop, he stopped to catch his breath. He shrugged out of his jacket, soaked with sweat from his exertions and the heat of the sun, and threw it across his shoulder. Turning, he looked back out to sea. The fog had completely rolled away, and the sun burned bright and hot. A thin line of haze demarcated the horizon in the far distance, and close in to the shore, he could see happily frolicking sea otters in the water.

She loved them so much, he thought, remembering her delight when they'd stop to watch the otters that splashed all along the coast here. But today he took no pleasure in watching them, unable as he was to share the joy with her.

How do I go on living? he wondered anew, feeling a sadness such as he had never known. But the sea, usually

5

a source of pleasure, of solace, of healing even, held no answers for him. It continued its eternal rise and fall on the sandy shoreline.

He trudged on down the road, alone in the unbearable silence.

BOOK ONE

Joanna and Josh
Spring and Summer 2000

1

Joanna Cameron Lawrence applied the brakes and slowed her elderly but immaculate Mercedes convertible to a crawl, carefully turning onto the narrow, twisting road that led up into the Santa Cruz Mountains. She'd been on the road before, but it had been a long time. Not long enough for her to forget that it was exceedingly dangerous, however, like the road to her own house in Aptos, nearby in the mountains.

Although it had two narrow lanes – in theory at least – in many places part of the road was washed out due to the inevitable mud slides during the heavy winter rains. Because the slides often left a mere sliver of blacktop, stop signs announced impending washouts so that traffic hopefully could come and go on the single remaining lane without major collisions.

She inhaled the cool, eucalyptus-scented air. To her left the mountain rose straight up from the road, its side adorned with houses that clung to it perilously. To her right, a ravine – a small canyon really – plunged dramatically, in places a hundred feet or more deep, to a creek that rose and fell with the seasons. Cypress trees, towering redwoods, eucalyptus, and pines created a canopy that permitted the sun to enter only at intervals.

Across the ravine, perched like commodious bird-houses on the mountainside opposite, she spotted occasional houses, rustic cottages most of them. They were isolated from one another, placed on large, almost vertical pieces of property. Most of them were reached by footbridges, some of which had been washed out in the winter floods – or dislodged by the periodic earthquake – and hung limply into the ravine. The inhabitants of these magical cottages had to park somewhere on this side of the ravine, then walk across the bridges to their homes.

They must be an intrepid breed, she decided, and she liked that about them. They dared to be different, to deal with all sorts of inconveniences to live in this dramatic setting.

She looked at the house numbers on the roadside mailboxes and saw that she was nearing her destination. The woman she was going to see had told her there was room to park – just – near her footbridge.

On the right she saw a big old rusty cream Jeep

Wagoneer, parked on the narrow shoulder off the road. It was the car the woman had told her to look for. Joanna slowed down and eased over onto the shoulder behind the Wagoneer, creeping as close to it as possible. She put on her parking brake and killed the engine.

Looking into the rearview mirror, she grabbed a brush from her big leather and canvas carryall and quickly ran it through her wind-tousled hair. There, that's good enough, she thought, inspecting it in the mirror once again. Then, grabbing her carryall, she threw her car keys into it, slung it across her shoulder, and slid out of the silver sports car.

I'll leave the top down, she decided. It's not going to rain, and it's nice and shady here so the interior won't get too hot. Plus, it ought to be safe.

She walked around the Wagoneer to the footbridge, and stood staring at it for long moments. It was about sixty feet across to the other side, and if there was anything in the world Joanna Lawrence feared, it was heights.

Oh, jeez, Joanna, she thought, cringing inside, *you've done it now, old girl. You have to walk across this thing. High up in the air over that deep, deep ravine. Nothing below your feet but a few puny-looking old boards.*

Taking a deep breath, she slowly put her right foot out onto the bridge, and at the same time she grabbed hold of the rustic wooden railing with all her might. She followed suit with her left foot, then stood still for a moment, exhaling. She could feel the bridge move slightly under her weight. She could also hear it creak.

11

Oh, Lord, she prayed, *protect me now!*

She remembered that someone had once told her to stare straight ahead under such circumstances – don't look down whatever you do! – and proceed slowly and steadily. Easier said than done.

She took another deep breath, looked firmly at the adorable cottage on the other side, and moved one foot in front of the other, slowly at first, then faster, faster, holding her breath and white-knuckling it all the way.

Reaching the other side, she stopped and shivered with relief. The short – but oh, so long! – trip was over. She turned slightly and looked back at the ravine. *Harmless*, she told herself. She hated this irrational fear, any kind of fear, but had never learned to conquer it. Straightening her shoulders, she glanced over at the cottage.

Like the footbridge, it was a gingerbread structure of batten board, weathered the color of the bark on the pines around it, with dark green shutters. Window boxes held cheerful red geraniums. The cedar-shingled roof was weathered a silvery brown, and the stone chimney and foundation were covered with moss and lichen. Fretwork decorated the eaves and the screened-in front porch, and vines grew all over the little house. A narrow stone path, which led to the front door, was bordered by all kinds of shade-loving shrubbery.

What a lovely, romantic place, Joanna thought.

She walked up the stone path to the front door. There was no doorbell, so she lifted the door knocker, a shiny brass pineapple that denoted hospitality, and knocked twice.

The door was opened almost immediately by a tall, slim woman about her own age, early thirties. She had sandy, shoulder-length hair and bright, alert eyes the color of tortoiseshell, a rich brown shot through with a golden yellow and amber. High cheekbones, beautifully arched eyebrows, a straight nose, and full, sensual lips were set off by healthy, very lightly tanned skin.

'Mrs Lawrence?' she asked with a friendly smile. Her lively eyes took in Joanna's crisp oyster linen blouse, matching trousers, and espadrilles. Casual but elegant.

'Joanna, please,' the visitor said.

'And I'm April Woodward,' the woman said. 'Come on in.'

She held the door wide, and Joanna stepped into the cottage. In the tiny entrance foyer, she noticed a wrought-iron stand, filled with assorted umbrellas, some with amusing animal heads as handles, and walking sticks of various lengths. A small pine console, over which a simple pine mirror hung, held a Staffordshire bowl with keys. On the floor was a kilim rug, old, faded, and multicolored.

'Joanna,' April asked, 'would you like something to drink? There's green tea, and I have some mineral water.'

'Oh, I love green tea,' Joanna replied. 'If it's no trouble.'

April shook her head. 'None at all,' she said. 'Sugar? Honey? Sweetener?'

'A touch of honey would be perfect,' Joanna said.

'Make yourself comfortable,' April said. 'I'll be right back.'

Joanna watched her stroll out of the room, noticing that April wore no-nonsense khakis, a pinstriped shirt, and loafers. Joanna headed for the big, comfortable-looking sofa in front of the stone fireplace, and sank into its deep cushions. She liked the feel of its slipcover fabric, which looked like natural linen.

She placed her carryall on the floor and glanced around the small room. It was paneled in knotty pine with built-in bookshelves that were filled to bursting with all sorts of books, well read from the looks of them. The big stone fireplace dominated one wall. It was a warm, cozy, and inviting room, to her mind in the best of taste. *Charming, simple, and unpretentious*, she thought. *Like April herself appears to be. A wonderfully romantic cottage, but not cloyingly sweet or overdone. Not extravagantly expensive either.*

April appeared with a small tray. On it were a teapot, cups, saucers, and a pot of honey. She sat it on the coffee table, then took a seat on the stone hearth.

'You didn't have to go to so much trouble,' Joanna protested.

'It's no trouble,' April replied. 'I enjoy doing it.' She poured their tea, put a small dollop of honey in each, and handed Joanna hers.

'Thanks, April,' she said.

'You're welcome.' April smiled and took a sip of the tea. 'Now, then,' she said. 'Let me get this straight. You told me you're interested in doing a sort of grotto?' She looked at Joanna with curiosity.

Joanna nodded. 'Yes,' she said. 'I've brought some pictures with me. I tore some of them out of magazines, and some of them are color Xeroxes from books I've got. They'll give you an idea of the sort of thing I have in mind.'

She set her tea down on the table and reached into her carryall, pulling out a large manila envelope. 'I guess it sounds a little crazy,' she went on as she opened the envelope and extracted the pictures, 'but I think you'll see what I mean.'

She handed the pictures to April, who slowly looked through them, one by one. When she was finished, she put the pictures down on the coffee table and smiled.

'These are fabulous,' she said excitedly, her tortoise-shell eyes sparkling. She tapped the pictures with a hand. 'And you're really serious about this?'

'Absolutely,' Joanna said, returning her smile. She was gratified that the pictures had excited April. 'I saw the fountain and garden walls you did at Ingrid and Ronald Wilson's house, and I loved them. They have such a sense of fantasy about them.'

'Thanks a lot,' April said.

'Anyway, something told me that you could do this,' Joanna said.

'Amazing,' April said. 'Nobody does this sort of thing anymore.'

'*I* do,' Joanna said, laughing. 'At least I want to. Even if it is a little crazy. There's this old stone building on

15

our property that used to be a stable. It's not too big, but it has a great view of the mountains.'

'A grotto's usually a cave, isn't it?' April said. 'Or like a cave.'

Joanna nodded. 'Yes, in the strictest sense. But I want this to be a sort of garden pavilion, not a real grotto. I guess I call it that because I want the whole room encrusted with seashells and pebbles. Walls, floor, and ceiling. With murals and architectural detail. Like the rooms you see in these pictures.'

April clapped her hands and laughed again. 'This is wonderful,' she enthused.

Joanna smiled. 'But I don't want to copy the pictures,' she said. 'I want us to come up with a plan of our own.' She paused and looked over at April. 'Hear that? I've already got you saying yes to the project, don't I?' she continued.

April smiled.

'Anyway, I have a few ideas. My husband and I are in the orchid business, and I want the murals to reflect that. You know, orchid murals made out of seashells and pebbles, that sort of thing?' She looked at April questioningly.

April took a sip of her tea, then set it down. 'Why don't I show you my portfolio?' she said matter-of-factly. 'I think you ought to have an idea of the kind of things I've done.'

'That would be great,' Joanna said.

'Excuse me just a minute,' April said. 'I'll just run and get it.'

As she left the room, Joanna noticed small water-colors on the walls that she hadn't seen before, and got up to look at them. There were several beach scenes, the dunes and sea, and some landscapes, featuring the local mountains.

April came back into the living room, carrying a large leather folder. 'Oh, I see you've discovered my little hobby,' she said. 'Or one of them.'

'They're lovely,' Joanna said. 'Really lovely.'

'Thanks,' April said, looking at them with a maternal eye. 'I'm working on botanicals now. Local flora. I'll show them to you before you leave if you like.'

'I'd love to see them,' Joanna replied. 'I love botanicals. In fact, I have a few in the car that I'm getting framed.'

'Really?' April said. 'Well, anyhow, in the meantime, let me show you some of the work I've done with shells and stones.'

They sat back down, both of them on the sofa, and April put the big portfolio down on the coffee table. She opened it and began flipping pages, showing Joanna photographs and drawings of various projects she'd worked on.

'This is fantastic,' Joanna said, pointing to a garden path created entirely of little pebbles set in elaborate patterns.

'Ummm . . . thanks,' April murmured. 'As you can see I haven't done a great deal, at least not with seashells, and most of it has been outdoors. Terraces, walls, paths, fountains, and such. But a lot of this work is along the same lines as what you're thinking about. Creating a formal layout, then designing the patterns to fill it in. Sometimes with tile and stone. Whatever people want.' She looked at Joanna. 'I'm sure I could do the same thing with seashells and stone. I have done one room sort of like you're talking about, but I don't have pictures.'

'Why's that?' Joanna asked.

'The client was this enormously rich man in Los Angeles,' she said, 'and he didn't want any photos taken. He didn't want them "leaked," as he put it. He was a little paranoid, I think.'

'You must deal with all sorts of people,' Joanna said.

'Oh, yes,' April replied.

Joanna nodded, then looked back down at the portfolio again. 'I see that some of your work is neoclassical, some of it's baroque or rococo.'

'Whatever the client wants,' April said with a smile. 'But I do try to put as much of myself into the work as possible. Making suggestions and such.'

'Well,' Joanna said, looking back up, 'I like what I see very much, April. The work is truly beautiful. I could go on all day about it, but I know you've heard it all before.'

She paused and took a sip of her tea. 'Do you think you'd be interested in my grotto?' she asked.

April nodded. 'Definitely,' she said, 'but I would like to have a look at the building first.'

'Great,' Joanna said enthusiastically. 'I just know it'll work out.'

She ran a hand through her hair, looking thoughtfully off into the distance. Then she turned her gaze to April. 'I've been collecting shells and pebbles for years. I have boxes and boxes and . . . well, you wouldn't believe!'

She laughed, her violet eyes dancing with light. 'You'll probably think I'm crazy when you see. Anyway, I've got catalogues from wholesalers, so I could order whatever we don't have that we need.'

'From the sound of it,' April said, 'the catalogues will come in handy, because this project is going to take a lot. Probably more than you realize. But, of course, I need to see the building first to get a better idea.'

'Well,' Joanna said, 'you can see it anytime that's convenient with you. How about tomorrow? I'd like to get started as soon as possible. That is, if you agree to take it on.'

'Let me check my appointment book,' April said. She rose to her feet. 'Why don't you come on back to the studio with me? You can look at those botanicals I was talking about.'

'Great,' Joanna said. She got up and followed April down a short hallway and into a small, high-ceilinged room that Joanna thought was probably added on to the cottage as a conservatory or garden room. It had windows on three sides, with French doors allowing access to the garden, and the ceiling was almost entirely skylights. It had been designed to allow as much natural light as possible. The room was dominated by a large worktable covered with jars filled with artist's tools: brushes, pencils, pens, charcoal, and such. Watercolor paper in various sizes lay helter-skelter all over it, and books were piled all around. Rolled-up blueprints filled tall urns, and little vases of flowers were everywhere. An enormous easel had a small watercolor in progress clipped to it. Some sort of flower, Joanna noticed.

'What a wonderful room,' she said.

'The heart of the house,' April replied, picking up her leather appointment book and flipping to the correct page. She studied it for a moment, then looked over at Joanna. 'Tomorrow's fine,' she said. 'Anytime you like.'

'How about around noontime, then?' Joanna asked. 'We could look over the building and have a bite of lunch?'

'Lunch?' April hesitated a moment, then smiled. 'Sure,' she said, 'why not?'

'About twelve-thirty, one-ish, then?' Joanna said.

'Okay,' she said. 'I'll be there.'

'Is this one of your botanicals?' Joanna asked, indicating the watercolor on the easel.

'Oh, yes,' April replied. 'Obviously not finished. This is a type of verbena. I've got the correct name written down.'

'I love the detail,' Joanna said, looking at it closely. 'Oh, and I love the little bugs you've put on it. How clever!'

April blushed slightly. 'Thanks,' she said. 'Let me show you some finished ones.' She opened a large leather portfolio on the table and started flipping pages.

Joanna drew up to the table beside her and looked

through it. 'They're really lovely,' she said. 'My favorite thing, though, is your imagination. Doing the flowers so correctly, then adding the little bugs and dewdrops and things.'

'Doing the flowers right is the easy part,' April said. 'It's making them interesting that's the difficult part. Hence my little additions.'

Joanna smiled. 'I'm so glad to see you enjoy doing these,' she said. 'Especially since I want to incorporate some of our orchids into the grotto.'

'It's a brilliant idea,' April said.

'I hope so,' Joanna said in a self-deprecating voice. 'Sometimes my ideas don't work out very well, but Ingrid Wilson assured me that you would at least understand me.'

'I don't think that'll be a problem,' April said.

'I don't either,' Joanna said. 'I can see by the way that you live – I mean, the way you've decorated your cottage and all – that we have very similar ideas and tastes. I meet very few people like that.'

'Surprised?' April asked with a little laugh.

'Sort of,' Joanna said honestly. 'And Ingrid told me you'd been married to Roger Woodward, that famous actor. So I guess I expected somebody more ... oh, I don't know ...'

'More glamorous?' April supplied, smiling. 'Somebody more Hollywood and with it?'

Joanna reddened slightly, then nodded. 'I guess you're right,' she said. 'Isn't that awful of me?'

'No,' April said. 'It happens a lot ... when people

find out I was married to Roger.' She looked at Joanna with a serious expression. 'But that was another world, a lifetime ago. Now I have a life that's entirely of my own making, and I like it very much.'

'That's wonderful,' Joanna said. 'I don't think many people can say that.' She paused, then said: 'I guess I'd better get on my way. It's been wonderful to meet you, and to see your house. It's so charming.'

'I look forward to tomorrow,' April said, smiling somewhat shyly.

'I'll just get my bag,' Joanna said, turning toward the hallway.

In the living room, Joanna picked up her carryall and slung it over her shoulder. 'Would you like to keep the pictures to study?' she asked. 'Or should I take them home with me?'

'If you could leave them, that'd be great,' April said.

'That's fine,' Joanna said, and went to the front door. She turned to April. 'See you tomorrow.'

April opened the door. 'Yes, see you then,' she said.

''Bye, April, and thanks,' Joanna said, starting down the little stone path to the footbridge.

''Bye,' April said. She closed the door, then glanced out a window, watching Joanna approach the bridge and cautiously step onto it, holding on to the railing for dear life.

What a lovely, lovely but odd *woman Joanna Lawrence is,* April thought. *And what an exciting but odd project she's come up with.*

Odd and wonderful, she thought, shaking her head.

Little did April know that her life was about to be changed forever by Joanna Lawrence.

Joanna reached her Mercedes and, leaning over, heaved her carryall onto the passenger seat. Then she opened the door and slid in. She threw her head back and took several deep breaths, trying to calm her racing heart. She could feel her pulse beating against her ear.

The trip back across the rustic footbridge had been no less frightening than the first time, and now, added to her adrenaline-generated fear, was the spark of excitement that coursed throughout her body.

After a few minutes her breathing began to slow and her heartbeat gradually returned to normal. She tested her hands on the steering wheel. They didn't shake, although they felt somehow electrified. She strapped on her seat belt, then extricated her sunglasses from her carryall and put them on.

She started the car, its powerful motor purring expensively. Then she carefully backed up on the thin shoulder and, after looking both ways, turned around on the narrow road.

She drove slowly, the wind whipping her hair about her face, the cool, scented air refreshing, stabilizing, although she still felt the excitement of her discovery coursing through her. The mountain's almost sheer side rose to her right, and the ravine, like a gigantic scar in the earth, lay on her left. She gradually picked up speed as she felt more confident of her driving. She had been negotiating these roads all of her life and had never had an accident.

Today won't be any different, she told herself, but then she remembered that so much had been different lately, that, in fact, her whole life had irrevocably changed.

Suddenly she laughed into the wind, tapping the steering wheel lightly with her hand. *You never know what fate has in store for you.* She shivered with excitement. She was watching the road ahead, but all she could see was the face and long, lean body of April Woodward shimmering before her in the dappled sunlight like some sort of chimera, enticing, alluring, and seductive, those tortoiseshell eyes of hers like a siren's call.

I think I've found her, she told herself. *At long last.*

She abruptly realized that she had reached the bottom of the mountain and would be back in lots of traffic, not far from the road that would take her back up into the mountains, back up to her own mountaintop aerie. But she wasn't going home yet. No, not now. She would go on down to Capitola, to a little custom framing shop she had used before, and finally get those botanicals properly matted and framed.

She headed north on the expressway, then took the Capitola exit, cruising slowly down into the little beachside village, chock-a-block with its lovely pastel Victorian cottages. She spotted the framing shop on the little main street and pulled over and parked. Reaching behind her seat, she retrieved the heavy folder that she'd stored the botanicals in.

A bell tinkled when she opened the door to the little shop. But, looking around, she didn't see Woody. She began looking at the hundreds of framing choices, many of them mounted on the walls, others glued to heavy board on large revolving racks. She bent over to look at an interesting piece of molding in a stack propped against the wall, and suddenly felt as if someone were watching her. She jerked up and looked around.

A young man stood regarding her, his darkly tanned muscular arms folded across his chest. His dark eyes traveled up and down her body, and Joanna felt herself blush under the weight of his assessing gaze.

He's undressing me, she thought, *or he sure seems to be.* He had done this on the several other occasions she had come, and she supposed she should feel flattered, but it made her uncomfortable. At least he knew his business.

'Oh, hello,' she said. 'I didn't see you when I came in.'

'I was in the back,' Woody said, maintaining his pose.

'I've got some botanical prints,' Joanna said, indicating her big folder. 'Six of them, and I want them matted and framed identically.'

Woody's demeanor changed to one more appropriate to a shopkeeper. 'Let's have a look. Over here.' He turned and walked over to a large, well-lit table.

Joanna followed him to the table and began pulling the prints out of the folder. She spread them out, then looked over at him.

'Nice,' he said, nodding his shaggy black curls. He came around to her side of the table to get a better look. 'Yeah, real nice.'

'We're in the orchid business, you see,' she said, 'and these are hand-colored prints from about 1815. I'd like to put them in my husband's—'

Suddenly she felt the heat and weight of his body press against hers and the light but definite brush of his hand across her buttocks.

Joanna turned steely eyes on him, and said, 'Stop that. Please.'

There was a smirk on his face. 'Hey,' he said, spreading his hands wide in a 'Who me?' gesture. 'Don't get the wrong idea. I didn't mean anything.'

She quickly gathered her prints and placed them in the folder, then turned to leave. 'I think I'll have somebody else do these,' she said, and headed toward the door.

'You do that,' the young man said in a snarl as she opened the door.

As she stepped out, she heard him add: 'Bitch.'

Joanna hurried to her car and got in, stowing the folder behind her seat. *What a bastard!* she thought, ignoring the Victorian charms of the little village as she headed back toward the expressway. He wasn't like that before.

But as she sped homeward, toward Aptos, her thoughts turned from the unpleasantness of the encounter to April Woodward.

April, she thought, *is the right physical type.* Tall, slim, and elegant, but not hard or brittle-looking. She wasn't a fashion victim striving too hard for chic. She simply had *it*. Her sandy hair, probably once blond, was well-cut, and those tortoiseshell eyes of hers were beguiling. Her features, while not traditionally pretty or beautiful, were striking. And her bearing, her attitudes and interests! They couldn't have been more perfect. She was extremely creative, but down to earth – a very important quality in the young woman she'd been looking for.

Still, Joanna thought, *there's no way to predict what will happen, whether or not she's actually perfect for my plan.* But something told her she wouldn't be disappointed. *April Woodward seems like the perfect young woman for what I have in mind.*

Joshua Lawrence was in the Stud Room, a small enclosure inside the greenhouse. Perched on a high metal stool, hunched over a wooden table, his sun-bleached hair falling forward into his ultramarine eyes, he was completely lost to the rest of the world, all of his powers of concentration on the task at hand.

The end of a toothpick projected from his mouth, rotating slowly as he maneuvered it around, gathering as much of his saliva as he could. After a few moments he extracted the toothpick from his mouth and held it up to the light with one latex-gloved hand. The toothpick gleamed in the light with a thick coat of his saliva.

'Ah, good,' he said aloud, although there was no one

around to hear him. His sensuous lips parted in a smile, and he nodded with satisfaction.

On the table where he worked were two rare and beautiful orchid plants, one of them a prize *Paphiopedilum* Screaming Eagle, the other a *Paphiopedilum* of a different sort. Quickly but delicately he began using the saliva-wet toothpick to pick up and transfer minuscule pollen capsules from one *Paphiopedilum* parent plant to the other.

Sex, he thought with wry amusement. *There's nothing quite like it.* For, in principle, that is what was happening. He was fertilizing one plant with the pollen of another.

It was a somewhat tedious process, the old-fashioned pollination process, requiring great patience and a skilled hand. But it was the only way to pollinate *Paphiopedilums*. They couldn't be propagated by tissue culture, a quick method that worked for many orchids. However, this old-fashioned, tedious work and the long wait for results – anywhere from six to eighteen years for the finished flower – was well worth the trouble. At least to Joshua Lawrence and a select clientele.

He had created some of the most extravagant orchids ever seen. With their waxy, glistening sacs, striking top sepal, and bizarre markings and colors, they had become much sought after by collectors the world over. While there were many other hybridizers, his hybrids were considered among the best, with large flowers, flattened petals, luscious folds, erect columns, hairs, warts, spots, and veins – all in extraordinary color combinations from the purest whites to near black.

He put the toothpick back in his mouth, working more saliva onto it. He wanted to make certain that he got plenty of pollen on the plant. Glancing idly at his watch, he noticed that it was lunchtime, and Joanna hadn't called him on the intercom they used here at home.

Strange, he thought. *She should have called by now, and she's usually so prompt, so efficient. Besides, she likes to hang out and watch me mate the plants.*

He was working in the small greenhouse in back of their mountaintop home, and usually ate lunch with Joanna when he was working there. This was a special greenhouse, distinct from the vast commercial ones they owned down in the valley. For it was here, close to home, that they kept some of the rarest, and therefore most expensive, of their orchid plants. They were protected by an elaborate alarm system, under constant lock and key, with video cameras and lasers trained on the precious stock night and day. The security might have seemed excessive to the casual observer, but some of the plants were worth a fortune. Several were valued at twenty-five thousand dollars apiece, and the parent stock was virtually priceless.

He reached over and punched the intercom button, calling to her. Once. Twice. Three times.

No response.

What the hell?

Turning his attention back to the orchids, he repeated

the process, meticulously applying the pollen from the parent Screaming Eagle to the other parent *Paphiopedilum*. After a few minutes, he sat back up, satisfied. He stretched his back and powerful, sunbronzed arms.

Reaching over, he tried the intercom again.

Still no response.

Shit! Not even Connie's picking up.

He shoved the pollinated orchid to the back of the table and pulled another one forward. He would be repeating the pollination process with several of the *Paphiopedilums*. Taking a fresh toothpick from the little box on the table, he stuck it in his mouth, still wondering where Joanna could be.

She hasn't been herself lately, he thought, maneuvering the fresh toothpick around in his mouth. *She's been distant and withdrawn. Maybe even a little secretive. Gone for hours at a time without any explanations for her time away. Not leaving word with Connie or me. She's even been short-tempered with Connie.*

That sudden realization was the clue that something must be very wrong indeed. Joanna Lawrence would never abuse Connie Cespedes, no matter how upset, angry, or harried she might be. Connie was like a member of the family, and Joanna admired her, believing that it was the ambitious struggles of people like Connie who had made this country the great place that it is.

He examined the new toothpick in the light, and began the pollination process again, trying to concentrate, but distracted by disturbing thoughts of his wife.

What could be wrong? he wondered.

Was it simply that her irritating older sister, Christina, had recently swept in unannounced for a brief but, well, a highly irritating visit? He doubted that. Even though he and Joanna both were left exhausted by Christina, the aftereffects of her drama-filled visitations were usually short-lived, and besides, Joanna's uncharacteristic behavior had started long before Christina's latest sojourn.

Could it be financial worries? he wondered. They lived extremely well, but the business did have its ups and downs. Lately, they'd been under pressure from the Rossi brothers, their chief competitors, to sell out. They wanted their land and greenhouses badly.

He heaved another sigh. *Maybe it's something really simple*, he told himself. *Like she needs a new project to work on.* She always had to be busy working on some kind of project, never content to run the house and help with the business. She'd done a beautiful book on orchids that had been well received, but that had been finished months ago. Maybe, then, it was simply the lack of a new project?

He put the toothpick back in his mouth, slowly shaking his head. *No*, he thought. *That's not it. No way. It's not that simple.* Lately ... just the last two or three months ... if truth be told, lately she hadn't seemed very interested in him. She hadn't snapped at him like she had at Connie, but she hadn't *wanted* him either. Not like she used to, that's for sure.

He took the toothpick back out of his mouth and, like the others, examined it in the light. Satisfied, he began pollinating again. *Could it be that she's grown tired of me?* he asked himself. *Could it be something like the seven-year itch? Or did that only happen to men? Besides, they'd been married for ten years now. The ten-year itch?*

He didn't know, but he was becoming convinced that something was very, very wrong. He heaved a sigh, moving the pollinated orchid out of the way, then began the procedure on another one. *Maybe,* he thought, *maybe it's because we still don't have any children. Maybe that's it.* They both wanted children, but they'd waited a long time to try. Then when they'd stopped using birth control, just a couple of years ago, nothing happened. Finally, they'd both gone to the doctor and gotten clean bills of health. Still nothing. At least so far. And now. Well, now, she didn't seem to be interested in even trying!

Suddenly, like a poisonous snake, an evil thought crept into his consciousness. *Joanna has found someone else.* He slumped forward, putting his head in his latex-covered hands, thinking about their years of bliss together. From the moment he had laid eyes on her, he had wanted her, beautiful, fanciful, yet practical creature that she was. And the same had been true for Joanna. Or so she'd always said. And their love, he'd thought, had only grown with the mounting years. They were lovers, partners, and friends.

What the hell was happening?

At that moment the telephone rang, jarring the quiet of the greenhouse.

Josh reached over to answer it. 'Hello?' he said.

'Josh,' the Hispanic-accented voice said, 'it's Carl.'

An involuntary tremor of nervousness ran up Josh's spine. Carl never bothered him at home unless it was extremely important. 'What is it, Carl?'

'I think you'd better get down here fast,' he replied.

'What *is* it?' Josh repeated.

'Something with the misters,' he said. 'I don't know if it's the computer or what.'

'Ah, shit!' Josh swore. Without another word he replaced the receiver on the telephone, threw down his latex gloves, and ran for the car.

Christina Cameron von Leydon luxuriated on the cool cotton Pratesi sheets, a champagne silk duvet thrown tantalizingly across her ample breasts and curving down between her firm tan thighs. She gazed across her vast bedroom's Carrara marble floor with its pale ivory and pink Aubusson carpet to the bathroom door. It stood slightly ajar.

She smiled to herself with satisfaction.

He was in there, and she could hardly wait for him to come back out again.

A Dunhill cigarette in one hand, and a vodka tonic in the other, she sipped the drink, then set it down on the draped table next to her bed. She puffed on the Dunhill, patting her expensively streaked silver and blond hair

– 'A dozen different shades, at least!' she would tell those who asked – normally a perfect helmet that defied destruction, now a tousled mess. Her makeup, which had gradually become more elaborate as she had aged, was in need of repair.

But it didn't matter. No, indeed. Not today. For he was responsible for her mussed hair and messy makeup. He and his ravenous appetite for her body. A sigh of pleasure escaped her lips.

All that yoga, the personal trainers, the two face-lifts, the breast implants – and subsequent reduction – the endless miles on the treadmill and stationary bike, to say nothing of the perpetual dieting – all of it had paid off for her. In her mid-thirties, her body was still youthful and tempting.

Even to a stud like Peter Rossi, she thought.

He came out of the bathroom, and she gloried at the sight of his body – all that thick, hard muscle, tall and suntanned, that fabulous toy between his powerful legs. With his dark eyes glittering in anticipation and a cocky smile on his sensuous lips, he strode to the bed and stood over her, taking pleasure in her obvious enjoyment of his body.

Christina quickly stubbed her cigarette out in an ashtray and reached over and brushed his hardening shaft with her hand. Then, sitting up and sliding her legs over the side of the bed, she encircled his hips with her arms and stroked his hard buttocks with her hands.

'Oooo, yeah, baby,' he crooned. 'That feels so good.' He took her breasts in his big hands, stroking them hard and squeezing her nipples between thumb and forefinger.

Christina moaned with pleasure, her tongue darting out to caress his heavy balls, then lick the length and breadth of his thick shaft. It throbbed with anticipation, and she was certainly not one to disappoint. Opening her mouth wide, she took as much of it as she could, licking and sucking, licking and sucking.

Peter groaned and put his hands on her head, moving his big thighs against her mouth harder and faster, harder and faster, until he suddenly stopped, his body tensing all over. 'Wo-ow!' he gasped. 'I'm getting too close, baby. Too damn close.'

He eased out of her mouth, then reached down, one huge arm under each of hers, and lifted her up off the bed to face him. 'You're too goddamn much, Christina,' he said, smiling. 'Too goddamn much.'

He pulled her hard against him then, kissing her hungrily, his tongue delving between her lips, exploring her mouth, his hands on her breasts again, stroking and squeezing, then moving over her buttocks and between her thighs.

Christina relished his body against hers, his hands all over her, the hardness of his cock against her, and gave herself up to him utterly. She could feel her own wetness between her thighs, and ground herself against him lasciviously.

Peter pulled back for a moment, both of them breathing hard, then eased her down onto the bed, where she lay on her back, already aching for his touch again.

Smiling down at her, he crouched over her on his knees, spreading her legs wider apart, his eyes devouring her hungry mound. He leaned down and slowly began to lick her thighs, his hands on her buttocks lifting her to him. Christina's moans of pleasure urged him on and on and on, until his tongue found her most magical of places and plunged lustily inside her, ravenous for her juices.

She gasped aloud and ground herself against him, her hands entwined in his raven-black hair, her body writhing from side to side, lost in an ecstasy of carnal delight.

He suddenly stopped, withdrawing from her, breathing heavily, and she groaned at the loss of him there. But she was not to be disappointed for long because he came up on his knees, spreading her legs wide again, and she saw his engorged manhood only for a moment before he plunged inside her, farther than she thought possible, and began to pump away at her like a man possessed.

In a rapture of desire, the fires of her lust inflamed by his need for her, she instantly responded to him, matching his rhythm, her body working with his, until in a mad writhing and pumping they reached orgasm at the same time, Peter bellowing with release and Christina screaming as wave after wave of ecstasy engulfed her body in shudders. Finally, he collapsed atop her, and they both gasped for air, utterly spent, their heaving bodies coated in a sheen of sweat.

'Oh, my God!' she rasped throatily. 'Oh, my God! That . . . that was so . . . so fantastic, Peter!'

He hugged her tightly, rolling onto his side and bringing her with him, staying inside her. He held her buttocks tightly, peppering her face with kisses, still catching his breath.

'Jesus . . . Christina,' he finally gasped. 'I didn't think . . . I didn't think it could get any better . . . any better . . . than the last time.'

She laughed lightly, as thrilled with his pleasure in her as she was in her own satisfaction. 'Me either,' she said.

He kissed her on the lips, slowly easing out of her, then sat up slightly, an arm around her shoulders, and looked into her eyes. 'You're one hell of a woman,' he said.

'And you, Peter Rossi,' she said, 'are one hell of a man.'

He reached over and took her cigarettes and lighter off the bedside table, then lit one and handed it to her.

'Thanks,' she said.

He lit one for himself and blew a streamer of smoke toward the ceiling. 'Your ex-husband must be crazy,' he said. 'Why the hell would your husband go looking for another woman?'

Christina shrugged. 'You tell me,' she replied. 'I don't know.' She took a drag off her cigarette, exhaled through her nostrils, then went on. 'But I do know that he was a prick just like all the others, and I hope he's happy with his trashy little whore because she's costing him a fortune.'

41

Peter barked a laugh. 'You took him to the cleaners, huh?'

'Bet your ass,' Christina said. 'Just like the two bastards before him.'

Peter laughed again. 'Serves 'em right,' he said, stroking her arm.

Christina looked into his eyes. 'I'm sure glad we ran into each other when I was up at Joanna's this past weekend,' she said.

'Yeah, me too,' he said, returning her gaze. He crushed his cigarette into the ashtray. 'I could get used to this.' He cupped a breast with a beefy hand and began fondling it. 'I think we make a real good team.'

Christina nodded. 'Yes, but we've got to keep this our little secret, don't we?' she said, leaning over and brushing her lips across his massive chest.

'For more reasons than one,' he said.

One of her hands crept down his chest and on down his stomach to come to rest at the base of his thick, instantly responsive cock.

'Whoa,' he said. 'We better not get started again. Don't forget, I've got to get to that meeting in Santa Barbara, and a bunch of business calls to make.'

'Oh, I know,' Christina said somewhat testily, removing her hand, then putting out her cigarette.

'Don't worry, babe,' he said. 'I'll come back tonight after it's over . . . if you still want me to.' He grinned over at her.

She socked him playfully in the chest. 'You'd better be back tonight,' she said.

*   *   *

Christina had soaked in a hot, scented bath and carefully applied fresh makeup, then slipped into a long silk dressing gown. She'd made herself a fresh vodka and tonic, then stood in the living room of her splendid neoclassical mansion, slowly sipping her drink, looking out the French doors, beyond the yards upon yards of shimmering silk draperies that decorated them, toward the misty Pacific Ocean in the distance. It lay far beyond the acres of elegant, well-tended gardens with their statuary and the huge swimming pool with its columned pool house. The beautiful, expensive view offered by her hilltop setting in exclusive Montecito gave her pleasure today, despite the wounds of her latest divorce. The reason, of course, being Peter Rossi.

What serendipity, she thought. That he'd been coming to Santa Barbara on business and could help her lick her wounds. *And how!*

Today the divorce decree had been handed down by the courts, and it was all official: Christina was free – again. Husband number three was history, and like she'd told Peter, she'd taken the son of a bitch to the cleaners. But good.

Sighing expansively, she turned and padded over to the downy comfort of an ecru, silk-covered chaise longue. Shoving a pillow covered with a fragment of scratchy antique tapestry out of her way, she made herself comfortable. She took a generous sip of her vodka tonic, then set the crystal glass down on the bronze and glass Giacometti table at her side. She noticed

43

the orchid plant sitting there, resplendent in its exotic beauty. Joanna had sent it down to cheer her up.

Well, this time around, she didn't need her sister's cheering up. No, siree. This time she'd lucked out. Ordinarily, she would be suffering from the excruciating loneliness and boredom that divorce brought on, from the terrible sense of loss and defeat that seemed to engulf her in the aftermath of a marriage gone wrong. But not this time, thank God. Peter Rossi had come along just in time.

She could feel her pulse begin to race at the mere thought of him. So tall – at least six-three or -four – and with a thick, hard, muscular body – the beefy body of the football player he'd once been. Black hair. Dark brown eyes. A very young near-forty. She knew that he'd come from the wrong side of the tracks, but she also knew that he was a ruthless businessman, very ambitious, very powerful, very rich. And unscrupulous. Oh, yes, she knew that too, and with a certainty. He had a mean streak a mile long. But she found the combination – the money and power and ruthlessness – a potent aphrodisiac, irresistible and compelling.

To top it all off, she thought with an almost guilty pleasure, Peter Rossi was her sister and brother-in-law's chief competitor. They loathed and feared him. And well they should. He and his brothers had built up a huge nursery empire, starting virtually from scratch, and now they wanted Joanna and Josh's business as well.

She smiled to herself. Peter Rossi was truly forbidden fruit – and nothing could be tastier to her hungry lips.

Picking up her drink, she glanced at the orchid. A *Paphiopedilum lowii*. *How like Joanna*, she thought. *To send the orchid.*

She reached over and plucked a bloom off the orchid. It was in full flower, its showy pink and green blossoms striated in some places, freckled with darkest purple in others. *Sweet*, she thought, even though Joanna knew she wasn't really crazy about orchids. They always made her think of her youth, the compost stench of greenhouses, and their father's twin obsessions, with orchids and the land.

She shivered, revolted by the thought.

How different my sister and I are! she thought. Joanna actually shared their father's interests and took great pleasure in these repulsive plants. She was content to live in what was a provincial backwater compared with the relative sophistication of Christina's world, content to live in their father's home, to carry on his business.

Joanna, she thought. *Joanna, who's always had everything. Everything any woman could ever want. She's strikingly beautiful and supremely healthy. She has plenty of money, even if she's not enormously rich like me. She has a beautiful home, even if it's not a spectacular showplace like mine. And, most of all, she's got Josh.*

Oh, yes! Joshua Lawrence, of the tall, muscular body, the sun-bleached hair, the blue, blue eyes, the strong, masculine good looks. And the perfect disposition to go with it. His was a confident masculinity, not a swaggering macho pose.

She lay back against the down-filled lounge, her

gaze directed at the orchid but not really seeing it. She'd always secretly envied her sister her happiness with him.

Well, she thought, *I'm not so sure I envy little sister anymore. No, indeed. Josh Lawrence seems somehow like a second-stringer compared with Peter Rossi. Josh might have more class, but class isn't everything. It certainly isn't the turn-on that money and power are. Or that mean streak, either.*

She idly continued picking at the orchid, thinking about Joanna and Josh, their land and business – the land and business that used to belong to *her* father. *I think I may have gotten a raw deal when Dad died*, she decided. *Just getting money while Joanna got everything else. It seemed fair at the time, but now . . . now I'm not so sure. I think I deserved more. Yes, I should have gotten some of that land, some of the business, too.*

Christina looked over at the orchid plant Joanna had sent. Its beautiful, exotic blossoms lay in a scrunched-up pile on the table and spilled over onto the floor. She had completely deflowered it.

Yes, she decided. *It's time for me to have some of the things Joanna's always had. Starting with the right man, then . . . well, we'll see, won't we?*

4

The atmosphere in the enormous greenhouse was like that of a tropical rainforest: warm, breezy, and humid. The smell of compost, to which Josh was all but inured, permeated the air with its ripe pungency. Something was missing, however, and the lack of that one essential ingredient could destroy hundreds of thousands of dollars' worth of orchids.

Mist, Josh thought with a scowl. *There's no goddamn mist.*

The computer-operated misters that bathed the plants in a tropical rain and created the humidity necessary for their survival had malfunctioned – or been tinkered with – and they didn't know when. It might have been anytime over the weekend, from Friday afternoon to

Monday morning. And that period of time can make the difference between life and death in a fragile tropical atmosphere.

Josh stalked through the big greenhouse, looking from side to side, examining the orchid plants, surveying them for damage.

'Christina was here the past few days so I didn't drop by over the weekend. *Damn!* One of the few weekends that ever goes by that I didn't drop by here.' He looked at his manager. 'I guess we lucked out, Carl,' he said.

'Yeah,' Carl Cespedes grunted in reply. The nursery manager, an unusually tall and broad Peruvian with Indio features, followed closely on Josh's footsteps. His face, normally a mask of passivity no matter what the situation, wore a worried expression. He treated the nursery as if it were his own, and he seemed as puzzled as Josh by the recent turn of events.

They had already examined the misting equipment for mechanical problems and had found nothing amiss. Then they'd reset the computer controls, and the misting system had kicked in perfectly. The problem obviously lay in the computer. Either it had malfunctioned for some unknown reason, or someone had reset it in a deliberate attempt to let the orchids dry out.

'Thank God the shades were working,' Josh said, 'or there might have been major damage already.'

Carl grunted again, looking overhead at the automatically controlled shades that ran the length of the greenhouse. They compensated for the shadows of passing clouds, and had they malfunctioned, the plants would have received either too much or too little light.

'One big catastrophe could practically wipe us out,' Josh continued. 'And that's just what the Rossi brothers would like to see happen. So they could come in and pick up the pieces.'

Carl looked at him. 'They still trying to get you to sell?'

Josh nodded. 'Yeah,' he said, walking on. 'They won't give up. This is the only direction they can expand in.' Then he abruptly stopped in his tracks and turned to Carl. 'I still don't understand how anybody could've gotten in,' he said, looking into Carl's dark eyes. 'If somebody did. Miguel didn't hear or see *anything*?'

'No,' Carl said, shaking his head. 'I called him at home when I saw that the misters weren't working. He said he didn't hear or see anything last night. Nothing or nobody.'

Josh scratched his head. 'Damn!' he swore. 'I just can't figure it out. We're going to have to get the people in who installed that mister, and we're going to have to call the cops.'

'The cops?' Carl said.

'Absolutely,' Josh said. 'We've looked for signs of forced entry and didn't come up with anything, but maybe they will. You know, maybe they'll see something we didn't.'

'I guess so,' Carl said, not really believing it. He didn't think most of the police he'd run across would be able to find anything he hadn't, even if they tried.

49

'And call Miguel,' Josh said. 'Tell him I want to talk to him.'

'I already did. He's waiting for you in the office,' Carl said.

Josh looked surprised for a moment, then smiled and said, 'Thanks, Carl, you're thinking ahead of me.' He turned and started for the greenhouse door practically at a trot, then turned and called out: 'If anybody needs me, I'll be in the office. Making phone calls and talking to Miguel.'

Carl nodded.

Josh sprinted to the big Victorian house rising in the flat, dun-colored fields, surrounded by greenhouses. The immaculate white house looked incongruous here, a nineteenth-century piece of clapboard wedding cake, decorated with all the froufrou a skilled carpenter could conjure up, now hemmed in on all sides by high-tech twentieth-century greenhouses.

Joanna's paternal family, the Camerons, had built the house before the turn of the century and had lived there, farming the hundreds of acres surrounding it. Brussels sprouts and strawberries, then later on artichokes, had been their primary produce, as it still was for many of the farmers in this area. But Mitchell Cameron, Joanna's father, had different ideas.

Mitch had been bitten by the orchid bug, was in fact a true victim of orchidelirium, a not uncommon obsession in Victorian England. He was also a dreamer and a romantic, who had begun buying orchid stock as a teenager, built a small greenhouse, and started hybridizing, creating new orchids. After inheriting the farm from his father, he had eventually shut down the farming operation and turned exclusively to orchid growing, and after a few years, money like manna had begun to pour in.

That was when he asked the beautiful Julia Lenoir to marry him. Her family had long owned the farm adjoining his nursery, and they had known each other since they were tots. Julia had accepted with alacrity, and he had commenced on the building of their dream house, a huge shingle-style mansion in the manner of McKim, Mead, and White. But the house wasn't here in the valley, it was high in the Santa Cruz Mountains, with its cooler breezes and fantastic vistas, away from the air laden with the smells of compost, fertilizer, insecticides, and the crops themselves.

Joanna and Josh lived in that house now, and as Mitchell Cameron had done before them, they used the old Victorian homestead as an office and for storage.

Josh dashed up the wooden steps to the porch, pushed through one of the double doors, and went into the airy hallway of the house. Luna, Carl's wife, sat behind a desk, typing at a computer keyboard, a telephone held at one ear by her shoulder. Josh wondered how she did it with her long, eggplant-colored fingernails. Half-Venezuelan and half-American, Luna had been born in the States and was legal. Carl's marriage to the fiery, tempestuous virago had gotten him a green card. They had fought like cats and dogs since the day they'd met, and were deeply in love.

'Hey, boss,' she said, looking up, her heavily painted lips, also eggplant, parted in a smile that revealed dazzling white teeth.

'Hey, Luna,' he replied, 'and quit calling me boss.' He looked at her, returning her wide smile. 'Please?'

'Sure, boss,' she said, ignoring him as always. She nodded her head toward his office, her long jet-black hair swinging with the motion. 'Miguel's in there,' she said, 'waiting for you.'

'Thanks, Luna.' He turned and walked to the glass-paned French doors that led to what had once been a parlor. Opening one, he went in and saw Miguel sitting in a chair. He was engrossed, playing with Lucy, the gray and white cat that lived in the house.

Josh took a seat behind his desk and looked over at Miguel. He was a short, wiry Mexican in his thirties. He was probably mentally retarded – Josh wasn't really sure – but he was very slow on the uptake in any case. The child of migrant laborers, he'd been given work by Josh when no one else would hire him. Miguel was harmless, even childlike, Josh told himself, and he was devoted to Josh and the nursery.

Miguel looked over the desk at him, grinning from ear to ear. 'Lucy, she like me,' he said. 'She play with me.'

'I know, Miguel,' Josh said. 'I've noticed how she really likes you.' He cleared his throat. 'Miguel, I need to talk to you about last night.'

Suddenly Miguel's face contorted in fear. His dark eyes widened, and for a moment he looked as if he might burst into tears.

'Don't worry, Miguel,' Josh reassured him. 'It's not serious. I just need to find out what you know.'

Miguel jerked his head from side to side, almost spastically. 'I don't see nothing,' he said. 'Nothing, nothing, nothing. I don't see nothing.'

Josh looked at him steadily for a moment, wondering about the wisdom of having a nightwatchman impaired as Miguel was. 'Are you absolutely certain?' he asked. 'You didn't see anything? Anything at all?'

Miguel jerked his head from side to side again, even more violently. 'No, I don't see nothing.'

'Did you hear anything?' Josh asked. 'Any little thing that you can remember? Maybe something that was different? Unusual?'

'No, no, no! Nothing!' Miguel continued to shake his head, closing his eyes, the troubled expression on his face fixed there.

He seemed to be in genuine anguish, Josh thought, and he hated to ask him any more questions. *What have I got to gain anyway?* he asked himself. But he felt like he had to know the answer to one more question.

'Do you think you might have . . . accidentally, I mean . . . fallen asleep, Miguel? I know the nights are long and lonely and—'

Miguel burst into tears, and Lucy tore out of his lap. 'No, no, no!' he cried. 'Never! I never fall asleep on the job. Never!'

Tears ran in rivulets down his dusty cheeks, and Josh felt like kicking himself. He got up and went around the desk to Miguel's chair. He put his hands on Miguel's shoulders and patted him. 'It's okay, Miguel,' he said soothingly. 'It's okay. Here.' He reached over to the desk and took a Kleenex out of a box there. 'Blow your nose and wipe your eyes,' he said, handing the tissue to him. 'It's okay now. No more questions. I promise.'

Miguel blew his nose, then wiped away his tears with his dirty hands. He looked up at Josh with pitiful eyes. 'Lucy, she run away from me,' he said.

'She'll come back,' Josh said. Then he suddenly had a thought, a brilliant idea, in fact. Or so he assumed. 'Hey, Miguel,' he said. 'What if I get a dog to keep you company at night? You'd like that, wouldn't you? A trained guard dog—'

Miguel shrank back from him in horror, his eyes widening again. Looking at Josh as if he were the devil incarnate, he began to tremble. 'I . . . I . . . I . . . scared of dogs!' he stuttered. 'Sc . . . sc . . . scared of dogs!'

Ah, Jesus! Josh thought. *Some days I just can't win.*

'Forget it, Miguel,' he said hurriedly, patting his shoulders again. 'Never mind. Forget I said it. We won't do anything to scare you. Here, look, Miguel, Lucy's come back. See?'

Thank God! he thought. *Just in time.* He reached down and picked up the cat and held her out to Miguel. 'Look, Miguel,' he said. 'She wants you to hold her again. See.'

Miguel looked up at the cat, and instantly he grinned. He took Lucy from Josh's hands, set her in his lap, and began stroking her, humming to himself softly.

Josh returned to his desk chair, sat down, and

thought: *No good deed goes unpunished.* He sighed. *Oh, well, what the hell? What's the harm?* He reached over and picked up the telephone receiver, then put it back down again.

'Miguel?' he said.

Miguel looked over at him.

'Why don't you take Lucy outside with you, and then get one of the boys to give you a lift back home? You've got to get some sleep so you'll be ready for work tonight. Okay?'

Miguel nodded. 'Okay,' he readily agreed. He got up and left the office, closing the door behind him carefully.

When he was out of earshot, Josh picked up the telephone and punched the number for the greenhouse. When Carl picked up, he said: 'Carl, get one of the boys to take Miguel home. Fast. I don't want him around when the cops get here. They'll scare him half to death, asking questions.'

Carl grunted. 'You got it,' he said, and hung up.

Josh then dialed the number for the company that had installed the computer-controlled misters. He'd call them before the police. Idly tapping a pencil against the desktop, he waited for someone to pick up, thinking: *I hope to God they'll check out the system and tell me it's malfunctioned, but somehow I don't think that's what they're going to say.*

Later, Josh sat in the office with Carl. The company that maintained the computer-controlled equipment

JUDITH GOULD

had come and gone. They had discovered nothing amiss with the equipment, and had told Josh that the only way the malfunction could have occurred was human error.

'In other words,' he'd said, 'someone tampered with the equipment.'

'Exactly,' the two technos had responded, nodding.

The police had arrived soon after and had done a thorough search of the perimeter and the greenhouses themselves. They turned up empty-handed.

'You sure nobody else has beepers to unlock the gates?' they'd asked him.

'No,' he'd said. 'Just Carl, me, and my wife. That's it.'

When he'd walked them to the car, one of the cops had turned to Josh and said: 'I think you'd better keep a close watch on your men, Mr Lawrence. Looks like an inside job to me.'

Josh had nodded his assent and thanked them politely, but deep down inside, he refused to believe that anybody who worked for him could have had anything to do with the malfunction.

It's got to be something else, he told himself. *We're practically like a family here.*

He looked over at Carl, sitting across the desk from him. 'I hate to do it,' he said, 'but I think we're going to have to get a guard dog.' He heaved a sigh. 'Maybe you can help Miguel get to know it, take him through it. If he just can't handle it, maybe I'll install video security or we'll just have to hire somebody new and put Miguel on something else.'

56

Carl nodded and rose to his feet. 'I'll try,' he said, 'but you know Miguel.'

'Yes, I know Miguel,' Josh said. 'Anyhow, I'll see you in the morning.'

'Okay,' Carl said, and turned and left the office.

Josh started to pick up the telephone to call Joanna, but it rang at that moment.

'Hello?' he said.

'Mr Lawrence?' the male voice said.

'Yes,' Josh replied, straining to hear. The caller was apparently on a cell phone and there was a lot of static.

'This is Peter Rossi.'

'Hello, Mr Rossi,' Josh said. 'Can you speak up? I'm having trouble hearing you.'

'I'm on the road,' Rossi said in a louder voice.

'What can I do for you, Mr Rossi?' he asked.

'I was just wondering, Mr Lawrence,' the man said, 'if you might have changed your mind about selling us your company. So many things can go wrong in this business. All those greenhouses and all that land are such responsibilities, don't you agree?'

Josh flushed red, and had to make an effort to control the anger he felt. 'No, Mr Rossi,' he replied. 'I don't agree. On the contrary, I've always welcomed the responsibility.'

And with that, he slammed the receiver down onto its cradle.

'Shit,' he said aloud. 'Shit, shit, *shit!*'

5

April poured herself a glass of wine, a relatively inexpensive but delicious Alexander Valley chardonnay that she'd discovered recently, and stirred the pasta sauce that was on the stove. Inhaling its aroma, she smiled to herself.

Woody will love it, she thought.

She'd sauteed some garlic in butter, put in a filet of cod, added some of her rich homemade tomato sauce, tossed in lots of capers and green olives with a little of their juices, and then sprinkled in salt and pepper with a couple of bay leaves.

Roger, her ex-husband, had always said she was a peasant at heart, and nothing reflected that more than her taste in food. She'd always preferred relatively simple, uncomplicated food, with seasonal, fresh ingredients, if possible, and the only complicated cooking she'd ever done was to satisfy Roger's taste for the baroque in all things. His motto had been the fancier the better – or embellish, embellish, embellish.

She turned around to the old pine kitchen table, placing her glass of wine on its well-worn surface, and then gave the salad a few more tosses. *Done*, she decided. She took a sip of her wine and then turned to check on the pasta sauce. *Perfect.* She turned it off. It would heat up in a minute, when she and Woody were ready to eat. Looking at her watch, she wondered where he was. He usually came early and stayed late. She sat back down, and began flipping idly through a garden magazine, thinking about Woody.

He nearly always brought a smile to her face. He was part Peter Pan, part teddy bear, part eternal surfer, part businessman. He was thirty-three, a year older than she was, and going on sixteen. He'd been a friend of Roger's growing up and now had a framing shop in Capitola. With his shoulder-length mop of curls, perpetually tanned muscles, and gleaming white smile, she'd thought he had come on to her in a major way. But he'd quickly backed off when he saw that she wasn't interested or wasn't ready, and he'd done it in the most gracious manner. Maybe that was in part because he'd been a friend of Roger's and had some sort of special respect for her. She didn't really know, but she was grateful there hadn't been any of the snarling backlash typical of the accomplished and cocky Casanova, none of the whimpering or pleading of the rebuffed suitor.

No, Woody had gradually become a pal – without the complications of a sexual relationship. While she suspected he wanted more, he was content to give her the space she needed without making demands.

She took a sip of her wine and flipped the magazine closed. *Where is he?* she wondered, looking at her watch again.

As if he were psychically attuned to her thoughts, she heard the living room door open and Woody's familiar voice.

'April?' his deep baritone called. 'Hey, kiddo, where are you?'

'In here, Woody,' she answered. 'The kitchen.'

He came rambling in, hands in his worn Levi's, a loud Hawaiian shirt hanging loose, making a production of twitching his nose in the air. 'I smell heaven,' he said, his dark eyes flashing mischievously. He kissed her forehead.

April laughed. 'Have some wine,' she said, starting to get up to get a glass for him.

'Sit,' he said. 'I'll get it.' He got a wineglass out of a cabinet, filled it, then sat down opposite her. 'Cheers,' he said, holding up his glass.

'Cheers to you, too,' April said, lifting hers and clinking it lightly against his.

'Did you have a busy day?' she asked after she'd taken another sip.

'Yeah.' He nodded his shaggy head and began tapping the table with the fingers of both hands, using it as a drum. 'Filled some old orders. Took a lot of new orders. Did some paperwork. You know. Same-old. Same-old.' He finished drumming with a flourish and looked over at her with a smile. 'You?'

'It was . . . different,' she said.

'Yeah?' he said. 'How different?'

'Well, I had an appointment with a lady who wants to do a grotto . . . sort of,' she replied.

'A grotto?' he asked, his dark eyebrows lifting quizzically.

'She has an old stone stable on her property,' April said. 'She wants the inside completely covered in sea-shells and stones. With murals.'

'No shit?' he said. 'Sounds like a huge job to me.'

April nodded. 'It would be.'

'You gonna do it?' he asked.

'I'm not sure yet,' she replied. 'I'm going over there tomorrow to look at the building and talk more about exactly what she wants.' She paused for a moment to take another sip of wine, then looked at him levelly. 'But if she wants what I think she wants, I hope it works out, because it would be really exciting. My biggest job to date.'

'Wow,' he said. 'Sounds cool.'

'Cool it would be, Woody,' she said. 'Murals of orchids and—'

'Orchids?' he said, his face screwed up questioningly.

'Orchids,' she repeated. 'They're in the orchid business.'

Woody suddenly sat up straight and looked at her with a serious expression. 'Who is she?' he asked.

'Joanna Lawrence,' she replied. 'She's—'

'I *know* who she is,' Woody said darkly.

'You do?' April said with surprise.

'Yeah,' he said. 'I've done some business for her.' He took a large sip of his wine and set the glass back down. 'She's like a lot of rich women, you know? Spoiled and arrogant.'

'She seemed like a very nice lady to me,' April said. 'A terrific lady, in fact.'

He finished off his glass, then poured himself another. 'Yeah,' he said in a sarcastic tone of voice. 'She *seems* like a terrific lady. But if you ask me, she's just another rich, smug *asshole*. You don't come from around here like I do, so you don't know. She comes from a really old family, big-shot father and all. Her older sister's some socialite tramp. You know. Makes the party circuit from San Francisco to L.A. and points in between. Wherever rich trash gathers.'

April looked at him. 'You sound a little resentful,' she said. 'And that doesn't sound like you, Woody.'

'Well, yeah. It's not important.' He heaved another sigh, then gave her a meaningful look. 'But I'm warning you, April.' He pointed a finger at her. 'You better watch your back. People like her are real bloodsuckers.'

April took a sip of her wine, looking at her friend across the table. She had seen Woody worked up before. He thrived on drama and created it where it was missing. But somehow this seemed different.

April nodded. 'I'm glad you told me,' she said. 'Most of the time I don't know what I'm walking into with clients. And some of them can be really screwy. In fact, I guess the richer they are, the screwier they are. Even if they're friends of friends. Anyway, Mr Pearlman!' She looked over at him and smiled. 'Are you hungry tonight?'

'You bet,' he said, smiling back, his gleaming teeth such a contrast to his darkly tanned skin.

'Then why don't you set the table,' she said, 'and I'll finish the food off and serve.'

'You got it,' Woody said, getting up and going to a kitchen cabinet to get out the dishes.

Later, after they'd finished the meal, they sprawled on the living room sofas, sipping coffee. Woody had built a small fire in the big stone fireplace to take the chill off the cool spring evening, and its light danced across their features as they talked, facing each other across the big coffee table.

'Guess who I saw last weekend?' Woody asked.

'Who?' April replied.

'David Jarman,' he said with a giggle.

'Arrrrgggghhhh,' April groaned between gritted teeth. 'And you just had to mention it,' she added.

'I thought you'd be interested,' Woody said, his eyes gleaming with a mischievous light. 'He was with a real Barbie doll. You know. Bleached blond hair, big blue eyes, perfect bod – biiig bozooms. Skin-tight leather mini.' He laughed helplessly.

April laughed, too. 'Sounds like he's found the perfect woman,' she said.

Woody nodded his shaggy-haired head vigorously. 'He's gonna marry the bimbo!' He laughed again.

'Marry her!' she said. 'Well, it's just what he deserves. But then, she may be a very smart, very nice person for all we know.'

'Oh, sure, April,' Woody said sardonically. 'Sure.'

April smiled. 'And I was just certain that he was waiting for *me*,' she said with amusement. She sighed dramatically. 'But those Silicon Valley millionaires are all in a hurry, aren't they? Don't have much time to shop around, they're so busy making all that dough.' She frowned then. 'To think I ever dated that . . . that big bag of testosterone! And you!' She pointed a finger at Woody. 'You introduced us!'

'Yeah,' he countered, 'but I didn't know the jerk was going to ask you out.'

'I bet,' April said.

'No,' Woody said, sitting up. 'I really didn't, April. When those loaded Silicon Valley types descend to the beach on the weekends, nine out of ten of them are looking for one thing, and one thing only.'

She nodded. 'All the more reason I wonder why you introduced us,' she said.

'How could I know he'd actually want to go out with you?' he said defensively. 'It wasn't like I was trying to set you up, you know?'

'Okay, Woody,' she said. 'Okay. But in the future, don't do me any more favors like that one. I didn't

think I'd ever get the aggressive creep out of my hair.'
She paused and sipped her coffee.

'It was interesting, though,' she said thoughtfully.
'He proved you don't have to be a controlling, ego-
obsessed actor in Hollywood to be controlling and
ego-obsessed. You can be a techno wizard that's made
millions of dollars in Silicon Valley and be just as
controlling and ego-obsessed.' She laughed. 'Just as
big a shit.'

'We're not all like that, April,' Woody said.

'No,' she said. 'I'm sure you're not. At least I don't
think you are. I guess I just haven't met the right one.'
She looked at Woody. 'I'm thirty-two years old now.
What are my chances?'

Woody got up from the sofa and came around to
hers. He sat down next to her and gave her a chaste
kiss on the forehead. 'You've always got me, April,' he
said, his dark eyes serious.

She looked up at him. 'Thanks, Woody,' she said,
squeezing his thick surfer's arm. 'You're sweet.'

Then she wondered seriously: *What* are *my chances?
I've dated lots of men since I was in high school. I've been
married. I keep meeting men that I guess a lot of women
would jump at the chance to go out with, even marry.
Why don't I seem to find the right fit? Is it* me? *And will
I always be alone?*

Suddenly she felt weird, being thirty-two and alone
in the world. No family except for distant cousins. No
real prospects in the husband category, if she excluded
Woody. But then, she reminded herself, she'd wanted

this independent life, and now she'd simply have to live with the consequences.

Deep down inside, however, something instinctual told her that her life was about to change, for better or worse, and that she had no control over it.

6

Josh cruised into the pea-gravel courtyard in front of their mountaintop house and brought his ancient yellow Toyota Land Cruiser FJ40 to a halt. He didn't see Joanna's Mercedes in the courtyard, and the garage bay where she kept it was empty, its door yawning wide open.

Well, he thought, killing the engine and jumping out of the big SUV, *Connie'll know where she is.* He saw that her old Plymouth Voyager was parked in its corner of the courtyard. Climbing the stone steps to the front door, he smelled the heady fragrance of the wisteria, then noticed that it was beginning to bloom. It draped in luscious-looking purple clusters from the pergola that ran the length of the house.

He started to go through the front door, then looked down at his boots. 'Crap,' he said. They were caked with muck from the nursery, as usual, and the door mat would never clean it all off. Turning to his left, he walked down the length of the pergola and opened the gate that led down a path through the garden to the little mud room around the side of the house. Opening the French door that led into it, he called out for Connie. No answer.

Sitting down on the old pine bench near the door, he quickly unlaced his boots, pulled off his socks, and wiggled his toes. Then he bounded down the hallway to the kitchen, where he was sure Connie would be.

'Connie,' he called again. Still no answer.

In the kitchen, he looked around and saw that no one was there. 'Well, hell,' he murmured. Then he spotted Connie through a window, outside on the terrace in the back, talking on the remote phone. He grinned. Connie, like her sister-in-law, Luna, loved talking on the phone. To whom and what about, he had no idea. As much Spanish as he knew, her rapid-fire conversations were completely lost on him. He didn't want to disturb her, so he backed away from the window.

He looked at the little blackboard near the refrigerator, checking to see if there was a note from Joanna. Nada. The big Sub-Zero refrigerator beckoned, and he opened it and took out a chilled bottle of white wine. It would be good, he decided, after a rotten day at the nursery. He poured himself a glass, then approached the window again, having already forgotten about Connie.

70

She glimpsed him from where she stood near a teak table, and he saw that she immediately punched the Off button on the telephone, then started toward the house with a smile.

When she came through the French doors to the kitchen, Josh said: 'Connie, you know you didn't have to get off the telephone because of me.'

'I know,' she said in her lightly accented English, 'but I was finished anyway. Just talking to my friend.' With her tiny fingers, she loosened her black hair from the rubber band that held it in a ponytail, then shook it and ran the fingers of one hand through it. She looked up at him. 'So, how are you, Josh?' she asked.

'Okay, Connie,' he replied, then added: 'Well, sort of.'

'What's wrong?' she asked, her pretty features suddenly lined with concern.

He looked at her and smiled grimly. 'You want a glass of wine or are you in a hurry?'

'You know I'm not in a hurry if you need to talk to me,' she said. 'I'll have a glass of wine.' She went to the refrigerator, got out the bottle, and poured herself a glass.

'You want to take it outside?' he asked.

'Sure,' she said. 'Let's go.'

She walked ahead of him, her petite, youthful body a vision in black. Simple black knit top with black jeans tucked into black cowboy boots. She looked like anything but a maid, he thought for the thousandth time, and she was wise beyond her years.

They walked out to the weathered teak table and chairs and sat down under the big market umbrella. The stone terrace was large, accessible from nearly every first-floor room in the horseshoe-shaped house. At its open end, across a bridge, was the swimming pool, its turquoise water barely rippling in the light wind. Beyond it, the dramatic peaks and canyons of the Santa Cruz Mountains were covered with spring's verdancy.

'What's bothering you, Josh?' she asked, after taking a sip of her wine.

He sighed. 'I . . . I just wondered if you'd noticed Joanna acting . . . well . . . sort of strange lately?'

Connie's dark eyes flickered in the afternoon light, then she looked away. 'Weeelll . . .,' she began, clicking pink-painted fingernails on the weathered teak, 'I don't know.'

He knew that she was holding back. 'Come on, Connie,' he said, cajoling her. He thought that once he got her started talking, she wouldn't be able to stop. Connie loved to conspire, whether with Joanna or him, but only in a very positive way. It was never conspiring *against* one or the other of them.

Connie took a sip of her wine, then set the glass down. 'Maybe the only thing that's been bothering Joanna is that bitchy sister of hers, huh?' She laughed and looked at him mischievously.

Josh couldn't help but laugh. 'Yeah, well, there is that,' he conceded, but then his expression became serious. 'But that's not it, Connie. I'm really getting worried,' he continued, 'and I need to know what you think.

Nobody knows Joanna better than you do, and I know the two of you don't have any secrets from each other.'

She took another sip of her wine, then set the glass down and looked at him. 'Well, Josh,' she said hesitantly, 'I guess so. You know.' She looked away. 'She has been gone a lot, and she's always thinking about something else. You know what I mean?'

He nodded. 'I know exactly what you mean,' he said. *Good*, he thought. *I've got her hooked*.

'It's like she's always on another planet,' Connie said. 'And she never tells me where she's going anymore.' She looked at him meaningfully.

'Me, either,' he said. He looked out at the swimming pool, then returned his gaze to Connie. 'Do you have any idea what might be going on?' he asked.

'Nooo,' Connie replied slowly. 'She doesn't tell me anything. I've started to wonder if maybe she's hiding something, you know?'

'Do you think she's worried about something?' he persisted.

Connie heaved a sigh. 'I don't know,' she said. 'I just know she's been ...' She looked at Josh and laughed. 'She's been a *bitch*, Josh,' she said. 'Sometimes, anyway. Over little things.'

Josh smiled. He knew that Connie loved Joanna like a sister and he took no offense at her remark.

'Yeah,' he said, 'and that's another thing that's worried me. It's not like her. Not one bit.'

Connie shook her head. 'No, it's not,' she agreed. She drummed her pink fingernails on the tabletop again. '*Misterioso*,' she said darkly, looking off into the distance.

'Do you think—' he began before he was interrupted by a very cheerful voice in the distance.

'Hello, you two!' Joanna called from a doorway. She set down several shopping bags and breezed out onto the terrace, all smiles.

Josh rose to his feet and planted a kiss on her cheek. 'Hi, beautiful,' he said. 'We're just having a glass of wine. You want one?'

'You bet,' she said.

He dashed off toward the kitchen.

Joanna brushed Connie's cheek with a kiss, then sat down. 'Did I interrupt a good gossip session?' she asked, her eyes glinting with amusement.

'Nooo,' Connie said. 'We were just, you know, enjoying the breezes.'

Joanna laughed. 'Since when have you ever stopped long enough to enjoy a breeze, Connie?' she asked, looking her in the eye.

Connie shrugged. 'Oooh, since now,' she said. Then they both laughed. She knew, of course, that Joanna guessed they'd been discussing her, and she also knew that Joanna wouldn't try to pump her for information, happy to let them enjoy their conspiracy.

Josh returned with Joanna's wine and handed it to her, then sat back down.

'Thanks,' she said, taking a sip. 'Ummm. That tastes so good.' She set the glass down and looked at Josh. 'How was your day?'

He frowned. She was in such a cheerful mood that he hated to tell her what had happened at the nursery, but he had to. 'I was working here in the Stud Room,' he said, 'and Carl called from the nursery. So I went out there. Either the computer-controlled misting system malfunctioned or somebody tinkered with it.'

'What!' Joanna exclaimed, her eyebrows rising with alarm. 'Oh, my God! Was there any damage?' *Oh, Lord,* she thought. *Why this on top of everything else that's happened to me lately?*

'Hardly any,' he said. 'We got lucky this time, but it could've been a disaster. We don't know how long it was off. It could've been out since last Friday afternoon. With Christina's visit, none of us were down there all weekend.' He looked at Connie. 'Your brother discovered it, so we have him to thank for saving the day.'

Connie, sipping her wine, simply nodded.

He looked back at his wife. 'Several people were in and out of that greenhouse, but Carl is the only one who noticed that the misters weren't functioning.'

'Oh, Josh.' Joanna paused for a moment, looking at him. 'And do you think that somebody might have deliberately fooled around with the system?' she asked.

He nodded. 'Maybe,' he said grimly. 'But the police didn't find any sign of forced entry. Nothing suspicious. The outfit that sold me the equipment has sent somebody out, and they say the computer didn't malfunction.'

'Excuse me,' Connie said, scooting her chair back and getting to her feet. 'I'd better get going.'

Joanna looked up at her. 'You won't have another glass of wine?' she asked.

'No, thanks. I really have a lot to do,' Connie said. She kissed Joanna on the cheek. 'See you in the morning.'

Josh stood up. ''Bye,' he said, winking at her. 'See you tomorrow.'

Connie wiggled her tiny fingers, turned, and quickly disappeared into the house.

Josh sat back down, and Joanna looked at him thoughtfully. 'Did you tell the police about the Rossi brothers wanting to buy us out?'

'No,' he said. 'I thought that might sound a little paranoid. Besides, they didn't find anything, so what was the point?'

'I guess you're right,' Joanna said, 'but something tells me that they might have had something to do with this.'

'I certainly wouldn't put it past them,' Josh agreed. He took a sip of wine. 'Peter Rossi called me at the office. Wanted to know if I'd changed my mind about selling out.'

'What!' she exclaimed. 'God, they've got a lot of nerve.'

'You bet they do,' he replied. 'From what I hear, when they bought the old Giglio place, they didn't want the buildings. They were just in the way. So instead of spending the money to tear them down, they paid somebody to drop a match, then collected the fire insurance.'

'I think these people are really dangerous, Josh,' she said. 'Capable of anything.'

76

'Well,' he said, 'I don't think it's anything I can't handle. Anyway, enough about my day,' he said, setting his glass back down. 'What've you been up to?' he asked, wondering if she would be forthcoming. Although he'd seen the shopping bags, he knew that she hadn't spent the entire day in the shops.

Joanna's expression immediately changed from one of concern and worry to a radiant smile. 'Oh, Josh, you wouldn't believe it!' she said excitedly. 'I've met the most wonderful lady!'

Josh looked over at her, gratified to see her smiling. 'Who?' he asked. 'Who is this wonderful lady you met?'

'You know the garden walls and fountain at Ingrid and Ronald Wilson's that you loved so much?' she asked.

'Sure,' he said. 'They were spectacular.'

'Well, I called Ingrid and found out who did them,' Joanna said.

'Was it somebody around here?' Josh asked.

'Yes,' Joanna replied. 'April Woodward's her name, and she lives nearby. Here in the mountains. So I made an appointment and went over to see her today.' She smiled and looked at him playfully, then took a sip of her wine.

'And?' Josh asked.

'And she's coming over here tomorrow to look at the old stone stable,' Joanna said. 'I think she's excited about my ideas for it.'

'That's great, honey,' Josh said, 'but are you sure you

77

really want to go through with this? I mean, I loved the Wilsons' place, but it's a lot of work and—'

'Oh, Josh, I've *got* to do it!' Joanna said, clapping her hands together. 'I'm so glad you mentioned the Wilsons' because it started me thinking. You know how I've been collecting all those seashells and pebbles for years and years and always dreamed of doing a sort of grotto.'

Josh laughed. 'Oh, God, Joanna, do I ever,' he said. He reached across the table and took one of her hands in his. He hadn't seen her this animated in a long time, and it reassured him that all was right with the world.

'You know,' he said, 'collecting all those shells and stuff is the only thing you've ever done that I thought bordered on an obsession.'

'I know,' she said, 'but I can't help it. Anyway, I took a bunch of pictures I've saved over to April's. You know, all those fabulous rooms made out of shells and tiles and things. And we talked about it.' She looked into Josh's bright ultramarine eyes. 'And you know what?'

'What?' he asked, smiling.

'She didn't think I was crazy!' Joanna laughed, and he laughed with her.

'I think she really understood what I want to do,' she said.

'Well, that's pretty amazing,' Josh said teasingly. 'Maybe she's crazy, too.'

'You devil.' Joanna squeezed his hand affectionately.

'No, really. She's even done something similar for somebody in Los Angeles,' she went on. 'Just not quite on this scale. So.' She paused and sat back in her chair. 'Tomorrow we'll see how it goes.'

'I hope it works out,' he said, 'but are you sure you want to start a project this big? I mean, it's—'

'I told you,' Joanna interjected. 'I have to. It's like ... well, it's like a kind of legacy. Like the orchid book I did.' She gave him a look that was at once both serious and wistful. 'Something with a little piece of me in it. It's something that I can leave behind in this world, Josh. Something that will be here when I'm ... gone.'

He looked at her with relief. He knew that he needn't have worried so much about her behavior recently. 'You're so much like your father,' he said.

'How do you mean?' she asked, knowing exactly what he meant, but wanting to hear it said.

'You're a dreamer and a builder,' he said. 'You have a creative impulse that's a bit different and that's got to be expressed. And, by God, you've got to leave your stamp on the world.'

Joanna looked down at the table, flushed slightly from the wine and his words. When she looked back up, she said, 'I guess we all want to contribute something, don't we? We want to give something back, to do something more than simply pass through this life, don't we? To make it a better place?'

'You know what?' Josh said.

'What?'

'I love you, Joanna,' he said in a near whisper. 'Truly and deeply.'

A smile trembled on her lips and unbidden tears sprang into her eyes. 'And I love you, Joshua Lawrence,' she said. 'More than you'll ever know.'

7

April maneuvered her trusty old Jeep Wagoneer up the dangerously narrow and curvy mountain roads with ease, slowing down to look for the road signs at turnoffs that Joanna had written down for her. It was a road very much like her own, beautiful and lethal at once, overhung with a sun-filtering canopy of fir trees, cypress, redwoods, eucalyptus, and live oak, complete with washouts where the road suddenly became a single narrow lane.

She wasn't quite prepared, however, for what awaited her after she made the last turn on Joanna's instruction sheet and climbed steadily uphill. Reaching a small plateau on the mountaintop, she slowed to a crawl, craning her neck both left and right, trying to take in the sheer magnificence that surrounded her on all sides: peaks and canyons of awesome heights and depths, all dressed in the fresh greens of spring dotted with vibrantly colored wildflowers. It was truly stunning, this mountaintop perch.

Ahead, she saw the driveway that led up to Joanna's house. She slowly turned onto it, taking in the old apple trees that lined both sides of the road. The short drive led to two massive stone gateposts, topped by copper lanterns with a verdigris patina. Heavy black iron gates were open wide, and looked as if they were always thus, ready to welcome visitors. The same iron was used in fencing that extended from either side of the gateposts, encompassing what appeared to be gardens surrounding the house.

Between the stone pillars she went, slowly pulling in to a large courtyard. On her left rose a large gray-shingled house with snowy white trim and shutters. A pergola, dripping with purplish wisteria, ran its entire length. Straight ahead was a four-bay garage, connected to the house by the pergola. On her right was another pergola, this one covered with old-fashioned-looking roses of the palest pink, thousands of them in riotous bloom. The whole had about it an air of solid, old-money affluence combined with loving and lavish care.

Pulling her big shoulder bag out of the Jeep after her, April walked up the stone steps to the front door. It was painted the darkest green, a green with a lot of blue in it. She rang the bell and waited.

The door opened and an extremely pretty petite young woman with jet-black hair and dark eyes greeted her.

'Hello,' she said cheerfully. 'You must be April, right?'

April nodded. 'Right,' she said, smiling.

'I'm Connie,' the woman said, opening the door wide. 'Come in. Joanna's waiting for you outside.'

April trailed after her, looking about. The loveliness of the exterior of the house hadn't prepared her for the immensity and old-fashioned grandeur of the interior. The spacious entrance hall was centered with a large round Regency table, over which hung a sparkling crystal chandelier, and an elegantly curving staircase led to the second floor. Following Connie, who was fast on her feet, April barely glimpsed rooms to the right and left, but the impression was one of burnished woods, polished silver and brass, and richly glowing fabrics and rugs.

Straight ahead, she could see that French doors at the back of the house framed a view across a stone terrace and verdant greenery to distant mountain peaks. She had been in many homes in this area, some of them belonging to very wealthy people, but April didn't think she'd ever been in one that exuded such luxurious tranquility. She wanted to reach out and brush fabrics between her fingertips, to stroke highly polished woods, to indulge her eyes in the visual feast that she sensed all around her; but Connie, who'd already reached the French doors, was standing there, an impatient smile on her face, awaiting her.

'Out here,' Connie said, opening the door.

'Thanks, Connie,' April said.

She saw Joanna seated at a big teak table under a market umbrella. Stacks of books and magazines were piled on the stone terrace and on the table. When Joanna saw her, she took off her sunglasses and rose to her feet.

'Hi,' she called. 'Welcome.'

'Thanks,' April said. 'It's so beautiful here, Joanna! I had no idea. I can't believe that after living here all this time, I've never been up this road before.' She looked out over the bridge toward the pool and beyond to the mountains and canyons. 'It's heaven!'

'It really is, isn't it,' Joanna said, reaching out a hand.

April took it, and Joanna didn't so much shake it as squeeze it affectionately. 'Here,' she said, 'have a seat and tell me what you'd like to drink. There's tea and soda and mineral water, whatever you'd like.'

April sat down and looked at Joanna's glass. 'What are you having?' she asked.

'Some iced green tea,' Joanna said.

'Oh, great,' April said. 'I'll have the same.'

Joanna turned to Connie, who stood waiting. 'Connie, why don't you bring a pitcher out?' she said.

'Sure,' Connie said, then turned toward the house.

Joanna sat down and looked at the young woman across from her. She was every bit as lovely today as she'd remembered.

'After you've had a drink, I'll show you around,' she said. 'Is that okay?'

'Yes,' April replied, looking about her, trying to take in all the plants, flowers, shrubbery, and trees. She breathed deeply, enjoying the mixed bouquet carried on the light breeze. 'I really can't get over this place,' she enthused. 'It's spectacular and . . . voluptuous, in a way. A quiet way.'

Joanna looked surprised. 'You've hit the nail on the head, I think,' she said. 'A quiet voluptuousness.'

'Have you lived here a long time?' April asked.

Joanna nodded. 'I've never really lived anywhere else,' she said. 'My father built the place when he and my mother married, so I grew up here. Then right after Josh and I got married, my father died and left it to us.' She paused and smiled. 'We were living in this little place down at the beach that Dad had given us as a wedding present. In the middle of nowhere near Pajaro Dunes. A beach shack really, but wonderful.'

'Well, this place certainly is,' April said. 'It's so un-Californian. I mean, the house and everything seem to have been here forever. You know what I mean? To have real *roots* here.'

Joanna laughed. 'Not like a lot of California. Covered up with vinyl-sided boxes that were built yesterday or the day before.'

Connie returned with a tray loaded down with a pitcher of tea and glasses, which she set on the table. 'There's real sugar, Sweet 'n Low, and honey,' she said, pouring a glass of iced tea for April.

'Thanks, Connie,' April said. 'I can do the rest.'

'Sure,' Connie said. 'I'll go finish lunch now, okay?'

'Yes,' Joanna said. 'We'll be ready in about half an hour or so.'

'Okay.' Connie rushed off, back to the kitchen.

'She's so pretty,' April said, 'and seems so energetic and happy.'

'She's a wonder,' Joanna said. 'Before Dad died, he practically adopted Connie and Carl, her brother. They were Consuelo and Carlos then, and had just moved here with their mother from Peru. Living in a little trailer in one of those horrible migrant labor places. Connie came to work here, and Carl works at the nursery.'

'They changed their names?' April asked, sipping her tea.

'Yes,' Joanna said with a nod. 'They wanted to be as American as possible. Still do.'

'Oh, so they're not legal,' April said.

'Carl is,' Joanna said. 'He married Luna Garber, a half-Venezeulan, half-Jewish American. She works at the nursery, too, running the office. But Connie ... well, it's so complicated.' Joanna laughed lightly.

'What?' April said, intrigued.

'Well, Connie found somebody to marry. You know, just a marriage of convenience. So we loaned her the five thousand dollars to pay the guy—'

'Five thousand dollars!' April interjected.

Joanna nodded. 'Seems to be the going rate. Anyway, they married, then when they had interviews at immigration, she didn't pass.'

'What?' April asked. 'But how's that possible?'

'The interviewer was probably having a bad day,' Joanna said. 'Anyway, he certainly smelled something fishy, because they couldn't answer all sorts of personal questions about each other. It was obvious that they hardly even knew each other, much less lived together as man and wife. So she didn't get her green card.'

'So what happened?' April asked.

'The way things stand right now,' Joanna said, 'is that we've hired a very expensive lawyer who specializes in these cases to help her out. He has a good track record, so we'll see. In the meantime, the fellow she married has disappeared with his cash.' She laughed again. 'There's always a little drama around here.'

'Sounds like it,' April said. 'It also sounds like you've been very generous with her.'

'Well,' Joanna said, 'Connie's worked here since she was about eighteen, and she's really like family. I'm as close to her as I am to my sister, Christina. She's been absolutely wonderful. She *is* wonderful. And smart and ambitious.'

'She's so pretty,' April said, 'I'm surprised somebody legal didn't sweep her off her feet right away.'

'It does seem odd, doesn't it?' Joanna replied. 'She dates some, but Connie is extremely particular. I mean, fussy beyond belief. A real snob when it comes to men. What they look like, what they do for a living. She's determined to get as far away as she can from that childhood of poverty in Peru. Plus, I don't think she's really fallen for anybody yet.'

'That does count for something, doesn't it,' April said with a laugh.

'Yes,' Joanna agreed. 'At least I think it does.' She saw that April had finished her iced tea. 'You ready to see the old stable?' she asked.

'Yes,' April said. 'I can hardly wait.'

'Well, follow me,' Joanna said, scraping her chair back from the table and getting to her feet.

She led the way across the stone terrace and over a little wooden bridge that brought them to the pool area.

'I love the bridge and the landscaping,' April said with enthusiasm. 'It's all so perfect.'

'Dad started it,' Joanna replied, 'but Josh and I have done a lot more over the years.'

They walked past the pool and on through lushly landscaped grounds until April could see the old stable about a hundred feet away, set on sloping ground surrounded with apple trees. From here the view of the peaks and canyons was even more dramatic than from the terrace.

'Oh, wow, Joanna!' she said. 'This spot is so beautiful.'

'I know,' Joanna said. 'That's one reason I think it would make a great place to entertain or just to meditate. You know, read, get away from the activity in the house. I discovered when I was working on the orchid book that as big as the house is, I could've used a separate place – a separate building – to get away to.'

They arrived at the stable and stood before it. Joanna

watched April's face for signs of what she might be thinking, but her expression was inscrutable.

Without saying anything, April slowly began walking the circumference of the small building, with Joanna trailing behind her. Then she stepped inside from the front, looking around her. Finally, arms akimbo and feet planted widely on the ground, she looked Joanna in the eye. Her expression was thoughtful.

'You know what I think?' she said in an even tone.

'What?' Joanna asked, a little worried that she might think the building unsuitable for what she had in mind.

April smiled widely. 'I think it's perfect,' she said. 'It's just right for what you want to do.'

Joanna felt a sense of relief rush through her. *Thank God!* she thought. *She'll take on the project.*

'Great,' she said. 'I'm glad you feel that way. I was afraid you'd think I was crazy wanting to fix this place up at all, much less do something elaborate with it.'

April shook her head. 'No, no,' she said. 'I really mean it. I think it's absolutely right.' She turned to what had once been stable doors leading to individual stalls. 'Look,' she said. Her speech became more rapid with her excitement. 'These openings are perfect for French doors. They're begging for French doors. They'd give a view of the mountains on this one side. Then,' she went on, 'the other three sides would be as they are. No doors or windows. Totally closed in.' She turned and looked at Joanna again. 'You'd be totally surrounded by architectural motifs and murals made of seashells and pebbles.'

Joanna's eyes brightened. 'You really do love the idea, don't you?'

'Oh, yes,' April said, nodding. 'It can be really fabulous, a real fantasy.' Then she added quietly, 'It can have real magic.'

Just the words I wanted to hear, Joanna thought. 'So you'll take on the project?'

'Well . . . we should talk about scheduling, terms, and so forth,' April said. 'But, yes.' She smiled. 'I'd love to take on the project.'

'That's wonderful, April,' Joanna said. 'I'm so excited.' She reached over and hugged April's shoulders, then kissed her cheek.

It was completely spontaneous and so unlike anything she would normally do with someone she barely knew that Joanna drew back and laughed nervously. 'I'm sorry,' she said. 'I . . . I know I hardly know you, but I'm just so excited.'

April blushed slightly. 'That's perfectly all right,' she said. 'I'm excited, too, and I . . . I already feel like I've known you for a long time.'

'I feel exactly the same way,' Joanna said. 'Like you're an old friend.' She paused thoughtfully. 'I guess we think a lot alike,' she said. 'We're both rather practical, I think, but we like a bit of fantasy, a bit of humor and whimsy in our lives.'

'Yes,' April agreed. 'I think we like the same things.'

Joanna took her arm. 'There's one more thing I want to show you, then we'll have lunch. Okay?'

'Sure,' April said.

'Over here,' Joanna said, indicating a corner of the stable.

April followed her to a corner where huge sheets of plastic hid whatever was underneath. Joanna pulled off the plastic sheets, and April saw that there must be at least a hundred or more neatly stacked boxes and storage bins. They towered from the floor nearly to the ceiling.

Joanna opened one of the plastic ones and turned to April. 'Look,' she said.

April drew closer and looked in. Her eyes widened in surprise at the sight of the colorful seashells packed inside the bin. Then she inhaled deeply. 'It's as if you've brought the ocean home with you. And they're beautiful,' she said.

'Yes,' Joanna said, 'there are thousands of them. All boxed by type.'

'Incredible!' April exclaimed.

'Anyway, I hope we can incorporate the ones I've collected,' Joanna said.

'That should be a priority,' April replied.

Joanna closed the plastic bin. 'Well, let's go have lunch now. That is, if you've seen enough.'

'Yes,' April said. 'For now anyway.'

Joanna led her up the slight incline, through the apple trees, back onto the lushly landscaped grounds, and on toward the pool and stone terraces.

'Connie is a great cook,' she said as they walked. 'She makes several Peruvian specialties. With her own added twist, of course. And they are delicious. The only

91

problem is that most of them are very rich. And hard to say no to.'

April laughed. 'Like so many good things in life.'

Reaching the table, she could see that it had been elegantly set with beautiful china and sparkling silver and crystal. There was even a white linen tablecloth with matching crisp white linen napkins. In the center of the table was a small pot of delicate-looking pale lilac orchids, so beautiful they themselves appeared edible.

'Everything's so beautiful,' April said. 'You shouldn't have gone to so much trouble.'

'Doing things beautifully is never too much trouble,' Joanna said.

April looked at her and realized that she meant it. This was a woman who would spare no effort to see that her world was as beautiful as she could make it.

'I've never seen lilac orchids quite like these,' April said.

'They're *Cattleya skinneri*,' Joanna said. 'Not rare or difficult, but a very pretty color, I think. Here,' she said, 'you sit over here.' She indicated a chair. 'And I'll sit here.'

They sat down, and as if by magic, Connie appeared from the kitchen, carrying a tray toward them.

The remains of the lunch lay colorfully on the exquisite china, testimony to Connie's skills in the kitchen. Bowls still pink from the creamy, rich shrimp soup that was perfumed with cilantro. Plates a mixture of greens, whites, and browns from a hearty *calsa*, a casserole of chicken breast, creamed potatoes, and avocado. The contents of the salad plates had merely been nibbled at, but the dessert plates looked as if they'd hardly been used, eaten clean of the delicious flan that Connie had made.

'That was out of this world,' April said, folding her napkin.

'Connie never fails,' Joanna said. 'You know, I've had people call from everywhere, even Europe, after they've eaten here. All of them want to know her recipe for shrimp soup.'

'Does she give it out?' April asked.

'Almost never.' Joanna laughed. 'There was one time when a great lady, a very rich orchid collector in France, called, and I begged Connie to give it to her. She's such a good customer, you see.'

'Did she?' April grinned.

'Well, she gave her a *version* of the recipe,' Joanna said. 'I've forgotten what she left out, but she did leave out something.'

They both laughed.

April caught herself brushing the orchid plant on the table with her fingertips. 'Oh, I'm sorry,' she apologized. 'It makes you want to touch it.'

'That's okay,' Joanna said. 'Like I said, these aren't rare or difficult. Why don't you take it home with you?'

'Really?' April's eyebrows drew up in surprise.

'Of course,' Joanna said. 'It's easy to take care of. I'll give you an instruction sheet before you go. We have

93

them for customers at the nursery. Would you like to see the little greenhouse before you go?'

'Yes,' April said. 'I'd love to. If I do work on this project, then I'm going to have to get on friendly terms with orchids.'

'Come on, I'll show you.'

April followed her across the little bridge to the pool area, then they followed a path around the pool house, which led to a small greenhouse a few feet away.

'You'd never know it was here,' April said. 'At least not from the house.'

'That was part of the idea of putting it here,' Joanna replied. 'These are really special orchids, for the most part. Rare and expensive. And Josh has his Stud Room here.'

'His what?' April asked with a quizzical expression. She almost snorted with laughter.

Joanna looked at her and smiled. 'You heard correctly. Stud Room. It's called that because that's where he pollinates the orchid plants. Manually. Some of them are very difficult. He's working on creating hybrids. That's one of the mainstays of the orchid business. *Our* orchid business, at any rate. Creating hybrids. Coming up with something new and different that will generate a lot of interest and *sell*. It's a long process, and you can't be absolutely sure what you'll get when you cross plants.'

She pulled a beeper from the pocket of her loose-fitting, sand-colored silk trousers. She punched in a code, aiming it at the greenhouse. There was a click, then Joanna opened the door.

'We have to have a security system here because the orchids are so valuable.'

As April followed Joanna in, her mouth almost fell open. 'Oh, this is like nothing else in the world,' she said in awe, looking about her at the riot of exotic blossoms and colors. Reds, pinks, purples, white, yellows, greens, near-blacks – every color of the rainbow and some she didn't think she'd ever seen before. The plants themselves, with their variable foliage and roots, were sights to behold, from tiny, potted orchids with strange foliage to orchids almost the size of trees.

'Wait till you see the nursery,' Joanna said. She could see where Josh had been pollinating the *Paphiopedilum lowii*. 'Do you like this one?' she asked.

April studied the plant. 'It's extraordinary,' she said. 'The greens and pinks and purples. Really beautiful.'

'Josh is trying to hybridize it with something else, I'm not sure what. Maybe several other orchids. To see what he'll come up with.'

'Did I hear my name being tossed about?' a deep male voice from behind them asked.

'Oh!' Joanna exclaimed. 'I didn't realize you were here.'

He took her in his arms, giving her a kiss on the lips. April watched, surprised by their unembarrassed display of affection for one another in front of someone else. They were so natural together, she thought, with such an easy familiarity.

'Josh,' Joanna said, 'this is my friend, April Woodward. And April, my husband, Josh.'

Josh leaned forward and took April's hand in his, and she shook it firmly, looking into his eyes.

Such eyes, she thought. *I've never seen such eyes before. They are almost mesmerizing in the depths of their blueness. And his smile! Those white, white teeth contrasting with his tanned body. And his hair!*

Suddenly she realized that she'd been staring at him, that she'd held his hand longer than she should have. She quickly let go and looked down at the ground for a moment, then back up at him. 'It's a pleasure to meet you,' she said. 'Joanna was just showing me some of your work.'

'The tip of the iceberg,' he said with a smile. 'What do you think of her project, April? Or have you had time to think about it?'

'I'm very excited about it,' she said, 'and I think we can work something out.'

'We've already been down to the stable,' Joanna said, 'and April really liked it.'

'Good,' Josh said. 'A lot of people don't really understand my wife's wonderful ideas, I'm afraid.' He took Joanna's hand and squeezed it. 'I guess that's one of the things I love about her.'

'Oh, Josh,' Joanna said, 'I think you've thought some of them were pretty crazy, too.'

He laughed. 'Yeah, that's true.'

'Listen,' Joanna said, 'how about you showing April the greenhouse while I run up to the house and get some things ready for her to take home with her? Is that okay with the two of you?'

April nodded. 'It's fine with me.'

'You sure you won't be bored to death?' Josh asked.

'Oh, no,' April said. 'Not with all these fantastic flowers.'

'I'll see you at the house, then,' Joanna said, and turned and left the greenhouse.

'So what did Joanna show you?' Josh asked, looking at April.

His eyes are like magnets, she thought. *I've got to stop looking at them. And his hair! I hadn't noticed before how sun-bleached it is, how streaked with gold.*

'Well,' April said, recovering herself, 'she was showing me something you're trying to pollinate over there.' She pointed to the *Paphiopedilum lowii*.

'Are you really interested?' he asked.

'Oh, yes,' she said, nodding.

He could see that she was serious, and he appreciated that. A lot of people were interested in the end product – a beautiful, exotic flower – but few had any enthusiasm for how it got to be that way.

He showed her how the sunshades and the computer-controlled misting system worked. Then he put on latex gloves and demonstrated how he used toothpicks to take pollen from one plant and pollinate another.

She watched with fascination as he took a saliva-coated toothpick from his mouth and swirled it around in one orchid, then transferred the toothpick, now laden with pollen, to the next orchid.

'Does this disgust you?' he asked, looking up at her.

'Oh, no,' she said, shaking her head. 'I think it's fascinating. You're more or less making them have sex.'

He grinned. 'That's exactly right.'

Afterward, they walked around the small facility, and he showed her various types of orchids, discussed their characteristics, areas of origin, and a thousand other details about them that became a confusing swirl in April's head.

Josh turned and saw the look on her face and laughed. 'I'm going too fast,' he said. 'And trying to cover too much ground for someone who doesn't know much about all this.'

'Yes,' April said honestly, 'but it's fascinating, and I can see that you have a real passion for it.'

'Uh-huh,' he said. 'I got it from Mitch Cameron, Joanna's father. He had the disease – orchid fever – and transmitted it to me. I've had it ever since.' He paused and looked at her. 'I came to work part-time at the nursery one summer while I was in college.' He paused and laughed. 'And I never left.'

'Really?' she asked. 'Just like that?'

'Yes.' He nodded and flashed a smile.

That *smile*, she thought.

'I fell in love with orchids, Mitch Cameron, *and* his daughter.'

'What an amazing coincidence,' she said. 'To fall into all this. It's such a . . . such a different life.'

'But then, so is yours,' he said. 'At least from what Joanna's told me.'

She looked at him. 'I . . . I guess you're right,' she said. 'There aren't many people who're interested in what I do, much less people who actually do it.'

'Do you love it?' he asked. 'I mean, really love your work, with a passion?'

He studied her face closely, and suddenly found that he had been ignoring her tall, slender body, her brown and golden amber eyes and sandy hair, and her strikingly beautiful features. Now that he had taken notice of her – real notice – he found it impossible to believe that he was actually noticing her for the first time. He'd been concentrating all of his attentions on Joanna when he'd first come in and had failed to realize that such an exquisite creature had been here all along.

'Yes,' she said, looking him in the eye. 'I do have a passion for my work. Whether it's working with shells or tiles or stone or simply doing my watercolors, I put everything I've got into it. I really do love it. It's what keeps me . . . I hate to use the word *centered* . . . but I guess that describes it.'

She paused and smiled ruefully. 'I guess if the rest of the world seems crazy and uncontrollable . . .' She sighed and shrugged.

'If the rest of the world is crazy and out of your control,' Josh finished for her, 'at least you have your work. And it's something you *can* control to some extent. You can decide where to put that piece of tile or shell, or how you want that watercolor to look. You can actually find peace in it.'

'That's it exactly,' she said, nodding.

How strange, he thought, *she seems to think just like Joanna. And me. And she has that remarkable self-possession, poise, and ease, that Joanna has about her. She also seems to be purposeful and practical like Joanna, despite her imagination. No wonder they are hitting it off.*

'I guess I'd better get up to the house,' Josh said. 'I left some paperwork here and have to get back out to the nursery.'

'Thanks a lot for the tour and all the information,' April said.

'I hope I didn't scare you off,' Josh said with a grin.

'No,' April said. 'Not at all.'

They left the greenhouse and walked back toward the house. On the terrace in the distance, Joanna was sitting at the table watching them, a hint of a smile on her lips.

They look so good together, she thought. *So perfect for one another. And I bet they're already finding it easy to talk to each other, to get to know each other.*

She lifted an arm and waved to them, and they both waved back. She could see that they were laughing together, sharing something humorous.

Perfect! she thought again.

When they reached the table, Josh leaned down and kissed Joanna's cheek. 'I've got to get some paperwork in my office. Then I'm going back out to the nursery.'

'You have to leave again?' she asked.

'Yes,' he said. 'All kinds of business to tend to.'

'Okay, darling,' Joanna said, 'I'll see you later, then.'

Josh turned to April. 'It was a pleasure to meet you,' he said. 'And I hope everything works out on the project.'

'It was nice to meet you, too,' April replied. 'And I'm sure the project will work out very well.'

As he walked toward the house, Joanna said to April, 'Have a seat for a minute and then I'll let you go.'

April pulled out a chair and sat down across from Joanna. 'Your husband's a very nice man.'

'He's pure gold,' she replied. 'In fact, he's like Fort Knox.' She and April laughed together.

'How lucky you are,' April said.

Joanna nodded and smiled dreamily. 'Oh, yes,' she said, her violet eyes looking off into the distance. 'Yes, indeed. And I don't mean to seem smug about it, but I'm the luckiest woman alive.'

April thought that she detected a certain wistfulness, possibly even sadness, in Joanna's eyes. She wondered what in the world could make this woman sad, but then decided she was imagining what she'd seen.

'Well,' Joanna said, looking back at April. 'I have some things for you to take home, and I think we should discuss some specifics now. If that's okay with you.'

'Sure,' April said. 'Fire away.'

'I don't know how you usually go about this,' Joanna said, 'but I was wondering if you could give me a rough sketch of what you propose to do and an estimate. I know that I'll have to choose orchids that I want you to use, but at least you can give me rough outlines of what you think would work.'

'When would you want this?' April asked.

'A week from today.'

'A week!' April almost gasped. 'That's awfully fast, Joanna.'

'I'm in a hurry,' Joanna said simply.

April looked at her and saw that she was serious. 'Well, okay then. I'll have to drop everything else, but I can do it.'

'Good,' Joanna said. 'Next week it is.' She paused, with a thoughtful expression on her face. 'Now then,' she began again, 'as for completion.'

April looked at her. She had the distinct impression that Joanna wanted this huge project finished yesterday.

'I would like to see the entire project finished within the next six months,' she said. 'At the latest. Four would please me even more, but I'll allow six.'

April gritted her teeth and grimaced. 'Ouch,' she said. 'Next week is one thing, but six months to finish? Joanna, that would be a tremendous challenge.'

'And I bet you love a challenge,' Joanna said.

'No, really,' April said. 'It would mean dropping or delaying practically everything else I have lined up.' She paused, biting on the end of a fingernail, then looked over at Joanna, seeming to have come to some sort of decision.

'Okay,' she said at last. 'Six months guaranteed. Four months, practically impossible, and I can't make any promises, but I'd be willing to give it a try.'

Joanna smiled. 'That's what I wanted to hear,' she said. She reached across the table and took one of April's hands. 'This will be a fabulous project, April,' she said. 'Believe me, you won't regret it.'

'I'm sure I won't,' April said, but she wondered if she wasn't already regretting it a little.

'Now,' Joanna said. 'I've got two shopping bags here for you to take home. In one is the orchid that was on the table, with instructions for its care.'

'Oh, thank you, Joanna,' April said. 'It's so lovely.'

'And,' Joanna continued, 'there's a copy of the orchid book I did a couple of years back. You can pick out some of your favorites, then next week the two of us will decide together which to incorporate into the murals. How's that?'

'Fine,' April said. 'And thanks so much. You've really been so generous.'

'Oh, you'll be paying me back,' Joanna said. 'So don't worry about it.'

'Well, I'd better get going,' April said. 'I've got tons of work to do between now and next week.'

'Should I give you an advance on this week's work?' Joanna asked.

'No, that won't be necessary,' April said. 'We'll see about it next week.'

They walked to the house, where the shopping bags were waiting for April at the front door. They exchanged kisses like old friends, and April left.

Joanna watched her pull out of the courtyard, then leaned back against the closed door, breathing a sigh of relief. I have *found her!* she thought. *Oh, yes, indeed, Josh. I've found the perfect woman!*

April slowly cruised down the dangerous mountain, her mind swirling with thoughts of the beautiful and decidedly different Joanna Lawrence. *What a woman she is*, she thought. *What a unique mind and what unique interests.*

And her world! April thought. So beautiful, so perfect! It was as if her universe were enchanted. Her magnificent mountaintop abode was lavishly elegant yet warm and inviting. The attention to detail was incredible, from the vine-laden pergolas to the way the table was set.

April stopped at one of the signs that indicated a washout, looked cautiously ahead, then proceeded on down the mountain.

I've got to concentrate on the road, she thought.

But inevitably her mind wandered back to the earthly paradise of Joanna Lawrence. There was, of course, the perfect completion to this heavenly picture: Josh Lawrence. Almost unearthly handsome with his sun-bleached hair and tanned skin, his Roman nose and square jaw, he was also possessed of a great charm and seemed to be gentle and patient, with a passion for life. His handsomeness, she decided, was particularly appealing because he seemed totally oblivious to it. Oh, yes, his was an easily worn masculinity, relaxed and comfortable.

Joanna and Josh Lawrence: What a couple! She could

only envy their easy affection for one another, and the picture-perfect life they had created together.

Turning onto the highway, heading south, toward her own humble but charming mountainside cottage, she ran a hand through her hair.

Yet, she thought, *yet . . . there is something decidedly off kilter about the two of them and their blissful world. No,* she corrected herself, *it's more to do with Joanna. Yes, Joanna. There's something definitely . . . well, not fishy exactly, but something that didn't ring exactly true.*

But what? she asked herself. *And why do I feel this way? Am I just looking for a bug in the ointment? Am I so skeptical that I refuse to accept what the surface appears to be? Can't a marriage, a world, like theirs appears to be, exist?*

Slowing down for her exit off the highway, she wondered if the feeling she had couldn't be the result of some instinct gone awry. Sometimes she didn't think she could trust her own instincts, these gut-level feelings that she had. Still, the feeling that something was amiss with the picture that the Lawrences presented to the world wouldn't go away. She couldn't put her finger on it, but something was telling her to be on her guard.

The sun in a last spectacular display of orange had gone down behind the mountains, and the evening air was beginning to cool. The landscape lighting dramatically lit carefully chosen trees and paths. The pool's lights rendered the water's blue a quieter shade of turquoise than the natural light of day. Big scented candles, all a refined honeysuckle aroma, burned in crystal hurricane holders placed on tables, on garden walls, and even around the pool itself.

It was Joanna's favorite time to swim. She had finished her nightly laps, and now lay on a float, staring up at the sky. She loved the early morning too, but if required to choose, her choice would definitely be for nighttime swims under the stars.

Ancient Japanese koto music wafted on the air from hidden speakers. Joanna found the music immensely relaxing – a quirk, she supposed, because it was unanimously vilified by her friends. Josh sometimes enjoyed it, but sometimes even he had to change the music.

Tonight she had the pool to herself, however, and the combination of the light, the water, the scented air, and the music was working its magic. Her mind and body – all of her senses – felt they had been afforded a particularly luxurious kind of massage, and the result was nothing less than a feeling of utter peace within.

Ah, yes, she thought, *tranquility reigns. For the moment at least.*

It's just what the doctor ordered, she decided, smiling ruefully. For she desperately needed these private moments – increasingly of late – to recharge. Sometimes she thought that, if not for these moments, she would go mad.

Tonight, she had managed to keep those feelings at bay, to enjoy this moment for what it was, and not worry about yesterday or tomorrow or next week or next month. No. She wouldn't worry about the trouble at the nursery tonight or Josh and all the responsibilities he had . . . and was going to have.

No. Tonight, she felt that she could count her blessings. And she had, literally ticking them off in her mind one by one, thanking her lucky stars – whatever powers that be – that she had been afforded a life of such abundance and joy and such love.

She rolled off the float and swam to the steps at

the shallow end of the pool, climbing up them and out of the water. She took a sip of the white wine spritzer on the table at poolside, then picked up a big, fluffy beach towel off a chair and began patting herself dry.

Suddenly, she felt powerful arms encircle her waist and a rush of warm breath on her neck. She was momentarily startled, but almost instantly recognized Josh's intoxicatingly masculine aroma.

'You look so beautiful,' he whispered, kissing her neck.

'And you feel so wonderful,' she responded. 'Even if you nearly scared me half to death.'

'Did I?' he asked, nibbling her ear.

'It's okay,' she said. 'I'll forgive you just this once.'

She turned to face him, and he kissed the tip of her nose.

'You're going to get soaking wet from me,' she said, kissing his chin.

'I don't care,' Josh said, smiling. 'You can get me wet anytime you want to.'

Joanna laughed. 'Are you as hungry as I am?' she asked.

'I could eat,' he said. 'In fact, I'm starved.'

'Good,' she said. 'Then you can help me prepare a simple feast.'

'What?' he asked, his eyebrows arching questioningly.

'Steaks,' she said. 'Juicy rib eyes. Some roasted potatoes with rosemary that I just have to warm up in the microwave, and a salad.'

JUDITH GOULD

'Sounds yummy,' he said. 'And let me guess what I have to do.'

'You got it,' she said. 'Grill the steaks while I get the salad ready.'

'It's a deal,' he said.

'Good.' She hugged him tightly, then let go. 'Let me get out of this bikini, and I'll be right back.'

'How about I mix up some killer martinis in the meantime?' he asked.

'Heaven,' she said, already walking across the terrace to the French doors that led into the house.

Josh followed, heading into the kitchen, where he got a bottle of chilled Stolichnaya out of the refrigerator, the vermouth from a liquor cabinet, and got busy mixing their drinks, gently stirring a mere whisper of vermouth into the vodka.

He had hardly finished before Joanna appeared in the kitchen, her hair still somewhat wet, wearing nothing but a short caftan made of a white gauzy crinkled muslin. The bodice was cut in a deep V, revealing lightly tanned cleavage.

'Ready?' she asked.

Josh gave the pitcher of martinis another stir, then flourished the glass stirrer in the air. 'Voilà,' he said with a grin. He filled their martini glasses nearly to the brim and handed her one.

'What, no olive? No twist?' Joanna joked.

'We wouldn't want to adulterate the pure and sublime taste of the alcohol, would we?' Josh replied, raising his glass to hers.

110

Joanna laughed. 'Not if you say so.'

They clinked glasses and took sips of their drinks.

'Whoa! That's powerful!' Joanna exclaimed.

'The better to render you powerless, my dear,' Josh said with amusement.

'Thought so,' she said. She set her glass down and went to the refrigerator, where she pulled out a plate with two steaks. 'These are for you,' she said. 'I'll pop the potatoes in the microwave and do the salad.'

'Rare as usual?' Josh asked.

'Charred on the outside, hardly cooked on the inside,' Joanna replied.

'At your service,' Josh said and picked up the plate of steaks, the pitcher of martinis, and his drink, placed them on a tray, and went back out to the terrace.

Within minutes, Joanna had tossed a salad of several different greens and fresh ripe tomatoes and dressed it with garlic, olive oil, and balsamic vinegar. The microwave *bing*ed and she took the rosemary-scented potatoes out. Placing everything on a tray, she joined Josh on the terrace, where the table had been set earlier. She sat down and sipped her drink.

'About done?' she asked.

'Soon,' he said. He sat down next to her and took a sip of his martini, looking over at his wife. 'You look a little tired,' he said. 'Is it getting ready for this new project?'

Joanna shook her head. 'No, no,' she said emphatically. 'I feel fine, and I think the project is going to work out wonderfully.' She paused and looked over at Josh. 'What did you think of April?' she asked.

111

'Well,' he began, 'I . . . I guess she seemed okay.'

Joanna laughed. 'You can surely do better than that, Josh.'

He grinned. 'Well, she seemed capable and enthusiastic and . . . well, I don't know.'

'Oh, come on,' she cajoled. 'Say it.'

'Say what?' he asked defensively.

'Her looks and attitude knock your socks off. Right?' Joanna watched him.

Josh reddened slightly.

Joanna felt a mixture of feelings begin to stir within her. *He really did like April*, she thought. *He really was affected by her. Otherwise he wouldn't be reacting this way.* She was glad, but at the same time, she felt a little . . . a little . . . jealousy? *Oh, God!* She hated to think she could be that way.

'Maybe I better scrap this project,' Joanna teased. 'I think you took a cotton to her.'

Josh reached over and took her hands in his, drawing her closer to him. He kissed her lips, then drew back, looking into her eyes.

'You know very well,' he said in a near whisper, 'that nobody else on earth could make me as happy as you.'

Joanna nodded slightly.

Without another word, Josh rose to his feet, pulling her up with him. He took her in his well-muscled arms and kissed her lips tenderly. 'Oh, I do love you so much,' he whispered. Then his lips traveled to her forehead, her eyes, her nose, her cheeks, her ears and neck. He began to kiss her more passionately, with more urgency, his hands moving down to her firm, rounded buttocks and pushing her against him.

Joanna responded at once, relishing the feel of him against her, his desire for her serving to increase her own. She ran her hands over his powerful back and shoulders, then suddenly gasped when she felt his hard manhood pressing firmly against her.

She drew back, looking into his eyes. 'Quick,' she said breathlessly, 'turn the grill off.'

Josh reached around behind him and switched the gas off, then took her in his arms again. *Oh, yes*, he thought. *Food can definitely wait.*

He kissed her lips again, then took one of her hands in his. 'Let's go to the bedroom,' he said. 'Okay?'

'Oh, yes,' she said.

Together, they walked inside and upstairs to their bedroom, where they quickly disrobed, leaving their clothes in a pile on the floor. Josh lit candles at the bedside, then stood relishing the sight of her body, splendid in the candlelight. Her pert breasts with their small rosy nipples beckoned to him from above a long, slender torso that culminated in the sweetness between her firm thighs.

Joanna went to him, her desire heightened by the sight of his tanned body, its classical proportions and hard muscularity accentuated by his leanness. His manhood, magnificent in arousal, brushed against her as she slid her arms around his thickly muscled neck, offering her lips to him.

113

Josh took her in his powerful arms, running them up and down her back and across her shapely buttocks, kissing her passionately, deeply, his tongue exploring her mouth. Then drawing back slightly, he led her to the bed, and she spread out on her back, looking up at him. He moved atop her, his knees between her thighs, his hands running up her thighs to her torso and on up to her breasts, caressing her tenderly. Then, leaning down, he took a breast in his mouth, kissing and licking it, while massaging the other with his hand.

Joanna moaned with pleasure and reached down, down between his strong thighs, and took his throbbing cock in her hand, squeezing it slightly. Josh tensed momentarily and groaned, then spread his thighs and let her lightly feather his testicles with her fingertips.

Aroused to a feverish pitch, he ran his tongue from her breasts down her torso, licking and kissing her flesh with urgent need, until he reached the mound between her thighs. He sat up and brushed the darkness there with his fingers, enjoying the look of carnal desire on her face, guiding her hand back to his cock again. Slowly and gently he inserted a finger between her swollen lips, playfully exploring her wetness as she stroked his manhood.

Joanna moaned again, her need overwhelming. 'Oh, Josh,' she whispered. 'Please, please. I can't wait.'

He withdrew his fingers and took her hand away from his cock, then spread her legs apart slightly. Leaning down, he buried his mouth between her thighs, licking and kissing her ravenously, teasing her unmercifully with his tongue.

Joanna writhed from side to side, moans of ecstatic pleasure escaping her parted lips. She didn't think she could hold back another instant, so close to climax was she, but he suddenly withdrew and then covered her body with his in one swift motion. His mouth hungrily sought out hers as he lifted his buttocks and plunged into her, all the way to the hilt.

Joanna gasped aloud and threw her arms around his back, opening herself to him, welcoming his need. They began to move together, their rhythm increasing in speed almost instantaneously. It seemed only moments before she cried aloud as wave after wave of heavenly contractions consumed her, engulfing her in a climactic ecstasy that only this man had ever given her.

'Oh, Josh,' she cried. 'Oh, my God. Oh, yes. Yes, yes, *yes!*'

With the sound of her cry, Josh let himself go, thrusting with all his might, not holding back any longer. When he came, he groaned with pleasure, his entire body tensing, then quivering, as his love for Joanna burst forth, filling her to overflowing.

He collapsed atop her then, his mouth peppering her face with kisses. 'Oh, Joanna,' he rasped. 'Oh, my God, that was wonderful.'

'Oh, yes,' she gasped between breaths, squeezing him to her. 'Oh, yes.'

He rolled off her, and they lay face to face in

the candlelight, kissing one another tenderly, stroking gently as their breathing slowly returned to normal.

At last Josh, his hands cradling her face, looked into her eyes. 'I love you so much,' he said. 'I don't think you'll ever know how much.'

'And I love you, Josh,' she said.

There was a hint of sadness in her voice and in her eyes that Josh didn't detect because a cool, powerful breeze caught the draperies at the open French doors, and they billowed out into the room like banners. The candles at the bedside sputtered and nearly went out.

Joanna shivered involuntarily, then laughed. 'Maybe we'd better bring the food inside,' she said. 'What do you think?'

Josh squeezed her gently and smiled. 'Maybe that's a good idea,' he replied. 'If the wind hasn't blown it away.'

In the breakfast room, Joanna laid down her knife and fork, then wiped her lips with a napkin.

Josh looked over at her and smiled. 'Are you quitting already?' he asked. 'I know the steak is terrible, it's so overdone, but it *is* edible.'

'It's okay,' Joanna replied. 'I've had plenty.'

Josh looked at her worriedly. It wasn't like her not to eat. She usually relished her food even if she did watch her portions and calories. But, he reasoned, there was probably nothing amiss. After all, the salad was now limp, the potatoes were overdone from two trips to the microwave, and the steak tasted like it had been boiled.

'It's not too great, is it?' he said with a grin.

Joanna smiled. 'Not exactly what I'd planned,' she said, taking a sip of her wine.

'Well, who cares?' Josh replied. He touched his fingers to his lips, then pressed them to her cheek. 'I'd rather have you for dinner anytime.'

Joanna smiled again. 'You bet,' she said, pressing his fingers with her hand. 'Maybe that's why I'm so full.'

She watched Josh finish eating, reflecting on the evening. Her swim had been wonderfully relaxing and invigorating, and their lovemaking had been nothing less than perfection. Nevertheless, the evening's magic was already beginning to dissipate, and she was beginning to feel uncomfortably edgy.

Oh, why, she asked herself, *do I feel this awful sort of darkness descending? Why do I feel as if I'm merely marking time here, with my beloved Josh?* But she knew the answer. She simply couldn't verbalize it yet, as if refusing to discuss it would keep its grim reality at bay.

No, she wouldn't give the awful truth credence. Not now. Not yet.

9

The sun had already burned off the morning's mist and was quickly warming up the day. Josh walked into the breakfast room, stretching his powerful arms and shaking his luxuriant head of hair.

'Good morning, everyone,' he announced.

He leaned down and nuzzled Joanna vigorously with his clean-shaven face, peppering her with an inordinate number of kisses.

Joanna looked up at him, smiling. He was like a kid, she thought. He beamed with the pride and satisfaction of a boy who'd discovered one of life's greatest secrets the night before.

Connie, who was busy in the kitchen shelling shrimp, looked through the arched doorway with a bemused expression. 'You're awfully cheery this morning, Josh.'

Josh winked at her. 'Had an exceptional night, Connie. An exceptional night!' He grinned. 'Slept like a bear, too.'

Connie laughed and shook an accusatory finger at him. 'You better behave yourself.'

'I always do, Connie,' he replied. 'Always do.' He sat down and picked up the newspaper that was laid next to his place at the table and started flipping through it.

The telephone rang, and Connie answered it in the kitchen.

'It's for you, Josh,' she called. 'Carl.'

He picked up an extension in the breakfast room. 'Carl?' He listened for a few minutes, grunting replies, then hung up the receiver.

'Anything important?' Joanna asked.

'No, not really,' he replied, going back to his newspaper.

Joanna pretended to be interested in the latest *Vogue*, idly flipping through it, nursing a cup of coffee. Despite the great sex, she had hardly slept at all, had tossed and turned all night. And when she'd finally dozed off, terribly realistic nightmares had haunted her in such a frightening way that she'd gladly relinquished them for an unhappy wakefulness.

Josh began heartily putting away the pancakes with strawberries and cream that Connie had brought to him, washing it down with hot black coffee. He looked over at Joanna. 'You've already eaten?' he asked.

'Yes,' she said, looking up from the magazine. 'I was up with the birds and went ahead.'

'What've you got planned for today?' he asked.

'I've got ten million errands to run,' she said, 'and a lot of telephone calls to make. The usual.'

'Home for lunch?' he asked.

She nodded. 'If you'll be here, I'll be here.'

'Good,' he said with a smile. 'I'll be here for sure.'

He finished eating quickly, then rose to his feet, and leaning down, kissed her on the cheek. 'I've got to run, but I'll be back from the nursery somewhere around twelve-thirty.'

Josh raced out of the house, and in the distance they could hear him fire up his ancient Land Cruiser. After he was out of earshot, Joanna put the *Vogue* down and headed for the bedroom. She shrugged off her bathrobe and quickly changed into khaki slacks, a lightweight cashmere pullover, and comfortable Gucci flats. Grabbing a straw sun hat and her shoulder bag, she went back out to the kitchen.

'I'll be out for a while, Connie.'

'Errands?' Connie asked, still peeling shrimp.

Joanna nodded. 'Yes.'

Connie looked at her with a puzzled expression but didn't say anything. Normally, Joanna would tell her exactly where she was going and how long she expected to be gone. Not today. She worried, like Josh, that something was truly wrong.

Joanna went out to the entrance hall, where she took her car keys from an Imari bowl set atop an

Irish Georgian console. She took her sunglasses out of her shoulder bag, slid them out of their case, and put them on. Finally, she put on the straw hat and looked at herself in the large gilt-framed mirror over the console.

'You'll do,' she told her reflection. She stepped out the front door and opened the garage door with her electronic beeper. Her old Mercedes convertible, a gift from her father years ago, appeared in its bay, and she hurried to it and slid in. The top was already down. She adjusted the chin strap on her hat to keep it from flying off, then fired the car up and drove out of the courtyard in a flash.

As she left the house behind and began the curvy descent down the mountain, she breathed a sigh of relief. *Thank God*, she thought. *I can get away from the house, from Connie, from Josh, the telephone.* From all the responsibilities, the decisions, that running the household entailed.

She had a million things to do, but she simply couldn't cope with any of that today. Shopping could wait, the grotto project could wait, the various orchid societies could wait, all of her charitable activities could wait. And her friends with their gossip, their problems, their little triumphs and defeats could wait, too!

I have to be alone, she thought. *Alone to think.*

Reaching the freeway ramps, she made a spur-of-the-moment decision to head south. South to – where? She didn't know, but she had to drive. Speeding along in the freeway's light morning traffic, she finally began to breathe easier. She let up on the gas, slowing her pace a little. She didn't want to be stopped by the highway patrol, and she could see that they were out in full force, as usual.

She gradually became aware of the sun's warmth on her body, of the wind whipping at her hat, of the terrain around her. She caught occasional glimpses of the Pacific off in the distance to her right, the sun glinting off it brightly.

On she drove, mindless of where she might end up, almost unaware of the fact that she exited the freeway somewhere in Watsonville and started driving down meandering streets but, inevitably it seemed, gradually climbing back up into those very same mountains she'd just left.

The road became a series of twists and turns with washouts and stop signs, almost indistinguishable from the one that wound up the mountain to her house.

Slowing down, she suddenly realized where she was. *My God*, she thought. *I must've been on automatic pilot or something.* It was as if some force greater than herself, some mysterious kind of magnet, had drawn her here. She had discovered that in this magical place the terrible headaches that had begun six months ago often dissipated, their pain blanketed for a while at least.

Approaching the turnoff on her left, she became excited. *I hope no one's here*, she thought, looking about.

She made the turn and slowly drove up the steep,

curving drive to the small parking area. She was pleased to see that there wasn't another car there. She looked over at the garden's high fence. It was lushly overladen with several different varieties of climbing roses, many of them huge, old plants. She strolled over, stopping to sniff Dainty Bess, a fragrant pale pinkish one, then found the familiar wooden gate and let herself in, careful to latch it closed against the deer.

She looked about her.

No one. Not another soul.

She smiled and took a deep breath. The air was heady with the perfume of thousands of rose blooms. She began slowly negotiating the garden paths, looking at the little markers to familiarize herself once again with the names of the roses that grew here. Many of them were of the old-fashioned variety, dating from the 1800s, and they were much more fragrant than most of the modern hybrid teas which had become so popular.

Kneeling down, she took a huge Comte de Chambord in hand and smelled its fragrance, noting that, according to its marker, it was from 1860. She walked on, smiling at the names. Duchess d'Brantes, Marchioness of Lorne, Lady Hillingdon, Bishop Darlington, Honorine de Brabant, Gruss an Coberg, Gruss an Aachen, Jacques Cartier, Louise Odier.

The beds were laid out in a haphazard manner, lined with old boards, and the paths were either dirt, black-top, or gravel. The fencing varied, too, from weathered wood to rusty wire. There was a guiding principle in this garden, however, Joanna thought, and that was beauty. The sheer beauty of the colors and the fragrances made up for the garden's apparent lack of formal structure and its rundown condition.

Certainly, she thought, *love has been lavished on this magical little clearing here in the midst of the redwoods.*

She strolled on, passing the small area devoted to potted roses that were for sale and stopped to look at the wooden stall that served as an office. The garden operated on the honor system, and there was a box with a slot in which to deposit checks or cash for roses. Joanna was always gratified that the system seemed to work and had for as long as she could remember.

Ahead she saw a wooden bench, weathered silver by time and weather. It offered a shady seat under a rickety wooden arbor, a venerable pink Cécile Brünner climbing up the arbor, then cascading down it dramatically. Sitting, she inhaled deeply again, savoring the mixture of perfumes, the warmth of the sun on her legs, the cool of the shade on her face. She closed her eyes for a few minutes, enjoying the peaceful quiet, as her mind, without the distractions of home, began to focus on the problem that she had to sort out.

I've got to talk to somebody about this, she decided. *And soon. I simply can't carry this terrible secret alone anymore.*

She had thought for some time now that she could bravely soldier along, bottling her problems up inside, not burdening anyone else. *I guess I'm not as brave as I thought,* she reflected. *Because I have to talk to somebody.*

I see that now. I have to share this terrible pain, this dreadful sense of loss, and the overwhelming fear.

Josh, of course, was the obvious choice. After all, he was her husband and her closest friend. *I must tell Josh first. It's only fair that I share this burden with him, despite the pain and suffering that he'll have to endure.*

Now she felt immensely pleased, with this place and herself. She felt some of the tremendous weight that lay so heavily on her shoulders lift. Perhaps now, she thought, some of the darkness that pervaded her nights and days would dissipate, too. After all, it was becoming increasingly difficult to hide the truth from him.

Yes, she thought. *I'll tell my sweet Josh. He deserves to know the truth.*

She lingered a while longer, ambling along the garden's paths, then decided to leave, but not before she'd said a prayer of thanks to this beautiful, magical place for the solace that it had afforded her, for the truths that it inevitably seemed to make evident to her.

Josh sat alone at the big dining table on the terrace, finishing the last of the two tuna fish sandwiches that Connie had made him. He always loved the flavor of cilantro that she put in it, but lately he'd come to the conclusion she was putting cilantro in everything.

Or maybe I'm just grumpy, he thought.

He looked over at the remains of the artichoke salad that had tasted so great. Did it have cilantro in it too?

He took a sip of the iced tea, then set the glass down and wiped his mouth with a crisp linen napkin. He looked across the table at the place that had been set for Joanna. *Great*, he thought. *Only there's no Joanna.* And that, he knew, was why he was in such a bad mood. She had done another of her disappearing acts.

In all the years of their marriage, they had dined together whenever possible, and few were the times when either of them hadn't been able to make it. Perhaps, he thought, he expected too much of her. After all, how many couples did he know who managed to live the way they did? Or wanted to, for that matter?

He realized that most of the couples they knew wouldn't *want* to live and work as closely as they did. He and Joanna, however, had found that this way of life suited them. They had been a team from the very beginning, and he couldn't conceive of their being any other way. He guessed it was because he was as in love with her now, after ten years of marriage, as he had been all those years ago when they'd first met.

Maybe that's the problem, he thought. *I'm still in love with her and she's—*

'Josh!' Joanna's unmistakably cheerful voice rang in his ears, interrupting his thoughts.

He turned and saw her rushing across the terrace to the table, all smiles. He slid his chair back and got to his feet. When she reached him, he kissed her breathless lips and hugged her to him.

'I'm . . . sorry I'm . . . late,' she said breathily.

'Where've you been?' he asked.

She sat down, dropping her shoulder bag to the

terrace beside her. Josh sat down too, taking another sip of his tea.

Connie appeared with a tray of sandwiches and salad for Joanna and began pouring tea for her.

'Thanks, Connie,' Joanna said. Then she looked at Josh. 'Oh ... I ... I had a lot of errands to run,' she replied.

He knew immediately that she was being vague. He hated to pursue the subject, playing the inquisitor, but he couldn't help himself. 'What kind of errands?' he asked, trying to sound as casual as possible.

'Oh, you know,' she said, taking her napkin and placing it in her lap. 'Little things. Dumb things like taking some clothes to the cleaners. You know, nothing important.'

Connie's heavy-lidded eyes narrowed to suspicious slits. She knew that Joanna had left empty-handed, and she also knew that she hadn't come back home with any shopping. She didn't say anything, however.

Josh gazed across the table at his wife with curiosity. He remembered the decision he'd come to out in the greenhouse, about having a serious talk with her. Now he felt compelled to continue questioning her, to probe further into her recent penchant for being aloof.

But then the memory of last night's wonderful intimacy swept aside any doubts he might have had about Joanna's behavior. She had been herself then, he thought. Loving, caring, and attentive, and the lingering sense of well-being and joy that their sex had left him with, that had made his morning so extraordinarily cheerful, reassured him that there was nothing really wrong.

Still, he thought, *maybe I should just mention her aloofness lately. Just ask her if there's something going on that I should know about, without making a big deal out of it.*

But before he could say anything the telephone bleeped, and Connie, who was putting his empty plates on a tray, picked up the remote that lay on the table.

'Hello?' she said, then listened for a moment.

She held the remote out to Josh. 'It's Carl,' she said.

Josh took the receiver from her. 'Thanks, Connie,' he said.

'What's going on, Carl?' he asked.

Joanna, munching on her tuna fish sandwich, watched him from across the table. She could see that he'd become visibly excited and wondered what Carl could be calling about.

The instant Josh punched the off button on the remote, she asked, 'What is it?'

Josh just looked at her and grinned like a Cheshire cat.

'What?' she repeated, really intrigued now.

'Guess who's coming in to the nursery?' Josh asked her teasingly.

'Who?' she asked, becoming exasperated, but enjoying his game.

'Guess.'

'Oh, Josh, stop it!' she cried. 'Who is it?'

'Mr Hara,' he said.

'Oh, heaven!' she exclaimed. 'This is heaven!' She jumped up from her seat and dashed to him, throwing her arms around his neck and planting a kiss on the top of his head.

'He called from his car,' he went on. 'He's on his way down from San Jose and will only be here today. So I'd better get moving.'

Joanna kissed his head again, then let him get to his feet. 'Do you want me to come with you?' she asked.

'No, you don't have to,' he said. 'I will happily deal with this.'

'Okay,' she said. 'I was going to go through some books to get more material together for April, but if you need me—'

'No,' he said. 'Do your thing.' He gave her a quick kiss. 'But how about helping me load up a few prize specimens from the greenhouse here to take down with me.'

'Let's go,' she said.

Holding hands, they headed toward the greenhouse, set aside the specimens Josh wanted, and made four trips to his Land Cruiser to load them up. When he left, Joanna was blowing kisses from the courtyard. Josh returned her kisses and waved out the window.

On his way to the nursery, he knew that he should be counting his lucky stars. Mr Hara was one of the world's richest and most important collectors of rare orchids, and just to have an orchid in his collection was deemed an honor among orchid growers and fanciers. He would spend as much as fifteen or twenty thousand dollars for a seedling in bloom, and Josh wouldn't be surprised if he spent a hundred thousand dollars or more today.

His enthusiasm was tempered, however, by a niggling awareness that had crept into his consciousness and refused to go away. It was an annoying feeling that something important had been left unsaid, that there was definitely something amiss on the home front.

I've got to have that talk with Joanna, he reminded himself. *Got to.*

10

Spring was turning to summer with a vengeance, and April cruised down the road in her old Jeep Wagoneer with all the windows open. The breeze filled the car with the overpowering aroma of Brussels sprouts. Some would call it a stench, she reflected, but she didn't mind it at all. There were acres and acres of them on both sides of the road here, in fields as flat as her kitchen table. On her right, they spread out as far as the eye could see toward the mountains, and on her left they swept straight up to the dunes that bordered the Pacific. She'd always marveled that such potentially expensive real estate would be used for growing vegetables.

She drove at a brisk pace, but kept her eyes peeled for the turnoff to Lawrence Nursery. She'd been down this road a thousand times on her way south to Monterey and points beyond, but she'd never noticed the sign for the nursery.

When Joanna had called yesterday and asked to meet her here, she'd assumed she was phoning to see if the preliminary sketches were finished. They were due tomorrow, and April thought that Joanna, like so many clients, might be getting anxious, perhaps even a little pushy. Instead, she'd been pleasantly surprised to be invited to meet her at the nursery today, without a single mention of the sketches.

She'd been glad to hear from her in any case. After being cooped up in the cottage like a hermit for the past week, working for hours a day drawing, erasing, and redrawing, she was more than ready for an outing. Woody had tried to cajole her into dinner, but she'd refused, so intent was she on meeting Joanna's deadline. When she hadn't been actually sketching, she'd been thumbing through all the books and pictures Joanna had lent her, searching for ideas, inspiration – anything to set her imagination on fire. And set on fire it had become, working feverishly, supplying her with more ideas than she could realistically use.

Now she felt as if her preliminary plans were more or less final, but she wanted to spend some more time with them tonight.

On her left, she spotted the sign that announced Lawrence Nursery. She'd never been to an orchid nursery before, and looked forward to the grand tour.

Joanna thought she should see as many orchid specimens as possible to get ideas for the grotto.

A quarter of a mile or so down the road, she saw the nursery on her right. Turning off, April pulled into the gravel parking lot. Grabbing her carryall, she slid out of the car and stood looking around.

Shielding her eyes from the sun with her hand, she gazed at the big Victorian house with its gingerbread trim, incongruously surrounded by greenhouses. It was immaculately kept, imposing even, but still, it looked oddly out of place.

She didn't see Joanna's Mercedes in the parking lot, but she followed the sign to a gate and a little walkway to the house. The fenced-in yard was tiny, with a few trees and shrubs, beautifully tended, but disproportionately small for the size of the house. She walked up the steps to the porch and opened one of the double doors into the cool of the office.

The reception area had obviously once been the entrance hall, an oddly shaped room, almost but not quite round. In the center was a desk, behind which sat a strikingly beautiful woman with jet-black hair and large dark eyes and too much makeup. She was talking on the telephone in rapid-fire Spanish.

When she looked over and saw April, she smiled slightly and pointed to a chair with her long carmine-lacquered fingernail, but didn't miss a beat in her telephone conversation. The torrent of Spanish continued at a furious pace, her eyes glittering, her free hand gesticulating wildly.

April sat down in the indicated chair and watched the woman with fascination. She could see that her lips were the brightest cerise, lined with a darker shade of red, and the heavy eye shadow above her dark brown eyes was a purplish brown. Her lashes were thick with mascara, and rouge highlighted her prominent cheekbones. Her perfect white teeth shone dazzlingly against her painted lips.

Suddenly the woman burst into a series of high-pitched giggles, said 'Ciao,' then replaced the receiver in its cradle. She looked over at April. 'Sorry,' she said in lightly accented English. 'A loco customer. Loco, loco, *loco!*'

'No problem,' April said, smiling. 'I'm supposed to meet Joanna Lawrence here.'

The young woman's eyebrows lifted. 'Joanna? Ah! Just a minute, please.' She pressed a button on the telephone and picked up the receiver, then looked at April again. 'What's your name?' she asked.

'April Woodward,' she replied.

'April,' the woman said, as if practicing. Then speaking into the receiver: 'There's a lady here. April Woodward. She's supposed to meet Joanna, but Joanna's not here.'

She listened for a moment, then hung up. 'Josh, Mr Lawrence, will be right out,' she said.

'Thanks,' April said.

The curtained French doors to her left opened, and Josh Lawrence stepped out of his office, beaming, his teeth no less dazzling against his darkly tanned skin than the secretary's. Dressed in khaki cargo shorts, khaki shirt, and work boots, he looked like the nurseryman he was. *He also looks drop-dead handsome*, she thought.

'April,' he said, holding out his hand for a shake. 'Welcome to our little operation.'

April rose to her feet and shook his hand. 'I hope I'm not imposing,' she said, looking into his blue eyes. 'Joanna asked me to meet her here. She's supposed to give me the grand tour.'

'No trouble at all,' he said. 'She's probably just running a little late. Did you meet Luna?' He indicated the secretary/receptionist.

'No,' she said, turning and extending a hand to Luna. 'Not formally.'

Luna stood up and shook hands across her desk. 'It's nice to meet you,' she said. She looked at Josh and let out another giggle. 'I was . . . I was on the telephone when she came in,' she said.

Josh grinned. 'As usual,' he said good-naturedly. He turned to April. 'Come on in, I'll see if I can get Joanna on the telephone.'

April walked into his office and looked around. *Must have been the parlor*, she thought. Facing her was a large Victorian desk centered in front of a bay window. The desk chair was on the window side, and on her side were two comfortable-looking leather-upholstered chairs.

'Have a seat,' Josh said, walking in behind her and closing the French door. 'I'll try to get Joanna.'

'Thanks,' April said, sitting in one of the chairs.

She watched as Josh sat on the edge of the desk and dialed a number, then she quickly averted her gaze. *Why do I feel as if I'm staring?* she wondered. *Trying to better see his blue eyes, his sun-bleached hair, those white-white teeth, and that wonderful tanned body?*

'Hey, Connie,' he said, 'is Joanna around, or has she left for here?'

He listened a moment, then said, 'Thanks, Connie, see you later.'

He hung up the receiver and turned to April. 'She's on her way,' he said. 'She refuses to get a cell phone, or I'd see how long she's going to be.' He smiled apologetically. 'I hope Luna didn't keep you waiting.'

'It's okay,' April assured him. 'I've got time.' Suddenly she felt slightly uncomfortable being alone in his presence. *How silly,* she thought. *He's Joanna's husband and a perfectly nice, perfectly harmless man.* Nevertheless, she found herself nervous as she tried to make conversation.

'Luna seems to be quite a lady,' she said.

He laughed. 'Luna's a little bit of a maniac,' he said. 'But she can juggle eight or ten phone calls at a time and get blood out of a turnip. Meaning,' he said, looking at her with amusement, 'she can get slow-paying customers to cough up cash. And fast.'

April smiled. 'Sounds like what every office needs.'

'She's great,' he said. 'Her husband's our manager. Carl. You'll meet him today. He's Connie's brother.'

'Oh,' she said, 'so you've got the whole family on the payroll.'

'Just about,' he replied, standing up. 'What do you say we go ahead and start the tour without Joanna? Is that okay with you?'

'That's fine,' April said, 'if I'm not taking too much of your time.'

'No,' he said, 'I can always spare time to get out of the office.'

April rose to her feet, and Josh ushered her out.

'Luna, we'll be looking around the greenhouses,' he said. 'Send Joanna on out when she gets here.'

Luna, her ear attached to the telephone receiver, nodded.

They went back out into the tiny front yard and through the gate, then turned onto a path leading to the greenhouses.

'This place is fascinating,' April said.

'Joanna's family built it in the eighteen hundreds,' Josh said. 'They were farmers. Then her father started the nursery, and it grew and grew. So he built the house we live in now and moved out of this place. But Mitch, her dad, always wanted to keep the house as office space. So we've kept up the tradition.'

They came to a high chain-link fence that surrounded the greenhouse area. The gates were open, and they walked on toward an enormous greenhouse.

'Good Lord,' April said, 'I've never seen a greenhouse this big before.'

'There are seven in all,' Josh said. 'They cover over eighty thousand square feet.'

'Eighty thousand!' April exclaimed.

'Uh-huh,' he said. 'Our business is almost totally wholesale. We ship thousands of relatively inexpensive, easy-to-grow orchids to nurseries all over the country.

139

We also supply a lot of the nurseries that sell through catalogues. Our specialty, though, is dealing in the rarities – they set us apart from other nurseries.'

He opened the door to the greenhouse and held it wide for her.

April stepped in and almost gasped at the sheer size of the space and what must have been thousands of orchid plants. As at the little greenhouse at their house, the air smelled of compost and was damp with humidity.

'It looks like you've got every orchid on earth here,' she said.

'Hardly,' Josh said. 'There're over twenty thousand species of orchids, and there're over a hundred thousand hybrid crosses registered so far.'

'I had no idea,' she said.

They started walking down a path between tables. 'This is one of what I call our bread-and-butter areas. All these are *Phalaenopsis*,' he said. 'What a lot of people call the Moth Orchid. It's one of the biggest sellers because they're relatively inexpensive and easy to grow at home. We have thousands of these. *Paphiopedilums* and *Cattleyas*, too, for the same reason. But we're getting so much competition from the Taiwanese with these varieties that it's a good thing we've always relied on our rarities for the really major money. That and our reputation for having the best stock available.'

'The Taiwanese?' she said. 'But how can they compete with you here?'

'Our government allows them to ship in orchid plants if they're bare roots, not in dirt,' he said. 'They've flooded the market with some varieties shipped in bare root, then potted here. Now what the Taiwanese have started doing is buying up land and building greenhouses all the way from Vancouver down to San Diego. They grow vast quantities without any regard to quality.'

'That's ... unbelievable,' she said.

'Believe it,' he said. 'Luckily, we have rarities and are known for extraordinary quality. That's what's kept us going while a lot of others have been wiped out.'

On they walked, through greenhouse after greenhouse, stopping here to admire a particularly flamboyant specimen, there to discuss native habitats. He patiently explained the computer-operated misters that periodically bathed the plants, and answered her questions about the automatic overhead screens that opened and closed to compensate for the shadows of passing clouds. He explained that conditions in the different greenhouses varied, depending on the orchids housed there, in an effort to reproduce their natural habitats.

'We have orchids from places as diverse as the temples at Machu Picchu, the Himalayas, and the most tropical parts of Brazil,' he told her. 'So we have to re-create their environments.'

Josh could see that she was truly interested in the nursery, even the technical aspects, and was gratified by her constant stream of questions. He met lots of orchid lovers, but very few people who were really interested in anything much beyond the beauty of their exotic blooms and where they came from.

'You know what?' she said after they'd been touring for quite some time, 'I've been so absorbed in all this that I completely forgot to make notes.'

'Make notes?' he asked. 'For what?'

'For the grotto room, of course,' she said. 'I wanted to pick out some of the orchids that would especially lend themselves to being re-created with shells and pebbles.'

'So you've definitely decided to take on the project?' he asked.

'Oh, yes,' April said enthusiastically. 'Definitely. I've become so wrapped up in it the last week that I couldn't say no.'

From behind them came an unmistakable voice. 'That's the first *I've* heard of it!'

Startled, April and Josh turned to look behind them and saw Joanna, arms akimbo, eyebrows knotted in a frown. For a moment April didn't know what to think of Joanna's posture, but then Joanna burst into gales of laughter and rushed forward to hug April and pepper her cheeks with kisses.

'I'm so thrilled!' she cried. 'I was afraid you might say no.'

Josh watched the two of them with a smile on his face. It was so wonderful to see Joanna this enthused by a project, and she'd obviously found the perfect person for it. *Yes*, he thought, *April is really . . . special.*

'I almost did say no,' April said. 'Because of the tight schedule and having to give up other projects, but after spending the last few days doing sketches, and now, seeing this place' – she shrugged eloquently – 'I guess I've sort of caught the bug.'

Josh's eyes widened with surprise, and he looked at her intently. 'You mean the orchid bug?' he asked.

'Well . . .' April began, 'I . . . I guess it's a combination of the grotto project with the shells and pebbles *and* the orchids. All mixed up together, it's a sort of rare and . . . well, seductive proposition.'

'I knew it,' Joanna said. 'I knew I'd discovered just the person.'

'Welcome to the family,' Josh said.

April looked up at him and smiled tentatively. 'Thanks,' she managed to say, not certain what she should make of his statement.

'Have you spotted some candidates for the grotto?' Joanna asked.

'I was just telling Josh that I'd completely forgotten to take notes,' April replied. 'But I've definitely seen some excellent choices.'

'Why don't I leave you two alone to do your work?' Josh said, 'and I'll get back to mine.'

'That's fine,' Joanna said. 'We'll be here for a bit, then we're going back up to the house.'

They kissed and he turned to April. 'See you later,' he said.

'Thanks a million for all your trouble, Josh,' she said. 'I really do appreciate it.'

He nodded and left.

'Now,' Joanna said, 'did you see everything?'

'I think so,' April replied, 'but I'm not really sure.'

'Well, what if we do a quick run-through,' she proposed, 'and I'll show you plants I've thought would be good to use. And you can show me the ones you like. We can make a list and then pare it down.'

The neoclassical conservatory at Joanna and Josh's had well-worn floors of old French limestone. It was filled with various kinds of palms, ferns, and, of course, orchids. In the center was a huge *pietra dura* table, its various marbles fitted together to create beautiful patterns, centered with doves in trees. Over the table hung a magnificent crystal chandelier with sixteen lights. It was the ideal place to work, Joanna and April decided, and it was there that April spread out her preliminary sketches.

After poring over them intently for several minutes, shuffling them this way and that, Joanna looked up at April, who had been watching like a slightly nervous mother hen for her reactions to them.

'They're beautiful,' Joanna said simply. 'And exactly what I had in mind.'

April let out a sigh of relief. 'Good,' she said. 'I've really done my homework this week, and was hoping you'd be pleased.'

'Just one or two things,' Joanna said in a take-command voice.

Oh, no, April thought with a sinking heart. *Now she's probably going to act like some clients and change everything I've done.*

Joanna saw the obvious look of consternation on

April's face, and her voice and demeanor immediately softened.

'Oh, dear,' she said. 'I've alarmed you, haven't I?'

'It's okay,' April said. 'Go ahead and say what it is that displeases you.'

'April!' Joanna turned and placed her hands on April's shoulders and looked her in the eye. 'It's nothing,' she said. 'I *love* your plans, but I want to make a couple of suggestions. That's all. Now look happy.'

April couldn't help but smile.

'That's better,' Joanna said, and she turned back to the plans, shuffling them around again, until she found what she wanted. It was a sketch of an interior wall, complete with a dado, niches, and other architectural elements, all made of shells and pebbles.

'Look at this, for example,' Joanna said.

April leaned down over the drawing with Joanna. She had worked so hard on these drawings that she couldn't believe anybody would want to change anything.

'This is a perfect interpretation of a wall in a neoclassical room,' Joanna said. 'I love it. And there's only *one* little change I want you to execute.'

April looked at her, and Joanna smiled.

'Blur the boundaries,' Joanna said.

'What do you mean?' April asked.

'Pretend this is a plan for a formal garden, if you will,' Joanna said.

'Okay,' April said, nodding.

'Now,' Joanna went on, 'pretend this garden is

145

planted, everything very neatly placed, as it is here. Every shell and pebble in its proper place.'

April nodded again.

'Now,' Joanna said, looking at her, 'let the plants get a little overgrown. Let them run a little rampant.' Then, carefully enunciating each word, she said: 'Let the formal lines blur. Allow a shell to creep over a line, or a pebble to do the same.'

April looked at her with dawning comprehension. 'I . . . I see what you mean,' she said.

'I thought you would,' Joanna said, smiling.

'I could get a little baroque around the edges,' April said, looking back at her plan.

'*Yes!*' Joanna said. 'Put the line there, then super-impose a curve on it. That sort of thing.'

'And that'll be a snap with the shells,' April said. 'Oh, you're a genius, Joanna!' she said.

Joanna laughed. 'No,' she said, 'I've just thought about it a lot. I can see masses of coral used as pediments over doors—'

'Coral?' April exclaimed.

'Why, yes,' Joanna said. 'What's wrong?'

'Joanna,' April said, 'coral is endangered. You are not, I repeat, *not* going to use coral in this grotto.'

Joanna looked at her and saw that she was quite serious. 'Well,' she said, 'I have tons of it that I've collected over the years, just waiting to be used. Why let it go to waste?'

'Because when people see what you've done here, some of them will want to try to copy it,' April said.

'They'll go out and buy coral wherever they can find it, and that'll only encourage shops to keep selling it. It's like a vicious cycle.'

'But—'

'No buts,' April said, shaking her head. 'Besides, there are substitutes. Things that aren't endangered that will work just as well.'

Joanna took a deep breath and sighed. *This is one gutsy lady*, she thought. *Sticking to her guns like this. She has real backbone, real principles.*

'You win,' she finally said with a smile. 'I have to admit I feel a little embarrassed because I knew that coral was endangered, but I wanted to use it anyway. But I see what you mean.'

'You know, there are going to be so many options,' April said, 'that I don't think you'll miss the coral.'

'Oh, I know,' Joanna said. 'Oh, by the way ...' She walked over to a long built-in bookshelf under one of the windows and started rummaging around, then pulled out a large stack of books and catalogues. 'Look what I've got,' she said, returning to the table and putting down her load.

'What?' April asked.

'You'll see,' Joanna said. She took a catalogue off the top of the stack and handed it to April.

April started flipping through it, and her eyes widened with amazement. 'This is fabulous,' she said excitedly. 'Oh, Joanna, how did you ever come by this?'

'I bought some shells in a shop in Monterey,' she said. 'There were so many that the lady packed them in a box from her wholesaler. So I called the whole-saler up in Oregon, pretended to be an artist who worked with seashells, and they sent me the cata-logue.'

April looked at her, and they both laughed.

'It was one of the hardest things I ever did,' Joanna said. 'I mean actually telling the lady I was an *artist*. Not only an artist, but one who worked with *seashells*. It felt so . . . goofy . . . and phony. But she bought it hook, line, and sinker. So did several others. Because I started going into shops and making little purchases and telling shopkeepers the same thing to get the name of their wholesalers.'

'You are *so* clever,' April said. 'We're certainly not going to have a problem getting enough shells or the types that we need. We'll pool our resources. I've used a couple of wholesalers in the past.'

'Plus,' Joanna said, 'we've still got the thousands I've collected, and I want to use them first, if possible. They have a lot of sentimental value for me.'

'I can see why,' April said, 'and I think that's a wonderful idea.

'Another thing we'd better discuss right away – well, two actually. One is the orchids, and the other is my estimate. I hadn't intended to give it to you until the meeting we'd planned tomorrow, but I have it with me and might as well go ahead and give it to you before we go any further.'

'Why don't we discuss the orchids first?' Joanna said with a laugh.

April smiled. 'I want to sketch a few of the ones here and photograph them, and some of those we saw today at the nursery.'

'That's fine,' Joanna said.

'But,' April said, 'I don't want to take them home with me to do the work. I don't want to be responsible for any valuable ones.'

'I understand,' Joanna said. She tapped her lips with a finger for a moment, thinking, then looked back at April. 'You're welcome to work on them here, if you like,' she said. 'You could use this room. The light's wonderful. What do you think of that?'

'I wouldn't be in the way?' April asked.

'Not at all,' Joanna said. 'Besides, you're going to have to be here a lot of the time anyway. So what's the difference?'

'Okay,' April said, 'if you really think so. I could use this as a base until the construction work is finished on the stable. Then I could move down there.'

'Perfect,' Joanna said.

'Now,' April said. 'My estimate.' She reached for her shoulder bag, which sat on a chair next to her, and took a folder out. She opened the folder and slid out her typed-up estimate. 'Here,' she said, 'study this and see if you have any questions. I've broken all the costs down as closely as possible.'

Joanna took the estimate from her and looked at it for a long time. April stepped away and looked out the windows toward the swimming pool, trying to give Joanna a degree of privacy.

'I see you've already priced the plumbing and carpentry and everything,' Joanna said.

April turned and nodded.

'I think it's fine,' Joanna said. 'I'll ask Josh to look at it when he comes in tonight, but I don't think there'll be a problem.'

'Okay,' April said, relieved once again. The cost of the project was huge, she knew, but it was going to take the next few months out of her life and require a lot of work.

Joanna approached her and gave her another hug, then drew back and looked at her. 'It'll be fine,' she said. 'So don't worry.'

She turned then and walked back to the big table and picked up a list she'd made. 'Now, let me see,' she said. 'Just a couple of things I've made a note to tell you. I'm going to give you a beeper for the gates out front. They're usually open, but you might find them closed sometime. Oh, and I'll have to give you a beeper for the greenhouse, so you can take plants back and forth anytime you need to.'

'That would be great,' April said.

'And, listen, April,' Joanna continued, 'don't hesitate to ask Connie for anything in the kitchen. Food or drink. Anytime. There's always too much of everything, so that would only be a help to us.'

April laughed. 'That's awfully nice,' she said, 'but I'll probably do like I usually do and bring my lunch.'

'Whatever suits you,' Joanna said.

'Right now,' April said, 'I'd like to go down to the

stable and do some more measurements and do some careful remeasuring. Plus, I might sketch some down there. Is that okay?'

'Sure,' Joanna replied.

'I'll probably be quite a while,' she said.

'Then why don't you stay for dinner?' Joanna said.

'Oh, no,' April said. 'I really shouldn't. I mean . . .'

'I won't take no for an answer,' Joanna said. 'We can have a little champagne to celebrate the beginning of my grotto.'

'In that case,' April said with a laugh, 'I can't say no, can I?'

'No,' Joanna said, shaking her head. 'Absolutely not.'

'Okay,' April said. She started gathering up drawing materials and shouldered her big bag. 'I'll see you later, then.'

'We'll probably eat about seven-thirty or eight,' Joanna said. 'And have that champagne before. Come on back up anytime, or I'll come and get you.'

'Fine,' April said, already heading out through the French doors toward the stable.

From the windows, Joanna watched her walk across the terrace, the little bridge to the pool area, and make her way around the pool until she was out of sight. She squeezed herself with delight.

This is so wonderful, she thought. *It's going to work out better than I had imagined.*

The light was beginning to dim inside the old stable, and April realized that it was later than she'd thought.

She had been so absorbed in her work that time had flown by. She gathered up her measurements, slipped them into a folder, and put it in her shoulder bag. Then she began gathering the few sketches she'd made. They were much more detailed than those she'd shown Joanna, and they also incorporated Joanna's advice about 'blurring the lines.'

She smiled to herself. *Normally,* April thought, *I'm as stubborn as a mule, determined to have it the way I want it.* Today, however, Joanna had taught her a valuable lesson. She could stick to the rules and use the formal structures she knew so well, but then she could play with them – just as she did in her botanical drawings – and actually improve them.

Packed up at last, she left the stable and started back up through the apple trees toward the pool area. The evening was beautiful, the air refreshing, and she felt a wonderful sense of accomplishment from the day's work.

As she crested the rise to the pool area, she heard laughter and water splashing. She came to a standstill when she got within sight of the pool. Candles in hurricane lanterns were all around the pool, set on tables and on walls. The setting was so romantically beautiful, April almost gasped.

Josh was in the pool splashing water up at Joanna, who was sitting on the stone terrace convulsed in laughter.

'That's what you get for dunking me!' he laughed, splashing her once again.

Joanna screeched with delight. 'Stop it!' she cried. 'I'll have to go change clothes now.' She stood up, surveying the damage to her slacks and blouse.

'Serves you right,' he said, his voice full of amusement. He climbed out of the pool and threw his soaking arms around his wife, planting a kiss on her lips.

Joanna squealed with delight again. 'Oh, now you've really done it, Josh,' she said. But she didn't try to struggle out of his arms.

April felt slightly embarrassed watching this sweet domestic scene, but she couldn't take her eyes off them. The picture was so perfect, everything she'd ever imagined a couple to be, everything she'd ever imagined having with a man.

And what a man he is, she mused. *So tall and strong and handsome, yet so tender, gentle, and playful.*

She felt the ache of a longing somewhere deep down inside. It was not the first time she'd ever felt that longing, but it had been a long time. It was almost as if desire were reawakening in her after having been extinguished by her unhappy marriage.

'There you are!' Josh shouted, and to her embarrassment, April realized that he had seen her.

She came completely into view, trying to appear as if she'd just reached the pool area. 'Hi,' she called back.

'Spying on us!' he said playfully.

'No,' she said. Then she laughed. 'But I did see you kiss.'

Joanna and Josh both laughed. 'Come have a glass of

champagne,' Joanna said. 'We were waiting for you to open the bottle.'

'That's so nice of you,' April said. 'But only if Josh promises not to splash water all over me.'

'I promise,' he said with a smile. He picked up a lightweight robe and tied it around himself, then started opening the champagne that rested in a bucket on the table.

April set her shoulder bag down on the terrace next to a chair and watched him.

'I'll be right back,' Joanna said. 'I've got to put on something dry.'

'Hurry,' Josh said, calling after her. 'We might drink it all while you're gone.' Then he looked at April. 'Take a seat,' he said. 'Make yourself comfortable.'

'Thanks, Josh,' she said, sitting down. 'It's so beautiful out here with the candles,' she said.

'It is, isn't it,' he agreed. 'You know, you're welcome to use the pool anytime you want to while you're working here.'

'Thanks,' she said. 'That's awfully generous.'

'Well, it's right here,' he said, 'so why not?' With a loud *pop!* the cork came free from the bottle and April watched a tendril of vapor escape into the air.

'Voilà!' Josh said. He poured champagne into three crystal flutes set on a silver tray. After putting the bottle back in its silver bucket, he handed a glass to April.

'Thanks,' she said, 'but don't you think we should wait for Joanna to have a toast?'

'Yes,' he said. 'You're right. I'm just a greedy pig.'

They both laughed.

'So I'll have a tiny sip, and she won't notice that it's missing from my glass,' he said. He paused and set his glass back down. 'But you will,' he continued. 'So I'd better wait on Joanna.'

April smiled.

'By the way,' he said, 'Joanna showed me your estimate, and I think it's fine. You did a very professional job of it.'

'Thanks,' April said. 'It's a big project so it wasn't easy to do. The construction and all isn't much of a problem, but figuring my own time wasn't easy.'

'I'm sure it'll work out,' Josh said, 'and I'm really glad because it makes Joanna so happy. She's so much like Mitch, her father, always having to be working on something a little creative. She fixed up the old shack at the beach practically by herself. She did her orchid book, and she's always doing something around here. Adding to the garden or redecorating a room, or just changing a color or something.'

'I think that's great,' April said. 'She could be spending all of her time shopping, like some women I know.'

He laughed. 'Thank God I'm spared that.'

'I'm back,' Joanna called. She walked over to the table and sat down. 'How nice,' she said. 'You waited for me.' She turned to April. 'Here,' she said, 'I brought you a shawl in case you get cool in the night air. We'll have dinner in about thirty minutes.'

'Oh, thanks, Joanna,' April said. She took the proffered shawl and wrapped it around her shoulders. It was a luxuriously soft pashmina and a beautiful shade of doeskin that looked good on her.

She noticed that Joanna had changed into a beige silk blouse with matching trousers. A white cashmere sweater was looped around her neck. It was a very casual look that April knew was not easy to achieve. *Like everything else about her*, April thought. She put a lot of hard work into making everything appear to be easy.

'Okay,' Josh said, picking up his champagne flute, 'I'm going to make a toast.'

Joanna and April followed suit, picking up their glasses.

'To the shell grotto,' Josh said, smiling. 'A cockamamie project I never thought Joanna would see to fruition.'

I only hope I do, Joanna thought.

But she laughed with them, clinking glasses and taking sips of the champagne.

April loved the way it was bubbly on her tongue and its smooth taste. She hadn't had expensive champagne for a long time. Or anything to celebrate, for that matter.

'Oh,' Josh said, raising his glass again. 'One more toast.'

'What?' Joanna asked, lifting her glass.

'To April,' he said, his swimming pool eyes shifting to April's, 'the only woman I've ever met who's listened to Joanna and actually heard what she was saying.'

'Hear, hear,' Joanna cried, watching the look that her husband was giving April. She felt a shiver of

156

excitement, seeing that the two of them were slowly developing an easy familiarity, and possibly more.

April sipped her champagne along with them, and felt that little ache of longing swell up within her once again. It was comforting, thrilling even, to be a part of this couple's lives, but she worried that that aching little feeling might be more than that – more than a longing to be a part of something so warm and welcoming, that it might center more directly on Josh Lawrence himself.

11

Full-fledged summer was now upon them as work progressed on the stable. The French doors had been installed, but hadn't been satisfactory until Joanna had hunted down and purchased – at great expense – just the right hardware. The simple brass door handles that had been installed were replaced with gilded bronze handles in – what else? – a shell motif.

April had assumed that once the work began, Joanna would, like so many of her clients, do a disappearing act, checking in only occasionally to review progress. She'd been surprised when she discovered that Joanna took very much a hands-on approach. With some clients this might have posed a problem. Joanna, however, had proved herself indispensable, offering advice and helping make crucial decisions.

She had rejected the small fountain that was to be placed in the center of the room as too ornate, for example.

'But I thought it would appeal to your sense of fantasy,' April had said.

'The fountain itself is only a base to work on,' Joanna had replied. 'It has to be very simple. The ornateness will come with the shells and pebbles that embellish it. Remember? Establish a rather severe line, then blur it.'

April had looked at her and laughed. She wouldn't forget again.

When the appropriate fountain was finally installed, Joanna had been right there alongside the plumbers, making certain that they adjusted the jets to the proper height and that each one was aimed in precisely the correct direction.

On the other hand, Joanna learned from April's experience. She noticed that April worked alongside the various tradesmen, cajoling them to do their best. When a piece of molding was 'almost level,' it was April who talked them into making it 'level,' extricating the little bit of extra time and work required for perfection.

The days flew by in such a whirlwind of work that when basic construction was actually finished and the time had arrived for April to begin working her own personal magic – embellishing the old stable-cum-grotto with shells and pebbles – she and Joanna were both surprised.

They had gradually become friends over the last few weeks, April often reflected, and one Friday morning in early June, while they were cooling off in the swimming pool together, April wasn't surprised when Joanna started talking about her sister, Christina.

'Christina's four years older, and she could be very bossy and very mean,' she said. 'But sometimes she was also very protective and motherly. We had some wonderful times together. She taught me about clothes and makeup and told me about the birds and the bees, and we had great talks about boys. Without a mother around, I can't imagine what it would've been like without her.'

'Are you still close to her?' April asked.

'Well,' Joanna began thoughtfully, 'we do have a history together, and we visit each other occasionally. I go down to Montecito a couple of times a year, and Christina . . . well, she might be here once a year or ten times. She's unpredictable.' She laughed. 'She was here a few weeks ago. But we are just so different.'

'Really?' April said. 'How?'

'In so many ways,' Joanna replied. 'Christina was always very ambitious, socially I mean. And money crazy. And man crazy like you wouldn't believe.' She looked at April. 'Maybe I should say crazy for men with money and power. Usually social standing too.'

They both laughed.

'I guess a lot of women are,' April said.

'Christina is, for sure,' she said. 'She's thirty-six and been married three times. All of them filthy rich, very

161

powerful, and very important socially. She runs around with a crowd that's strictly Montecito, Palm Beach, like that. Rich and idle. They follow the sun and maybe the horses. Polo crowd, some of them. Most of them have big trust funds and have never worked.'

'That doesn't sound like you at all,' April said.

Joanna shook her head. 'No way,' she said. 'And you know, the strange thing is, a lot of these people are really miserable. I don't mean all rich people are, but Christina always seems to fall in with a crowd that's bored and restless and really unhappy.'

'No goals or ambitions,' April said.

'Exactly,' Joanna said. 'They obsess on their problems all the time. You know, like their hair, their clothes. Their face-lifts and jewelry. Their latest lover. All that vital stuff that can really be a problem.' She smiled.

April returned her smile. 'People like that need to get outside themselves,' she said. 'I think that's the best therapy when you're feeling blue. Try to do something for somebody else.' She looked at Joanna. 'Does that sound corny?'

'That sounds exactly like something I would say,' Joanna said with a laugh. 'I've said it a million times. What Christina needs to do is some hands-on charity work. Get involved outside of herself with something, just like you said.'

'You said you're close,' April said. 'Do you get along well? Being so different, I mean?'

Joanna shrugged. 'Okay,' she said. 'I guess you could say we've agreed to disagree about things. And be friends, regardless. Before Dad died he asked us how we wanted to break up the estate. It was going to be either land and business or money. Christina immediately jumped for all the money, and I was really happy because I wanted the land and business.'

She paused for a moment, looking off into the distance, then continued. 'It's worked out beautifully, I think, even though it was really an uneven split. This house and the beach shack and the business and land weren't worth nearly as much as the stock portfolio and cash that Christina got.'

'That's pretty amazing,' April said. 'That the *worth* of one sister could be so much more and not create bad blood.'

Joanna nodded. 'It is, isn't it? But we've never feuded about it at all. I told you. We're completely different. I didn't really care about the money, and Christina couldn't have cared less about the business.' She paused, a thoughtful expression on her face. 'Or at least she didn't used to.'

'What do you mean?' April asked. 'She does now?'

Joanna frowned and shook her head. 'I don't know,' she said. 'I don't guess so, but she's been asking all kinds of questions about the nursery lately. Stuff she usually doesn't give a hoot about. It's odd.' She laughed. 'Maybe it's because she's just bored between husbands or she's suddenly getting sentimental about family and the business.' She shook her head. 'I don't know. Oh, anyhow,' she said smiling, 'suffice it to say that we've grown apart, no doubt about that. Taken *very* different paths in life, but in some ways she mothered me when I was little, and I'll always appreciate it. I'll never forget it.'

'What happened to your mother?' April asked. A few weeks earlier she wouldn't have felt comfortable asking this question, but she and Joanna had reached such a stage of intimacy that she didn't think twice about it now.

'Right after I was born,' Joanna said, 'she drowned.'

'Oh, my God,' April said. 'I had no idea.'

'It happened in Monterey Bay, down near the beach shack. Dad had a sailboat, and the two of them were out sailing alone. A squall came up suddenly and a pea-soup fog rolled in with it. There were big swells, and they were rushing to get back to shore. Anyway, they'd both had a few drinks, and she wasn't wearing her safety harness. She fell overboard and drowned before Dad could save her. He searched for a long time and radioed for help, but it was useless. She washed up on shore the next day, almost in front of the beach shack.' She looked at April with huge sad eyes.

'How terrible for you,' April said. 'I always wondered about your mother because I've heard you and Josh both talk so much about your father.'

'It wasn't really so terrible for me,' Joanna replied. 'After all, I was a baby. I don't remember her at all. Christina barely remembers her, and sometimes thinks she doesn't really remember her at all but just thinks she does from the pictures of her or the stories about her.'

'And your father never remarried?' April asked.

Joanna shook her head. 'No,' she said. 'I don't think he ever even looked at another woman.' She coughed a little. 'He was a wonderful madman. After Mother drowned, he set the boat on fire and watched it sink, then he quit drinking. He never had another drop.'

'Did he always blame himself?' April asked.

'I think so,' Joanna said. 'And he tried to make it up to us. He devoted himself to Christina and me, lavished us with love. Sometimes I think he waited until we were both married, then – and only then – allowed himself to get cancer and die. He knew that we were taken care of and he could call it quits.'

'That's extraordinary,' April said. 'You were really lucky to have him, weren't you?'

'Oh, yes,' Joanna said with a nod of her head. 'He was the best father – and man – imaginable. I always thought that it was so unfair – so *cruel* – that he died such a horrible death. So slow and painful. He suffered so much at the end, after living such a decent, generous life.'

She paused, then looked at April with a serious expression. 'I guess I lost any faith I had in any kind of benevolent God then, and I don't know whether I've ever regained it or not. I'm still trying to come to terms with the unfairness, with the cruelty, that life can dole out.'

She laughed lightly. 'I didn't mean to get so serious,' she said. 'I can tell you this. Christina and I were blessed. No two girls were ever loved so much, or spoiled, I guess.'

'Well, you don't seem spoiled to me,' April said. 'You seem to know what you have and appreciate it.'

'Thanks, April,' Joanna said. 'Anyhow, I'm keeping you from your work.'

'Speaking of which,' April said, 'I've got Woody coming over to help me for a while today.'

'Is he the one you told me about?' Joanna asked. 'The one with the shop?'

'Yes,' April replied. 'He's worked for me before on big jobs. He helps me when I use quick-setting cement to do some of the shell and pebble placement. If it has to be done really fast, I get somebody to help me. It saves a lot of time, and he's good at doing quick simple background stuff. I won't let him do anything elaborate.'

'What does he do about his shop?' Joanna asked.

'He has somebody running it for him, you know,' April said. 'Then he sacrifices some of his surfing time to catch up on the shop work.'

Joanna didn't want to tell April that she knew Woody Pearlman, at least not yet. She certainly hadn't forgotten her trip to his shop and the pass he'd made at her. Still, he'd done good work the two earlier times. Maybe, she told herself, he'd just been having a bad day.

'He must like you an awful lot to drop everything and help out,' Joanna said. 'Is he by any chance in love with you?'

'No,' April said. 'Well . . . not exactly . . . love. Oh, hell, Joanna. I don't know.'

'How do you feel about him?' Joanna asked.

April smiled, then laughed. 'I'm not in love with him. At least I don't think so. We've been like pals for a while. He was a friend of my ex-husband's, so we've known each other for years, but it's more like a brother-sister thing. At least I think it is. I've certainly never had any weak-in-the-knees, heart-fluttering moments with Woody, at any rate. Woody's the kind of guy I go to the movies with. You know, for company.'

Joanna felt relieved to hear this news but didn't say anything to April. *Woody Pearlman isn't worthy of April,* she thought. *I'm sure of it.* She knew that she would have mixed feelings about any man April was seeing, that she had proprietary feelings about her. But remembering her own brief encounter, she was certain that Woody was a heart-breaking Casanova of the first order. *He's after one thing and one thing only, that man.*

How, then, she asked herself, could you explain their friendship, which was obviously pretty close? She was certain that after he got enough of what he wanted, Woody would move on to the next woman. April would no longer be a challenge.

April climbed up out of the pool. 'I'm going to change and watch out for Woody,' she said.

'Okay,' Joanna said. 'I'll see you at lunch.'

'You're sure I'm not wearing out my welcome, Joanna?' April said.

'Don't be silly,' Joanna replied. 'Besides, today's special. The construction's finished and the real work begins. So it's time to celebrate.'

'We already did,' April said. 'Remember?'

167

'One can't have too many celebrations in this life,' Joanna laughed.

'Well, I'll be there,' April said. She turned and walked off toward the pool house to change, guiltily wondering if Josh would be at lunch today.

Woody stood with his hands in his pockets, eyeballing the stable with curiosity. Finally, he shook his shaggy head of black hair and whistled.

'I gotta say, April,' he said with admiration in his voice, 'this is gonna be one cool room.'

'Well,' April replied, 'it was Joanna's idea, not mine.'

'Yeah, but you did all the design work,' Woody said, 'and now you're doing the shell work.' He turned and looked at her. His dark eyes glittered with intensity. 'Give yourself some credit, you know.'

'Thanks, Woody,' April said. 'Anyhow, now you've seen the layout and what's got to be done. Are you sure you can spare the time to help? I'll only need you for the fast work.'

'Yeah,' he said. 'I can make the time for you, April.' He looked around again. 'What's gonna be the fast work anyway?'

April laughed. 'Large spaces filled in with mostly identical shells or pebbles. No intricate designs. Look.' She motioned for him to come over to the work-table she'd set up in the room. Plans were spread out all over it.

'Look at the design for that wall,' she said, indicating the south wall with a hand. 'See these large areas between moldings? Areas like that can be done with quick-setting cement. They call for identical shells or pebbles.'

'I understand,' Woody said. 'It's the simple, boring stuff any idiot can do.'

'Exactly,' April said. 'I've saved the hard, more stimulating stuff for myself.'

Woody laughed. 'You're the boss.'

April looked at her watch. 'Listen,' she said, 'I'm going up to the house for lunch, so I've got to run. You can find your way back out?'

'Sure,' Woody said. 'No problem. Mind if I stay a while, though? I'd like to study these plans to see how much of that simple, boring stuff there is.'

'That's fine, Woody,' she replied. She was surprised that he was taking such an interest. She knew that he worked very well, quickly and efficiently, because of his help in the past, but she'd always thought he was simply passing the time, not really caring much about the work.

'That way,' he said, 'when we get started Monday, I'll have a good idea of exactly what areas I'm going to be working on. I can set little goals.'

'Oh, Woody,' April said with a laugh, 'you're so funny.' She gave him a kiss on the cheek. 'I'd better run. I'll see you tonight. Okay?'

'Later,' he said. 'Have fun.'

She turned and left the grotto, walking up to the pool area. Woody's eagle eyes followed her until she was out of sight.

*   *   *

'No, keep your seat,' Joanna insisted. 'I've got this under control, and I don't need any help.'

'If you're sure,' April said.

'Believe me, she's sure,' Josh said with a grin.

Joanna headed on into the house carrying a tray laden with dirty dishes. They had finished lunch – all but dessert – and she was going to get coffee and the simple dessert she'd made herself.

'Is Connie off today?' April asked.

'Yes,' Josh said. 'I don't know what she's up to. She takes off every now and then without any warning, but it's not a problem. Anyhow, Joanna loves going it solo in the kitchen when Connie's gone. I think she likes it so much because it's like this rare treat.'

April laughed. 'Makes sense,' she said. 'I enjoy the kitchen a lot more if I'm doing something special for my friends.'

'That's the way I am,' Josh said. 'Sometimes it's fun to cook a special meal for Joanna and myself, or maybe make something special to contribute to a dinner party. If it were routine, well, I don't think I'd like it so much.'

'Growing up,' April said, 'sometimes I'd make a big deal out of making myself a sandwich or something. Make it really special. Like put chocolate sauce on peanut butter.'

Josh laughed. 'I did exactly the same thing!' he said. 'I'd make a sandwich out of sardines and then pour ketchup all over it. Or put ketchup in a can of soup.'

'Ugh! It sounds so awful now,' April said, 'but when you're little and alone, you do crazy things to entertain yourself.'

'You sure do,' Josh said with a thoughtful expression. 'We do really nutty things to make life . . . better.'

'Yes,' she agreed.

'You seem to have made a very good life for yourself,' he said. 'You've got your storybook cottage Joanna told me about, and your work. And you seem like a pretty happy camper to me.'

April nodded. 'You're right, Josh,' she agreed. 'I'm a pretty happy camper. It's not always heaven, but it's a hell of a lot better than it used to be. And projects like this with you and Joanna help make it that way. Speaking of which, where *is* Joanna?'

'If I know Joanna, she's in the kitchen putting the finishing touches on dessert,' he said, 'which could mean quite some time.' He looked at her and smiled again. 'She's trying to do whatever it is perfectly, needless to say. And I'm sure you know something about that.'

From the conservatory windows, Joanna had been watching the two of them. The dessert was ready to serve, the coffee was made, but she hadn't been able to tear her eyes away from the scene she had seen unfold before her.

Tears of both sadness and joy, and relief, had rolled down her cheeks. Simply observing the friendly camaraderie that was developing between Josh and April – the camaraderie she had prayed for – had churned up a cauldron of conflicting emotions within her that she had never expected.

Now, torn between a glorious sense of elation and a terrible sense of loss, she had to recommit herself to the dangerously tricky path she had set out upon. This was unchartered territory, for an intimacy was developing between all three of them, a potentially destructive intimacy, and she began to doubt the wisdom of her decision.

Who do I think I am that I can play God? she asked herself.

But then she reminded herself that she *must* take this bold gamble, that she *must* see to fruition the plot that she had hatched.

After all, what have I really got to lose? she asked. *Absolutely nothing.*

And what have they got to gain?

She knew the answer to that, too: *Everything.*

Woody turned out the lights in the grotto and began weaving his way through the apple trees up toward the pool area. On the wind, he could hear the sound of soft voices engrossed in conversation, almost as if they were whispering, punctuated by an occasional tinkle of ice in a glass.

When he came within view of the terrace, he stopped and stood, unseen, in the shadow of one of the old apple trees. Josh Lawrence. Big, bright, rich Josh Lawrence, one of his hands on one of April's. And April. Eating it up. Obviously.

Woody would have liked to spit on the spot. He scowled maliciously, then turned on his heel and quietly backtracked, going around the terrace so as not to be seen.

How could she do this? he wondered. *How could she let herself be taken in by that rich bitch's handsome stud?* She was practically drooling over the son of a bitch, from the looks of things.

Why won't she give me what I want? he wondered. *Why that lousy bastard?*

When he reached the courtyard, he took out his car keys and started toward his van. He saw Josh Lawrence's old Toyota Land Cruiser sitting there. *Really old*, he thought. *Really perfect condition.* He took his car key and, walking along the side of the big RV, he firmly held the key against the fading canary yellow paint, slicing a thin line of paint from the metal, all the way from the back to the front.

Serves the prick right, he thought, getting into his van and starting the engine. Spewing gravel, he spun out of the courtyard and started down the hill, feeling little satisfaction from his wanton act of destruction. Wondering what he could do to really get even.

12

Christina walked up the concrete steps to the board-walk, her expensive Gucci stiletto heels clicking loudly, and grimaced with distaste, wishing herself invisible. She had tried to get Peter Rossi to meet her somewhere else, but he had insisted on this dreary place – some shop at the southern end of the Santa Cruz boardwalk. He was in a hurry and had some business to do at a place here, he'd said, and it wasn't especially busy on an early evening in the summer, so no one they knew would see them here.

Not likely, Christina thought. *God knows, nobody I know would be caught dead here.*

Besides, Peter had told her, there were dozens of places close by where they could spend a couple of hours together. Still, she wondered if he wasn't testing her, just to see what sort of mettle she had, to see if perhaps she was too grand to mix it up with a guy that had come from the wrong side of the tracks.

In this case, Christina thought with a smile, *he could be from Mars and it wouldn't pose a problem.*

The piping of cheerless calliope music filled the air, but was almost overcome by the roar of the Giant Dipper roller coaster, its constant din punctuated by the shrieks of fear and shouts of laughter that erupted from the evening revelers. The smell of corn dogs and cotton candy, underlaid with beer, suntan oil, and sweat, permeated the air. It was a stench in her nostrils.

God! she thought. *I feel so out of place here.*

She felt nothing but contempt for the particular stripe of humanity that was attracted to the amusement rides, cheap food, and the countless tacky souvenir shops that sold T-shirts, seashells, jewelry, and other trinkets. She glanced at a group of filthy, leather-clad bikers and their dingy girlfriends with barely concealed disgust, then noticed that the boardwalk police in their khaki shorts were circling their bicycles near the group, making their presence felt.

She looked away, smiling to herself. The cops might not look so tough on their bicycles, but she knew they were.

She strolled up the boardwalk, ignoring the rides and the beach on her left, staying closer to the well-lighted shops on her right, looking for the one that he'd named.

Finally she glimpsed it just ahead: Poseidon's Garden. Just one slightly shabby trinket shop like so many others. She slowed her pace, seeing if she could spot him through the glass double doors, but her view was blocked by a peroxide-blond, muscle-bound couple, she in a tiny orange bikini that left little to the imagination, he in an almost nonexistent flesh-colored posing strap that left even less to wonder about. Their bronzed bodies, pumped up from steroids and weightlifting, filled both doors as they edged their way out, laden with shopping bags.

The fools must be freezing, she thought, for the early evening air was cool.

She watched them leave, noticing that their slow, deliberate movements seemed to emphasize every ripple and flex of their muscles.

She looked back through the shop doors, craning her neck to try to see Peter. There he was. So tall and handsome. So big and strong. She could swear she felt her heart skip a beat. He was standing between shelves of – what? Seashells? She couldn't tell from here. She took a deep, calming breath and pushed her way in. He didn't turn around and look to see who'd come in, but a clerk at the counter near the door looked over at her with a blank expression.

'Help you?' the clerk asked in a zombie's voice, looking as if the last thing she wanted to do was make a sale. She was slumped on the counter, chin in hands, two fingers alternately twirling the blond skunk stripes in her pitch-black hair and the rings in her nose, lips, and eyebrows. Tattoos decorated her skinny arms.

'I'm just looking, thanks,' Christina said, trying not to cringe.

She started toward the back of the store, and could feel her pulse quicken as she approached Peter, who still hadn't seen her. 'Hello,' she said, sidling up to him.

He turned to her and smiled. 'Hey, there,' he replied.

'What are you so engrossed in?' she asked.

'Just looking at these postcards,' he said.

She noticed that he was holding cards that depicted huge sharks, caught and laid out on a pier for show, a horrendous bloodbath surrounding them.

'Pretty,' she said sarcastically.

He replaced the cards in the rack without replying and picked up a seahorse in a box of shells nearby. 'Bizarre, aren't they?' he said, looking at her.

She looked at him and nodded. 'Yes,' she agreed, 'but very beautiful.'

'Fragile, too,' he said. 'You can snap them in two between your fingers.' He smiled a shark's smile.

She stared mutely at his handsome face, not quite sure what to make of his comment. Was it some sort of less than subtle threat? But then, why would he threaten her? She wasn't certain, but she knew he was a . . . a dangerous man. And that really turned her on.

'Let's get out of here,' he said. He took her arm and quickly led her back outside onto the boardwalk, then south a few feet and down a flight of concrete stairs to the street.

'I've got us a room in a motel down the block,' he said, his powerful arm around her shoulders now, rushing her along beside him.

No asking, she thought. *Just telling.* She liked that. She liked that a lot.

It was all she could do to keep up with his pace in her high heels, but she did, excited by his rush, by her own aroused sexuality, and the secrecy of their meeting.

They crossed the street and entered the courtyard of a small, nondescript motel. It was pink stucco with a garish neon sign: *The Seabre ze*, it flashed in red.

At the entrance to room number 9, Peter took the key out of his trouser pocket and unlocked the door. He held it open for her, and she stepped inside, looking around. *Thank God*, she thought. *At least it looks clean.*

He closed the door behind them, then turned to her, taking her in his massive arms roughly, kissing her hard on the lips, his powerful body almost slamming her against the closed door.

She felt a thrill rush through her entire body, and gasped as he began pushing her skirt up, running his huge hands up her thighs and around to her firm buttocks, then pulling her even harder against him. She could feel his tumescence and almost swooned with desire.

'Glad to see me, babe?' he whispered.

'Oh, God, yes,' she breathed, her legs quivering, damp already between her thighs.

Without another word, he began unceremoniously

pulling her clothes off, then quickly undressed himself and led her to the bed. He mounted her like an animal, tearing into her with a merciless and selfish abandon, pounding away at her savagely, relentless in pursuit of his own satisfaction.

She loved it, her body almost instantly responding to his brutal thrusts by contraction after ecstatic contraction, her juices flowing freely as with a bellow he rammed himself into her with a final mighty thrust and released a flood that filled her to overflowing.

It was over almost before it started, so excited were they both, and they panted feverishly, a glistening sheen of sweat coating their bodies as they lay entwined, letting their breathing return to normal. Neither of them spoke, but they steadily looked into one another's eyes as their hands slowly began stroking, exploring, discovering.

It was only moments before they were devouring each other again, ravenously but this time a little less fiendishly, taking the time to savor their bodies, to thrill one another in various ways, until they finally climaxed in a spent heap of shining flesh.

Only when they'd caught their breath did Peter light cigarettes for them both.

'Glad you could come up here and meet me, babe,' he said, kissing her on the cheek and slapping her fanny playfully. He handed her a cigarette.

Christina took it and inhaled a long drag. 'Oh, God, me too,' she said, appreciating the fact that he'd said that, imagining that Peter Rossi rarely told anyone he was glad to see them.

'Your sister and brother-in-law don't know you're here, do they?' he asked.

Christina coughed a laugh, cigarette smoke sputtering out of her mouth. 'No way!' she said. Then she looked at him with a sly smile. 'But I'm not worried about it, Peter. If somebody happens to see the Rolls or me, I'll tell Joanna I've been to see friends in San Francisco or something. Just passing through.'

He smiled. 'You got balls,' he said, playfully slapping her fanny once again.

'Why do you say that?' she asked, relishing his attention. 'Because I'm sleeping with the enemy?'

'That's right, babe,' he said, taking a drag off his cigarette. 'Maybe even helping out the enemy a little bit, huh?'

They both laughed. 'I'm going to humiliate that fucking brother-in-law of yours till I have my way,' he said. 'Down the road, they're going to beg me to buy them out.'

She could hear the amusement in his voice, and couldn't help but share the joy he took in his wicked intentions. She knew that their secrecy and the pure evil of their actions only served to heighten the ardor of their sexual encounters – heightened it, in fact, to levels Christina had never before experienced.

And, she thought smugly, *I have experienced a great deal.*

'Well, from what I hear,' she said, looking over at

him, 'they're beefing up security.' She blew a streamer of smoke out her nostrils. 'So it might be harder to do anything.'

'We'll see,' he said. 'You can keep me posted.'

She nodded. 'I'll find out what I can from Joanna without showing too much interest,' she said. 'I certainly don't want her to get the idea that I'm *too* interested in what's going on, if you know what I mean.'

She looked over at him. 'You see? They could suspect *me*. I'll be taking risks for you, Peter.' Her voice was almost petulant. She looked at him again, expecting some sort of show of support.

Peter Rossi's eyes seemed to harden, becoming glints of obsidian that bored through her. He stubbed out his cigarette and then slowly smiled. 'You can handle it, babe,' he said mildly, still looking into her eyes. He pulled her naked body to his, squeezing her. 'For us, huh?'

'For us,' she echoed. Then she smiled. 'Hmmm,' she said, putting out her cigarette. 'I think I can do it.'

'Yeah,' he nodded. 'I thought so.' He leaned down and kissed her again, on the lips this time, lingering there, his tongue parting her lips, exploring her slowly, almost tenderly. Then he pulled back, reluctantly and just as slowly, and smiled.

'You want to know what we're going to do next?' he asked.

She looked at him questioningly and nodded but didn't say anything.

He cupped one of her breasts in a hand, fondling it

gently, then leaned over to her ear, his tongue brushing it teasingly, before whispering into it, telling her what she had to do next.

When he'd finished, he began kissing her again, harder, more passionately, and his hand brushed lightly down her stomach, trailing on down to her mound. He teased her there, inserting a finger, then drawing it out.

'Oh, Peter,' she moaned quietly. 'Oh ... oh ... oh, my God.' She began to move her hips against his hand, delighted that her body was once again responding to this man. But he suddenly removed his hand and his lips, pulling away from her.

'What—?' she gasped, looking at him.

'Give you something to remember me by, babe,' he said. 'Till the next time, you know?' He smiled his shark's smile.

She was sorely disappointed, but knew that she would get hot just thinking about the next time, just thinking about the unfinished business they had in bed.

'Okay,' she said with a sigh.

'Now,' he said, 'I'd better get out of here. Get my ass back home.'

He got out of bed and began to get dressed. She lay there watching him, hating to see him go but enjoying the sight of him dressing, watching the movement of his tanned muscles against his expensive clothing.

When he was finished, he went over to her, leaning down and kissing her deeply for long moments. Then he drew himself back up to his full height and smiled. 'I'll be in touch,' he said.

She nodded. 'Can't wait,' she said, meaning it.

Then she watched as he went to the door, tossing the room key onto a dresser on his way. He turned at the door, blew her a kiss, then was gone.

She began dressing then, slowly, savoring the tiredness of her body, the feeling of utter satiation that engulfed her in a pleasant contentedness. Despite the complications of their seeing each other, she couldn't wait until the next time.

She both loved and hated these clandestine meetings, but they were a necessity. They must not let anyone see them together. For one thing, he was in the process of divorcing his wife, and he had to look like an angel until it was final. And for the other, she was a traitor.

Yes, I'm a traitor, she thought. *Sleeping with the enemy. Betraying Joanna and Josh. Helping him ruin their business in any little way I can. Giving him information. And oh, oh, oh! they have another little surprise waiting for them soon at the nursery. But I don't care*, she decided. *Joanna and Josh have always had everything. Everything! And it's a small price to pay to have Peter Rossi. To have his power and money. And that sexy mean streak that turns me on so.*

Ah, yes, Christina thought again, *I'm a traitor. But for a very good cause*: me.

13

Josh picked up the telephone on his desk at the nursery. 'Hello?' he said.

'Mr Lawrence?' the deep voice asked.

Despite himself, Josh felt a chill run up his spine. He knew the voice and it gave him the creeps, but after a moment anger replaced his initial reaction. Trying to sound as matter-of-fact as possible, he said, 'Yes, Mr Rossi.'

'I was wondering,' Peter Rossi said, 'if you'd had a change of heart about selling out.'

Josh could hear amusement in the thug's suave voice, and it only infuriated him more. He couldn't keep a lid on his anger any longer.

'No!' he shouted. 'I am *not* selling out. Not to you. Not to *anybody*!'

He slammed the receiver down in its cradle, then put his head in his hands. *The fucker*, he thought. *The goddamn lowlife motherfucker.* He took a few deep breaths, trying to compose himself, his mind racing around in circles.

I should call the police right now, he thought. *But for what? What am I going to tell them? That every time we have trouble here at the nursery Peter Rossi calls me afterward wanting to buy me out?*

He got to his feet and went out to the reception area, slamming the office door behind him.

'Luna,' he said, without glancing at her. 'I'm headed home. Take any messages.'

'Sure, boss,' she said, her eyes wide as she watched him slam the front door behind him.

Josh let the mud room door slam and sat down on the old pine bench with a loud *thunk!* He slowly unlaced his boots, kicked them off, then pulled off his sweaty socks and threw them on the floor.

'Joanna!' he called out with a scowl on his face. 'Joanna!'

There was no answer. He stood up and kicked one of his boots, sending it sailing across the floor to bounce off a table leg.

'Joanna!' he cried again. 'Joanna!' He started toward the kitchen, determined to find his wife.

Where the hell is she this *time?* he asked himself. He was getting sick and tired of not being able to get hold of her. Nobody had picked up the telephone here

186

all afternoon, and the damn woman wouldn't have a cell phone.

Her refusal hadn't bothered him at first, but now it was making him crazy. It was as if there were a plot against him.

He looked around the kitchen. No Joanna. No Connie. No note. He walked through the downstairs rooms calling. No Joanna. He dashed up the stairs to the second floor, calling. No answer.

Where is she when I really need her?

He tromped back downstairs and retraced his steps to the mud room, where he slipped into a pair of Top-Siders. Then, walking out onto the terrace, he looked toward the pool.

Nobody in sight.

He crossed the little bridge to the pool area and looked around the plateau that the pool was built on.

Nothing. Nobody. Shit!

He stomped toward the old apple orchard, heading in the direction of the grotto, and almost bumped into April, coming from between the trees.

'Whoa,' she said. 'What's the hurry?' Then she saw the look on his face. 'What's wrong, Josh?'

'Joanna,' he said between gritted teeth. 'Joanna is what's wrong. I mean, something is going on and I'm getting pissed off.'

'Ooooh,' she said, 'you really *are* upset.'

'I'm sorry,' he said. 'I'm just . . .'

'You're at your wit's end,' she finished for him. 'And it's okay. You want to talk about it?'

'No,' he said. 'Well, I don't know. Maybe ...'

She took his elbow and steered him uphill toward the pool area. 'Come on,' she cajoled. 'Let's go sit down. I think you need to cool your heels.'

They sat at one of the tables that was situated poolside. Although it was hot and humid, there was a slight breeze, and April thought that just looking at the pool helped cool her off.

April saw the look of sad defeat on Josh's face and felt disturbed by it. *He's always so genial, so happy-go-lucky*, she thought, *but he's not unflappable, after all.* She decided to let him do the talking, if he wanted to, because she certainly didn't want to pry, even though he had given her an opening.

'Did you see her at lunch?' he asked, looking at her questioningly.

April shook her head. 'No,' she said, 'I haven't seen her all day. She was already gone when I got here this morning.'

'That's weird,' he said. He looked more perplexed than ever.

'She's probably just running errands, Josh,' April said with a smile, trying to pacify him, but not really believing her own words. Who ran errands at eight o'clock in the morning? Besides, she knew that it was unlike Joanna not to be home for lunch.

Josh looked at her steadily across the table. 'Maybe,' he said, 'but I somehow doubt it.'

'Didn't she leave a note like she always does?' April asked.

He shook his head. 'No,' he replied, 'and it really has me worried.'

'Oh, come on, Josh,' April said. 'She's nearly always here for you, isn't she? Morning, noon, and night.'

He heaved a sigh. 'Yes,' he conceded. 'I guess she is, but lately . . . I don't know. It seems like something's going on.'

'I think maybe you've just had a rough day,' April said. 'Maybe you're overreacting a little bit.'

He nodded. 'Yeah, it's been a rough day, all right.' He stretched his arms. 'And that's putting it mildly. It was the *worst*, April.'

'What?' she said. 'Mr Hara didn't stop by and drop another hundred grand in your pocket?' She was making an effort to lighten the atmosphere for him, but it didn't work.

Josh grimaced. 'No,' he said. 'I wish.' He slumped in his chair. 'But this is really serious. I think somebody's been trying to sabotage the nursery.'

'Are you serious?' she asked, surprised.

'Dead serious,' he said.

'But how do you know?' she asked.

He sat straight up. 'Let's have a glass of wine, okay?' he asked.

'Oh, Josh,' April said, 'I really shouldn't. I ought to get going in a few minutes.'

'Just a glass?' he said.

She could hear the plea in his voice, and knew that he needed to talk to somebody. 'Well . . . okay,' she said, 'but just one glass.'

'I'll run get a bottle and glasses,' he said. 'Be right back.'

April watched him hurry toward the kitchen, wondering what could be going on at the nursery that was upsetting him so much. Maybe it's not really that serious after all, she thought. Maybe that and Joanna's errand-running or whatever, maybe the two together, make it all seem much worse than it really is.

Her reverie was interrupted by Woody, who suddenly appeared at her side.

'Oh, my God, Woody!' she said. 'You scared me half to death.'

'You're crazy,' he said in a near whisper, his glittering dark eyes riveted to hers.

'What?' she said.

'You're playing with fire, April,' he said in the same barely audible voice. Then he turned and stomped off, back toward the orchard, skirting the terrace area, leaving work for the day.

Jesus, April thought, *what's his problem? I'm going to have to have another little talk with him.* She wondered now about the wisdom of hiring Woody to help her with this job, never suspecting that he would behave this way. But then, she realized, on past jobs, when Woody had helped out, she hadn't been involved with the clients like she was here.

Josh returned with a bottle of chilled white wine. 'Here we go,' he said, pouring them each a glass. He handed April hers, then sat back down.

April took a sip of the cool wine. 'Okay,' she said.

'Tell me about this nursery business. You really think it's sabotage?'

'Definitely,' Josh replied. 'It started a few weeks ago. The computer-operated misting system malfunctioned. If Carl hadn't been paying attention, a lot of orchids could've been lost. Either soaked to death or dried out.'

'I remember Joanna told me about it,' April said. 'But I thought it was just a computer problem.'

'The technicians that came out didn't think so,' Josh replied. 'They think that somebody had tinkered with the system.'

'Could they have been trying to cover their own asses?' April asked. 'So their system wouldn't look bad.'

'I doubt it,' Josh said. 'They've got a great reputation in this area.'

'But if it was sabotage,' April asked, 'who could it have been? And why?'

Josh looked at her steadily. 'I have a good guess,' he replied. 'The Rossi brothers have been trying to buy us out. They're a huge operation with land on both sides of us, and they want to expand.'

'And you've refused to sell,' April guessed.

'Yes.' Josh took a sip of his wine and set the glass back down. 'We could get enough to retire if we wanted to or go into something else, but Joanna's father really treasured that land. And the business. He spent his whole life building it up. And Joanna feels very strongly about it, too.'

April looked at him. 'And so do you,' she said. 'You've got the orchid bug, and you're devoted to that business.'

Josh nodded in agreement. 'Yeah,' he said, smiling, 'You're right about that.' He fell silent, lost in thought.

'So you think it might be these Rossi brothers who're trying to sabotage you,' she said.

'Yes,' Josh said. 'After the computer mister episode, Peter Rossi actually called me to make another offer.'

'What?' April said. 'You're serious?'

'Yep,' he said. 'It's almost like they're playing with me.'

She looked at him with a stunned expression. 'Did you tell the police that?'

'Yes,' he said. 'For what it's worth. There's nothing they can do. Nothing they can act on.'

'I can see that,' she replied. 'And now something else has happened?'

Josh sighed. 'There's been an outbreak of some kind of fungal disease in one of the greenhouses. *Phytophthora*, I believe. It's a black rot fungus that's attacked some of the *Phalaenopsis*.'

'Oh, Lord, no,' April exclaimed. 'Is it serious?'

'I don't know yet,' he said. 'It's contained to that one greenhouse. All *Phalaenopsis*. We're having the bacteria analyzed to see exactly what it is, but it doesn't really matter. It's good-bye to some of the plants, and a long period of nursing for the ones we can save. A lot of them were due to be shipped, so we have to buy more stock or lose orders.'

'That's horrible!' April said.

'The weird thing is, the environment for those orchids was perfect. Exactly as it should be. Air, temperature, humidity, spacing between plants, all of it perfect. The fungus should never have appeared.'

'Did you call the police again?' April asked.

'Yes,' he replied, 'and like the last time they couldn't find any sign of forced entry. Nothing. And like the last time, Miguel, the night watchman, saw and heard nothing out of the ordinary. And he says that the watchdog we got hasn't raised any alarms, either.'

He paused and took another sip of wine. 'Of course,' he continued, 'this being a fungus, somebody could've come in like a customer during regular hours and deposited it in the *Phalaenopsis* greenhouse. But I don't think so, because we have very few walk-ins and they're usually with a salesperson.'

'Oh, Lord,' April said. 'It gets more and more difficult to pin down.' She flicked a bug away from her wine. 'Did you get a telephone call this time?' she asked.

'Yep,' he said. 'That too.' His eyes locked on to hers. 'See what I mean about being played with?'

'Oh, God, this is creepy,' she said. 'Was it the same guy, uh, Peter—'

'Peter Rossi.' He nodded. 'I'm beginning to think it's getting a little creepy, too. These people have a reputation for being ruthless and unscrupulous, but jeez, I can't believe the gall he has to call like this. I mean . . . he seems to have no fear whatsoever.'

'So what are you going to do?' she asked.

'I don't know, April,' he said. 'I really don't know. That's one reason I was so angry about Joanna not being here. I need to talk to her about this.'

April sat staring at him. He had slumped in his chair again and looked defeated. She wished she could make him feel better, but she knew that she couldn't.

'I'm sure Joanna will be here soon,' she finally said. 'She's probably been shopping or something and just paid no attention to the time. You know how she gets distracted.'

He looked up at her then. 'Thanks for listening,' he said, 'and trying to cheer me up.' He smiled. 'You're really . . . special.'

April felt that peculiar uncomfortable feeling again, that longing that he seemed to arouse in her, and knew that she was blushing slightly.

'Thanks, Josh,' she said. 'You and Joanna are very special, too.' She took the last sip of her wine and set the glass back down. 'I'd really better get going now,' she said. 'I've got a lot to do at home.'

He sat up. 'I'm sorry,' he said. 'You've been stuck here working all day, and I've kept you way over-time.'

'It's okay,' she said, smiling. She rose to her feet and reached down, picking up her carryall. 'I don't mind at all. That's what friends are for.'

Josh, on his feet too, picked up their glasses and the

bottle of wine. 'Well, thanks a lot anyhow.' He looked at her. 'And I'm glad you can call us friends.'

'Me, too,' she said, already walking toward the house. 'Me, too.'

The beach stretched before her, an almost entirely deserted expanse ranging from dark gray, where waves lapped at the shore, to beige, to a dry white at the dunes. Driftwood lay beached like prehistoric sea creatures, and kelp, rubbery and tubelike, was strewn in generous clumps across the sand. To the south, she could see a lone fisherman casting a line, and far beyond him the towering stacks of the power plant near Moss Landing.

She turned and looked north, the wind whipping her hair across her face. Using both hands, she swept it out of her eyes. She could barely make out what she knew to be Santa Cruz, although the fog, which was rolling in off the ocean in great pearly clouds, would soon render visibility nil. In the near distance, she could see Joe Camel, her name for the huge upright piece of driftwood with its camel's head that marked the path in the dunes leading to the old beach shack.

She had walked for miles and miles and lost all track of time, even though the position of the sun and its relative intensity were a reminder that time was fleeting. She should have been home hours ago.

Today, she had decided, would be different. She had left for the beach immediately after Josh went to work, not leaving a note, not letting anyone know what she was doing. It was a luxury, this willful, self-centered escape, but she had no apologies. She wanted to be alone here at her father's old shack, on the beach that she had loved with all her heart, all her life. No place had ever meant more to her than the simple, rustic cabin where she had spent weekends and holidays with her father and sister, and where she and Josh had spent the first exquisite months of their marriage.

As she neared the camel's head, her legs and arms suddenly became weary. She eased herself onto the sand, carefully setting down the heavy plastic bags of shells she'd collected. There were hundreds, she supposed, a few of them perfect specimens, the vast majority broken. But they would have their use, she told herself. Every last one of them. Whole or incomplete, beautifully colored or uninterestingly dull, it didn't matter.

She faced the horizon, which was gradually disappearing in the encroaching fog, and saw that the sun was beginning to set. The end of the day, she thought. The end of the day. Tears came into her eyes, and she let them flow silently down her face. Normally, she would have tried to hide them, but now she let them stream unchecked, down onto her sweater, wherever they might fall. Sobs began to wrench her body, and she put her arms across her stomach. Despite the roar of the wind, she could hear her own choking wails of agony, could hear them as they became louder and louder shrieks alternating with barely discernible mewls of pain.

Her screams were answered only by the roar of the

wind and surf, the screeches of birds, the sounds of her plastic bags whipped by the wind.

When her fury was finally spent, her body aching with exhaustion, she collapsed on the sand, her chest heaving, the salty sand sticking to her wet face. She rested there for a long time, catching her breath, murmuring and sighing, gradually becoming conscious of her surroundings.

When at last she sat back up, she could see that dark was fast approaching. She stood up, brushing the sand off her clothes, off her face, fatigue almost overwhelming her. Picking up the bags of shells, she trudged through the dry sand, slowly making her way over the dunes to the sea shack. She passed the outdoor shower at the foot of the steps leading up to the big screened-in front porch, but she ignored it. She didn't care about tracking sand throughout the house.

Inside, she laid her shells on a chair, then flipped on a light. She padded across the worn wooden floor to the bathroom and, flipping on a light there, looked at herself in the mirror. 'What a mess you are, old girl,' she murmured to her reflection. She started to laugh, but quickly checked the impulse. She didn't want to cry anymore. She washed her face, then brushed her hair in long, even strokes. That done, she flipped off the light, then went back out to the living room.

I should straighten up the bedroom, she thought. *And put away the wine and glasses and—*

'Forget it,' she said aloud. *Nobody much comes here*

anymore but me, she thought, *and what difference does it make anyway?*

She gathered up her bags of shells, closed up the house, and went out to the car. For a few minutes, she sat silently, taking deep breaths of air, then she started the car, feeling finally that she could go home and play the good wife.

Josh turned off the hot shower and stepped out onto the cool marble floor. Taking a big, fluffy white towel, he started drying off, humming tunelessly to himself. When he heard the car in the courtyard, he threw the towel down and grabbed his terrycloth bathrobe off the brass door hook. He went through the bedroom and down the hallway in the direction of the stairs.

Finally, he thought, sailing down the steps. *Now, let's see what Joanna's been up to – or says she's been up to.*

He reached the bottom of the stairs just as the front door was opening, and Joanna started edging her way in, her arms loaded down with heavy plastic bags.

'Hi,' she chirped, smiling, radiantly cheerful.

Josh felt a sense of relief surge through him, coupled with that familiar joy that her sparkling presence never failed to evoke.

'Wait a minute, honey,' he said. 'Let me help you.'

He rushed over and held the door wide, at the same time trying to extricate some of the plastic bags from her hands, an impossible task as they were entwined with her fingers.

'Ouch!' she said. 'My hands are trapped!'

'Just drop them,' he said.

'But they're filthy, Josh!' she exclaimed. 'Covered up with sand and who knows what else.'

'Never mind the dirt, just drop them,' he said.

Joanna eased the heavy bags down onto the hallway's marble floor, then drew herself back up and planted a kiss on his lips. 'Hi, handsome,' she said. 'I'm glad you were here to help. I didn't realize these were so heavy.'

He immediately detected the smell of alcohol on her breath and was surprised. Joanna, who always smelled of an exotic citrus and vetiver perfume, had come in reeking like a Bowery bum. Then he noticed that her hair was a mess and her clothes were too.

'What've you got here?' he asked. 'Smells like the fish market.'

'Oh, you wouldn't believe!' Joanna said excitedly. 'I've been shelling, and I got oodles of all kinds of things!'

He smiled, swept up in his wife's charm and innocent excitement.

'Look,' she said, rummaging around in one of the bags. 'A whole bagful of little bits of mother-of-pearl! Great for filling in background in the grotto.'

'Yeah,' he said, 'looks like quite a haul you got for yourself. I'll get some garbage bags in the kitchen to stick these into, so just leave them here.'

'Clever,' she said. 'You're so clever.'

She followed him out to the kitchen. Opening the refrigerator door, she said, 'A nice chilled white. Just what the doctor ordered after lugging all that weight.'

'I put a couple of bottles in earlier, so they should be chilled,' Josh said, taking some garbage bags from a box.

'You too?' she asked. 'Want some vino?'

'Sure,' he replied. 'I'll be right back.' He started out of the kitchen, then turned back to her. 'Do you want me to put these in the laundry room so we can start soaking them?'

'That'd be great, Josh.'

He went back out to the entrance hall while Joanna opened the bottle of wine, retrieved two crystal glasses from a cabinet, then took the bottle and glasses out to the terrace table.

She sat down under the big umbrella and looked out toward the swimming pool. Fog, in cottony wisps, was swirling all around, and it would be a beautiful time to relax in the pool. She'd missed her swim this evening, but she decided she was too tired to go near the pool. In the distance, she could see huge fog banks enshrouding the mountainsides.

Josh approached from behind her and put his powerful hands on her shoulders, massaging her lightly.

'Oh, that feels so good,' she said, looking up at him and smiling dreamily. She closed her eyes and gave herself up to the sensuous feel of his hands on her.

'Aren't you hungry?' Josh asked. 'It's past dinnertime, and Connie's got tons of stuff in the fridge ready for us.'

'Dinnertime,' she said, sitting up. 'Is it that late?'

'Uh-huh,' Josh said.

'Oh, my gosh,' she said. 'I had no idea.'

'Have you by any chance been drinking?' he asked lightly. 'It's not like you to forget dinner.'

'Yes,' she exclaimed. 'It was wonderful, too. I stopped off at Umberto's and had some wine and watched the sunset from their terrace.'

'Umberto's?' he asked. 'You hate that place.'

'It was perfect just this once,' she said. 'For the sunset. I didn't even notice all the plastic flowers and furniture.'

Josh laughed. 'You are in a mood, aren't you?' He gave her shoulders a final pat, then sat down next to her at the table. 'Alone?' he asked as casually as possible.

She nodded sleepily. 'Um-hm,' she said. 'Just me and my lonesome.'

Josh didn't know whether to believe what she was saying or not, but he had the distinct feeling that she was lying. Obviously she'd been shelling and obviously she'd been drinking, but Umberto's? With all those kids and surfer types and tourists?

He wanted to know what she'd really been up to, but he looked at her sleepy eyes and knew that he wouldn't pry any further. *I wish I could talk to her*, he thought. *And I need to tell her about the problems at the nursery today. But now is definitely not the time. Not when she's high from drinking.*

'April was here when I got home,' he said, changing the subject.

'How was she?' Joanna asked, taking a sip of her wine. 'I missed her today.'

'She was fine,' he said, 'but I think she had some questions to ask you. Wanted your approval on some things.'

'There's always tomorrow,' Joanna said. 'Besides, I trust her implicitly.' She leaned back in her chair and closed her eyes again.

'Oh,' Josh said, 'I almost forgot. Christina called. Just a little while ago.'

Joanna sat back up and opened her eyes. 'And what does my precious sister want?' she asked.

'She wants to know if you're coming down to visit like you said you would,' Josh replied.

'Oh, God,' Joanna said. 'I'd forgotten all about it. With this project going on and all.'

'I told her I didn't know,' Josh said. 'I didn't even know you'd called her and told her you were going down there.'

Joanna averted her gaze, looking off into the distance. 'Well, I thought she could use the company,' she said. 'I know she's very unhappy after the divorce.' She returned her gaze to Josh. 'I've been terribly neglectful,' she said. 'Christina's really suffering and I just . . .'

He reached over and took one of her hands in his. 'Don't worry about it now, Joanna,' he said gently. 'Come on.' He rose to his feet, bringing her hand with him. 'I'll whip up something to eat, and we'll put something in that empty stomach of yours.'

Joanna let him pull her to her feet, then stood there next to him. He drew her closer, against his nearly naked body, and kissed her tenderly.

She felt his warmth and inhaled his clean masculine aroma and realized that he was aroused. *Oh, Lord,* she thought. *I hate to disappoint Josh, of all people, but I'm just so very, very tired.*

She looked up into his eyes. 'Josh,' she whispered. 'I'm . . . I'm really exhausted. I think I ought to take a quick shower and go straight to bed.'

'You're sure?' he asked, not wanting to take no for an answer.

She nodded. 'I'm exhausted.'

'Okay,' he said, the lusty excitement in his eyes dimming. 'I'll be in a little later.' He let his arms fall from around her.

''Night,' Joanna said. She gave him a quick kiss on the lips and walked off toward the French doors leading into the kitchen. He supposed he should be angry with her, but he just couldn't summon up those feelings. She'd looked so happy when she came in and had looked somehow so . . . fragile just now.

Josh watched her disappear into the house, then sat back down and took a sip of his wine. He felt more mystified than ever, and couldn't make any sense of her behavior. *She's gone all day and comes home a little high on wine,* he thought. *Says she's been to a café she detests. Forgot she'd promised her sister she'd be down for a visit. She won't eat.*

But worst of all, he told himself, *is that she doesn't want to make love.* He couldn't remember when she'd last refused him. In all the years of their marriage, it had happened only a handful of times. She'd either been

203

really sick or really upset about something. But now? He didn't think she'd ever said she was too tired.

Doesn't she want me anymore? he wondered. He told himself that thinking that way was ridiculous. Just plain paranoid. Hadn't they made love several times lately? And hadn't it been as great as always? *Then what the hell's going on?*

14

J osh sat on a stool in the marble bathroom, staring down at the package in his hand. His eyes were filled with tears, and he had the look of a wounded animal.

Why didn't I take the time to have that talk with her? he asked himself once again. But he knew why, of course. At the nursery, the last few days had flown by in a haze of relentless work, everyone working overtime, getting orders out, isolating and nursing the fungal-infected plants, acquiring more stock.

And all the while, his home life – his relationship with his wife – was becoming a nightmare.

Staring down at the package, he felt as if Joanna had become someone else altogether, someone devious, uncaring, and unloving. *Or*, he thought, *maybe I never really knew her at all.*

He was going to turn in early because he was exhausted. He had been looking for her to kiss her good night. She'd been in her little office earlier, doing something on the computer, so he'd gone there first. But the computer had been turned off, and she wasn't there. He'd looked in the bathroom next to it to see if she was there, and saw instead the offensive package on the marble counter. In plain view.

He'd been stunned at first. Then the pain came, a hurt so intense that he didn't yet feel the rage that he was certain must come. He'd sat down on this stool and tried to figure out what to do next.

I have to confront her about this. And right now, he decided. *No more putting off a talk. No more being too busy. No more excuses. This does it.*

He snatched up the package and headed downstairs for the kitchen. She'd probably be in there or in the sunroom. When he reached the kitchen, he saw that she was pouring herself a glass of wine.

She saw him out of the corner of her eye. 'Would you like some?' she asked. She topped her glass, then turned to face him.

Josh planted himself in front of her and held out the offensive package. 'Why?' he asked, his voice an anguished plea.

Joanna saw the package in his hand, and her face went a ghostly white. She let the wineglass slip from her fingers, and it crashed onto the Mexican tile floor, glass and wine flying everywhere.

'Why, Joanna?' Josh repeated. As much as he loved

her, at this moment he wanted to hit her, something he had never done. Something he could never have even imagined wanting to do before tonight.

'I . . . I . . .' Joanna stuttered. Suddenly she emitted an animal wail of anguish, tears coming into her eyes, and she rushed over the splinters of glass, ignoring them, past him, and out of the kitchen.

Josh stood glancing down at the shattered glass and wine for a moment. Then he opened the cabinet with the garbage bins and tossed the package of birth control pills in. He slammed the cabinet door shut with all his might, then turned and headed back upstairs to the bedroom. He was determined to have that talk with her. And tonight.

He tried to open the bedroom door, but it was locked. 'Joanna,' he called, 'please, honey, open the door. We've got to talk.'

There was no response, and he pounded on the door with his fists. 'Joanna,' he cried, 'we've got to talk about this. *Now.* Open up.'

He put his ear to the door, but not a sound could be heard from the other side. He raised his fists and started to bang again, but dropped them, feeling suddenly ridiculous.

She is already miserable, he thought. *I don't want to compound that.*

He went down the hall to a guest room and, heading toward the bed, noticed the bar setup for guests. There were several bottles of liquor and glasses on a large silver tray. The ice bucket was empty, but it didn't matter. He poured himself a large dollop of scotch, then threw off his bathrobe and spread out on the bed, staring up at the ceiling, sipping the scotch. He'd never slept in this room before, and it felt strange not to have Joanna at his side. He wondered if he would be able to fall asleep. His mind was still such a whirlwind of mixed emotions that he doubted he'd get a wink. He looked at the glass of scotch, but decided he didn't want a fuzzy head on top of everything else in the morning.

But no matter what, he decided, *tomorrow is D day. We're going to discuss this come hell or high water.* Then, so exhausted was he, he fell into a deep undisturbed sleep.

Josh came awake with a start. He instantly knew that he wasn't in his own bed and, eyes open, scanned the room quickly. Even in his slightly disoriented state, he knew where he was. Then he remembered last night, and what had happened.

He sat up slowly and glanced at the clock on the bedside table. Nearly seven. Looking toward the windows, he could tell from a chink in the curtains that the light was a uniform gray. The fog hadn't burned off yet, probably wouldn't for a few hours yet.

He slid his legs around and put his feet on the floor, then noticed his bathrobe where he'd thrown it off last night. He slipped it on, then rose to his feet. He stretched his arms and rolled his head around, yawning loudly.

'I've got to go find Joanna now,' he said aloud. 'This

very minute.' He knew that he had to act fast before the chance slipped away. Joanna might dash off somewhere before he could talk to her.

He padded out into the hallway toward their bedroom. The door was ajar, but he listened at it for a moment before going on into the room. Silence. And then he heard her in the bathroom.

She's crying, he thought miserably.

He rushed through the bedroom and opened the door into Joanna's big marble bathroom. She was sitting at her vanity table, her head in her hands.

'Joanna!' he said. 'Joanna, what is it? What's wrong?' He flew to her, gently putting his arms around her, trying to comfort her.

When at last her sobbing stopped, she turned and looked up at him with a pained expression. Her tear-streaked face was flushed, and her eyes were puffy and red. She let her head drop against his robed shoulder.

'Joanna, darling, Joanna. Please tell me what's wrong,' he said in an anguished voice, hugging her closer.

She remained silent, then got up and went to the sink, where she turned on the cold water tap. She quickly splashed her face several times with the icy water, then patted it dry with a thick white towel.

When she was done, she turned back to him, looking up into his blue eyes. As long as she had put off the inevitable, she realized that she had to tell him the truth now. He had discovered the birth control pills, and her disease was progressing at such a rate that she couldn't hide it from him much longer.

'We have to talk,' she finally said, hugging herself with her arms.

'What *is* it, Joanna?' he asked, going to her and wrapping his arms around her.

She could see the panic in his eyes and could only think of the torture this wonderful man was going to be put through because of the terrible words she was going to utter.

She reached out and took one of his hands in hers. 'First, why don't we grab some coffee downstairs and take it outside on the terrace?' she said. 'Is that okay?'

'Sure,' he said, squeezing her hand in his.

Together they went down to the kitchen and went through the early-morning ritual of making coffee as if nothing were amiss. As they stepped outside, the morning fog floated around the terrace in endlessly shifting swirls. They sat under the big umbrella, still in their bathrobes, sipping hot coffee.

Josh reached across the space between them and took her hand again. He didn't know why he was so unnerved, but he didn't remember ever feeling such fear before.

'I . . . I've known that something was wrong for a while, but if this is because of my anger last night, finding the pills—'

She shook her head vigorously. 'No, no, Josh,' she said. 'Don't even think about blaming yourself for anything.'

She looked down into her coffee, as if searching its depths for the right words, the most painless way to tell him what she must. But, she decided, there was only the simple truth.

She looked back up into his handsome eyes. She could see the fear there and wished she could dispel it. 'I'm going to die,' she said calmly.

She felt his hand jerk in hers. It was as if he had been bitten by a snake. She held it more fiercely in her own. She saw his sad eyes widen, and his mouth open as if to speak.

'I didn't want to tell you,' she continued, 'but I don't have any choice now, Josh. I'm going to die.'

'Die?' he finally whispered.

She nodded. 'Yes. The disease is progressing—'

'What disease?' Josh said, almost angrily. 'What in God's name is wrong with you, Joanna?'

'It's cancer, Josh,' she said. 'Brain cancer. And it's terminal.'

For a moment he looked at her as if she'd gone mad. Then he got out of his chair and, getting down on his knees, put his arms around her waist, his head on her bosom, and held her tight.

'Are you certain about this, Joanna?' he asked, his voice almost a whisper.

'Yes,' she said, nodding. She stroked his hair with her fingers, tenderly, lovingly. 'Absolutely, Josh.'

'But . . . but . . . there must be something we can do!' he cried. 'We'll stop at nothing. You'll see all the best doctors. The best doctors in the—'

'Josh!' she said with firm authority. 'You must listen to me.' She paused, then continued. 'Doctors might be able to prolong my life by a few months at the most. Using horrible invasive procedures and radiation and chemotherapy.'

'Then—' he began.

'No!' she cried. 'Listen to me. I am *not* going to try to gain a few months that will only be misery for me and everyone else.' She took his shoulders in her hands and squeezed them hard. 'I am not going to die like my father. Suffering on and on and on. In constant pain. I am going to die my way, Josh. With dignity.'

'But . . . but—' he began again.

'No, there are no buts,' Joanna said softly. 'Don't you see? The symptoms have already started. Some headaches and nausea. And now they're getting worse. There's even been some blurred vision—'

'But how did you find out?' he asked. 'When did you go to the doctor?'

'Last January when I went to San Francisco on that shopping trip, I saw a doctor at Stanford. Because of the headaches.'

'But you never said a thing,' he accused. 'You hardly even mentioned having headaches.'

She nodded. 'I know,' she said in a matter-of-fact voice. 'I wanted things to be as normal as possible. For as long as possible. And I still do. Besides, the doctor's given me some medication that helps with the headaches. It's just that you have to be aware of the symptoms now, and the decisions I've come to.'

'What decisions?' he asked.

'That I die with dignity,' she said. 'Here at home. I

don't want to go to the hospital, and I don't want any treatment that will only prolong my life.'

'But—'

'I've already told you, Josh. No buts. And don't try to change my mind. It's made up.' She paused and hugged him fiercely. 'We've had a wonderful life together, darling. We've had the greatest gift there is – our love for one another. I can die in peace knowing that. Don't you see?'

He nodded, but he wasn't certain that he did see. His eyes had filled with tears, and he fought to hold them back. Nothing of what she'd said had truly sunk in yet. It all seemed so unreal, as if their lives had suddenly become someone else's, as if this were a movie.

'Josh?' she said, taking both his hands in hers. 'Josh?'

'Yes?' he said, looking into her eyes.

'I want to ask a very important favor.'

'Anything,' he said, tears spilling from his eyes.

'I meant it when I said that I want our lives to go on as normally as possible,' she said. 'As if this didn't exist. I know that's going to be difficult, but that's the way I want it. And I don't want anybody to know that doesn't have to. The one thing in the world that would make me happiest is to go on as usual.'

He nodded, not trusting himself to speak. Tears streamed from his eyes unchecked.

'I want you to go to work as usual,' she went on, 'and I'll carry on here as usual. I know that's not going to be easy, but that's what I want.'

'Who . . . who's your doctor?' he managed to say.

'I've made a list for you,' she said. 'It's in the top right-hand drawer of the desk in my office. All the doctors and their telephone numbers are there. There's also a couple of articles about the particular kind of cancer I have. They'll help you understand it better.'

He put his head in her lap, and she stroked his hair again, running her fingers through it gently, savoring the feel of his warm breath on her.

Funny, she thought. *I thought I would cry when I finally told him. I thought I would hardly be able to get it all out. But ... having him here, holding me ... our being together, has made it easy.*

He abruptly looked up at her. 'This is why you took the birth control pills, isn't it?'

She nodded. 'I found out about the cancer right after we started to try to have a baby, so I decided I'd better not. I might not have lived till full term. There could've been all sorts of complications.' She didn't tell him that she wanted him to have a child with someone else, that she hoped he would father a child that would have both its parents. No, she would wait to tell him that. And a lot more.

'Oh, Joanna, you're so brave,' he said. 'To have held this inside for all these months. I wish you'd told me before, so you wouldn't have felt so alone with it. It makes me ... it makes me angry, I guess, that you haven't included me.'

'I've had to come to terms with it myself,' she said. 'And I didn't want to talk about it until then, Josh. I didn't want to leave you out, but I simply couldn't tell you till I was ready.'

'I'm glad you did,' he said.

'I am too, Josh,' she said. She paused, then ruffled his hair. 'Now, I want you to get up and go get ready for work. Let's have a normal day. Remember? April will be coming soon and so will Connie. There's a lot to do.'

'You're crazy, Joanna!' he said. 'A normal day after this?'

'I'm not crazy,' she said evenly. 'And yes, I want us to have a normal day. As normal as possible.'

'You really mean it?' he asked in disbelief.

'Oh, yes,' she said. 'And I'll be upset if you don't go right now and get ready. Please try to do this for me, Josh. I know it's hard, but it's really what I want. It'll make it so much easier for *me*.'

He stood up then, and looked down at her. She thought she detected a look of determination in his eyes. *Good*, she thought. *He's going to try to be brave.* But then, she wouldn't have thought otherwise of him.

'Go,' she said. 'And then come down and kiss me good-bye before you leave. If you can, come home for lunch as usual.'

He stood there, immobile, reluctant to move.

'Go, Josh,' she said again, very quietly.

Finally he walked off toward the house, and she watched him, trying to fix in her mind his every footstep, every subtle twist in his shoulders, the slight movement in his arms. For a moment she thought that her love for him would overwhelm her, but she was determined to remain dry-eyed, to be calm and in control.

Nevertheless, she had to finger a tear from her eye. *Josh, Josh, Josh*, she thought. *I will miss you. Miss you so very much.*

Then she straightened her shoulders and took a sip of coffee.

I may be dying, she thought, *but my work in this life isn't finished yet. Not by a long shot. I've got a lot to do before I go.*

BOOK TWO

April and Josh
Fall and Winter 2000

15

April sat at the big table in her kitchen, sipping coffee and nibbling on toast with butter and jam, blackcurrant on one slice and orange marmalade on the other. The morning newspaper was spread out on the table, and she eyed it while eating. When the telephone rang, she reached over to get it, her eyes still on the paper.

'Hello,' she said distractedly.

'April?'

Josh?

She instantly put down the paper, her antennae on full alert. Why on earth would he be calling her?

'Hi, Josh,' she said. 'What's going on?'

'I ... I need to talk to you,' he said hesitantly. 'If ... if you don't mind.'

What's wrong? she wondered, her curiosity piqued. His voice held none of its customary cheer, she thought. In fact, it was downright grave.

'Of course I don't mind,' she replied lightly. 'I'm all ears, Josh. What is it?' When he didn't answer immediately, she added: 'You don't sound like yourself.'

'I'm not,' he said. 'I . . . well . . . I'd rather discuss this in person, if you don't mind. It's . . . it's something very important, April. I hate to bother you, but I really need to talk to somebody. It's . . . it's really important.'

'Sure, Josh,' she said. 'That's fine. Do you want me to come up there?'

'No,' he said. 'I don't think so.' He paused, then asked, 'Do you mind if we meet someplace? I really need to discuss this in absolute privacy.'

My God, she thought, *he sounds so . . . desperate.*

'Why don't you come on over here, Josh?' she offered. 'I'll put on a fresh pot of coffee. How's that?'

'That'd be great, April,' he said, sounding somewhat relieved. 'I'll come straight on over, if that's okay.'

'That's fine, Josh,' she said. 'Do you know how to get here?'

'Yes,' he replied. 'Joanna's told me all about it. I don't think I could miss it.'

She could hear a hint of familiar amusement return to his voice and felt relieved. Perhaps whatever he had to discuss wasn't so serious after all.

'I'll see you in a half hour or so,' he said. 'Okay?'

'Perfect,' she said.

'See you in a bit.'

''Bye.' April hung up the telephone and sat staring off into space for a few minutes, then turned her attention back to the newspaper, but she couldn't seem to read the print, much less concentrate. Finally, she folded it up and laid it aside, then got to her feet to make a fresh pot of coffee.

What the devil could be going on up there? she wondered. *Josh Lawrence wouldn't be calling me unless it was important. And he certainly wouldn't be asking to meet me in private unless it was very important. But* what? *Had they suddenly decided they didn't like her work? Could they have decided to call off the project for some reason?*

Dumping the old coffee grounds in the garbage, she missed the can and grounds went flying in wet clumps.

'Damn!' she exclaimed. When she went to the sink and dampened some paper towels to clean up the mess, she realized that her hands were shaking.

Why am I so nervous? she asked herself. But deep down inside, she knew the answer to that question. Despite her efforts to suppress her feelings for Josh Lawrence, they had only grown more powerful. And they were not the feelings of a sister for a brother. No, indeed.

And now this! she thought. *Whatever* this *might be.*

Cleaning up the mess on the floor, she promised herself anew that no matter what Josh might have on his mind, she would put the skids on her own volatile emotions for Joanna's sake. For Joanna had come to be the sister she'd never had, and she wouldn't want anything – nothing in the world, especially not her feelings for Josh – to get in their way now.

Cruising up the mountain road, Joanna eyed the small package in its burnt orange box with the brown bow. It lay on the Mercedes passenger seat next to her. She smiled with delight just thinking about it. When she'd seen the beautiful Hermès scarf with its fanciful shell motif, she'd known immediately that she must get one for April.

Now, freshly coiffed, she'd decided to swing by April's house on her way home and surprise her with it. She'd been waiting for just the right time to give it to her, and something told her this morning that she should take the package with her to the beauty parlor, then drop by April's.

She braked at one of the stop signs on this treacherous stretch of the road and waited for an oncoming car to negotiate the narrow pass before continuing on ahead. She glanced over at the cottages across the ravine on her right. Some of them were barely discernible in the junglelike growth around them, but that was part of their charm, she thought.

She slowed down because she knew that April's cottage was just ahead, around the next corner. She hoped she'd be able to park behind April's car, but as she slowly rounded the corner she saw that the narrow shoulder behind the old Wagoneer was already occupied.

By Josh's ancient Land Cruiser. Unmistakably Josh's.

Joanna put on the brakes, her mind racing, her heart pounding. Then she swiftly stepped on the gas and sped on up the mountain road. Though she thought it doubtful they would, she didn't want them to see her car passing from across the ravine.

When she reached a crossroads, she made a left and pulled over to the side of the road. There was a wide shoulder here, and she put the car in park and sat staring through the window. Her heart was still racing, and she could feel a pulse in her ear.

My God, she thought. *Even my hands are shaking.*

She took a few deep breaths, trying to steady her nerves and clear her mind. After a few minutes, she looked over at the beautiful package on the seat next to her. The gift she'd so excitedly bought for April. Suddenly she began to laugh, a barely audible sound at first, but gradually increasing in intensity until her entire body shook with hilarity and the car was filled with the sound.

I've done it now, she thought. *Oh, yes, I've accomplished almost everything I set out to do. Only I didn't expect to feel quite so . . . jealous! Quite so . . . left out and . . . betrayed by it all!*

Her laughter quickly dissolved into tears, and she quietly cried, hating herself for her own jealousy – a feeling that she despised owning up to – and at the same time hating Josh and April for the bond that she

223

could see had developed between them. A bond that she had helped create, that she had nourished like a mother hen.

Of course he would come straight to her, she thought. *And it's only natural that he should. I should count my lucky stars and be grateful that Josh has her to talk to. God knows, he needs somebody.*

When her tears at last subsided, she took off her sunglasses and wiped her eyes with a Kleenex. Then she suddenly began laughing again, less raucously this time, but helplessly laughing nevertheless.

The irony of it all, she thought. *I've gotten exactly what I wanted. So I should be thrilled.*

But now she realized that she would have to grow accustomed to the success of her project. *How stupid of me,* she thought. *Not to have had the foresight to realize that I would be so powerfully affected by Josh's attraction to someone else. Even if it was someone of my own choosing.*

She finally put the car in drive and eased back onto the road. She would take an alternate route back down the mountain, then go on home, she decided. As she drove, she gradually began to feel a little less anxious, and reflected back on the history of her illness.

When she'd first learned that she was sick, Joanna had immediately decided that she must find another woman as her replacement in Josh's affections. She knew that despite his good looks, charming personality, and a strong masculine presence, he needed the support

224

of a partner. Physically, emotionally, and spiritually. But then, she supposed, didn't everybody?

It was her love for Josh that drove her to search for someone to replace her when she was gone. First, there had been the up-and-coming interior decorator Julie Gillette. Joanna had hired her to help with ordering wallpaper and fabrics that were available only through decorators, and had become intrigued by her. Initially, she had seemed as if she might be the perfect second wife for Josh. But after only a matter of days Joanna discovered that Julie, for all her good qualities – and they were many – was too aggressively upwardly mobile and obsessed with being a friend of the very rich and very social. There was nothing wrong with that in and of itself, Joanna thought, but Julie's relentless social ambitions simply didn't fit with Josh's idea of a way to live. They wouldn't have made it past first base, she decided.

Next, there had been Rachel Lewis, a photographer. Joanna had met her when she was working on her orchid book. At the time she'd thought that photographs of the flowers would accompany the text – rather than the drawings she later decided on – and she'd interviewed several photographers, examining their work. She'd met Rachel, who was both a great photographer and a great beauty. Over the course of their discussions, she discovered that although Rachel was indeed a wonderful woman, she lacked one essential ingredient: She was emotionally weak and lacked an inner strength that Josh could rely on. Rachel, it seemed, could barely keep her own fitful demons at bay, much less lend moral support to someone else.

There had been others that she'd briefly considered pursuing as candidates. Frieda, the beautiful, divorced bookshop proprietor, who she soon discovered would be ideal but for the fact that she was a lesbian. Then there'd been Laura, the young, wealthy horsewoman who was extremely poised, strong of character, and as well-bred as one of her Arabian horses. Unfortunately, she was also both unintelligent and ill-educated, though she'd been to the very 'best' schools.

Joanna sighed with relief as she zipped along the highway, headed back toward home. All of those defeats were in the past, she thought happily. After giving up the search and reconciling herself to the fact that Josh would have to make his own way in the world, April had fallen into her lap. *Their* laps, she reminded herself. April, the perfect mate for Josh. April, whose inner strength and character were more than enough to lend Josh the support he needed. April, who gladly gave of herself and would happily receive.

Joanna smiled to herself, her fears and conflicted feelings conquered – for the moment at least. She could hardly wait until Monday, when she could give April the beautiful scarf with its colorful shells. She could hardly wait to see the look of delight that she knew would cross her lovely features when she opened the package. *She will love it*, she thought with satisfaction. *They will both love it.*

*   *   *

'And she just told you about it?' April asked, her face etched with concern.

Josh nodded. 'She wouldn't even have told me today if I hadn't discovered that she was taking birth control pills.' He paused and looked into those compassionate eyes of hers.

'You see, April, we'd waited a long time to try to have a baby. Then we finally decided the time was right. So she stopped taking the pill. A year later, she was diagnosed.' He paused again, shaking his head. 'So, she immediately started taking the pill again. She didn't know if she could carry a baby to term, and she didn't want to endanger an unborn child.'

April sat staring at him, her mind a maelstrom of conflicting thoughts and emotions. She felt as if she were in shock, so stunned was she by the news. It didn't seem real somehow. Not yet, at least.

'Oh, my God, Josh,' April said, making an effort not to cry. 'I don't know what to say except that I'll do everything humanly possible to help. Just say the word. Anything at all, and you know that I mean it.'

Josh looked into her eyes. They were huge and sorrowful, but she hadn't shed a tear. The tears would come later, of that he was certain. He looked down at the mug of coffee on the kitchen table in front of him, then looked back up at her.

'Thanks, April,' he said. 'I . . . I know that you love Joanna or I wouldn't have told you. I felt like I *had* to tell you. Not just to unburden myself, but because

I thought you should know. I thought you had a right to know.'

April reached across the space between them, and placed a hand on his. 'I'm so glad you told me, Josh,' she said. 'I'm really honored that you did. And you're right, of course. I love Joanna dearly. She's so wonderful, so ... I don't know. Like no one else I've ever known. And I've said it a dozen times, but she's been like the sister I always wanted.'

Her voice choked, and she paused a moment until she trusted herself to speak. 'I ... I love you both, Josh,' she finally said, looking directly into his sad blue eyes. Her face suddenly burned brightly with this admission, but she continued. 'And I'll be there for you both. Whatever it takes.'

Josh swallowed hard and squeezed her hand in his. Oh, my God, he thought. *I wish I was brave enough to tell her that I feel the same way. That we both love her, too. That I love her.* But he felt as if it would be a betrayal of his love for Joanna to say the words. Even thinking them felt like a betrayal.

'I knew I could rely on you,' he finally said with a tight smile. 'You've been so great to us both, April, that we feel like you're family. I hope you understand that. I think you do.'

She nodded. 'Yes,' she said simply. She looked out through the windows at the luxuriant foliage that surrounded the cottage, then shifted her gaze back to him. 'One thing, Josh,' she said.

'What's that?' he asked.

'I don't think I should tell Joanna that you've told me,' she said. 'I think I should wait for her to tell me herself.'

He nodded silently.

She removed her hand from his and ran her fingers through her hair nervously. 'I'm sure that she will, and I hope it's soon.'

'I think it probably will be,' he replied hoarsely. He cleared his throat before continuing. 'She ... she's beginning to have more problematic symptoms. More frequent headaches and some blurring of vision. Medicine takes care of some of it, but she's going to have to confide in you soon, I'm sure. You know ... to explain what's going on.'

April nodded. 'Well,' she said with quiet confidence, 'I'll be there.'

'Thanks again, April,' he said. He shifted in his chair uncomfortably. 'I guess I'd better get going. I don't know when Joanna will be back home, and I want to be there. I'm a little afraid for her to be alone, even if she wants things to be normal.'

'It's that bad, you think?' April asked.

'Getting there,' he answered. He rose to his feet, and April followed suit.

'If there's anything I can do between now and Monday morning,' she said, 'let me know. Call me anytime, Josh. And I mean it. Anytime. I'll be here puttering around all weekend.'

'Thanks,' Josh said. He smiled sadly. 'We'll just have to play it by ear, you know?'

'Yes,' April said. 'I guess so.'

She walked him to the front door, then to the foot-bridge. 'Remember,' she said, turning and looking up into his eyes, 'don't hesitate to call if you need me.'

Josh returned her gaze. 'I will,' he promised. He wanted desperately to reach out and embrace her, to thank her, to feel the warmth and support of her body against his.

At that moment April, as if sensing his need, put her arms around him and hugged him to her. 'We have to be strong for Joanna,' she whispered.

'Yes,' he said, returning her embrace. Then he drew back and started across the bridge to his car.

April watched until he'd pulled out, waving as he left. Then she turned and went back into the house. She closed the door behind her, and leaned back against it, her feelings more confused than ever. The tears she'd so long delayed for his sake began to flow. She wept and wept. Tears for Joanna, for Josh, and for herself.

Josh drove into the courtyard and was relieved to see Joanna's Mercedes there. He parked and leapt out, heading toward the mud room, anxious to see her. His visit with April had, he reflected, made him feel stronger. He didn't know why exactly, but supposed it was just the knowledge that he would have her moral support in dealing with Joanna's illness.

He also realized that after sharing his secret, he felt a new and more powerful bond with April. It was a wondrous feeling, but at the same time it made him feel a little guilty. He had really enjoyed being with her, had enjoyed being in her little cottage – with its feeling of warmth and charm and coziness, of beauty tinged with a sense of fantasy.

The same kind of feeling that Joanna creates in her surroundings, he thought.

In the mud room, he realized that he was wearing spiffy-clean Top-Siders and didn't need to take off dirty work boots. He headed toward the kitchen, but Joanna wasn't there or on the terrace outside. In the entrance hall, he shouted upstairs, but there was no answer. On an impulse, he turned and walked back to the kitchen and out the French doors to the terrace, over the little bridge to the pool area, and down through the apple trees to the grotto.

He saw her before she realized that he was there. Standing outside the doors, he watched her. She was idly walking about the room, brushing her hands across the shell-encrusted surfaces, then standing back and studying them with a critical eye. Then she would step closer again and touch them anew.

He stepped into the room. 'Joanna?' he said in a soft voice.

She turned to him, not at all startled. He was surprised to see a beautiful smile on her face. She appeared to be calm, serene and happy even. 'It's becoming truly beautiful, isn't it?' she said, taking one of his hands in hers.

'Yes,' he nodded, giving her hand a gentle squeeze.

'It'll have a bit of me in it, don't you think?' she asked, looking up at him.

'It's pure Joanna,' he replied. 'Your ideas, your imagination at work.' Tears suddenly formed in his eyes.

Joanna reached up and brushed them away with a fingertip. 'None of that,' she said. 'Remember? We have to be strong, and you have to go on for me. Keep building what we've started together. Always building, making everything more beautiful.' She paused, then kissed his lips lightly. 'And not on your own,' she said.

Early the next morning, Joanna woke with a start. Something was definitely wrong, but she wasn't certain what it was. She reached over for Josh, but didn't feel his familiar warmth next to her.

That's it, she thought with relief. *Josh isn't in bed. He's already up and about. Funny, how we become so accustomed to sleeping with someone that their absence can set off alarms.*

She slid out of bed and slipped into her bathrobe, then padded into the bathroom on bare feet and took the first pill of the day, a preventative painkiller. She washed her face and brushed her teeth, then ran a brush through her hair, looking at her reflection in the mirror.

Odd, she thought. *I don't look sick at all. In fact, I look pretty damn good.* She smiled and flipped off the light. *Now to find my husband.*

She started down the hall to the stairs, but passing

by his office, she saw that the door was ajar and the lights were on. Peeking in, she saw Josh at his desk, the computer screen bright with words or figures she couldn't read from here. Piled up on the desk next to him were several stacks of paper, some of them she guessed to be the articles and notes she'd told him about, some of them apparently printouts that he'd run recently.

She tapped lightly on the door, then went on into the office. 'Josh?' she asked.

He jerked up and turned around. She saw at once that his eyes were bloodshot and weary-looking, with dark circles. His hair was a tousled mess, and his clothes were rumpled. The room was airless and smelled stale.

'You look exhausted,' Joanna said worriedly.

He nodded and smiled grimly. 'I am,' he said.

She went to him and put her arms around his shoulders, then ran her fingers through his hair affectionately. She didn't have to ask what he'd been doing because she was certain she knew, but she did anyway.

'What've you been up to?' she asked.

'I . . . I've been surfing the Net,' he said hoarsely. 'I . . . I've been trying to find out as much as I can about your . . . your—' He looked up at her with wounded, sorrowful eyes.

'You can say it, Josh,' Joanna said quietly, looking into his eyes. 'It's not a disgrace, you know. *Cancer*. See? It's just a word.'

'I . . . I'm sorry, Joanna,' he said. 'I still . . . I still find it hard to believe.' She could see that he was fighting back tears.

She hugged his head to her closely, then leaned down and kissed it tenderly. *I've got to be brave*, she told herself, holding back her own tears. She loved him so much and knew she was breaking his heart by being sick.

'You'll come to terms with it eventually, my darling,' she said. She forced cheer into her voice, and once again tousled his hair. 'Now, tell me what you've been doing.'

'I was finding out as much as I can,' he said calmly. 'The American Brain Tumor Association, the Brain Tumor Society, the National Cancer Institute, the National Brain Tumor Foundation. On and on and on. I've been up all night going from one website to another, seeing what I can find out. I called Dr Saltzman in Palo Alto yesterday, and he filled me in on everything and answered all my questions. But I thought maybe I could learn something else.'

'No wonder you're exhausted,' she said. 'Come on, let's go down and get some coffee. Or do you want to shower and go to bed?'

'No,' he said. 'I'm too wound up to sleep. Let's go get that coffee.'

They walked hand in hand to the kitchen, where Joanna ground beans and put on the coffee while Josh made toast, poured fresh-squeezed orange juice, and set the table out on the terrace. When they finally sat down to eat, the warm morning sun was already burning off the fog.

'I saw that your doctor is listed on Best Doctors, Inc., website,' Josh said, after sipping his coffee.

'I know,' Joanna said. 'That's not where I found out about him, but I think I've probably visited every website there is that deals with my form of cancer.'

Josh set down his coffee cup and looked at her, his eyes burning with an unfamiliar intensity. 'Joanna,' he said, 'you know that there're a lot of new techniques out there that make treatment for brain cancer a lot more effective than it used to be. And there're a lot—'

'Josh,' she said firmly, looking him in the eye. 'I know *all* about them, believe me. I've studied the literature, and I've talked to umpteen-million doctors about my case.' She took a sip of coffee and set her cup back down. 'And they all say virtually the same thing. They can only buy me time. And not much of that.'

'But what about some of the experimental studies, Joanna,' he persisted. 'You know—'

Joanna slammed her hand down on the table. 'No!' she cried. 'Stop it! Right now! I don't want to hear any more!' Her voice broke and tears came into her eyes.

Josh quickly jumped out of his chair and, kneeling down beside her, put his arms around her. 'Oh, Joanna,' he cried, 'I'm sorry. I just . . . I just don't want to see you give up so easily. I keep thinking there might be something, some miracle that will make you well. It just can't . . . end . . . this . . . way.'

'Look at me, Josh,' she said calmly.

He looked up into her eyes and saw a resolute determination shining there that he knew no one could defeat.

'I've told you before,' she said. 'I don't want to die like Dad did. I don't want all that pain and misery. The terrible lingering. And I will not be a guinea pig. Don't you see, Josh? I might be alive, but I wouldn't be living. I've made up my mind about this, once and for all, and I hope that you can respect that.'

After a moment of silence, he slowly nodded his head, knowing that nothing he could say would change her mind, and yet he couldn't quite fathom what seemed to him her acceptance of this awful death sentence.

'Joanna,' he said, 'aren't you angry? Don't you hate this?'

Her eyes flickered briefly with recognition, then she nodded. 'Yes,' she said. 'I've been angry, Josh, and I've cursed God and the world and everybody in it. At first, anyway.' She took a deep breath, then continued. 'But now,' she said, 'now I've reconciled myself to it. To its inevitability. To my . . . my powerlessness over it.'

She looked at him and smiled, not with amusement, he thought, but a little sadly. 'I've come to a kind of peace, Josh,' she said finally, 'and I hope you will, too.'

She leaned down and kissed him, and he hugged her tightly. 'Now,' she said, 'let's finish breakfast, because I've got a busy day.'

'What?' he said, rising to his feet and sitting back down in his chair.

'I've got to start packing,' she said. 'I'm going down to Christina's for a little visit. I hate to leave you here alone, but you'll be busy at work. Anyway, I want to tell her what's going on. And in person, not over the phone.'

He looked at her almost with astonishment, marveling at her composure. 'Do you think you really ought to take a trip like that?'

'I told you,' she said. 'We've got to carry on as usual, and I meant it.' She laughed. 'It's not so much that I'm anxious to go down to Christina's, but it's only fair, Josh.'

He nodded as if in agreement, but he still didn't *feel* it. Not really.

'Are you going to the nursery today?' she asked.

He shook his head. 'No,' he said. 'I don't have any appointments this weekend, so Carl can handle everything. I thought I'd stay here and get some work done in the Stud Room.'

'Why don't you try to get some sleep first?' she said. 'You're exhausted.'

'I'll try,' he said.

'Promise?'

He nodded. 'Yes,' he said with a smile. But he knew he wouldn't. He couldn't. Not yet.

16

April was up on the scaffolding, lying flat on her back, the ceiling only two feet above her. She was embedding circular scallop shells, in shades ranging from off-pink to orange, in the quick-drying cement. She was carefully following the lines she had sketched out because making a mistake and having to redo was painstaking and time-consuming.

Argopecten circularis, she thought with wry amusement. *I'm learning more about shells than I ever dreamed I would. Or wanted to, for that matter.*

She had been at it all day, with a short lunch break. Woody had left, and she was working late. She was doing as much overtime as she possibly could in light of Josh's revelation. Plus she wanted to surprise Joanna with the progress she'd made when she returned from Montecito.

In her fantasies the ceiling would be completely finished, and although that wouldn't really happen, she would nearly be finished. The ceiling was the hardest part by far, due to the simple fact that she had to do it flat on her back, up in the air. Despite the fans they'd set up, the heat was still suffocating, and the work was dirty.

Placing the last of the scallop shells at the end of the line she'd marked out, she breathed a sigh of relief. *This is going to be it for the day*, she said. *And I mean it.* She'd told herself that several times, only to keep going, trying to get a little closer to completion of this section of the ceiling.

'Hello up there,' Josh called from one of the French doors.

'Hi,' April called down.

'It's getting late. Don't you think it's time you quit for the day?'

'I'm just finishing up,' she replied. 'This *is* the last one for the day.'

Josh stepped into the room and stood looking up at the ceiling. He could see from the work so far that it was going to be a spectacularly beautiful and exotic room, unlike anything he had ever seen. The difference between the sketches and the reality was startling. But then, he told himself, so was the enormous time and patience the work required.

April scooted over to the edge of the boards she lay

on, then eased herself down to the next level of the scaffolding. When she finally reached the floor, she pulled off the latex gloves she wore, then stretched her arms and shoulders and rolled her head around.

'This kills your arms and shoulders.' She laughed. 'I don't know how Michelangelo ever did it. I don't know how any of those guys did it. They must've all died cripples.'

Josh laughed. 'It's paying off, though, isn't it?'

It was good to hear him laugh, April thought. There had certainly been little laughter since Joanna had left. She looked up at the ceiling and then looked at him with a pleased expression. 'I think so,' she said. 'I think it's really going to be terrific.'

'Listen,' he said. 'You want to stay for dinner? Connie's made something, and I hate to eat alone again. Besides, I'd say you deserve a good meal after what you've put in today.'

April looked at him and for a moment didn't know what to say. Then she decided she was being silly. She wanted to stay for dinner, so why not? Besides, it might do Josh some good should he want to talk.

'That'd be great,' she said. 'But ... oh, my Lord! Look at me. I'm filthy. Covered up with cement dust and stuff.'

'That's okay,' Josh said. 'You can wash off if you want to or take a shower.'

'I'll just wash off,' April said, untying the big painter's smock she wore. 'That is, if I won't offend you looking so ... well ...'

'Like a working artist,' Josh said. 'There's nothing wrong with that.'

'I'll just straighten up my things here,' April said, 'then come on up. How's that?'

'Great,' Josh said. 'You can come up to the house and clean up in a guest bath or use a pool house bath if you want to.'

'The pool house bath is fine,' April said. 'I'm getting to know it quite well.'

Josh laughed. 'Okay,' he said. 'See you up on the terrace.'

After he left, she quickly straightened up the room, getting ready for the next morning, and gathered up her tools that needed washing. She placed them in a bucket as she did every day, picked up her carryall, flipped off the light, and left, closing the French door behind her. In one of the pool house's two bathrooms she cleaned her tools and dried them off.

She looked in the bathroom mirror. 'Hopeless,' she said to her reflection. She washed her hands and arms, scrubbing them clean of cement and dust, then washed her face and neck. Toweling off, she looked in the mirror again.

'My hair!' she cried. Cement dust coated it in a thin white layer. 'I look like an actress in a high school play. Trying to age her appearance. And failing miserably.'

She grabbed her hairbrush and started brushing, brushing, brushing. 'Hopeless,' she repeated. 'Hopeless.' Finally, she put the brush down and sighed. 'Screw it,' she said. 'I'll just have to be me. And Josh'll have to like it.'

She flicked white dust off her shoulders, her arms, her bust, then picked up her carryall and headed out toward the pool, then across the little bridge to the terrace that adjoined the house.

The area had been transformed while she'd been in the bathroom. Candles burned in hurricane lamps all around, and the table had been beautifully set, as always, with a crisp linen cloth and napkins. Provençal plates, shiny silver, and crystal wine goblets. A potted orchid sat in the middle of the table, its abundance of small, delicate blooms cascading down onto the table. She walked over to take a closer look. The flowers made her want to reach out and stroke them.

'They're real beauties, aren't they?'

She turned and saw Josh, approaching from the house, a bottle of wine in hand.

'They're gorgeous,' she said. 'So fragile-looking.'

'*Barkeria spectabilis*,' he said. 'One of the *Cattleya* Alliance.' He pulled a chair out for her. 'Here, take a seat. Connie's bringing the food in just a minute.'

April sat down in the proffered chair. 'Thanks, Josh,' she said.

He sat down opposite her and filled her glass with wine, then poured some for himself. 'To . . . to you, Michelangelo,' he said, lifting his glass. 'I guess that's Michelangel*a*,' he amended, 'and the crazy, beautiful grotto ceiling.'

April smiled and lifted her glass to his. 'And to you,' she replied, 'and beautiful, beautiful orchids.'

They sipped their wine, and Connie came with a tray of food. 'I'm going to let you serve yourselves,' she said, setting the tray on the table, 'because I've got to get going.'

'That's fine, Connie,' Josh said. 'And thanks for sticking around to do all this.'

'That's okay,' she said, smiling at Josh. 'You know that.' With a barely perceptible lift of her chin, she gazed at April, her eyes sleepy-looking, as if they veiled a deep dark secret. 'Have a nice dinner.'

'Thanks, Connie,' April said.

Connie turned and hurried back into the house.

When she was out of earshot, April said, 'Sometimes I think she doesn't really like me very much.'

Josh's eyebrows lifted in surprise. 'Why would you say that?' he asked. He began to serve them from the tray, putting salad on their plates, then chicken, roasted new potatoes, and green beans.

'Thanks,' April said. 'This looks delicious.'

'And it'll taste better than it looks,' Josh said. 'The way she spices things. Anyhow, tell me why you think she doesn't like you.'

'Oh, I don't know,' April replied. 'Just little things. I mean, she's friendly, but a little guarded. I get the feeling she doesn't like our being friends.'

'You mean, you and me?' he asked.

'No, that's not what I mean,' April said. 'Well, maybe that, too.' She laughed lightly. 'I don't think she likes my being friends with Joanna, either. Maybe she feels as if I'm encroaching on her territory or something. I know she and Joanna are very close.'

'Oh, yes,' Josh said. 'You can bet on that. But Joanna has other friends, and Connie doesn't seem to mind.' He began chewing on a piece of fried chicken.

'Well, maybe I'm wrong,' April said with a shrug, 'but I get that feeling. Maybe it's because I'm around nearly all the time, and Joanna and I spend a lot of time together. Time that she might normally spend with Connie.'

Josh stopped eating and looked at her. 'I hadn't really thought about it,' he said, 'but you might have something there. Joanna's always confided in Connie. Connie's always been like a member of the family.'

'I know,' April said. 'And I don't want to . . . well . . . interfere with that. Especially not now.' She tasted the potatoes. 'Oh, these are fabulous.'

'I told you so,' Josh said with a grin. 'But listen, April,' he said. 'Seriously, I want you to know that you're not interfering in anything. It's only natural that Joanna's been confiding in you. She's taken to you like a fish to water. You know that, and vice versa, I know.'

April nodded. 'Oh, yes,' she agreed.

'That's what I mean,' Josh said. 'So don't worry about it. Believe you me, Connie can handle it. She may be petite, but she's got really thick hide. It's just that Joanna has found a sort of sister in you, and I'm truly grateful for that.'

April smiled. 'I am, too,' she said. 'I haven't had a friend like her since . . . well, I don't think ever in my life.

Not like Joanna.' She paused and took a deep breath. She felt tears threaten, and she certainly didn't want to cry. Not in front of Josh. She quickly picked up her glass and sipped her wine, aware of Josh watching her from across the table.

Joanna decided to check her makeup one last time before the dinner party. She flipped on the light in the luxurious marble and mirror bathroom and was startled as always by the multitude of reflections that bounced back at her. All of herself. The scent of gardenias was cloying, from the three bushes that decorated the enormous length of the vanity. Edging up to the mirror over one of the twin gold sinks, she looked closely at herself.

Not bad, she thought, leaning back again. *No, not bad at all. I do seem to have a glow about me.* She smiled ruefully. *A glow of life and health? Ha!*

She leaned in closer to the mirror again. *But . . . I could use just a tad more blusher.* She reached over for her little compact and lightly brushed another hint of Givenchy's Sunset onto her cheekbones.

She stood back and looked again. *That's fine*, she decided. *There'll be bronzed flesh all around me tonight, so I'll fit in a bit better.* Christina and her friends constantly globe-trotted, worshiping the sun all over the planet, and were generally very darkly tanned the year round. *Too dark*, she thought, *for their own good.* A lot of them paid doctors a fortune to repair the sun damage, then went right back out and did the same thing again.

246

She snapped the compact closed and stood back, looking at herself full length. She did a quick twirl in front of the mirrors, then stopped. The outfit was beautiful, she thought. It had a big, flowing, golden silk mousseline blouse with long sleeves, worn with a shawl that was made of yards of the same silk. The lightweight wool jersey pants were the same color. All by Chanel. And very much her cup of tea. She knew that she looked elegant, but casually so, as if no effort had been expended in achieving the look.

If they only knew the time it takes to look as if you've spent no time putting yourself together.

She flipped one of her drop earrings with a fingernail and watched it glint in the light. She loved these earrings because Josh, who couldn't really afford them at the time, had somehow scraped together the money and given them to her for a wedding present. They were gold drops, set with small rubies and diamonds. Later, on their first anniversary, he'd given her a matching necklace. She didn't wear them often, but welcomed the chance. Tonight, she'd made a special effort for Christina because her sister always did if she was coming up to one of Josh and Joanna's rare parties, and besides, she wanted to look her best when she gave Christina her news.

She went back out into her bedroom, inhaling the sweet aroma of the beautiful arrangements of fresh flowers. *Christina has tried to make everything perfect*, she thought. She leaned over and stuck her nose in an enormous pink rose. 'Luscious,' she said aloud. The bed had been made with the finest pure linen, and the latest books and magazines had been neatly stacked on a table. There was a mini-fridge, well stocked with all sorts of drinks, a bar, and fresh fruit. The bathroom had been supplied with the gardenias and a host of luxurious toiletries. Christina knew how to pamper guests.

Joanna sat on the edge of the bed and slipped into her high-heeled Manolo Blahnik sandals. She looked at them admiringly, sticking her legs out in front of her and wiggling her toes. They matched her outfit beautifully, and she adored the tiny crystal posies at the toes.

I guess I'm silly, she thought. *To be so concerned about such frivolous things at a time like this, but at least they're . . . distracting.*

She wasn't really looking forward to a dinner party, not tonight, but had decided to be a good sport for her sister. She'd come down to Montecito to tell Christina her news in person – she'd thought it was vital that she did so – and had hoped to have a sister-to-sister tête-à-tête. She'd also reasoned that Christina could use the company since her divorce and, gruesome as her own news was, had hoped that it would distract Christina from her own woes.

Christina had surprised her, however, by being in a cheerful, even expansive, mood. She'd not once mentioned Rudi, her ex-husband, or the loneliness that invariably accompanied the periods between husbands.

What's going on? Joanna wondered idly. She knew her sister well enough to know that something big was percolating in Christina's mind. What else could explain the joie de vivre that had so uncharacteristically taken hold of her sister?

She picked up her handbag at the bedside. Rummaging through it, she took out a small bottle of pills, took off the lid, and jiggled two out. Then she reached for the glass of mineral water on the bedside table and took the pills. *Just a precaution*, she told herself. *In case I feel one of those terrible headaches coming on.*

But I'm fine, she reassured herself. *Really. Only I'd better talk to Christina. And tonight.*

She'd been putting it off ever since she'd gotten here, telling herself that there was plenty of time. But the time had flown by, and now she had to be getting back home. And still she hadn't broached the subject. They'd been so busy doing a thousand things, and besides, Christina had seemed so happy and excited that Joanna didn't want to upset her.

There was a soft knock at the bedroom door, and Joanna walked over and opened it.

'Are you ready, darling?' Christina asked, looking into the room with wide, worried eyes.

'Yes,' Joanna said. 'I'm ready.'

'Oh, you look beautiful!' Christina exclaimed, coming into the bedroom. 'Absolutely beautiful! I don't know how you do it. Without even half trying. Not like me, spending hours and hours, working myself half to death, just trying to look presentable.'

Joanna rolled her eyes. 'Christina,' she said mildly, 'you look fabulous and you know it. But if you're fishing for compliments, you've come to the right place. You really do look wonderful, and that dress looks like it was made for you.'

'It was,' Christina exclaimed. 'By Josephus Thimister, in Paris. It took four – not the usual three, darling, but four – fittings.' She swirled around in the exquisite floor-length gown, then stood looking at Joanna. 'Divine, isn't it?'

'Breathtaking,' Joanna said. And she really meant it. The dress was an artful blend of tatters, made of silk and tulle in palest pink, almost flesh-toned. Christina had gilded the lily with huge diamond earrings, a diamond necklace, and diamond bracelets and rings.

'Well,' Christina said, tossing her many-shaded blond tresses, 'let's go in, shall we? We can have a little drinkie before the hordes arrive.'

Leading the way, Christina left the bedroom with Joanna following, and they went out to the huge marble living room to await the guests.

The dinner was over and the guests had left. Joanna and Christina were seated in Christina's opulent sunroom, a vast neo-classical space that faced the beautifully lit gardens, the pool, and a cascade of water that fell down the hillside as far as the eye could see.

Joanna thought the room was slightly eerie because of the many marble busts on plinths that lined the walls, and the plethora of statues and fragments of antiquity that were everywhere. *So much cold marble*, she thought. *So many long-dead people. So many body parts.*

Christina looked over at her and could tell that she was anxious to talk. She took a drag off her cigarette. 'Did you enjoy yourself tonight?' she asked, exhaling a plume of smoke.

'Yes,' Joanna said. 'It was amusing, and very different from the dinners I usually go to.'

Christina stared at her for a moment. 'Amusing?' She coughed a laugh. 'Well, I guess *that's* the death knell. You didn't have a good time, did you?'

'I did, Christina,' Joanna exclaimed. 'I just . . . I guess I was just a little distracted, that's all.'

Christina's expression turned serious. 'Don't tell me,' she said, 'you're having trouble with Josh.'

Joanna shook her head. 'No, it's nothing like that,' she said, laughing.

'You can tell me, Joanna,' Christina said, inching closer to her on the sofa. 'I know how men are and, believe me, sister dear, they're all *pigs*.' A thoughtful expression crossed her face momentarily. 'Well . . . most of them anyway,' she amended.

Joanna laughed again. 'No, no, *no!*' she cried merrily. 'You've got it all wrong, Christina. It's got nothing to do with Josh at all.'

'What, then?' Christina asked, exhaling another plume of smoke.

Joanna looked about her. 'Why don't we go out on the terrace?' she said. 'I don't want any of the help to hear me.'

'Seriously?' Christina asked. 'They're making so much noise in the kitchen they couldn't hear a gunshot.'

'This is a deep dark secret, Christina,' Joanna said. 'I would feel a lot more comfortable.'

Christina immediately rose to her feet and extended a hand to Joanna. 'Let's go,' she said. 'You've got me so excited about this secret, I'd walk from here to Santa Barbara to hear it.'

Joanna took her hand and got to her feet, then followed Christina out onto the terrace, where they spread out on adjoining chaise longues. There was a steady breeze, and Joanna relished the feel of it on her skin.

'All right,' Christina said, fighting the breeze to light another cigarette, 'tell me what's going on.'

Joanna looked into Christina's eyes steadily before she spoke. 'What I'm going to tell you must not go further,' she said. 'And I mean it, Christina. Do you promise?'

'You know you can trust me.'

'I mean you can't tell anybody,' Joanna said. 'This has to be like when we were little girls conspiring against Daddy. Only it's a lot more important.'

Christina's eyes went wide with wonder, but she didn't say a word.

'Still promise?' Joanna asked.

Christina nodded slowly. 'Yes,' she said. A sense of dread was coming over her because she'd never seen Joanna in a mood like this before.

Joanna looked into her sister's eyes. 'I'm going to die, Christina,' she said simply.

Christina's body heaved, almost as if she were going to be sick. 'Wh ... wh ... what do you *mean*?' she stammered, the whites of her eyes huge in the near darkness.

'Just what I said,' Joanna said calmly. 'It's brain cancer, and I have a few months at the most.'

Christina's features collapsed into a knot of disbelief, fear, and horror all at once. 'But ... but ... but,' she blubbered, tears beginning to form in her eyes. 'Joanna! You can't mean this!' Her voice was a dramatic, hoarse whisper.

'It's true,' Joanna said, 'and I wanted you to know. Because you're my sister and have a right to know what's going on.'

Christina jumped up from the chaise longue and sat down next to Joanna, pushing her over with her hip, then taking her by the shoulders with her hands. 'Tell me you're lying,' she cried. 'Tell me you're lying.'

Joanna gently took Christina's hands off her shoulders and held them in her own. 'I'm not lying, Christina. I've never been more serious in my life.' She looked up at her sister, who had begun to weep uncontrollably. 'I hate for you to have to know,' she said, 'but I had to tell you.'

Christina's hands jerked spastically within Joanna's, and she choked back her tears. 'But what about Josh?' she whispered. 'Does he know?'

Joanna nodded. 'Yes,' she said. 'And I'm going to tell you what I told him. I want everything to be as normal as possible till the end. Can you understand that?'

'Normal?' Christina burst out.

'Yes,' Joanna said, looking with steely eyes at her sister. 'As normal as possible. For my sake.'

Christina stared at her for a moment. 'I guess I understand,' she finally said.

'I'm asking us all to be very strong,' Joanna said, 'and I know it's difficult.'

Christina drew herself up and looked at her sister. Her eyes burned bright with tears. 'You know I can be strong!' she said. 'You know that no matter what comes along, no matter what a mess my life always is, deep down inside, I'm as strong as an ox! I'll do anything I can for you!'

Joanna pushed herself up and put an arm around Christina's shoulder, then planted a kiss on her cheek. 'I know you will,' she said. 'And I love you for it.'

Christina hugged her close to her. 'If you need any help, any help at all, Joanna, I'll be there,' she whispered.

As if the breeze had caught her words and then brought them back to her like an echo, Christina wondered whether or not she meant them. She squeezed her eyes shut and tried to clear her mind. *I don't know,* she thought with confusion. *I don't know what I feel anymore. I don't know what I really think. I have to think of myself . . . of Peter . . .*

Josh took a sip of his wine and looked across the table at April. 'I'm like you,' he said. 'I've never had a friend like Joanna, either.'

April heard the wistful note in his voice, and hoped that she hadn't steered the conversation in a painful direction.

254

'Joanna could've had almost anything or anybody, but—'

'*You* were for her,' April said, pointing a finger at him.

Josh smiled a little sadly. 'You bet,' he said. '*We* were for each other.' He looked off into the distance a moment, then returned his gaze to April.

'It was like a miracle,' he continued. 'When Joanna and I met, I didn't have a thing,' he said. 'Nothing but the job her father had given me. Maybe two dollars left over at the end of the week.' He laughed. 'But it didn't matter at all. Not to Joanna. She was beautiful and fun and imaginative and creative. And she believed in me. God, we've been happy.'

He stared off into the distance again, and April saw the anguish that came into his eyes.

'I've thought you were the luckiest couple I've ever met,' April said, trying to fill in the silence. 'Since the very first time I met you.'

He drew his gaze back in and looked at her. 'Did you?' he asked. 'Really?'

'Yes,' she said, noticing that his eyes were shining with unshed tears. 'You both seemed so good for each other. Still do. Like everything I ever wanted. Everything *most* people want.'

Josh looked into her eyes, and realized that she meant it. At the same time he understood that she was lonely, or if not exactly lonely, then hoping for someone special in her own life.

His heart went out to her, and he reached over and

touched her hand. 'I'm sure the same thing will happen to you, April,' he said. 'You'll end up with the greatest man in the world for you.'

She had almost jerked away when he touched her, but she quickly reminded herself they were friends, after all. Confidants even. And it was completely innocent. Nevertheless, she felt a familiar pinprick of guilt, knowing that she enjoyed the touch of his hand upon hers.

'A woman like you,' Josh went on, 'is bound to find someone. Just because the first time turned out lousy doesn't mean it won't happen.' His hand lingered on hers for another moment, until it occurred to him that he might have been a little forward. He told himself that it was merely a gesture of compassion and friendship, however, and April didn't seem to mind.

If it weren't for Joanna . . ., he thought. He quickly took his hand away, and a blush of guilt burned his ears. *I shouldn't even be thinking this way*, he told himself. *Especially not with the way things are now.*

'Thanks for the vote of confidence,' April said, forcing a smile. 'I need that sometimes. I guess I don't always feel as good about myself as I should.'

'What was he like?' Josh asked. 'I mean Roger Woodward. Or is that being nosy?'

'No, no,' April said quickly, 'not at all.' She paused, thinking. 'Roger was an adorable shit,' she finally said, her voice full of amusement. 'We were married for four years, but sometimes it seems like it was two weeks. Two fuzzy weeks in my memory.'

'Do you miss Hollywood and all that?' Josh asked.

'It must be so different here after being married to a movie star and all.'

'No,' April said emphatically. 'When we met, Roger was totally unknown and I was an architecture student.' She looked at Josh and shrugged. 'It's an old story. I quit school to support him while he took acting classes and went to auditions. With the promise that when he hit it big, I'd go back to school. But' – she paused and thrust a finger in the air – 'when Roger got the Big Break, he didn't want me out of his sight. Like a lot of actors, he was an egomaniac. Wanted me to be a slave to him and his career. I decided I didn't fit the bill. I wanted to have a career of my own.'

'So that's what caused the split,' he said.

'More or less,' she agreed. 'I started doing work for a friend, designing garden structures, working with tile and stone.' She looked at Josh and grinned. 'And shells.'

He laughed. 'And it's a good thing, too,' he said.

'Anyway, we finally agreed to a divorce,' she went on, 'and I bought the cottage up here with my teensy settlement.'

'Teensy?' he asked. 'Why?'

'Because I didn't want to feel like I owed anybody anything,' she said. 'Especially him. I wanted a life of my own. Anyway, I had a big commission up here, and I really loved it. So . . . the rest, as they say, is history.'

'And I know you're happy in your work,' he said.

She nodded. 'Oh, yes. I love it. There's nothing wrong with being a housewife, but it's not the only thing I want to do. I guess I want to have my cake and eat it too,' she said. 'Because someday I do want a family.' She looked at him. 'Kids and all.'

Josh's expression became sober. 'Yeah,' he said. 'Me too.' He was silent for a moment, his head hanging. Then he looked up at her with curiosity. 'Were you a happy kid?' he asked.

'I . . . I . . . well . . . a lot of the time, I guess,' April stammered. 'I was alone a lot. My mother was divorced and worked, and my father lived on the East Coast, so I almost never saw him.'

'Sounds familiar,' Josh said. 'My parents were divorced, too, and I almost never saw my dad. And my mom worked, so I was left to my own resources a lot.'

'And I bet you were very resourceful, too,' April joked.

He smiled. 'You bet I was,' he replied. 'Always up to something. I guess you'd say I had a very early education about the ways of the world.' He looked at her. 'You too?'

April shrugged. 'Well, yes and no,' she said. 'I had a lot of freedom, but I was always trying to . . . well, I guess you'd say I was always trying to make things *look* better than they were. To make myself better than . . . better than the situation I was living in.'

Josh detected a long-buried pain in her voice and saw it in her bright eyes and immediately identified with it. 'Things weren't so great at home, and you wanted to get away from there? To have a better life for yourself?'

April nodded. 'Yes,' she said. 'To be perfectly honest . . .' She laughed and looked at him. 'I hate that expression,' she said, 'because I know I'm about to be lied to if somebody says it.'

Josh grinned. 'That one, or "to tell you the truth." You know you're going to be lied to.' He took a sip of wine and set his glass down. 'Come on,' he said, 'finish what you were saying. I want to know all about you.'

She could see that he really meant what he said, and felt a curious sort of thrill that he would really want to know about her. To know *her*. She looked down at her fingernails, as if studying them. 'Well, I was going to say that I . . . I was ashamed of our . . . our being poor . . . our cheap clothes . . . and our cheap little studio apartment in West Hollywood.'

She looked away then and cleared her throat. 'I feel a little guilty now, in retrospect. But I really was ashamed,' she continued. 'We lived so close to Beverly Hills, and most of the kids I knew had bigger houses and fancier cars and beautiful clothes. Sometimes brothers and sisters, too, and sometimes both parents.'

Josh sat staring at her mutely, his face suddenly burning bright red, his teeth clenched in his square jaw, his hand rigid on the glass he held.

April saw the effect her words had had on him and felt acutely embarrassed, as if she had been too personal. She felt a blush rising from the top of her chest, up her neck, and suffusing her face with its heat. She quickly took a sip of her wine, fumbling with the glass.

Oh, my God, she thought. *I've ruined everything*

now. This wonderful man was truly interested in me, and I've completely turned him off with my stupid, sad little story. Nobody, but nobody, wants to hear about my dreary past.

Then, through the pulse that beat a violent tattoo against her eardrum, she heard his gentle voice.

'April,' he was saying, 'I think we grew up in the same place.'

She turned and looked at him. All the tension had gone out of his body. Those mesmerizing ultramarine eyes of his bored into hers, and there was a hint of a smile quivering tentatively at the corners of his lips.

'What? . . . I'm . . . I'm sorry,' she stammered. 'What did you say?'

'I said, April,' he continued in a near whisper, 'that we grew up in the same place.'

He astonished her by reaching over and taking one of her hands in his. 'What I mean to say is, we both grew up in shame. We both grew up poor, surrounded by . . . well, what we thought were our betters.' He squeezed her hand again.

Tears, unbidden, sprang into April's eyes, threatening to spill over. She couldn't trust herself to speak.

'I knew there was a reason I took such an instant liking to you,' he said, 'or thought I did. It wasn't just that you and Joanna think so much alike and share the same interests. It was this, this past you carry around with you, that I recognized. Because I identify with it so strongly. I guess I somehow sensed it in you because it's something that's so much a part of me.'

'It . . . it is?' she finally uttered.

'You can bet on it,' he said. He picked up his napkin and, reaching across the table, tenderly brushed the tears from her eyes. 'There,' he said, 'that's better, isn't it?'

'Yes,' she said, wishing that she could give him a hug. 'Much better. I . . . I feel like such a fool, Josh,' she said. 'I'm sorry. I feel like I've made a scene and—'

'Hush,' he said quietly. 'You haven't made a scene at all. You simply told me something about yourself that's painful. And you happened to tell just the right person.' He beamed across the table, his perfect teeth dazzling in the candlelight. 'So cheer up,' he said. 'You're in good company.'

'Oh, Josh,' she said. 'Oh, thank you. I thought I'd made a terrible mistake, being too personal. It's just that you and Joanna have been so wonderful and warm and have shared yourselves with me so generously that I sort of got carried away, I guess.'

'You're allowed to be yourself with us, April,' he said. 'You're safe here, remember that.'

'Thanks, Josh,' she said. 'Oh, I feel like an idiot!' She laughed lightly.

'Because you've exposed a little of yourself,' he said. 'You've been honest. That's all. Now you can appreciate what it took out of me to confide in you about Joanna.'

They both laughed, delighting in their understanding of one another, this common ground that had proved to be a link between them.

'I guess one reason I was drawn to Joanna and her father,' he said seriously, 'was that their world was so different from mine, so beautiful, so ordered and calm. The orchids, too. A way to make the world more beautiful, and with my hybridizing maybe even create a new beautiful specimen.'

'I know what you mean,' she said. 'Absolutely. It's why I was drawn to architecture and design, and why I do my botanical drawings and my garden work. And now grotto work.' She smiled. 'I've been trying to make order out of chaos, trying in a way to make things more beautiful, and all the while—' She shrugged.

'You felt like an outsider sometimes?' he suggested.

April nodded again. 'Exactly. Like I don't really belong. Anywhere, really. Like the rest of the world is part of this club that I'm not part of. Sometimes I bridge the gap quite well.' She looked at him. 'Like when I met you and Joanna.'

Josh smiled. 'It's always been the same with me,' he said. 'And I think it goes right back to the shame and so on.'

April saw the wisdom of his words at once. 'I'd have to agree with you,' she said. 'So . . . we make the best of it!' She looked at him with a bright-eyed expression.

Josh's eyes lingered on her for a long moment, then he abruptly clapped his hands together. 'Dessert!' he said. 'I hope you've got room for more.'

'More?' April said.

'Yep. Connie's special flan,' he said. 'And you keep

your seat while I run up to the house and get it, okay?'

April watched his tall, lithe body walk up to the house and at that precise moment knew that she had fallen in love with him. She couldn't deny it to herself, shameful though it made her feel.

I'm hopelessly in love with Josh Lawrence, she thought. *A new friend. And worse, my new best friend's husband. My sick—*

She couldn't finish the thought. Guilt washed over her. *I can't do this to Joanna,* she thought. *Or Josh. Or myself. I'll have to discourage any contact outside of work. Especially when Joanna isn't around.*

Suddenly she wished that Joanna hadn't gone to Montecito, as much as she relished her time with Josh. She quickly poured a splash of wine in her glass and took a large swallow. Its taste was no longer quite so delicious on her palate. Now it tasted of guilt and remorse, of a longing unfulfilled, of awful treachery and betrayal.

When Josh returned with their dessert, Connie's flan, she smiled, performing as best she could under the circumstances.

Josh looked at her with an almost wary expression for a moment, then returned her smile. He had experienced a frightening realization in the kitchen: He was falling in love with April Woodward. Now he would have to control the powerful urges that drove him toward her, that made him want her so desperately, despite the guilt that he was already experiencing.

Oh, my God! he thought. *How could I even think of*

such a thing? Especially considering Joanna's . . . condition.
Nevertheless, the feeling would not go away. It was
there, real, almost a tangible feeling that could not
be denied.

17

April had filled the popcorn maker and positioned the large metal pot under its spout, waiting for the big, fluffy kernels to come spewing out. Woody was standing at the stove, melting a lot of butter, she noticed, to pour over the top. The popcorn popper had a little metal cup for melting butter, but it didn't hold enough.

She laughed over the noise of the popper.

Woody looked over at her and grinned. 'What's so funny?' he asked.

'Has it ever occurred to you how silly it is to have this expensive air popper when we're just going to pour a ton of butter over the popcorn anyway?' she asked.

'Yeah,' he said, 'it's pretty silly. Except the popper's really great.'

'There is that,' she agreed. Popcorn had begun to shoot out of the spout like BBs, and April couldn't resist trying a few. Lousy, she decided, without all that yummy butter and salt.

When she'd come home from work, there'd been a message on her machine to please call Woody. She was still a little miffed with him because of his stupid comments that time he'd seen her talking to Josh, but she decided to let bygones be bygones. They'd worked together very efficiently, if a bit quietly, since then, and April thought it was time to clear the air. Besides, Woody's voice on the machine had been endearingly contrite and pleading. But, she told herself, she was definitely going to have to talk with him about his obnoxious behavior.

She'd called him, and he'd apologized, then he'd begged to take her out to dinner. April had said no, that she was going to have a quick nibble at home, take a bath, then pile up in bed and watch something on television. That was when Woody had proposed one of their popcorn-and-video nights, which he knew April found almost irresistible.

'You win,' she'd told him. 'Come on over in an hour or so. Just don't bring one of those videos with tons of blood and violence. And I mean it. I'm not in the mood to see one of those tonight. Not even for a goof, Woody.'

Now she was glad he was here – *and* his warm, sweet

self instead of the sneering macho creep she'd seen at Josh and Joanna's. And he'd brought *Ridicule*, a French movie she'd yet to see, but had heard had beautiful costumes. *He really does feel contrite*, she thought with amusement. *Otherwise, he'd never have shown up with this movie.*

The popper had spewed out its last popcorn, and she looked at the big pot, then turned to Woody. 'Do you think this is enough?' she asked.

Woody looked over at the pot and shook his shaggy black curls. 'No way, April,' he said, grinning. 'For two people? With a good movie to watch?'

She smiled. 'Thought so,' she said. She got out another big pot and filled the machine again to pop some more. 'You want to go ahead and butter and salt this while it's hot, Woody?'

'Yeah,' he said. 'Will do. Then I'll put on some more butter.' He got the pot, poured butter over it, dashed lots of salt on, then put the lid on and began shaking it, doing a sort of Carmen Miranda with castanets.

'You're so silly,' April said, laughing.

He finished his act and set the pot down. 'I know,' he said.

'What got into you, anyway?' April asked. 'Up at Joanna and Josh's that time? Making those stupid remarks.'

'Uh ... I don't know, April,' he said, putting more butter on to melt. 'I just think those people are really snakes in the grass, you know?'

'That is ridiculous, Woody,' she said. The popper

began firing out popcorn, and she made certain the pot was in position. 'In fact, they are super-nice people.'

Woody shrugged. 'Have it your way, April,' he said, 'but I still wouldn't trust 'em. She's like this spoiled rich bitch, tooling around in her old Mercedes like she owns the world, and he's just like her. An arrogant bastard. Tooling around, flexing his muscles, teasing the local babes.'

April looked at him in amazement. It was as if they weren't even talking about the same people. 'You are demented, Woody,' she said. 'That's just plain crazy. I don't know whether they're rich or not. I guess they're well fixed, at least, but they don't act spoiled or arrogant. And Josh Lawrence wouldn't run around teasing the local babes, either. They're the most devoted couple I've ever seen.'

He slid her a look out of the corner of his eye. 'Like I said, have it your way, April,' he said off-handedly. 'But I know different.'

He turned the burner off and rolled the melted butter around in the pot, then looked over at her. 'I could tell you stories I've heard about her sister that'd make your hair stand on end,' he said.

April stared at him for a moment. 'Well, I don't know anything about her,' she said, 'but I do know them. And you're wrong about them, Woody.'

She could envision Joanna and thought of her extra-ordinary generosity of spirit, of her loving friendship, and of her illness, and she couldn't listen to another word of his stupid allegations.

'Woody,' she said, her eyes fiery, 'I don't want to discuss this again. Ever. And I don't want to hear another word against either one of them. Hear me?'

His expression changed to one of irritation. 'If I'm so wrong, April,' he said, 'then why was Josh Lawrence looking all goo-goo-eyed at you? Huh?'

'That's ridiculous,' she said defensively. 'He was telling me about some problems at work, that's all.'

'That's not the way it looked,' Woody said. 'And I'm not blind, April. You know? That guy's creaming over you.'

'Oh, *you*,' she said. 'I said I don't want to discuss it anymore, and I meant it. So let's forget it. You're not rational about them.'

'Okay,' he said. 'Okay. But you asked me my opinion, and I gave it to you.'

The popper shut off, the last few pieces of popcorn trickling out of the spout spastically. 'Here,' she said, 'more to salt and butter.'

They walked into the bedroom and piled up on her big bed with lots of pillows, putting the popcorn bowls between them. April idly watched as Woody fed the tape into the VCR, but her mind was elsewhere. Woody might be an overgrown boy in many ways, but he was not stupid, she reminded herself.

He was a fairly astute observer, as a matter of fact, and she worried about what he'd seen. The intimacy he'd detected between her and Josh when he'd seen them talking. If he'd sensed it, then wouldn't Connie? And wouldn't . . . Joanna?

April felt a sick feeling in the pit of her stomach, and reached into a bowl of popcorn and took a handful, then began chewing on it, but not really tasting it. She realized what her feelings for Josh Lawrence were – there was no denying them – but she hoped they weren't too obvious. As for the way Josh felt about her, could Woody be right? Did Josh really feel as strongly about her as Woody suspected?

She sensed that the bond between them was becoming more than friendship, and that he was enjoying it as much as she was. But she wasn't certain, and she didn't want to think about it right now. Deep down inside, she felt little warning bells going off. She was afraid that Woody might have sensed something that others could, something that could break Joanna's heart. That, April decided, she couldn't live with. No matter what.

'Ready?' Woody asked, snapping her out of her reverie.

She nodded. 'Ready,' she said. 'In fact, I have a head start on the popcorn.'

Later, as they lay together, Woody's eyes slid sideways, observing April, who was watching the movie as if hypnotized. She was eating it up, like the popcorn, enjoying every minute of it, he thought. He felt gratified, even though the movie didn't particularly appeal to him. He liked pleasing April, but then, he enjoyed pleasing any woman. Well, any woman he wanted, that is. Any woman he found desirable. And he thought April was one of the most desirable women he'd ever met. She was a challenge, too, and he liked that. His eyes moved down to her breasts, outlined against the T-shirt she was wearing. *She'll come around*, he thought. *I know she will. They all do for Woody Pearlman, don't they?*

18

Josh walked slowly through the greenhouse, Carl at his heels, looking from side to side, eyeballing the replacements for the fungal-infected *Phalaenopsis* that had been destroyed. They had finally arrived, at great expense, but they were of excellent stock. Unfortunately, when the fungus had attacked, there was enough damage that the plants couldn't be nursed back to health in time to fill the orders they had. They'd decided to purchase very expensive stock just so they wouldn't lose orders and potentially damage future business.

'I still think we need to spring for more security,' Carl said. 'Strategically placed video cameras.'

Josh shook his head. 'I don't think we'll need to, Carl,'

he said. 'We've got Miguel and the guard dog at night now. And during the daytime somebody on the staff has to be with anybody that comes in. Like an escort.'

'Yeah, but Josh,' Carl argued, 'we were requiring escorts when somebody planted the damn fungus. And I don't know how much good Miguel and a guard dog are going to be. Why are you being so stubborn about this?'

'I'm not being stubborn, Carl,' he replied testily. 'You know, we could've gotten some stock that had already been contaminated and just took a while to show up,' he went on. 'That's a real possibility. And besides, we didn't have *everybody* go through with an escort like we do now.'

'No,' Carl agreed, 'not everybody. But it's much more likely that this was done at night. You know what I think?'

'What?' Josh asked.

'I think you're still trying to deny that anybody would deliberately do this,' Carl said. 'And you're fooling yourself if you don't think that this is sabotage.'

Josh didn't want to tell Carl that he'd hardly given the problem any thought since Joanna's news. He'd found it difficult to concentrate on business.

'Josh! Josh!' It was Luna calling him from the other end of the greenhouse. He and Carl saw her running toward them, her large breasts heaving against her tight-fitting blouse, her stiletto-heeled shoes kicking up sawdust and gravel. Carl laughed, and Josh couldn't help but smile.

She reached them breathlessly.

'What is it, Luna?' Josh asked.

'Mr What . . . what's . . . his name,' she sputtered. 'He's . . . in the . . . office.'

'Who?' Josh asked. *Luna's information leaves something to be desired*, he thought with amusement.

'That . . . that Japanese man!' she blurted.

'Which one?' Josh asked, growing excited.

'You know,' she said. 'He has black hair and . . . oh, he's one of the really rich ones.'

'Why didn't you page me?' Josh asked. 'Or use the intercom?'

'I was too excited!' she said. 'He said he must see you *now*!'

'Thanks, Luna,' he said. *It has to be Mr Hara*, he thought. *Back to buy some more orchids. Or maybe even Mr Nakamura*. He took off at a fast pace, practically running, heading toward the office.

Josh leaned back in his desk chair, staring happily at the ceiling. *There may be a God after all*, he thought. Mr Nakamura had spent a small fortune, enough even to cover the costs of replacing the lost *Phalaenopsis* stock with a little bit left over. Visits like this were becoming more frequent occurrences as he and the nursery gained an international reputation for their stock, but Josh had still not grown used to it. He certainly hadn't been spoiled by it.

I've got to tell Joanna, he thought. *Right away.*

He swung forward in his chair and, picking up the

receiver, dialed the number. Connie picked up after three rings.

'Connie,' he said. 'Let me speak to Joanna, please.'

'She's not here, Josh,' Connie replied.

'Where is she?' he asked. 'I've got to chase her down.'

'I don't know,' Connie said.

'You don't know?' he said, bewildered. *Goddamn it*, he thought. *Joanna shouldn't be off alone without our knowing where she is. What if—*

'All I know,' Connie said in exasperation, 'is that she's acting really strange.'

'What do you mean?' Josh asked. He felt a chill run up his spine.

'Ooooh, I don't know.'

'Come on, Connie,' Josh cajoled. 'Tell me what you know.'

'Well, like when I went down to clean the beach place,' Connie said.

'What about it?' Josh asked.

'You wouldn't have believed it.'

'Why?' Josh asked. 'Come on, Connie. Tell me.'

'It was a *wreck*,' Connie spat, 'and I mean a *wreck*.'

'How do you mean, a wreck?' Josh asked, becoming increasingly distressed.

'Oh, you know,' she said. 'Empty wine bottles all over the place. Half-empty bottles sitting out uncorked. The bed looked like somebody had died in it. Sand and stuff all over the floor.' She paused, and when she spoke again her voice was angry. 'It took me hours to straighten up.'

Josh felt a knot twist in the pit of his stomach, and beads of sweat broke out on his forehead. He felt sick. He knew that Joanna must have been there sometime in the last few weeks, licking her wounds most likely. All alone. It was too terrible to contemplate.

When he found his voice, he said, 'I'm sorry about that, Connie. You should've told me.'

'I didn't want to worry you.'

'Anyhow, I'm coming on home,' he said. 'I'll see you there in a while.' He decided that it was probably time that they told Connie what was going on so that she would understand Joanna's unusual behavior.

'Okay,' she said, then hung up.

Josh sat at his desk, staring off into space. How a few minutes could change your mood, he thought. The elation over Mr Nakamura's visit had drained away completely, replaced by a looming sense of fate that threw everything else in shadow.

What difference does anything *make now?* he asked himself. *Except Joanna.*

He got to his feet and went out into the reception area. 'Luna,' he said. 'I'm leaving for the day. If anything comes up, you can get me at home.'

Luna, telephone receiver plastered to her ear as usual, put her hand over it for a moment. 'Okay, boss,' she said with a smile. 'Don't worry about anything here.' She removed her hand from the receiver and immediately began speaking in rapid-fire Spanish again.

Out in the parking lot, Josh hopped into his big Land Cruiser and headed out to the highway, toward home.

Rolling north in the heat, he glanced over at the Rossi brothers' property on his right.

'Goddamn,' he cursed aloud. He almost slammed on the brakes and pulled into their lot, but then thought better of it. He cruised on north, fresh worries plaguing his already overburdened mind. Carl's truck – unmistakably Carl's – had been parked right out in front of the Rossi offices.

What the hell is Carl doing there? he asked himself. *And if he has some legitimate business for going there – although I can't imagine what it could be – then why didn't he tell me about it?*

Shit! He slammed the steering wheel in anger, and only succeeded in hurting the palm of his hand. *Is the whole world turning against me?*

Josh pulled into the courtyard at home and parked the Land Cruiser. Joanna's car wasn't there, but he saw April's Jeep Wagoneer and Connie's van. He went in through the mud room, slipped out of his dirty boots and put on clean Top-Siders, then went to the kitchen.

Connie looked up at him from a kitchen counter, where she was busy making something. 'Hi,' she said. Her eyes held that sleepy expression that he knew indicated that she would not discuss anything further with him.

'Hey, Connie,' he replied. 'I guess you haven't heard from Joanna.'

'No,' she said, shrugging. 'She's still not here. Just

that April down at the stable and the man working with her.'

Josh heard the disdain in Connie's voice. He wondered why she didn't like April – was it jealousy? He still wasn't sure, but he wasn't going to pursue that right now.

He went out through the French doors and headed across the terrace and down through the apple orchard to the old stable. He poked his head through an open door and looked around. April was up on a scaffold, and her partner was working on the south-facing wall. Dozens of boxes of shells and pebbles, many of which he recognized, lined the north wall, some open, some shut.

'Hey,' he said. 'How's it going with you two?'

'Josh,' April said, pulling down her paper face mask. 'It's going great.' She hurried down from the scaffold and snapped off her latex gloves.

Woody looked over from the south wall, where he was fitting small pieces of mother-of-pearl into an area of background. He watched the two of them for a moment, then turned silently back to his work.

'Look,' April said excitedly. 'The ceiling's finally almost finished.'

Josh looked up and surveyed the finished work for the first time. He was stunned by the beauty of the design. The ceiling was a night sky complete with many of the constellations, all of it worked in seashells and pebbles.

'My God,' he said. 'It's really beautiful, April. I had

no idea it was going to be so intricate. And the colors are spectacular.'

'Thanks,' she said. 'It's really coming together now, isn't it?'

He shook his head. 'You can say that again.' He looked at her. 'Has Joanna seen this yet?' he asked.

'No,' April said. 'She saw it when she got back from Montecito, but not since then. I can't wait for her to get home. I think she's really going to be pleased.'

'I know she will be,' Josh replied. 'I've never seen anything like it. Abalone, trochus, scallops, mother-of-pearl, cowries, cones, spiders, turbos, cockles, even thorny oysters. You've worked in shells I would never have imagined.'

'I didn't know you knew so much about them,' she said.

'He's the one who got me so interested in seashells in the first place,' came Joanna's voice from behind them.

They both turned to see her standing just inside the doorway, smiling happily at the two of them. She was carrying shopping bags, which she eased down onto the floor, and walked over to them.

'Hello, darling,' she said, kissing Josh on the cheek.

'Hi, beautiful,' he said, glad to see her.

Joanna brushed April's cheek with a kiss and hugged her. Then she backed away and looked up at the ceiling for a long time.

'April,' she said, turning to her in almost a swoon of delight, 'you are nothing less than a magician! A sorceress! This is already so beautiful I want to move into the room. It's . . . heavenly!'

April laughed. 'Well, that's the idea with the ceiling.'

'You know what I mean,' Joanna said, smiling. 'It's really perfect. Now I long to see the rest of it finished.'

'We're working as fast as we can,' April said. 'Oh, by the way, Joanna, the plaster busts for the wall niches came today. They're over there, lined up with the boxes of shells, if you want to see them now.'

Joanna abruptly looked over at Josh. Her face was contorted in pain. 'I . . . I'm going to go lie down,' she said.

Without another word, she swept out of the room and disappeared, leaving her shopping bags behind.

Woody turned and watched her leave with a smirk. *Yeah, I bet she's got to lie down*, he thought. *Seeing the two of them together's put her to bed. Serves her right.*

April looked at Josh, whose face held a worried expression. 'I'd better check on her,' he said quietly.

'Tell her I hope she feels better,' April said, herself alarmed by Joanna's sudden departure. It wasn't like her, April thought. No, not at all.

Josh opened the bedroom door and saw that the room was in complete darkness. The curtains were shut, and all the lights were out. He could just make out Joanna, lying on top of the bed in a short silk bathrobe. He approached the bed quietly and sat down next to her.

'Are you all right?' he asked worriedly.

'Yes,' she said. 'I just need to rest.'

'You're sure?' he persisted.

'It's nothing,' she assured him. 'Don't worry, Josh, I
. . . I really just need to be alone and rest.'

'Okay,' he said, getting the message. 'I'll be here if
you need anything.'

'Thanks,' she murmured.

He left the darkened room and shut the door behind
him. Suddenly, he leaned against the wall in the hallway, his heart heaving in his chest. *Oh, God, he prayed.
Please don't make her suffer.*

Fear, like a palpable force, gripped him in its claws
and held him there, immobilized, for what seemed an
eternity. Finally, weak from its clutches, he went into
his study, where he poured himself a straight scotch
and spread out on the daybed, unable to concentrate,
exhausted by the terrible feeling that had begun to eat
away at him.

He felt so alone.

19

Joanna looked through the open doorway to the grotto and saw that April and Woody were busily working away, applying shells to cement. She didn't want to interfere, but just to watch them work for a while. There had been more and more days recently when she'd simply had to rest, reading in her bedroom or the conservatory, storing up her energy in order to perform only those tasks she really had to do. So she hadn't been down here for several days and was anxious to see the progress.

'April?' she asked.

'Oh, Joanna,' April cried, turning her head toward the door. 'Come on in, stranger. I didn't realize you were down here.' She was up on the scaffolding, working in a corner where wall met wall.

JUDITH GOULD

'Do you mind if I watch a little while?' Joanna asked. 'I promise to be quiet as a mouse. I would just love to watch it coming together a bit.'

'Of course, that's fine,' April said. 'Pull up a chair and get comfortable. Just keep a little distance so you don't get covered up with cement dust.'

'Thanks,' Joanna said. 'You won't even know I'm here.'

Woody glanced at her out of the corner of his eye, but didn't say anything. He continued filling in background space on a wall.

Joanna scraped a little bistro chair over to a corner and sat down, looking around her. Happily, the work on the grotto was progressing on schedule, and there were days when the dramatic effects of all the hard work put into it could easily be seen. Sometimes, though, days passed, even a week at a stretch, when the tedious and time-consuming work didn't seem to accomplish anything.

Today, Joanna was happy to discover, was one of those great days when she could see the work coming together. As she looked about the room, she felt a sense of joy and fulfillment, of a cherished ambition nearly realized. The ceiling with its constellations was a marvel to behold, and the niches, which would hold fanciful shell-encrusted busts on pedestals, were completely finished. Various kinds of shells had been used to create the effect of fantastic moldings all around the ceiling, the doors, and the niches. April had even created a dado with them, below which the

284

walls appeared to be paneled in a dozen different kinds of precious stones.

She could see where blank spaces had been left. These, she knew, were to be filled in with shell orchids. Joanna had to bite her tongue to keep from enthusing about the work, but she could withhold her praise until lunchtime. April had promised to eat with her today, so she'd discuss it with her then.

April continued working silently, carefully positioning shells, but despite her concentration, she was constantly aware of Joanna's presence. For months Joanna had come and gone quite a bit, coaxing April into having lunch or dinner with her, but her visits had begun to become less frequent in the last two or three weeks. April knew why, of course, but did her best to act unconcerned, because she knew that that's the way Joanna wanted it to be.

She also realized that Joanna was becoming impatient, but realized, of course, what her anxiousness stemmed from: She feared that she wouldn't live to see the grotto complete. But there was nothing April could do to hurry the project along. She was working as hard as she could, working overtime, in fact, hoping against hope that she would finish in time.

She placed the last shell in her box into position, held it there a moment, then let go and sat back on her haunches to eye the line she'd created. It was fine, she decided. Straight as could be.

'Woody,' she said, 'would you be an angel and hand me another box of the leafy carditas, please?'

'Just a second, April,' he replied, carefully positioning a piece of mother-of-pearl in a background spot.

April looked down at him, where he sat in a lotus position facing the wall, working diligently, covered from head to toe with cement and fine white cement dust, like herself. She smiled at his comical appearance. They'd complained to one another about having to wash their hair every night, but they'd decided that was preferable to wearing a shower cap all day.

'Hey, Woody,' she said, 'those beautiful black curls of yours are getting gray before their time.'

He laughed. 'Yeah, well, I wouldn't talk if I were you. That blond hair of yours is looking pretty much like an old lady's,' he said. He shifted around and got to his feet, then found the box of leafy carditas and took them over to the scaffolding and handed them up to her.

'Thanks, Woody,' she said, placing the box on the boards where she sat.

'No problem,' he replied. He went back to his spot on the floor, assuming the lotus position again and getting back to work.

Joanna sat for a long time, watching them from the corner. They had an easy camaraderie that she'd noticed ever since Woody had first started helping April, and they worked together very well, so attuned to each other that they almost seemed to have a secret code between them.

Like the secret language of very close friends, she thought. *Or lovers.*

She had to admit that Woody was very attractive –

physically, at least – and she could see that he would have great appeal for a lot of women. Especially women who were looking for good sex with a few laughs, lots of muscles, and no commitment.

After watching the two of them for several weeks, she'd seen that he was extremely protective of April, and she sensed that he was even jealous of her relationships with other people. One thing was for sure, Joanna thought. If Woody wasn't in love with April, then he wanted desperately to add her to his list of conquests and, Joanna believed, he would play the big brother for a very long time just to try to get her in the sack.

In the course of her conversations with April, Joanna saw that April was almost convinced that Woody really was a big brother she liked to have around. She'd laughed at his antics with other women, not believing that she herself could be hurt by him. But Joanna was afraid that April would be deeply hurt by him, and wondered what to do about it. Plus, she told herself, she didn't want anything or anybody to interfere with April's friendship with her – or Josh.

'You've been so quiet,' April said, approaching Joanna from across the room.

Joanna almost jerked, so lost in thought she'd been. She laughed. 'I told you I'd be a little mouse,' she said. 'The work was going so beautifully I didn't want to interrupt.'

April looked around, smiling. 'It really *is* coming along wonderfully,' she said with pride in her voice.

'You're still having lunch with me?' Joanna asked.

'Yes,' April said. 'I'm just going to run up to the bathroom at the pool house and clean up a little bit.'

'Okay,' Joanna said. 'I'll meet you on the terrace. I think I'll sit here for a few more minutes and just soak up some of the atmosphere that's beginning to develop.'

'You're so funny,' April said with amusement, 'but I know exactly what you mean. See you in a few minutes.' She turned and started out the door, then turned around. 'Woody,' she said, 'I'll see you in an hour or so.'

'You got it,' he said. He stood across the room from Joanna, busily wiping his hands off on a rag.

Joanna watched him for a minute, then cleared her voice. 'Do you go home for lunch, Woody?' she asked. They were still playing the game that they'd never met each other before.

Woody continued cleaning his hands and didn't look up. 'Sometimes,' he replied. 'But usually I grab something close by here.'

'You'll have to stay for lunch one day,' Joanna said, more out of politeness than sincerity.

'Ah, I usually meet a friend for lunch,' Woody said. 'But thanks.' He threw down the rag. 'See ya,' he said, sauntering out the door.

You bet you will, Joanna thought, watching his cocky strut up the hill.

20

Christina arrived first, creeping through the thick fog into the lot and parking at the south end as Peter had instructed her to. Looking about, she saw only one or two other cars parked here.

She got out and slowly made her way through the thick swirls of fog over to the wooden ramp that led up the dunes to the cedar-shingled condominiums. Luckily, his was the southernmost, because she couldn't see where the buildings began and ended.

Jesus, she thought, *why does it always have to be like this? Meeting in such spooky places.* But of course she knew the answer to that question. They couldn't be seen together. Thus, today they were meeting in a condo he kept on the beach as a secret hideaway.

Huge eucalyptus trees and wind-tortured pines shivered loudly in the heavy breeze coming off the ocean, and sand, fine and gritty, blew up at her face, stinging it ferociously.

My God, she thought, pulling a silk scarf out of her handbag and holding it up in front of her face. *This is plain creepy.* But she didn't care. Not today. Because today she was going to meet Peter, and she could hardly wait.

She carefully started up the wooden ramp, holding on to the old railing for support, her high heels making the steep climb that much more difficult. *I should have worn flats*, she thought. But then she nixed that idea. *No, Peter likes to see me all dressed up. He thinks I look classy like that.* His word, *classy*. She almost giggled aloud, thinking that what they were doing was anything but.

At the top of the ramp, the fog was even thicker. She stood there, the scarf still held protectively up to her face, catching her breath, her eyes searching for the sign that would direct her to the correct condo.

I'll never find it in this fog. Then she made out a small wooden plaque with weathered brass numbers and arrows on it, almost right in front of her. The arrow pointed to her right for unit 803. She followed the arrow until she reached the sign indicating 803, at the top of a flight of wooden stairs.

Christina took a deep breath, then started up, her eyes on the aqua-painted door above. She reached the top and stopped, cursing the cigarettes she smoked and her thirty-six-year-old lungs. Then she went down the walkway and, standing on her tiptoes, reached up, her fingers searching the top of the light fixture next to the door for the key.

Yes, there it is, she thought. *The key to nirvana.*

She let herself in, taking the silk scarf away from her face at the same time, then closed the door behind her. Kicking off her murderous high-heeled shoes, she looked around her. Straight ahead, all the way through the dining area, the kitchen, and the living room, she could see a huge floor-to-ceiling window that looked out over the sea. Today the view was exclusively of the grays and whites of the fog.

She picked up her shoes and walked through to the living room. The condo was decorated entirely in shades of white and furnished with big comfortable modern sofas and chairs, also white, and inexpensive wooden tables. *Boring but serviceable,* she thought. Dropping her shoes in front of the sofa, she idly flung the silk scarf over a shoulder, then walked to the window and stood in front of it, trying to see if she could make out the sea at all.

The fog was almost mesmerizing, she thought. She stood there, all sense of time suspended, her eyes searching to no avail.

It occurred to her that the old beach shack that Joanna and Josh had fixed up so beautifully was just down this beach, one of the few surviving old-fashioned cottages that used to be sprinkled along the coast. Now huge developers and agribusinesses – owned by smart men like Peter – had swallowed up nearly all the land hereabouts. *The old beach shack must be worth a fortune,* she thought, still looking toward the invisible sea.

She almost screamed aloud as she felt huge arms encircle her and the warmth of a large body press firmly against hers. She could feel his breath on her neck. Almost as quickly as he had crept up behind her, wrapping those powerful arms around her, she realized that it was Peter.

'Oh, my God,' she wailed, her knees suddenly weak, her body beginning to shake. 'You – you—!'

'Scare you, baby?' he asked quietly, his mouth going to the nape of her neck, his tongue licking the wind-driven salt and sand that coated her from head to toe.

'Oh . . . Jesus . . . Peter!' she gasped. 'Who wouldn't be? You could've been a . . . a crazy rapist or something. There's nobody around out here.'

He laughed, turning her roughly to face him, his obsidian eyes staring hard into hers. 'Yeah, but I wasn't, was I?' he said.

She looked up into his eyes and knew that he was enjoying her fear. 'I – I—'

He jerked her harder against his huge muscular body and kissed her on the mouth. Ravenously, fiendishly. Then pulled back, leaving her gasping, and whispered, 'You like it, don't you, baby?'

Christina felt her body begin to quiver again, but not from the shock this time. It was as if something in the deepest, darkest recesses of her being was responding to him of its own accord. And it was something over which she had no control. She could feel a wetness between her thighs, and her pulse had begun to race. She was breathy with desire now, and any reservations she might have had were gone, as if picked up by the fog swirling at the window behind her and carried away into some netherworld.

'Yes,' she whispered, 'I like it, Peter. Oh, yes. I like it.'

'Yeah, baby,' he said. 'I thought so.'

He pulled the silk scarf from over her shoulder and quickly whipped it into a long blindfold. She watched his adroit movement with fascination. Then, before she realized what he was doing, he had placed it around her head – tight and thick across her eyes – and tied it firmly at the back.

'Peter!' she gasped, her body trembling. 'I can't . . . I can't see a thing! I—'

'Shhh,' he breathed. He grabbed her hands in his and led her across the carpeting into a bedroom.

'What . . . what are you doing?' she almost whimpered.

'Shhh,' he breathed again. 'You're going to like it, babe.'

She felt him begin to take her clothes off, quickly and unceremoniously, anxious to get to her naked flesh. When he finished, she stood trembling before him, but she knew that the fear and sexual excitement held her in its thrall.

She heard him undressing himself and wished that she could watch, but sensed that she should remain still.

293

How she would love to see that magnificently powerful body, every inch of it, gradually exposed to her hungry eyes! How anxious she was to feel it against her again! On her! *In* her!

As if her thought was his command, she felt his hands on her again, running lightly over her breasts, then trailing down her torso to the soft damp mound between her thighs. Then brushing across her buttocks and up her back.

Christina thought she would go crazy with desire but continued to hold her tongue, stifling a gasp of utter pleasure, afraid to interfere with this scenario he had conjured up.

Now his hands were at her breasts again, squeezing them gently, then more firmly, thrumming away at her rosy nipples, lightly at first, then harder and harder, until she thought she couldn't stand the pleasure turning to pain another second. But he abruptly stopped, and she felt his hot, wet mouth on her right breast, his tongue licking it slowly, slowly, then more rapidly as his hand found her mound and stroked it gently before pushing a finger up into her mounting wetness, exploring, massaging, caressing.

'Ah . . . ah . . . ah!' Christina cried, unable to hold her tongue any longer. 'Ah, my God, Peter!' She reached out for his cock, but he grabbed her hands with one of his and held them behind her, at the base of her spine.

Then she felt his free hand on her shoulder, pushing her down, down onto her knees in front of him. He let go of her hands and pushed her head into his groin, rubbing her face against his loaded balls and rock-hard shaft.

Christina's tongue began licking him frantically, like a woman starved, and he finally guided her blindfolded face to his shaft. Her mouth took him, and she almost cried as she felt his enormous manhood within her. She worked her tongue around it, licking and licking, taking as much as she possibly could.

His hands forced her head harder against him, moving it back and forth on his shaft, until she couldn't possibly take any more. That's when he shoved the hardest, choking her for a long moment before finally relenting and jerking her head back off him.

'Yeah, baby,' he whispered. 'You really like that, don't you? Huh?'

Christina's eyes had filled with tears from the choking, but she was more enthralled than ever by his powerful, commanding body. 'Oh, yes,' she rasped.

He pulled her up and led her over to the bed, where he picked her up and practically threw her on it. 'Ah!' Christina gasped on an expulsion of air.

But before she could protest, before she knew what was coming next, he was on top of her, spreading her legs with his knees, then mounting her like a vicious beast, plunging into her up to the hilt of his shaft, filling her as she'd never been filled before.

For a moment she thought he had torn her apart, despite her wet readiness, but as he began his ruthless movements, ramming into her with merciless abandon, her body quickly responded, moving with his, welcoming his huge shaft, almost crying out for it when he pulled all the way out, only to ram it in again, harder yet, pinning her to the bed with it.

Stars burst before her blinded eyes, and her body began to writhe wildly as wave after wave of ecstatic orgasm convulsed through her, her body pumping madly against his. Peter rose up and rammed inside her one final time, then bellowed like a bull as his massive cock exploded, flooding her with his juices, his body convulsing atop hers. She let out a scream, unable to hold back any longer, and felt her body go completely rigid before she contracted a final, mighty time, her floodgates opening as never before.

They collapsed in a tangle of sweaty flesh, gasping for air, still holding on to one another, his throbbing cock still inside her. It was long moments before either of them could speak, and it was Christina who spoke first.

'Oh . . . Jesus . . . Peter,' she rasped. 'You . . . you can . . . blindfold . . . me anytime.'

They both laughed breathlessly, then he slapped her fanny in his playful way and rolled off her onto his side.

'You liked it, huh, babe?' he asked, a hint of pride in his voice.

'Oh, yes, I liked it, all right,' she said. She reached up, pulling at the silk scarf, but Peter pushed her hands out of the way and reached around and untied the scarf himself. He pulled it loose, then wrapped it around his fist, like a boxer's bandages, and began stroking circles on her belly with it.

Christina blinked and looked down at his hand on her stomach, then up into his eyes.

'We'll have to play with this some more,' he said, his obsidian eyes staring into hers. 'You know? Maybe get a few more. Make it more exciting.'

Returning his stare, she knew that he wasn't kidding, that he wanted to up the ante, so to speak. And while something deep down inside her found his suggestion weird, repugnant even, Christina decided she didn't really give a damn. She wanted this man, and she wanted to keep him. Besides, she'd never had such exciting sex. So why not?

She nodded then, still staring into his eyes.

With a smile he leaned down and kissed her on the lips, then drew back and sat up, reaching for the pack of cigarettes and lighter he'd put on the bedside cabinet when he'd undressed.

He lit a cigarette and handed it to her, then lit one for himself. Christina scooted up, leaning her head on his shoulder, and he wrapped a big arm around her shoulders.

'So what's up with your sister that we've got to talk about?' he asked, exhaling a plume of blue-gray smoke. 'They upset about their latest little problem?'

Christina wriggled even closer to him. 'You're not going to believe it,' she said.

'Try me,' he replied.

'It's a lot more than the latest little problem at the

nursery,' she said. 'Joanna's sick. She's going to die.' Her voice was emotionless, but she felt a twitch of discomfort in her stomach.

He looked at her with a quizzical expression, then his lips slowly formed a smile. 'You're shitting me,' he said.

'No,' Christina said, smoke curling out of her nostrils. 'She has a few months at most. Cancer.' She stubbed her cigarette out in an ashtray, then turned back to him. 'So,' she said, tracing a fingertip across his lips, 'if you just bide your time, the place will be yours. The whole kit and caboodle. Josh'll be glad to get rid of it.' She smiled. 'I'm sure of it.'

Staring at her, he put out his cigarette and took the finger she was brushing across his lips. He opened his mouth and began to lick it, running his hand down her arm, then over to her breast, his fingers latching on to her nipple.

Christina's breath caught in her throat, and her body eased down farther on the bed, her eyes still staring into his. In only moments he was riding her again, fast and hard, worshiping her body with his own as no one ever had, as if her information had served to feed the fires of his desire.

This is worth it, she thought ecstatically, her body beginning to writhe beneath his. *This is worth any price I have to pay.*

21

The big Morris Beige Rolls-Royce Corniche rolled majestically into the courtyard, its beige top down. Christina was in the driver's buttery-soft beige leather seat with its beige piping. The ubiquitous cigarette was between two of her bejeweled fingers, as if it were a fashion accessory.

Connie, who had heard the car, peeked out a window to see who it was and gasped aloud. 'Oh, shit, no!' she exclaimed to herself. 'The plastic bitch has flown in on her expensive broomstick.' She hated Christina with a passion that she could barely conceal – and sometimes didn't – and dreaded her visits. She went back to the kitchen, where April was helping her get a simple lunch ready to take down to the poolside.

April looked up and smiled when she came into the room. 'What's wrong, Connie?' she asked, seeing her look of distress.

Connie leaned against the doorjamb with a distasteful expression. 'Joanna's sister is here,' she spat.

April's eyes widened. 'Here? Uh, unexpectedly?'

'Yes,' Connie said. 'Out front in the courtyard. In the big broomstick she flew in on.'

April couldn't help but laugh. She knew about Connie's intense dislike of Christina – and all women of her ilk – and she knew that it was tolerated by Joanna and Josh, even gleefully so at times.

What none of them realized, however, was the depth of Connie's hatred. Nor did they understand that Connie ached to live exactly like Christina, to have everything Christina had. In short, they didn't fully understand that Connie's hatred was a result of a deep-seated envy.

'I'll go greet her, Connie,' she said. 'You can stay here if you want. And there's no need to go get Joanna and have her come all the way up here. I'll take her sister down to the pool.'

April put down the tray she'd loaded with dishes and cutlery, and rushed off toward the front door. She pulled it open and stared for a moment at the astonishing sight that greeted her eyes.

The much-talked-about Christina von Leydon was dressed as if for an afternoon stroll on the Via Condotti. She stood at the trunk of her enormous Rolls-Royce convertible, her hair wrapped in a brightly colored

Hermès scarf tied at the base of her neck, over which she wore a black gaucho hat, secured beneath her chin. Huge Jackie O-type sunglasses virtually hid her face. A white silk blouse was tied in a knot at her waist – and unbuttoned down to there. Beneath that were tight white silk capri pants and cherry-red stiletto-heeled sandals. On her arm was a shiny candy-apple red Vuitton carryall.

'Christina?' April called questioningly.

Christina turned around and pulled her sunglasses down her nose, the better to look at April. 'Yes?' she responded haughtily. 'Who are you?'

'Sorry,' April said, walking down the steps and approaching her. 'I'm April Woodward,' she offered, holding out a hand to shake. 'I'm doing some work for your sister.'

'I see,' Christina said, looking her up and down, but ignoring the proffered hand. 'It must be rather dirty work, huh?'

April looked down at remnants of the cement dust that she'd tried unsuccessfully to clean off her clothes before lunch. 'Well, yes, it is,' she said.

'Humpf,' Christina grunted.

'I don't believe Joanna is expecting you,' April said, unwilling to let this unpleasant woman intimidate her.

'No. This is a surprise visit, and it would hardly have been a surprise had I told her, would it?' Christina replied with undeniable logic. She looked over April's shoulder, toward the house.

Connie slowly descended the front steps, eyeing Christina suspiciously.

'Oh, Connie,' Christina cried. 'How nice to see you – and how convenient. Be a dear and take my luggage in.'

'Is there a lot?' April asked.

'Hardly a thing,' Christina said airily. 'Connie can handle it.'

'Good,' April said. 'If you want, you can come with me. Joanna's down at the grotto, and I know she'll want to see you.'

'Grotto?' Christina asked. 'What grotto? What the hell's going on?'

'You'll see,' April said mysteriously. 'It's something Joanna's been working on.' With April leading the way, they headed down to the grotto.

Connie looked into the big car's trunk, her features set in a glare. *Louis Vuitton luggage*, she thought. *Of course! And tons of it. Aren't I lucky?*

'You look marvelous,' Christina said, holding out her skinny, tanned arms.

Joanna, who'd been settled into a chaise longue relaxing, watching the progress, rose to her feet. She hugged Christina, and they exchanged air kisses. 'And you look . . . very glamorous,' Joanna said.

'Pish!' Christina exclaimed. 'I look every bit the face-lifted, liposuctioned harridan that I am.' Then she smiled, her expensively bonded teeth dazzling white. 'But that ain't so bad, is it?'

Joanna laughed. 'No, indeed it's not.'

302

'Now,' Christina said, 'what is this ... this grotto business?' She took notice of the room for the first time, and stood with her arms akimbo.

'Why, Joanna, it's beautiful!' she gasped as she looked around in the grotto.

'Well, you have this young woman to thank for that,' Joanna said, indicating April, who stood watching the two of them in fascination. 'Although you've more or less met, April, this is my sister, Christina, and Christina, this is the resident magician who's done all this work.'

April nodded. 'It's nice to meet you, Christina.'

'It's nice to meet you, too,' Christina said, eyeing her more critically.

'Oh, and this is her helper,' Joanna said, indicating Woody, who was cementing abalone in place. 'Woody, this is my sister, Christina.'

Woody looked up from his work, a frown on his face, and simply nodded his shaggy head and grunted.

'Lovely to meet you, too,' Christina said, her voice tinged with sarcasm. Then she looked at Joanna and winked. 'This really is an enormous project,' she said.

'Yes,' Joanna said. 'It's taking thousands and thousands of shells and a lot of work.'

'Well, it's absolutely marvelous,' Christina said, 'if a bit over the top. But I mean, why, Joanna? Especially now ...'

Christina realized her mistake the instant the words were out of her mouth and quickly blurted, 'I mean, it just seems a little over the top, if you know what I mean. You've done so much work on this old place.'

303

April tried not to cringe inside, but Christina, whose eagle eyes seldom missed anything, was certain that she detected a knowing look in April's eyes.

She knows about Joanna, Christina thought. She wondered why a stranger – a common worker – would be privy to such intimate information and made a mental note to ask about it later.

'I'm doing it because I want to,' Joanna said, knowing there was no way her sister could argue with such an answer. 'Anyway, we're just about to have lunch at the pool. You want to freshen up and join us?'

'That's heaven,' Christina said. 'And I do need to freshen up a bit first and see to my things.'

'I'll take you up to the house, then,' Joanna said. She turned to April. 'Lunch will be just a little late, April,' she said, rolling her eyes. 'We'll be back down shortly.'

April smiled and nodded.

Joanna led Christina toward the French doors and back outside, where they walked through the apple orchard up toward the pool, Christina carefully negotiating her way in her stiletto heels.

'Who *is* she?' Christina asked when they were out of earshot.

'April?' Joanna said. 'She's an absolute angel who works in shells and pebbles and such. We saw some garden work she did for Ingrid Wilson, and we both loved it, so we hired her to make a grotto out of the old stable. She's turned out to be a real joy to have around. A real friend.'

Christina, who had always been irrationally jealous of her younger sister's friends, did not like what she heard. 'And the guy?' she asked. 'Who's he?'

'That's Woody Pearlman, a friend of April's,' Joanna replied as they arrived at the pool area. 'He has a framing shop in Capitola but helps her out sometimes on big projects.'

'He's a real cutie,' Christina said, giggling almost girlishly. 'But he's awfully rude.'

'That's Woody,' Joanna said, not wanting to discuss him any further.

'Hmm,' Christina said. 'Too bad, really. He looked like he has a terrific bod under those work clothes. Bet he'd be a good roll in the hay.'

'Christina!' Joanna laughed. 'Sometimes I don't believe you.'

'Oh, I'm not serious,' Christina replied. 'But . . . well, he does look hot.'

'You are shameless,' Joanna said with amusement. They reached the house and went into the kitchen.

Connie had a loaded tray in her hands, and was getting ready to go down to the pool. 'Your luggage is in your usual guest room,' she said to Christina.

'Did you unpack everything?' Christina asked.

Connie looked at her with deceptively sleepy-looking eyes. 'Noooo,' she said. 'I thought your things are so special that only you would know what to do with them.'

Christina looked at Joanna, her face a mixture of amazement and anger.

Joanna shrugged helplessly. 'I'll help you unpack,' she said.

'No, no,' Christina said quickly. 'I can handle it myself. Besides, I'm sure you need to rest . . . or something . . . before lunch?'

'I'm fine,' Joanna said. 'We'll meet out by the pool in a few minutes.'

'Fine,' Christina said. She swept out of the kitchen and headed toward the entrance hall to the stairs.

Joanna turned to Connie. 'Connie,' she said, 'I know you don't like Christina, and I know she's a real pain. But couldn't you be a little bit more civilized?'

Connie looked at her with those same heavy-lidded eyes. 'What? You think I don't like her? I'm not nice to her?'

'I *know* you're not,' Joanna said. 'And *you* know I know.'

'I don't even give the plastic bitch a thought,' Connie said spitefully.

Joanna sighed, then went back out onto the terrace. She had almost laughed aloud at Connie's comment, but she didn't want to encourage her dislike of Christina. Her sister was enough of a handful without Connie complicating matters. She walked on out to the pool and sat down under one of the big market umbrellas.

She was tempted to call Josh at the nursery to tell him that Christina had arrived unannounced, but she decided not to bother him with the news.

Poor Josh, she thought. *He's having a hard enough time coping without Christina around.*

I should never have confided in her, she decided. Christina's intentions might be the best, but Joanna knew that her sister would drive her and Josh crazy in a matter of days, if not hours. She also realized that Christina was incapable of acting as if everything was normal, the way she wanted it to be.

Now what? she wondered.

She knew that Christina would try to be *too* helpful in all the wrong ways. And in the process, her manipulative and controlling behavior would completely alienate Connie, Josh, and April, at the very least. In other words, those closest to her.

I've got to do something to remedy the situation, she thought, *and I might as well start right now*.

She got up from the table and headed toward the grotto. She would start by asking April to dinner, even though she was already having lunch with them. Aside from the fact that Joanna wanted her there, April would act as a sort of buffer zone between herself and Christina. She knew that Christina wouldn't discuss her illness in front of someone she considered an outsider.

Lunch had gone smoothly, with Christina dominating the conversation, regaling Joanna and April with the latest antics of the rich and spoiled from San Francisco to Montecito. Now dinner was over, and Christina and Joanna were placing the last of the dishes on big trays to take to the kitchen. Connie had made excuses to leave rather than stay and help serve and clean up as she usually did when there was company. Joanna knew the reason, of course, but she hadn't objected to Connie's leaving.

'Please,' April asked for the second time, 'let me do something?'

'No,' Joanna said. 'You're a guest, and besides, Christina and I will have this done in no time.'

'And,' Christina chimed in, 'we want to have a nice sister-to-sister talk, don't we, Joanna?'

'Oh, yes,' Joanna said to humor her.

They finished loading the trays and headed off to the kitchen, leaving Josh and April alone at the dinner table on the terrace. Josh took a sip of his coffee and looked over at April with a smile. 'What do you think of big sister?' he asked.

April returned his smile. 'Weeeell,' she drawled, 'she's certainly larger than life. She's beautiful and intelligent and can be really sharp and funny, but . . .' She looked at him and shrugged.

'But what?' he asked.

'Well,' April ventured, 'she also seems bossy and sarcastic and supercilious and mean and . . .' She stopped and looked at Josh with a sheepish expression.

He laughed. 'Go on,' he encouraged her. 'Don't stop now. It was just getting interesting.'

'I . . . I'm sorry,' April apologized. 'I think I've overstepped my bounds here.'

'You know you shouldn't feel that way, April,' Josh said. 'You're like one of the family.' He laughed again. 'And like all families, we have our differences.'

'I didn't mean to be unkind,' April said. 'Or so judgmental. I mean, I hardly know the woman.'

'Well,' Josh said, amusement in his voice, 'I think you've hit the proverbial nail on the head.' He looked off into the distance. 'I wish she wasn't here, and I know Joanna feels the same way. I don't think Joanna really wants her here' – Josh paused and looked at her knowingly – 'not until the end. If then.'

Despite herself, April felt a quiver of fear rush through her. Joanna seemed so healthy most of the time, even though she did rest a lot, that her illness still seemed unreal somehow, and speaking of it made it seem all too real. It was, she thought, like acknowledging the existence of evil. She felt compelled to change the subject.

'How're things going down at the nursery?' she asked. 'Joanna hasn't mentioned anything to me lately.'

'Okay,' Josh replied. 'Knock on wood.' He tapped the table with a fist. 'I hope we don't have any more bad luck. We sure don't need it.' He looked at her and smiled. 'I don't have to ask you about how your work is going,' he said. 'Joanna is thrilled with it, and I am too.'

April felt herself blush and looked away. She loved to hear his praise, despite the twinges of guilt she felt. *Every time he says anything the least bit appreciative of me, I feel that I'm somehow betraying Joanna because I like it so much. But I want to hear even more! Oh, what am I going to do?*

* * *

Christina glanced out the library window as she settled down on the big leather Chesterfield sofa. She smiled tightly, then turned away, nervously fluffing her multicolored hair with long, Jezebel Red-lacquered fingernails. Heavy gold bracelets, set with small, glinting gemstones, clanked dully on her thin wrists. She took a large swallow of her brandy, then chased it with a long pull of her cigarette.

So, she thought, *the little gray wren from the grotto stays to dinner. And she's in like Flint with Josh, too. How cozy.*

Her features contorted into an ugly mask. *I don't give two hoots about Josh Lawrence, but I'll be damned if some meddling little nobody is going to come in here – to the house I grew up in – and take over. Acting like Miss Goody Two-shoes, when it's obvious she's nothing but a little tramp from nowhere. I'll break this up, and now!*

She smashed her cigarette out in an ashtray and got to her feet, heading for the terrace. Joanna almost collided with her, returning to the library from the powder room.

'Where are you going in such a hurry?' she asked Christina.

'I was just going out to the terrace,' Christina said. 'I see Josh and that April person out there looking awfully cozy.' She arched a brow at Joanna.

Joanna laughed. 'Sit back down and leave them alone,' she said. 'They're perfectly fine, and we can have that talk.'

Christina hesitated before finally sitting back down

on the big leather Chesterfield. 'What kind of a name is April, anyway?' she said in a nasty voice.

Joanna laughed again. 'You can be so mean, Christina, and April is the nicest person in the world.'

'I bet she is,' Christina said sarcastically. She lit a cigarette and looked over at Joanna, exhaling a long plume of smoke. 'Do you think she's making it with that hunky Woody person?'

'I don't have the faintest idea,' Joanna said, slightly exasperated. She didn't like this interest of Christina's in Woody.

She cringed inside. Christina was like all of her ex-husbands in that respect. While they'd all been promiscuous, invariably taking up with other, usually younger, women, Christina herself relished the occasional toy boy.

No, Joanna decided, she didn't like this one bit. She could see a potentially explosive dalliance in the making, and it was a complication she hadn't anticipated.

Then suddenly it came to her – what she must do. She had already formulated a plan that involved the sullen Mr Woody Pearlman. Now she would simply carry out her plan earlier than expected, and kill two birds with one stone. Pleased with herself, she gladly turned her full attention to her sister.

'Now then, Christina, darling,' she said, 'when did you say you were leaving?'

22

Josh rushed down the hallway toward the bedroom, almost out of breath. He had raced home from the nursery after April called him.

She was coming toward him, and before he could say anything, she put a finger to her lips. 'She's sleeping now,' she whispered.

'What . . . what is it?' he asked, gasping for air. 'What happened, April?'

He felt her hand on his shoulder, patting him lightly. 'Let's go downstairs,' she said, taking his hand for him to follow her. The gesture was so natural that neither of them was aware of it.

Together, they walked down the stairs and out to the terrace, where they sat down at the big teak table.

Josh looked over at her anxiously. 'Tell me what happened, April,' he said. He was making an effort to control the hysteria in his voice.

April gripped his hand in her own as if for strength. 'We were down at the grotto,' she said calmly, 'and Joanna started having a severe headache and some blurring of vision. So I called the doctor and had him paged.'

April took a deep breath before continuing. 'I've given her a very heavy dose of the pain medication, and sleeping pills, too, like the doctor told me to. She'll probably sleep for quite a while, then be okay when she wakes up.'

Josh's eyes never left April's face, and his fingers began stroking her hand. 'Thank God you were here,' he said. 'This is . . . well, it's going to be so difficult for all of us. Especially with her staying here at home. And you know you don't have to do these things. I can hire—'

'Stop right there, Josh,' April said in a firm voice. 'Don't even think about it. Joanna is fine most of the time, and I love having her down at the grotto with me. I can keep an eye on her that way. So . . . forget about a nurse or whatever.'

'I really appreciate that, April,' he said quietly.

'I told you I would be here for Joanna,' she said, 'and I meant it.'

Just then he noticed that she was in her work clothes, her hair a disheveled mess and a liberal sprinkling of cement dust all over her. 'You've had your work interrupted,' he said, indicating her clothes.

'Oh, this,' she said, laughing lightly. 'Well, that's not important, is it?'

He smiled. 'No, I don't think so under the circumstances.' Frowning, he asked, 'Where were Christina and Connie when all this was going on?'

April shrugged. 'I don't know,' she replied. 'I know that Christina went somewhere this morning because Joanna mentioned it. Shopping or something, I guess. Connie came in and did some cleaning, then left to go do some grocery shopping, I think.'

'She's still gone?' he said.

'Yes,' she nodded. 'I know she had a lot to do with Christina being here and so on. Joanna mentioned it. We were down at the grotto. You know, just chattering away about some of the shells to use and the best orchids to try to do in shells. Stuff like that.'

She paused and looked off toward the pool, her eyes beginning to tear. 'We were having such a good time, and that's when it happened.' Her voice broke, but she continued. 'Suddenly, with no warning.'

Josh took her hand again. 'You've been so brave, April,' he said.

She shrugged. 'Joanna's the brave one,' she said.

They sat in silence for a moment, then April looked at her watch. 'I'd better get back to work,' she said. 'I was going down to the nursery later to finally decide which orchids to use for the grotto, but Woody's not here today, and I've got a lot to do.'

'He couldn't come in?' Josh asked.

'I don't know,' April said. 'He was supposed to be

315

here, but he didn't show up. It's not like him to do this, so I don't know what's going on. Maybe he had a lot of work to catch up on.' She looked at Josh and smiled. 'I guess it's just a crazy day.'

'I guess so,' he said.

'But listen, Josh,' she said, 'don't worry about Joanna. If you need to get back to the nursery, I'll run up to the house every now and then and check on her. The doctor says she should be out for quite a while. So I can handle this end of things.'

'No,' he said. 'I appreciate the offer, but you can get back to work. I'll call Carl. He can handle whatever comes up at the nursery, and I'll stick around here. Maybe get some work done in the Stud Room.'

'Okay,' April said. 'But I'll still be running up to check on Joanna every now and then.'

He gave her hand a final squeeze. 'Okay,' he said. 'Between the two of us, we ought to be able to handle this.' He looked thoughtful for a moment. 'I wonder if Christina will come back expecting lunch,' he said.

'Well,' April said, 'if she does, she's a grown woman, and she knows where the refrigerator is, doesn't she?'

Josh's face actually lit up. 'That's the spirit,' he said with a laugh.

Christina lay spread-eagled on the big king-size bed, her wrists tied to the headboard and her ankles to the footboard. Her Hermès scarf that he had so efficiently wrapped and knotted around her eyes rendered her blind.

Her body quivered in a mixture of fear and anticipation. After three husbands and numerous lovers, she'd never been this sexually aroused. Every fiber of her being was concentrated on Peter Rossi and what he would do to her next, how he would indulge her insatiable appetite for him.

She had already feasted on his big, thick shaft, had already made love to those huge balls of his, so heavy with nectar, and he had ravished her entire body in turn, his powerful hands and sensuous lips and tongue torturing her with a thousand delights.

Now she could sense movement about the room, could feel shifts in air currents, almost as if the fog outside were curling around the room, undulating in wisps that she felt ever so lightly on her body.

What is he doing? she wondered. Then she could sense his presence near her, his tall, muscular body hovering over her at the side of the bed, preparing to mount and assault her mercilessly. Her thighs trembled anew, so hungry was she for him, and when she felt his hand suddenly clap onto her mound and his thick fingers ruthlessly enter her, she cried out at once, a cry of both alarm and ecstasy, relishing his control over her and her own submission to his every desire. He explored her brutally, and her body gave up its sweet juices as she lay panting, whimpering, then almost screaming out, begging for more, more, more.

As swiftly as his hand had entered, he withdrew it, and he crawled onto the bed over her, poised, she was certain, to enter her with his massive manhood. And he did, savagely plunging into her, his hands under her buttocks, ramming her up against him with mighty thrusts.

She came at once, screaming as her body uncontrollably writhed and contracted around his cock, spasm after spasm engulfing her in a primal ecstasy she had never thought possible. When he exploded into her with the growl of a beast, she ached to fling her arms around him and sink her nails into him, pulling him ever closer, to savor every ounce of his hot, copious juice.

When it was over, they both lay panting like winded animals, their bodies covered with a fine sheen of sweat. The scents of their bodies commingled in the heady perfume of sex, of spent lust and desires fulfilled.

When her breathing had at last returned to normal, Christina merely cooed a long 'Hmmmmmm,' momentarily unable to find the words to describe her satisfaction, her utter satiation with this powerful man.

Without uttering a word, he rolled off her, then got off the bed.

What's he doing now? she wondered, her body still aching for his touch.

She heard him moving around. It sounded as if he was getting dressed. *Jesus*, she thought, *what does he think he's doing?*

She wriggled against the restraints that held her to the bed, growing alarmed by his continuing silence and the sound of his dressing.

'Peter?' she gasped at last. 'What – what are you doing?'

She heard the sound of the zipper on his pants, the sound of him cinching his belt closed, then the swish of fabric as he put on his jacket.

'Peter?' she said again, louder this time, irritation in her voice. 'What the hell are you doing?'

Still there was silence, and she wriggled against the restraints again, more frantically this time. 'Peter,' she almost shouted, 'let me go.'

Then she heard sibilant whispering.

Whispering?

Her mind spun in a thousand different directions, and she couldn't think. Fear, like a poisonous vice, was beginning to take her in its grip, and she broke out into a sweat that coated her body anew.

'Peter!' she screamed, wriggling frantically again. 'Let me go! *Now!*' She began to whimper like a child until—

Laughter?

But not his deep, masculine laughter.

No, it was the tinkle of a woman's laughter. Cruel, mocking laughter.

Christina thought for a moment that she would faint, and she began to jerk like a demon possessed at the restraints that held her so securely, her body lurching up off the bed. Then she began to scream and cry at once, begging him to let her go.

Suddenly she felt his weight on the bed and his hand clapped over her mouth, and she frantically gasped for breath.

'Cool it, babe,' he said calmly. 'Just cool it. I'm right here.'

319

She whimpered, still panicked, wondering what was going on.

'I'm going to take my hand off now,' he said, 'but I'll put it back on if you make one fucking sound. You got that?'

Christina nodded wildly. *Anything, anything,* she thought. *Just to get this over with.*

She felt his weight shift slightly, then he said, 'Go wait out at the car.'

There was another heave of laughter – *the woman's laughter!* – as if she were trying to control it, and then she heard footsteps, very light and quick, exit the room. She heard the condo's front door slam.

Christina felt her entire body begin to tremble uncontrollably, but it was with fear and exhaustion, not the delight of sexual anticipation.

She felt him get off the bed, but she didn't say anything, so shocked was she by the turn of events.

'I'm going to untie you now, babe,' he said. 'Then I'm going to go. Got that?'

She nodded again but didn't speak.

She felt him first free her right leg, then her left, as quickly and efficiently as he'd tied her down. She began moving her legs about, shaking them gingerly, to get the blood moving. Then he moved to the headboard, where he untied her left arm.

As fast as he had started, he stopped. 'Now I'm going to split, babe,' he said. 'You can untie your other arm, then go. Just close the door behind you.'

'What – who—' she began.

320

'Just do what I say,' he said, his voice menacing.

'But, Peter,' she whined miserably. 'Who – who was that? And what about – what about us? What—?'

'There is no *us*, babe,' he said nastily. 'I don't need you anymore. So forget about it, or you're dead. Understand?'

For a moment Christina couldn't believe her ears. Then her mind turned white-hot with an all-consuming rage. She wanted to lash out at him with her nails, her teeth, anything to tear him to pieces. But fear kept her silent.

'Ciao,' she heard him say lightly. Then she heard him leave the room and the front door close.

Frantically, she began wrenching the blindfold off with her free hand. It wasn't easy because he'd tied it securely. When she managed to yank it off at last, she opened her eyes and blinked several times, adjusting to the light. She looked around. There was no one in the room, of course. Quickly, she began untying the restraint that held her right arm, fumbling in her nervous hurry but finally succeeding. Her arm free at last, she shook it repeatedly and rubbed her wrist, trying to get the circulation going again.

She jumped to her feet and dashed to the front door of the condo. Edging the door open, she peeked out at the parking lot, but she could see nothing in the fog. Nothing and nobody. There was only the sound of the myriad sea birds, their cries a lonely plaint in her ears.

She went back to the bedroom and dressed. Only

321

when she was fully clothed did she sit down on the bed and begin to cry, heaving silently at first, her head in her hands, then gradually letting go, wailing aloud and slamming her fists into the bed as the tears flowed.

When she was finally exhausted, her body aching from convulsions, she rose to her feet, tottering on her heels, and went into the bathroom. She switched on the light and looked into the mirror. *What a pretty sight!* she thought. She snatched Kleenex from a box on the counter and quickly wiped away trailing mascara and the remainder of tears. Then, before fresh tears began to flow, she retrieved her handbag from the bedroom, returned to the bathroom, then fished around in it until she'd found all of her makeup.

Looking into the mirror again, she began applying fresh makeup to her face, trying to control her still shaky hand. When she had repaired the damage as best she could, she threw the makeup back into her handbag and started to switch off the light. Then on second thought, she fished around in her handbag again until she found her eyebrow pencil. Taking it out, she held it poised in front of the bathroom mirror for a moment.

No, this won't do, she thought. *Too easy to clean up.*

She went back into the bedroom, where she slipped out of her heels and climbed onto the bed. Removing the badly drawn seascape that hung above the bed, she threw it against the mirrored closet doors. The mirror cracked in a spider web, and the glass covering the drawing shattered.

Good, she thought, though there was no real joy for her in the destruction.

Taking eyebrow pencil in hand, she began to write on the wall, going over and over the letters to make them thick and bold. When she was finished, she eased down off the bed, slipped into her heels, grabbed her handbag, and walked to the bedroom door. She turned and looked at her handiwork: FUCK TRASH, it read. Centered beneath the first line, the second read: PIG. An arrow pointed down to the bed.

Pleased with her literary endeavors and the paint job that would be required to conceal it, she turned and left the apartment without looking back.

23

The sun had burned off the fog and streamed in through the breakfast room windows. Josh had left for work, and Connie was busy upstairs. April had said a quick hello, then gone on down to the grotto. She had been working alone for several days because Woody was catching up on work at his shop and wouldn't return until next week. Joanna and Christina sat alone at the table, sipping the last of their morning coffee.

'I feel great,' Joanna said, and she meant it. It had been a week since her last bout with the headaches and vision problems, and the episode, though frightening, seemed like a distant memory.

'Have you already called Vincent?' she asked.

'Oh, yes,' Christina said. 'But only after you told

325

me last night that you had appointments and would be tied up all day. So I was up with the little birdies, and got on the horn right away.' She drummed her long fingernails on the table with nervous energy.

'And Vincent was up and at it that early?' Joanna asked.

'Yes, indeed,' Christina said. 'Making his awful jokes about early birds getting the worms. In his case, a very different sort of worm, I should think.'

Joanna smiled. 'But your hair is perfect, Christina,' she said, noting that her sister was wearing full makeup. 'As good as they say Vincent is, I don't understand why you want to do anything to it.'

Christina patted her dozen shades of blond hair with a bejeweled hand. 'It's never perfect, darling,' she said. 'And Vincent, despite the fact that he's in this backwater of a place, is one of the best haircutters I've ever run across. He can do it without it looking like you've had a haircut, and that's what I like.'

'I see what you mean,' Joanna said, not really paying attention. She couldn't fathom the amount of time and money her sister spent on her looks. She would be bored out of her wits. But then, she supposed, boredom was what led Christina to obsess on her appearance anyway.

'Too bad you can't come with me,' Christina said, although she'd been certain Joanna would turn her down before she'd asked her. 'We could get Vincent to do something really exciting with your hair. It'd be fun.'

'No,' Joanna said. 'I've got several errands to run, and I can't spare the time. Anyway, I like the way Jonathan cuts my hair.'

'But you never change it!' Christina exclaimed.

'And I never will,' Joanna countered.

'Oh,' Christina said, 'what a bore!'

'Anyway,' Joanna said, 'I'll drop you off on my way, if you like. Unless you want to take your car.'

'I'll be quite a while,' Christina said. 'I might do some poking around in shops, too. Explore some of the new places. So maybe we ought to go our separate ways.' Then she paused and lowered her voice. 'Are you certain you're okay to be out on your own? I can always stay here or go with you.'

'Oh, no,' Joanna replied. 'Thanks for being so concerned, but I'm fine. Really. You go ahead.'

'If you say so,' Christina said. She rose to her feet and stretched. 'I'll get a jacket and get on my way, then. I don't want to keep Vincent waiting.' She leaned down and gave Joanna an air kiss. 'See you later, darling.'

''Bye,' Joanna said. 'Have fun.'

'Oh, I will,' Christina chirped as she left the room.

Joanna sat staring out the window. Christina had been behaving awfully strangely, she thought. She'd been somewhat tearful a time or two, until Joanna had chastised her for it, but for the most part she'd been uncharacteristically cheerful, busying herself out and about. The local shopping trips – let alone getting her hair cut here – and her dinners and lunches with friends Joanna didn't know she had: This was a new Christina, one that surprised Joanna.

Oh, well, she thought, *as long as she's happy.*

Then Joanna decided she'd better get busy with her errands. *Time's flying*, she thought, *and I don't want to waste a minute of it.*

Joanna drove out of the courtyard and started down the treacherous mountain road. She was at her bank within ten minutes, where she had to park and go inside. The business transaction she had in mind couldn't be done by machine or drive-in teller. After a considerable delay, she returned to the Mercedes, gratified that her shoulder bag had a big, fat envelope in it.

She headed toward the charming little village of Capitola. Within twenty minutes, she reached the ocean-side town with its brightly painted Victorian houses and its plethora of pricey boutiques, many of which featured the work of area craftspeople.

Being a weekday, it was easy to park, right in front of the shop, in fact. She got out of the car, hefting her shoulder bag. Then she walked straight to the shop.

Squaring her shoulders, she opened the door and looked around. A teenage girl piped up from behind a counter, 'May I help you?' She had long bleached hair and a dark, dark tan.

'I don't think so,' Joanna said. 'I need to speak to Mr Pearlman.'

'He's not here,' the girl said.

'Do you know if he's at home?' Joanna asked.

The girl hesitated before she answered. 'I . . . I really don't know,' she said. 'I can take a message.'

Joanna stared at her for a moment. The girl was lying, that much she was sure of. 'No,' she said, 'I'll stop in later.'

'Okay,' the girl said.

Joanna turned and walked out of the shop, then went around to the side of the building, where a wooden staircase led up to the second floor. She knew that he lived upstairs, and she knew about the staircase from April's mentioning it. Joanna had asked her about a limp, and April had told her about slipping on the wet staircase leading up to Woody's apartment the night before.

Joanna looked up the sun-bleached gray steps and took a deep breath. *Here goes*, she thought, and started climbing. At the top of the stairs, she opened the rusty screen door and knocked on the apartment's faded wooden one with her knuckles. No response. She knocked again, louder this time. Still no response.

Then she saw the little once-white buzzer button attached to the door frame. She put her finger on it, hoping it worked. And it did, because she could hear it buzzing loudly inside.

The door opened a crack, and Woody peeked out. His large dark eyes widened in surprise, but for a mere instant before his face assumed a casual, what-do-I-care demeanor.

'Hey,' he said. 'What ya need?'

'Could we speak in private?' Joanna asked.

'Uh, I'm really sorta busy right now,' he said.

'This is extremely important,' Joanna said. 'And I think you'd be a poorer man if you didn't hear me out.'

'Well, uh, give me just a minute,' he said. 'I gotta put something on.'

'Fine,' she said, noticing for the first time that he seemed to be holding a towel around his waist.

He disappeared from sight but left the door open a crack. Joanna patiently waited outside, dreading what she was about to do, but determined to go ahead.

Woody returned and opened the door. 'Come on in,' he said, cocking his thumb toward the room.

Joanna stepped into the apartment and looked around. She was surprised to see beautifully framed prints and paintings hung chock a block on all the walls, many she recognized as being by local artists. The furnishings were expensive but modern and austere. From down a hallway she could hear jazz, its sound muted by a closed door.

'I hope this won't take long,' he said, 'because I've got to get downstairs.'

'I'll only be a minute,' Joanna said, suddenly uncertain of how she would broach the subject.

'What's on your mind?' he asked, studying her from across the room. In nothing but a pair of baggy shorts, he looked bigger and more muscular than ever, his curly black hair seemed shaggier, and his dark eyes shone with intensity.

Joanna felt extremely uncomfortable, but she forged

ahead. 'I hate to be too personal,' she said, looking him in the eye, 'but it's very important for me to know something.'

'What?' Woody asked with a haughty stare. He was rocking on the balls of his feet slightly, his big arms folded across his chest. He seemed to enjoy her discomfort, although Joanna could tell that he was nervous. 'I don't have any secrets,' he added. 'Fire away.'

'Are you in love with April?' Joanna asked, her eyes staying riveted to his.

He stopped rocking and stood perfectly still. His eyes shifted from her to the floor, then back up again. He stroked his chin with one hand. 'I don't think that's any of your business,' he said at last.

'I thought you didn't have any secrets,' Joanna said in a quiet but firm voice.

'I don't,' he said angrily.

'Then what's—' Joanna began.

'I think you're being a little too personal,' he broke in, his voice and manner haughty again, 'but if you have to know, yeah, I think I may be in love with April.'

'You "think,"' Joanna said, echoing him. 'Then you aren't certain that you're in love with her?' she persisted, her heart sinking, hoping that he wouldn't say yes. She had come here convinced that Woody was an egotistical, testosterone-driven seducer who operated on the principle that no woman should be denied the vast pleasures that his body offered.

'Well. . .' Woody said, scratching his head, 'I've known April a long time, knew her ex and all, you know? She's really talented and smart and sexy and . . .'

He shrugged, and Joanna felt the knot of worry in her stomach dissipate, replaced by a stir of impending triumph.

'And how do you think she feels about you?' Joanna asked.

'Like a friend,' he said without hesitation. 'Sort of like a big brother, I guess.' He grinned. 'Except big brothers usually don't want to screw their little sisters.'

Joanna grimaced, but forged on ahead. 'From what April's told me, that hasn't happened.'

His grin disappeared, replaced by a frown. 'If you know so damn much,' he snarled, 'then what are you doing here?' He paused, folded his muscular arms across his chest again, and began rocking on his heels. 'Besides,' he went on, 'April might get to like it, you know? Every other woman does.'

His posturing didn't impress Joanna, nor did it frighten her. 'Would you consider leaving April alone?' she asked. 'What I mean is, making some excuse to her, then simply walking out of her life? Forever.'

He glared at her, his dark eyes shiny in the apartment's semi-gloom. 'What the fuck're you getting at?'

'I think you know,' Joanna said, her eyes remaining on his, despite the malevolence she saw there.

'What if I paid you off? Think you could handle that?'

'Paid me off?' he said, his thick brows knitted in a question.

'Well, could you?' Joanna persisted. 'Could you handle that?'

'You're crazy,' he said.

'Maybe,' Joanna said. 'But that doesn't answer my question. If I gave you, say, fifty thousand dollars, would you disappear from April's life? And I do mean forever.'

'Fifty thousand dollars?' he parroted.

Joanna nodded silently.

'You're . . . serious?' he asked.

Joanna nodded again.

He continued his slow rock, then finally began to nod his head, hesitantly at first, his shaggy hair falling over his forehead, then more definitely. He quit rocking and looked at her. 'Yeah,' he said at last, 'I'd fuck off for fifty grand.'

'You'll call and make some excuse,' Joanna said, 'and really stay away?'

'Yeah,' he said. 'I'll call her tonight. Tell her I met Miss Right. Tell her to stay away, or she'll fuck up the picture. I'll disappear from her life for good.'

Joanna decided she believed him, even though he was a first-class creep. She reached into her shoulder bag and withdrew the fat manila envelope. 'Here,' she said, holding it out to him. 'I expect you to keep your word.'

Woody nodded and took the envelope from her. He didn't want to give her the pleasure of seeing him open it in front of her to have a look at the money, but he couldn't resist and tore it open immediately, satisfying himself that there was fifty thousand dollars in it.

'Not a word about this to anyone,' Joanna said. 'If you tell April about this, she'll drop you like a hot potato because she'll know about the bribe.'

Woody carelessly pitched the envelope onto a couch. Joanna's eyes followed it, then suddenly stopped, dumbstruck by what she saw. A pair of spike-heeled black leather Gucci sandals, identical to Christina's, lay on the floor in front of the couch. Tossed on the couch was a pony skin jacket, also from Gucci, also identical to Christina's. And resting atop the jacket was a black leather handbag. Needless to say, Gucci and identical to Christina's.

Joanna's heart began to pound. She was certain that she must have turned white as a sheet, and she took several deep breaths to steady herself.

Woody saw her staring at the couch, then saw the look on her face.

After a moment she looked back over at him with a grim smile on her face.

'What can I say?' he said. 'They all want me, you know?'

Joanna turned to leave, pausing at the door. 'Not April,' she said. Then she started down the stairs.

Woody stuck his head out the door and called after her, and Joanna turned to look at him.

'What if I hadn't ... gone along with you?' he asked.

Joanna smiled. 'I was certain you would.'

Then she continued down the stairs to her car. She started the engine, pulled out, and raced down the village street to get away from Woody and the sordid scene in his apartment. A scene she herself had engineered, only to discover that her precious sister had upped the sleaze factor considerably.

God, she thought, *I guess we're more alike than I ever wanted to admit.*

At the next light, she had to stop. Across the street in a parking lot, she spotted a Morris Beige Rolls-Royce Corniche.

Christina's, she thought. *It has to be. So she was there for certain.*

The light changed, and Joanna stomped on the gas, anxious to leave Capitola. The ugly scene had left her with the feeling that she needed to take a bath to wash the filthy memory of it away.

Well, I certainly have no right to be angry with Christina, she thought miserably. *I'm no better. I've never stooped so low. Bribery! And it's someone who, despite his flaws, April has come to rely on.*

But she wasn't sorry, she decided. Oh, no. For she had effectively removed him from April's life, paving the way for Josh to replace him. Of course, she hadn't factored in Christina.

What on earth would that come to? she wondered. But Joanna didn't know, and decided she really didn't care. Woody was out of April's life, and that's what mattered. Hadn't she seen the proof of Woody's true character firsthand?

No, Joanna thought. *Sinner that I am, I'm not one bit sorry that I've done this. It's for the better. I'm sure it is now.*

24

Joanna crossed the little bridge to the pool area and spied Christina spread out on a chaise longue, big straw hat shielding her face from the sun, huge sunglasses making reading possible. She was wearing an orange bikini and, as she'd always done, was letting all of her body tan while protecting her face from the worst of the sun's aging effects.

As she drew near to her sister, Christina looked up. 'You're up,' she said gaily, as if nothing were amiss. 'How do you feel today, darling?'

'Fine,' Joanna said.

'Are you sure?' Christina asked.

'Yes,' Joanna said, trying not to sound too exasperated.

'Why don't you have a seat?' Christina said. 'I'm having a look at the slicks. Italian *Vogue* right now. All the winter goodies coming up.'

'I don't think so,' Joanna replied. 'I'm going down to the grotto for a while to see April.'

'Oh,' Christina said. 'Well, I hope you won't wear yourself out down there in all that filthy cement dust. You could be relaxing here in the bright, clean sunshine.'

'Don't get too comfortable,' Joanna said, looking down at her sister's prone body, 'because I would like it very much if you left no later than tomorrow morning.'

Christina laid the magazine on her lap and slipped her glasses down her nose. 'What . . . do you mean?' she asked innocently.

'I think I made myself perfectly clear,' Joanna said. 'I would've told you yesterday, but I didn't see you since you came in so late last night.'

'Well,' Christina said, 'I . . . I—'

'Never mind, Christina,' Joanna said. 'Just be ready to leave after breakfast tomorrow. I have enough to deal with right now without dealing with you, too.'

'But—' Christina protested.

'Just go!' Joanna said from between clenched teeth. Then she went on past Christina and down the short trek to the grotto. She didn't want to discuss yesterday's events with Christina. She had no idea what Woody had told her, and she didn't really care. She just wanted Christina out of her sight.

When she entered the grotto, April was on a ladder, working alone. 'Hi,' she said, smiling at Joanna as she walked through the door. 'I'm so glad you're here. If you want to visit, I can get down in just a minute, and we can look over some orchid drawings I've done.'

'Wonderful,' Joanna said. She looked around the big room, smiling to herself. 'I know I've said it a thousand times, April, but it's turning out to be more fabulous than I ever expected.'

'Well, like I've said a thousand times, you've had a lot to do with it,' April replied. 'But thanks anyway.'

Joanna brushed off a chair seat with a clean paper towel and sat down. 'Where's Woody, by the way?' she asked casually. 'Isn't he helping out today?'

April started climbing down the ladder. 'I'll tell you about it in a second,' she said. When she reached the floor, she took off her dusty smock and draped it over a ladder rung, smacked off her hands, then rubbed them and her face on a clean towel kept on a hook just outside. When she was finished, she came back in and poured some mineral water into a glass.

'Do you want some?' she asked Joanna.

'Not now, April,' Joanna replied. 'But thanks.'

April took a big swallow of water, then scooted a little bistro chair over to where Joanna sat. She sank down onto the chair and heaved a sigh. 'You came at the perfect time for a break,' she said.

'Oh, good,' Joanna said. 'I really hate to interfere, but I love looking in on you and watching when it doesn't bother you.'

'It never bothers *me*,' April said, 'but I think it bothered Woody sometimes.'

'I see,' Joanna said. 'I don't think he's crazy about me.'

'Well, you won't have to worry about that anymore,' April said.

'What do you mean?' Joanna asked.

'He called me to tell me he's quit,' April said. 'He's too busy with his own work. But' – she held a finger up in the air – 'get this piece of news. Not only did he call to say he'd quit, but he told me that he's met somebody special. He says she's the one, Miss Right. So . . . he doesn't want to see me anymore.' She looked over at Joanna, a happy smile on her face.

'How do you feel about all this?' Joanna asked. 'Are you upset? I know you and Woody were friends and all.'

'To tell you the truth, it's an odd feeling right now,' April said. 'I haven't quite gotten used to it yet, but I'm sure I will. He'd come over if I felt blue. We'd go to a movie or out to dinner. Since I moved up here, he's always been there for me, you know? So I was never really lonely.'

'You've told me,' Joanna said, nodding.

April took a sip of her water, then laughed. 'The thing is, Joanna, I was beginning to get a little nervous about Woody. He was starting to get a little too close, a little too cloying, and I hated to give him the old heave-ho and hurt his feelings. Underneath all those muscles is a very insecure guy.'

'I'm sure he'd have gotten over it,' Joanna said.

April nodded. 'He'd have gotten over it pretty quickly, I imagine,' she said. She looked at Joanna and grinned. 'From what he's told me, he'd had oodles of women in the past, and I know from going out with him that he attracts them like flies.'

'I bet he does,' Joanna said.

'Anyway,' April continued, 'he was really becoming too dependent on me, I think. And too protective. At least for someone I considered just a friend. And vice versa, I suppose.' She laughed. 'Sometimes we're better off dealing with our loneliness alone, aren't we?'

Joanna nodded. 'I know what you mean,' she said. 'We have to learn to rely on ourselves, our inner resources, and if we depend on somebody else to distract us from ourselves, well . . .'

'In that case, we never really get to know ourselves, do we? We never learn to be alone with ourselves.' April looked thoughtfully into the distance for a moment. 'The long and short of it is, I'm relieved because he was pressuring me about sex – not aggressively, but I always felt it. And it just wouldn't have worked for me. Not with Woody.'

'I'm glad you don't feel hurt,' Joanna said. 'And I'm sure there'll be somebody to take his place.'

April chuckled. 'Yes, but who's going to help me out here? That's the million-dollar question. I've got to start looking for help.'

'Let me help you,' Joanna said.

April looked at her with astonishment. 'You? Help me? But, Joanna . . . I mean . . .'

'You mean in my present condition,' Joanna said. 'With my cancer.'

April stared at her with widened eyes, her face flushing red, but she didn't utter a word. She didn't know what to say.

'Yes, I know that you know,' Joanna said in a soft voice. 'And it's all right.'

April's eyes shifted to the French doors, and she unconsciously clenched her hands together before her gaze returned to Joanna. 'How . . . how did you know?' she finally asked.

'Oh, little things,' Joanna said. 'Little looks. Little concerns. Not to say that you weren't always concerned with me, but maybe a little more so than usual now. And I know that you picked up on Christina's silly faux pas when she came down to see the grotto.'

Then she laughed lightly. 'Of course, the clincher was seeing Josh's car at your place the very day I told him.' Joanna smiled mischievously. 'I'd come by to see you and didn't stop because I knew he was confiding in you.'

April looked at her with a stunned expression.

Joanna began to laugh again, and April finally joined in. 'I'm just glad Josh felt comfortable confiding in you,' Joanna said.

'And I'm glad he felt that way, too,' April said, almost sheepishly.

Joanna chucked her under the chin. 'Don't worry,

April,' she said quietly. 'About the confidences that you and Josh share. It . . . it delights me more than you'll ever know.'

April looked at her with a mixture of wonder and love, not certain how to respond.

Joanna smiled ruefully. 'Anyway, I'm happy that you know, and happy that just because I'm dying, you don't think I should stop living. That I should just stop with this project. You know as well as I do that it's part of what I want to leave behind. For Josh. And you, too.'

April felt tears threaten, but she was determined not to cry. 'I think you're so brave,' she said, when she could trust herself to speak.

'I'm just doing what feels right and natural for me to do,' Joanna said. 'I think you and Josh are the brave ones,' she added. 'To be able to go on as you have, knowing what you do about me. I assumed that Josh would tell you because he needs all the support he can get.'

April nodded. 'Yes,' she said. 'He needed to talk to someone.'

'I'm pleased that he chose you,' Joanna said. 'He's very vulnerable, April, like you and me.'

'I know,' April said.

'We've been very much a team since we first met, Josh and I,' Joanna continued. 'And my one great sorrow is that part of the team will be missing when I die. I . . . I want more than anything for Josh to be part of a team again . . . after I'm gone.'

Her violet eyes looked piercingly into April's. 'Josh

has loved this life – the life we've had together – and not just because of me. The business and everything have meant so much to him, and I hope he'll go on with it. Keep fighting those Rossi brothers. But I know Josh, and I know he's better off with a partner in life, and that's one reason that I hope, desperately hope, that he'll marry again. The sooner after I die the better.'

Joanna turned the full wattage of her gaze on April, looking at her with an intensity April had never seen there before. 'It would mean more than anything else in the world to me,' Joanna went on. 'For him to have somebody to go on with, to continue to build on the beautiful life that we've had together.'

April held her gaze, but her entire being was caught up in a vortex of conflicting emotions. She was rendered speechless by Joanna's words, and was certain that she detected the message that lay behind them.

Suddenly, she felt almost faint with the significance of this moment, but she knew that she must be as strong as Joanna thought she was.

'Now,' Joanna said in a blithe tone of voice, 'you must show me where to begin.' She rose to her feet and placed a hand on April's shoulder, smiling. 'You've got to show me how to do Woody's job.'

The day had been more exhausting than usual, April reflected as she reached the courtyard where her old Wagoneer was parked. Added to her own painstaking work had been patiently teaching Joanna what to do.

Luckily, Joanna was both a quick study and a determined and motivated pupil, an excellent combination. By day's end, she was doing Woody's job as well as he had, although she hadn't yet built up his speed.

April knew that what had really exhausted her was the emotional toll that her conversation with Joanna had wrought. Joanna's intimate revelations had moved April to the very core of her being. She had wanted to weep but had kept her emotions in check all day long.

Now, she thought, climbing into her Wagoneer, *I feel like an old dishrag, and one that's been wrung out to dry at that.*

She was closing the door when she heard her name being called. Christina was approaching her from the house, and she waited to start the car, curious as to what she might want.

'Hi, Christina,' she said, when Joanna's sister reached the car. She noticed that Christina, as usual, was groomed to perfection and dressed luxuriously in a printed silk blouse and silk pants. Her jewelry glinted expensively in the evening's fading light.

'I'm *so* glad I caught you before you left,' Christina said in an ingratiating voice. 'Could I have a word with you for just a moment?'

'Sure,' April replied, wondering what on earth Christina could have to say to her. 'What is it?'

Christina couldn't help but eye April with a somewhat superior air, although she was making an effort to act sincere. 'You're such a nice person,' Christina said, 'that I'm sure you'll understand what I have to say.'

'Yes?' April said.

'Woody Pearlman, dear,' Christina continued, 'the young man who used to help you?'

'Yes,' April said. 'What about him?'

'I know you were friends and all,' Christina went on, 'for a long time, I gather. And anyway, I just wanted to let you know that he and I are seeing each other now. Quite seriously.'

April made a supreme effort not to show her surprise. 'I see.'

'So,' Christina continued, 'I hope you'll be the lady that Joanna thinks you are and keep your distance. From Woody, I mean.'

April stared at her for a moment, then said, 'I don't think that'll be a problem, Christina. Woody doesn't want to see me anymore.'

'Well,' she said, 'sometimes we have a change of heart, don't we? Even Woody might.' She lowered her voice and grabbed April by the upper arm, clenching it fiercely. 'So stay the fuck away from Woody, understand?'

'I understand perfectly,' April said. 'And I wouldn't think of interfering in your . . . relationship . . . in any way. I think you and Woody are absolutely perfect for each other.'

'Really?' Christina said enthusiastically.

'Yes,' April said. 'He's had nearly every woman in the country, and from what I'm told, you've had most of the men, so you'll make a great pair.'

With that said, April removed Christina's hand from

her arm, slammed the door shut, and fired up the engine. Christina backed away, her face a mask of fury.

Shoving the car in gear, April tore out of the court-yard as if leaving the scene of a particularly odious crime.

Christina glared after her, her face flushed red, her features twisted. 'You little fuck!' she spat under her breath. 'I'll get you!'

25

'You know, April,' Joanna said, 'this is the most fun I think I've had in years.'

'Seriously?' April replied, turning to look at her.

'Well . . .' Joanna demurred, 'maybe the most fun I've had except with Josh.'

They both laughed, then turned back to their work. They'd been working well together, chatting away all the while, discussing everything from life in general to just plain gossip. With Christina gone, it was as if the air had somehow become cleaner, and certainly less tense.

In the beginning, April had worried that their working together would interfere with their friendship. But now that she and Joanna had been more or less closeted together in the grotto for the last couple of weeks, their easy friendship had only grown that much stronger.

Familiarity, April decided, does not always breed contempt.

But one thing that worried April continuously, always in the back of her mind, was her encounter with Christina the night before she left. She had repeatedly asked herself if she should tell Joanna about it.

As if she had read her mind, Joanna resolved the problem for her. 'By the way, April,' she said, 'I've wanted to tell you something for the last few days, but I've been having trouble finding the right words to say it.'

April looked over at her with curiosity. 'That doesn't sound like you, Joanna,' she said. 'I can't imagine what you would find difficult to tell me.'

Joanna laid down her trowel and looked into April's eyes. 'I . . . I've been holding out,' she said seriously. 'I've wanted to tell you that, believe it or not, Christina and Woody have taken up with each other. It happened sometime after they met here, and I . . . I've just been sort of nervous about telling you.'

A smile slowly came to April's lips, and then she burst out into laughter.

Joanna looked at her in amazement. 'What – what's so funny?' she asked.

April's infectious laughter continued for a minute, and Joanna helplessly joined in.

'I – I've been doing the . . . the same thing!' April finally managed to say. 'I knew about it, and I've been agonizing about telling you!'

350

'No!' Joanna said. 'But . . . how? How did you know?'

'The night before Christina left,' April said, 'she came outside when I was leaving for the day. She told me in no uncertain terms to keep my hands off Woody.'

Joanna looked at her in amazement again. 'I don't believe it,' she said. 'But I do! It sounds just like Christina.'

April then told her about their conversation, and she and Joanna both laughed heartily. It was as if they were exorcizing the demon that was Christina and her troublemaking at last.

'She was on her strangest behavior the whole time she was here,' Joanna said. 'This time and the last. Disappearing to shop and go to lunches and dinners with friends I never heard of. Visiting the nursery even. And that is something she almost never does.'

She looked at April with a serious expression. 'I guess I never really knew my sister,' she said, 'at least not as well as I thought. She's still a sort of enigma to me, and I guess she always will be.' She paused, then gazed back at April. 'But you know what?' she asked, not waiting for an answer. 'It's not really important now. You're important, and Josh is important. Not much else matters, really.'

April reached over and touched her tenderly on the cheek, and Joanna took her hand and kissed it. They sat like that for a moment, then Joanna abruptly let go of April's hand.

'I – I've got to go rest,' she said. Suddenly a look of fear and panic came into her eyes, and she wobbled to her feet. April immediately jumped up and went to her side. 'Here, Joanna,' she said. 'Let me walk you to the house.'

Joanna simply nodded and took her arm.

Josh and April sat together out on the terrace as they had before, trying to comfort one another while Joanna slept in a heavily sedated state.

April didn't think that she'd ever felt as sad and fearful, but she had told Joanna and Josh that she would be here for them. And it felt right and natural, as Joanna might have said. She looked over at Josh. His face looked older, grayer somehow, with sorrow and anxiety. The cheerful, tanned boyishness was gone, for the time being at least.

He looked over at her and put a hand on top of her hands, patting them. He smiled sadly. 'I'm so glad you were with Joanna when this happened,' he said, almost in a whisper. 'I can't imagine what would've happened otherwise. Just thinking about it—'

April placed her hands on his shoulders. 'Listen, Josh,' she said firmly. 'I *was* here, and if I hadn't been, Connie could've handled it. So don't drive yourself crazy thinking about what-ifs. Somehow, we'll work this out so that Joanna can stay at home, like she wants to. Hell, I'll move in if I have to.'

He held her hand more tightly, fighting the urge to get up and hug her, to kiss her. 'I guess we can handle it together.'

April felt that familiar stirring within her, the one

that was such a thrill, even if guilt inevitably followed it. Josh had said 'we,' whether realizing it or not, and April couldn't help but feel a rush of warmth and pleasure.

'I'd better go check on her now,' April said, reluctantly removing her hands from his. 'I know she should be out for another couple of hours, but I just want to be sure.' She rose to her feet.

'I'll come, too,' Josh said, getting up.

Together, they walked up to her room. Joanna lay on the bed in semidarkness, her lovely face serene. Her breathing was calm and seemed normal. The dampness of her hair, however, gave evidence of the recent agony that she had endured.

Josh reached down and gently took one of her hands in his. He held it for long moments, stroking it tenderly, while April stood watching. 'Joanna,' he whispered. 'You're going to be all right.'

Joanna didn't move or acknowledge him in any way. Obviously the heavy sedation was still at work. Josh, nevertheless, continued to whisper to her, to stroke her hand, to encourage and comfort her with his words.

Tears formed in April's eyes, but she quickly brushed them away with her fingers. His love for Joanna touched her so deeply, stirred something deep down inside her so powerfully, that she was almost overcome by emotion. She didn't think that she would ever forget these few moments in this room with these two people.

After several minutes, Josh leaned down and brushed Joanna's forehead with his lips, then straightened back up and turned to April. His face was etched with anguish. 'We'll come back in a while,' he said.

April nodded and they left the room, returning to the terrace. They sat down, and April looked at her watch. 'It'll most likely be another hour or so before she wakes up. Do you want to get something to eat?' she asked. 'Connie's gone for the day, but I could rustle something up in the meantime.'

'Sure,' Josh said. 'I'll help, but first I'd better go call the nursery. Carl'll be leaving soon, and I'd better check in with him. I think I'll try Connie, too. I'm going to have to tell her what's going on and see if she can work some extra hours.'

'That's probably a good idea,' April said. 'Besides, I think it's only fair at this point that she knows the truth.'

Josh nodded. 'You're right,' he agreed.

They got up and went into the house.

'I'll be here in the kitchen,' April said, 'seeing what our options are.'

'Be back in a minute,' Josh said. He turned and went down the hallway to the library to make his telephone calls.

April started rifling through the refrigerator, and discovered that Connie had left tons of food already prepared. Her famous shrimp soup, for starters. Lots of fried chicken and her casserole of chicken with avocado and potatoes. *Bless her*, thought April. *She's been awfully busy making sure everybody eats – and well at that.*

She took out the container of shrimp soup, got out a

pot, and started heating it up. She thought that it would probably be all they would want tonight. Before it was even warm, Josh was back.

'All's well at the nursery,' he said.

'Good,' April replied. 'And Connie? Did you get her?'

'No,' he said. 'She must be out. I'll have to try her later tonight or talk to her in the morning.'

'Look,' April said. 'She's left a wealth of food, but I thought the shrimp soup would fit the bill. What do you think?'

'Perfect,' he said, smiling at her.

They finished eating and checked up on Joanna, who was still sleeping peacefully, and decided to sit out on the terrace, despite the chill night air.

'I was supposed to go down to the nursery tonight,' April said. 'To pick up the orchids we finally decided to use. Joanna gave me a beeper for the gate today.'

Josh couldn't help but grin. 'You mean you two finally made up your minds?'

April nodded. 'Finally,' she said. 'It's only taken us months. Anyway, I thought that I'd go on down there, if you don't mind, and pick them up. I could always come back here and spend the night if you want me to.'

Josh shook his head. 'No,' he said. 'You've done enough for one day, April. I'm sure everything here'll be okay. Just don't feel like you have to go all the way down there tonight.'

'I really want to,' April said. 'I need to take those

355

orchids home so I can draw them. And the sooner the better.' She looked over at him. 'I . . . well, I feel like time is of the essence. I know that Joanna said it was from the very beginning, but now I really feel it. More than ever.'

Josh nodded and looked down at the table.

April reached over and took his hand. 'I . . . I didn't mean to upset you, Josh,' she said.

'That's the last thing you could do,' he said, looking up at her. 'I don't know what I'd do without you.' He stared at her for a moment longer, then in a cheerful voice, said, 'Now, get on out of here and go get those damned orchids for Joanna.'

April drove down the freeway, careful to observe the speed limit. The highway patrol seemed to have a special affinity for this stretch of highway, and she didn't want a speeding ticket. The windows were rolled down, and the evening air felt good on her skin and in her hair, especially after the grueling day. In fact, she thought, the drive was almost therapeutic, and she looked forward to seeing all the orchids again.

The ones she was picking up weren't rare and expensive specimens, so she'd decided she could keep them around her house for several days to try to figure out the best way to render them in seashells. Sometimes, she'd discovered, she would get an idea about a particular way to render a flower or plant simply by living with it a few days, acquainting herself with it in different lights, at various angles.

She got off the freeway and breezed on down the road toward the nursery. She pulled into the parking lot and hopped out. She'd never been there at night before, and it was eerily quiet, with the exception of the cacophony of nocturnal insects. She followed the path out toward the greenhouses, and when she arrived at the main set of gates, she pressed the code into the beeper. The gates made a metallic clicking sound, then quietly parted. She went through on one side, then started down the path toward the *Phalaenopsis* house.

She saw no sign of Miguel and idly wondered where he and the guard dog were. *Probably catching a little shut-eye*, she thought. *And why not? If the dog was as good as they said, then there was nothing to worry about. He would alert Miguel to any intruder.*

She was continuing down the path toward the *Phalaenopsis* house when she suddenly felt a chill run up the nape of her neck.

I'm not alone, she thought, alarm bells ringing in her head.

She stopped in her tracks, pricking up her ears. She was certain she had heard something, but what? Come to think of it, why *hadn't* she heard the guard dog yet? He should have been barking like crazy by now, shouldn't he?

There! She heard it again. On the other side of the hedge that lined the path. A sort of gasping. And groans. *Oh, my God*, she thought, is somebody hurt? Could somebody have broken in and injured Miguel?

357

She dared not move yet and remained still as a statue, listening with all her might. *There, again.* But two distinctly different groans, she decided. *One male and one female.*

She took three quiet steps, practically on tiptoe, then stopped at the point where the hedge ended. She listened again, holding her breath. She could hear more clearly now and knew at once that she'd been right. It was two people, a man and a woman.

She cautiously peered around the hedge, trying not to make a sound and—

She almost gasped aloud at the sight that greeted her eyes, but she caught herself, quickly jerking her head back behind the cover of the hedge.

She felt a cold snake of fear and revulsion slither up her back and neck, then slip on over the top of her head. Beads of sweat broke out on her forehead, and she began to shiver involuntarily. At the same time she felt a bizarre urge to laugh aloud. She took several deep breaths, then as quickly as possible retraced her steps to her car.

When she got in, she started the engine and crept out of the parking lot, not turning on her lights until she was well clear of the nursery.

Only when she hit the main highway, headed back north, did she feel that she could breathe easy. Then she suddenly realized the absurdity of her fear and revulsion and, slapping the steering wheel, gave vent to the urge to laugh that she had tried so hard to control. Relief, sweet, sweet relief, immediately swept over her body, relaxing her tensed-up muscles and giving her a fresh perspective on what she'd seen.

Just wait till I tell Joanna and Josh, she thought. *Are they ever going to get a kick out of this.* Then just as suddenly as the laughter had come, it died in her throat.

Oh, my God! What a fool I am! This means ... almost certainly means ... that I've found out who's been causing the trouble at the nursery. And Joanna will be ... devastated. Josh, too, for that matter. She knew that she could be wrong, but she seriously doubted it.

She wondered about whether or not she should tell Joanna at all. Perhaps, she decided, she should go straight to Josh, tell him, then he could make the decision about whether or not Joanna should know.

I'd better wait until tomorrow, April decided. *Not bother him tonight. It was definitely not a good time to break the news. Not after today's events.* She could probably catch him alone in the morning. It all depended on how Joanna was doing.

April stepped on the gas, her mouth set in a grim line. *I don't like being the bearer of bad news,* she thought miserably. *But I don't have a choice, do I? No. I have to tell him what I saw. And the awful truth, painful as it may be, will be out in the open at last.*

26

April pulled into the courtyard earlier than usual, hoping to catch Josh the first thing. She parked next to Connie's Plymouth van and hopped out of her old Jeep, making a beeline for the kitchen.

'Hi, Connie,' she said cheerfully, her nose happily inhaling the smell of fresh, strong coffee.

Connie looked up from a counter where she was chopping vegetables. 'Good morning, April,' she said. 'You're early.'

'I need to talk to Josh for a minute,' April said. 'Is he around?'

Connie nodded and laughed. 'Look right in front of you,' she said. 'Out the door. They're on the terrace.'

April had been in such a hurry that she hadn't even

seen them. 'Oh!' she said. 'Stupid me. I guess I'm not awake yet.'

'Go on out,' Connie said. 'I'll bring you some coffee, okay?'

'That'd be great, Connie,' she said. She went on outside, waving at Joanna and Josh, who had seen her and were gaily beckoning her to them. She couldn't help but be astonished at the change in Joanna since last night.

'Good morning,' she said cheerfully as she approached the table. She leaned down and kissed Joanna on the cheek, then kissed Josh on the top of the head.

'You're early,' Joanna said, 'but I'm so glad.'

'How're you feeling this morning?' April asked, sitting down next to Joanna.

'Fabulous, now that you're here,' she said. 'Like a new person.'

'Honestly?' April asked, looking from her to Josh.

'It's incredible,' Joanna said. 'I don't feel any after-effects at all.'

'I'm so thrilled,' April said. Joanna really did look perfectly normal and, if not exactly lively, she was very much herself.

'April,' Joanna said, 'I . . . I know that my insisting on being at home is making things difficult for you. And everybody else, for that matter.'

'Don't say that,' April said. 'Don't even think that way, Joanna.'

'But it's true,' she said. 'And I just want to thank you for all you've done. I really want to be here.'

Josh put an arm around her shoulders and hugged her to him tenderly. 'You are, my love,' he said. 'And you will be. Make no mistake about that.'

Joanna patted his back. 'Thanks,' she said. 'Both of you. For indulging a crazy lady.'

'You're not crazy,' Josh said. Then he laughed shortly. 'Well, maybe a little.'

The three of them laughed together, but April couldn't get her mind off of the news that she had to tell Josh.

Connie came out onto the terrace then. 'Josh,' she said, 'telephone. It's Carl.'

Josh's laughter died away, and his expression changed to one of concern. 'I'll be right back,' he said, getting up. 'Better see what this is about.' He walked off toward the house.

When he was out of earshot, Joanna turned to April. 'There's some paperwork I need to take care of this morning,' she said, 'but I'll be down later to help. Okay?'

'Good Lord, Joanna,' April replied. 'You don't have to do a thing. Except take care of yourself. Maybe you should rest today. What do you think?'

Joanna shook her head. 'Seize the day and all that,' she said, smiling. 'Speaking of which, I wanted to tell you something . . . something that I guess sounds silly, but . . .'

'Go ahead,' April said. 'You've said silly things before.'

They both laughed, then Joanna looked at her seriously. 'I hope that after I'm gone,' she said, 'you won't let the memory of me . . . of our friendship . . . prevent you from living the fullest life possible. And sooner than later.'

April looked at her with a curious expression. 'What—?'

Joanna squeezed her hands. 'You should have a husband and children, April. You told me you want them. And I want them for you. I want you and Josh both to have full and rich lives once I'm gone.'

'But . . . ?' April began.

Joanna reached up and touched her fingertips to April's mouth. 'Shhhh,' she whispered. 'I love you both.'

April had been working alone in the grotto for about twenty minutes when Josh appeared in the doorway. She looked up and knew immediately that something was wrong. She quickly stood up and went to him. 'Josh?' she asked softly. 'Josh, what is it?'

His head was lowered. 'There's been damage to the lab,' he said. 'Some of my orchid crosses deliberately destroyed.' He shook his head. 'Just when they were beginning to grow.'

'Josh—' she broke in, but he continued.

'Which means,' he went on, 'a huge loss this time. At least in terms of my time. I *created* those little seedlings from crosses I made.' He sighed and looked up at her. 'There's just no winning, April.'

'Josh,' she said, 'you've got to listen to me. I got here early this morning because I had to talk to you about the nursery.'

'What're you talking about?' he asked.

'Last night,' April said, the words tumbling out in a rush, 'when I went down there, I heard these strange noises. I went to investigate, and I saw Miguel and Connie having sex—'

His eyes widened in surprise. 'What?' he exclaimed. 'You've got to be joking!'

She shook her head. 'They were just off the path that runs into the greenhouses. In fact, right behind the lab, back behind the hedge. I looked around and the watchdog was muzzled, chained up to a stake. Right next to them. It looked at me like it wanted to tear me to pieces.'

'Oh, Jesus,' Josh exclaimed.

'And Connie and Miguel were going at it like . . . well, like I don't know what,' April said.

Josh put an arm around her shoulder and drew her to him. 'April,' he said, 'I'm so sorry you had to see something like that.' He shook his head. 'I don't *believe* it!'

He suddenly removed his arm and started pacing the room, then stopped and looked at her. 'Connie's been practically like a sister to Joanna,' he said, 'and Carl's been like a brother. I just can't believe Connie could have anything to do with this.'

'If you say so,' April said. 'But I think you ought to seriously consider this. Joanna's told me herself how upwardly mobile Connie is. How she despises most of her own people. How she's so proud and snobbish and determined to get ahead.'

365

Josh was becoming increasingly disturbed by her words, but he let her continue.

'You've also told me,' April went on, 'that she only dates hot up-and-comers. *Anglo* up-and-comers, at that.' She looked Josh in the eyes. 'I know you don't like hearing this, or even thinking about it, but why would Connie be down there at the nursery making it with Miguel? He's a poor simpleton, like you said. Connie wouldn't give Miguel the time of day, Josh, and you know it.'

He hung his head. 'I've been such a fool,' he said, 'not wanting to believe what's right in front of my face. This is going to break Joanna's heart.'

'Maybe . . . maybe she doesn't have to know,' April said, although she thought that Joanna would definitely want to know, regardless of the awful betrayal involved.

'We'll see,' he said. 'But before I do anything else,' he said, 'I'll have to talk to Miguel and see what I can get out of him. Then I'll go from there.'

'Sounds like a good plan,' she said.

'I should get down to the nursery right now,' he said.

'Then go,' she said. 'I'll be here if Joanna needs anything.'

'It's amazing,' he said, looking at her. 'She's in her study doing some paperwork. Seems as content as can be. Says she's coming down here to help you.'

'Good,' April said. 'So we've got this front covered. You go on to the nursery.'

366

'I will,' he said. 'And I'm really sorry you saw what you did, April. I know it must have been a shock.'

She nodded. 'I'll get over it,' she said, smiling ruefully.

Then he hugged her and quickly let go. 'I'll see you in a while.'

He turned and left, and April's heart was pounding as never before. *Oh, Lord*, she thought. *Forgive me, but I . . . I really do love this man, and I think he loves me.*

Miguel shifted uncomfortably in the chair in front of Josh's desk. He didn't come into the office often, and he didn't like it. Luna always teased him, and usually when Josh wanted to see him here it was for something serious.

Josh looked over the desk at Miguel, dreading what he had to do. He cleared his throat. 'Miguel,' he said calmly, 'does anybody ever come to see you when you're here at night?'

Miguel shook his head violently from side to side, clenching his eyes shut. 'No, nobody,' he said quickly. 'I'm always by myself.'

'Are you sure about that, Miguel?' Josh asked.

Miguel didn't look at him. He clenched his eyes shut again and began to shake his head. 'Nobody, like I said,' he muttered. 'Never. Never, anybody.'

As he did all of the people who worked for him, Josh knew Miguel very well. Now, watching him across the desk, he knew without a shadow of a doubt that Miguel was lying to him. It saddened him, but he could hardly hold Miguel responsible for his actions. Miguel had the mind of a child, after all.

'Miguel,' he finally said, 'I think you've forgotten something.'

'Nooo, Mr Josh. I didn't forget nothing,' Miguel said, shaking his head more slowly this time.

'I believe you did, Miguel,' Josh said. 'Because I think Connie's been down here to visit you, hasn't she?'

'Connie?' Miguel repeated, his eyes widening.

'Yes,' Josh said, 'Connie. You've been seen together here . . . having a very good time together, I hear.' Josh forced himself to smile.

Miguel looked up at him and grinned hugely, forgetting himself. Almost as soon as he did, he realized his mistake and let out a yelp that sounded like a puppy's. Then the inevitable tears began to flow.

'I'm sorry, Mr Josh,' he sputtered. 'I'm sorry.'

Josh hated himself for making Miguel cry, but he had to get to the bottom of this. He got up from behind the desk and went around it to Miguel. Kneeling down, he put his hands on the boyman's powerful shoulders.

'It's okay, Miguel,' he said calmly, patting him softly. 'It's okay.'

Miguel choked and sobbed but wouldn't look Josh in the eye.

'Listen, Miguel,' Josh said. 'You've got to help me. You're the only person who can. Did you know that? The only person. Do you think you can quit crying and do that? Can you help me save the nursery?'

Miguel finally looked over at him. 'Me?' he said.

'Yes, you, Miguel,' Josh replied. 'You can do it. Just tell me if Connie did anything while she was here. Did she . . . tinker with anything?'

'Tinker?' Miguel looked perplexed.

'Did she mess with anything?' Josh persisted. 'Did she . . . go into any of the greenhouses or the lab?'

Miguel regarded him silently.

'Think, Miguel. It's very important. Remember, you can save the nursery,' Josh said. 'What did she do while she was here?'

'We just had fun,' Miguel replied.

'Where, Miguel?' Josh asked. 'Inside? Outside? Where?'

'Different places,' Miguel said. 'Sometimes in the greenhouses. Different ones. The lab. She . . . she made me open them.'

'And the last time it was the lab?' Josh ventured.

Miguel nodded. 'I think so,' he said. 'The one with all the shelves full of glasses.'

Josh gave Miguel's shoulders a squeeze, then sat back on his heels, letting go of him. He didn't want to believe what he'd heard, but there was no mistaking the truth. Connie was working for the Rossis. Had to be. Ever-faithful Connie, of all people, had betrayed them.

Josh felt a bitter wave of bile rise in his throat. The knowledge of her treachery almost made him physically ill, and at the same time he felt saddened and disgusted. It was as if his best friend had suddenly turned on him for no reason.

He slowly rose to his feet. 'Okay, Miguel,' he said. 'Let's go. I'll take you home now.'

Miguel got up, and Josh held the door open for him. In the reception area, Luna looked up from behind her desk, quickly put the telephone down, and smiled, her Hershey bar lipstick emphasizing the gleaming whiteness of her teeth.

'Miguel,' she cooed. 'You look so handsome today. I love those torn jeans. So sexy.'

Miguel made tracks out the front door, and Josh scowled at Luna. 'Lay off him,' Josh said.

Her smile immediately disappeared, and was replaced with big pouty lips.

'I'm going home,' Josh said. 'You and Carl hold down the fort.'

'You just got here,' Luna said in a petulant voice. 'But sure, boss,' she added. 'Whatever you say.'

She was picking the telephone back up as Josh left, hurrying after Miguel. Hurrying home.

Pulling into the courtyard, Josh saw Connie's old Plymouth van. He hopped out of his Land Cruiser and started to head into the house, but decided to check up on Joanna first. He skirted around the house to a gate that led down to the pool area, hoping that she would be down at the grotto with April.

As he approached, he was surprised to hear laughter. Joanna's laugh – unmistakably hers, musical, throaty, rich, and mirthful. He couldn't help but smile at the sound and stopped short of the grotto amid the apple trees to listen and watch.

Just inside one of the grotto's French doors,

Joanna sat on the floor, her legs crossed, covered from head to toe with cement dust. April and some young man – *who's he?* he wondered – were sitting on the floor near her. They were all drinking from iced tea glasses. It was obviously break time. When the laughter subsided, he could hear Joanna and April chattering away. It was as if they didn't have a care in the world.

He stood for a moment longer, reluctant to intrude upon their happy camaraderie, and finally decided to go back to the house and get his confrontation with Connie over with.

When he got to the house, she was in the kitchen, peeling potatoes, humming tunelessly to herself.

'Josh,' she said, smiling up at him. 'You're back so soon.'

'Yes, Connie,' he said. 'Actually ... I came home because I need to talk to you about something.'

Connie continued peeling as if he hadn't said anything.

'It's pretty serious, Connie,' he said.

She shrugged and replied, 'Don't worry, Josh. I already know what you're going to say.'

'You do?' he said, surprised.

'Joanna told me all about her cancer,' Connie said. She shrugged again. 'I had to know because I would see her sick.'

Josh remained silent, digesting this news.

'I'm really sorry,' Connie continued, glancing at him out of the corner of her eye. 'I remember when it happened to my uncle. It was terrible. It can happen to anybody, even Joanna.'

Her voice was so matter-of-fact, so devoid of emotion that Josh was shocked. She had been so close to them for so long, had been like a member of the family. Was it simply a fatalistic attitude? he wondered. He wasn't sure, but he only had to remind himself of the reason he'd come to talk to her to understand that Connie was not the woman he'd once thought she was.

'I didn't come here to discuss Joanna,' he said.

'Oh?' Connie said, peeling away. 'Then what's on your mind, Josh?'

'You've been seeing Miguel, down at the nursery,' he said. 'Haven't you, Connie?'

Connie dropped the peeler and sputtered in laughter. 'Miguel!' she cried. Then she began to laugh hysterically, practically collapsing with laughter. Her face reddened, and she slapped her thighs with her hands.

Her dramatic response seemed forced to Josh, as if trying to make her lies seem convincing.

'Miguel?' she repeated. 'Did he tell you that?'

Josh nodded. 'Yes, Connie, he did.'

'Well, he's a *mongolito*, isn't he?' she said with a derisive laugh. 'So why do you believe him, Josh?'

She started peeling potatoes again, looking up at Josh, her pretty face alight with seeming amusement.

'You've been *seen* there with him, Connie,' he said.

The look of amusement disappeared, replaced by an angry glare. 'Who told you this?' she demanded, the peeler poised in her hand but not moving.

Josh didn't answer but stared at her sadly.

'Who?' she cried angrily. 'Who tells you this lie?'

'April,' Josh said.

'That's crazy,' Connie said. '*She's* crazy.'

'No, Connie,' he said. 'She's not crazy, and you know it. Why would she make it up? Huh? Why would she make up the fact that she saw you screwing Miguel outside the lab?'

The anger and defiance slowly ebbed from Connie's face, and she laid the potato peeler down carefully. She knew that any further denials on her part would be futile. The jig was up.

'Why, Connie?' Josh asked her quietly. 'Why would you do this to us? We've loved you so much and thought you loved us.' He paused, staring at her. 'Did the Rossi brothers pay you that much?'

'I don't know what you're talking about,' she said, angry again.

'I think you do,' he said. He sighed wearily. 'I hate to believe it,' he went on. 'You and Carl and Luna – all of you have been like family to Joanna and me. We've only tried to help you. Jesus, Connie, right now a lawyer is working away, trying to get you a green card. Because we love you enough to pay him to.'

Connie's face burned brightly, but she was still defiant. She slipped off her apron and flung it down on the granite kitchen counter. 'I don't have to listen to this,' she said arrogantly. 'And I don't need your help anymore. I don't need your fucking lawyer anymore.'

Her glaring eyes locked with his for a brief instant.

'Peter Rossi's going to marry me!' she spat. 'He likes me more than he likes Joanna's whore sister!'

'What – what are you talking about?' Josh asked her in amazement.

'Christina was screwing him while I was doing all the dirty work,' she cried, 'but I got him. Not her! And now I'll be richer than you are!'

Before Josh could respond, she turned and stormed out of the kitchen in triumph.

He stood and watched until she'd disappeared from his view, then sighed again.

It's like the end of an era, he thought. *A happier and more innocent era. And the future seems to promise nothing but bleak loneliness.*

He started to head back down to the grotto, but decided he didn't want to inflict his somber mood on the happy trio down there. Besides, he needed to talk to Carl right away. Yet another unpleasant task. He had to tell Carl that his sister was working for the Rossi brothers, causing the trouble at the nursery. Just then he remembered seeing Carl's truck parked at the Rossi brothers' nursery some time ago.

He can't be in on it, too? Can he?

He didn't know, but he decided he'd better find out fast. He rushed out of the kitchen to the courtyard, and tore down the road to the nursery once again.

The pool area was aglow with the flickering light from dozens of candles. They burned along the retaining walls, hung suspended in lanterns from the trees, graced the tables in big hurricane lamps, and even floated on the surface of the placid turquoise pool. The dining table was centered with a large orchid, a *Miltonia spectabilis* var. *moreliana*, its exotic blooms ranging from a dark fuschia to the most delicate pink, cascading down onto the table.

The dinner was delicious and hearty fare. Josh had grilled thick filet mignons on the terrace, baked potatoes, tossed a salad of mixed greens, and served it all with a very fine Château Latour he'd been saving for a special occasion.

'That was fabulous,' Joanna said, setting down her wineglass.

'I'll second that motion,' April chimed in.

'Thank you, ladies,' Josh replied with a nod. 'My pleasure.'

'And to what do we owe all your culinary endeavors?' Joanna asked.

'Oh, I was just in the mood,' Josh replied good-naturedly.

'I see,' Joanna said. 'And where's Connie? I thought she was going to be staying late and helping out.'

Josh and April exchanged glances. He had briefed her earlier in the kitchen while Joanna was changing clothes for dinner. He knew that he was going to have to tell Joanna about Connie's treachery, but he'd wanted to delay it. He'd hoped tonight the three of them could have an enjoyable dinner without discussing the day's events, but he could see that was not to be.

'Come on, Josh,' Joanna said. 'Something's going on, and I want to know what it is.'

'Well . . .' he began hesitantly, 'Connie's left.'

'Left?' Joanna said with alarm. 'What do you mean "left"? She would never just leave.'

Josh hated to tell her the truth. 'Well,' he said, 'I noticed that all her things were gone when I came home this evening.'

Joanna stared at him for long moments, her eyes shining intensely. Finally she expelled a deep sigh. 'She betrayed us,' she said, 'didn't she?' It was a statement, not a question.

Josh looked over at her and nodded.

Joanna's face registered an immense sadness, but only for a fleeting moment. April, watching her closely, didn't think she would ever forget that look of sorrow. Brief as it was, it had such poignancy that it bespoke a profoundly abiding bond that had been cruelly severed.

'She caused the trouble at the nursery, didn't she?' Joanna said.

Josh nodded again but remained mute.

Joanna looked at him, his anguished features, before shifting her gaze to April, whose face was a solemn mask.

Suddenly she threw back her head and roared in throaty laughter, stunning both of them. She laughed deeply, barely able to contain her mirthful outburst.

April and Josh exchanged bemused glances. Joanna's laughter would normally have been infectious, but neither of them knew what to make of it.

When she finally calmed down, Joanna looked at them again. 'Wipe the solemn looks off your faces,' she exclaimed. 'You can only laugh at such a betrayal. That or you cry. And I, for one, would rather not do that.'

Nevertheless, they saw tears come into her eyes, which she deftly wiped away. 'All those years of trust and friendship,' she said wistfully. 'I hope they paid her awfully well.'

'At least now you know the source of the trouble,' April said. 'Not that it's much consolation.'

'That's my girl,' Joanna said. 'You've got the right attitude, looking on the bright side.'

April wasn't certain whether Joanna was being facetious or not. 'Are you serious?' she asked.

'I'm quite serious,' Joanna said. 'It's time to move on.' She looked at Josh. 'Did one of the Rossi brothers call as usual?' she asked.

Josh nodded. 'Yes,' he replied. 'Peter, as usual.'

'Well, finding out about Connie doesn't mean the Rossi brothers will stop trying to buy us out or force us out, but at least they don't have an insider working against us.' She paused and looked at Josh. 'They don't, do they?'

'I thought maybe they did,' he replied. 'But—'

'Who?' Joanna asked anxiously.

'Carl,' he said. 'But I was wrong, thank God. I'd seen his truck at the Rossi place and got worried, especially after finding out about Connie, but it turned out they'd asked him there for a legitimate job interview. Offered him a lot of money to leave us, in fact. But he wouldn't take it.'

'That's a mercy,' Joanna said. 'He restores a bit of my faith in people.'

'Not so quick,' Josh said. He decided he might as well tell her the rest of it, now that she been dealt the hardest blow.

'There's *more*?' Joanna asked, looking at him.

He shook his head. 'Apparently,' he said, 'Christina had been seeing Peter Rossi.'

'What!' Joanna looked at him in amazement.

'How did you find out about this?' April asked, as stunned as Joanna by the news.

'Connie,' he said. 'I don't know exactly what to believe, but from what she said, Christina had been fooling around with Peter Rossi. He was probably just getting information out of her. Now, at least from what Connie said, he dumped Christina, and he's going to marry Connie.'

Joanna was silent for a moment, then shook her head as if to clear it of the news. 'I guess I should be shocked,' she said, 'but I'm not. Not really. A little surprised, maybe.' Then she looked over at April. 'I guess she went running to Woody when Peter Rossi dumped her.'

'Poor Woody,' April said. 'But then I guess they deserve each other.'

She and Joanna laughed, and Josh finally joined in.

'So, we've been betrayed by Connie and Christina both,' Joanna said quietly. 'Not a good track record, I suppose, but' – she looked from Josh to April – 'we've got each other, don't we?' She reached out and held hands with both of them.

'You bet,' Josh said.

'You bet,' April echoed, squeezing Joanna's hand lightly. Then her face became serious, and she looked at Josh. 'And the damage this time?' she asked, after their laughter had stopped. 'How bad is it?'

Josh groaned. 'I don't even like to think about it.'

'We've got to,' Joanna said. 'The sooner it's dealt with, the better.'

'Some of the cultures in the lab were destroyed,' Josh said. 'I'm not sure exactly which ones yet.'

Joanna groaned.

He turned to April. 'The cultures were from crosses that I've made – between orchid plants – so it's a big setback, no matter what. They'd just started to grow in the lab.'

'So what do you do about it?' April asked.

'It means starting over from scratch on whatever's been destroyed,' Josh said. 'It could only be worse if they decided to torch the place. First, I'll have to see exactly which cultures were destroyed. They're all numbered, so that'll be easy, just tedious. Then I'll have to try to replicate the destroyed ones. Very time-consuming.'

'I'll be glad to help in any way I can,' April offered. 'I know I'd have to learn, but I'd give it a try.'

'That's really thoughtful of you,' Josh replied, 'but I think you've got your hands full here. By the way, who was the guy helping out today?' he asked.

'Randy Jarvis,' April replied. 'He's worked with me

once or twice before, so I called to see if he could pick up the slack for Woody. Luckily, he was available and came on over.'

'That's great,' Josh said. 'Because I know you've got a lot to do.'

'You bet,' April said. Then she looked at Joanna. 'We've got a grotto to finish,' she said. 'Right?'

'Damn right, and fast!' Joanna said. Then she looked at April and smiled somewhat slyly. 'You can help out at the nursery later. In the future.'

They all laughed, but April felt as if she was being not so subtly pushed in a definite direction. She didn't mind. *No*, she told herself. *I don't mind at all. In fact, I like it very much.*

27

The days flew by in a whirlwind of activity, with April and Randy both working overtime to finish the grotto. Joanna often joined them, helping out, and sometimes she would spread out on a chaise and simply watch them, taking pleasure in the progress they made. But there were frequently days now when she retreated to the house, to rest alone in the privacy of her bedroom.

April never questioned her decisions, never made suggestions, or offered help. She knew that Joanna would ask for whatever help she needed, and she didn't want to intrude on her sense of self-reliance, of privacy, and of dignity. Nevertheless, she felt a deep-seated sorrow more powerful than any she had ever known before. It threatened to overwhelm her at times. But working on the grotto gave her a goal outside of herself. It was something to focus on, rather than giving in to the awful awareness of approaching death.

She knew that Joanna was slowly slipping away from them, but she knew that she was powerless over the outcome. Sometimes she could see a faraway look in Joanna's eyes, almost as if she had already left them or had glimpsed another, more desirable place and was only waiting patiently to go there.

April recognized the pain that Josh was suffering, but pleaded with him to go on as usual. He respected Joanna's wishes as much as possible, coming and going to work as if nothing were out of the ordinary, all the while aching inside.

It's no less than Joanna's doing, he often thought.

Work, fortunately, proved somewhat therapeutic. He lost himself in cataloguing the orchid crosses that had been destroyed and trying to re-create them. As winter approached, he also hoped that a special hybrid he'd created would be ready to show Joanna soon.

About a month after the last trouble at the lab, April went up to the house to have lunch. Joanna was feeling particularly well today, her eyes dancing, laughing and chatting away as if all were well.

Connie's replacement, a Peruvian cousin of Carl's named Elizabeth, had served dessert – a flan very much like Connie's – and Joanna and April sat at the table in the conservatory eating the last of it.

'That was delicious,' April said.

'It was, wasn't it?' Joanna agreed. 'We're so lucky

to have Elizabeth. She'll never be the confidante that Connie was, but ... well, maybe she'll be a little less treacherous.' She laughed lightly, and April couldn't help but laugh, too.

'Which reminds me,' Joanna said, picking up a local newspaper that lay on the chair next to her. 'I thought you might be interested in this.' She handed the newspaper to April.

April instantly recognized the woman in the photograph of a bride and groom. 'Oh, my God,' she uttered in disbelief. 'I ... I know what she told Josh, but still ... I can hardly believe it.'

CESPEDES-ROSSI VOWS EXCHANGED

Connie Louise Cespedes and Peter Anthony Rossi, both residents of Watsonville, were married Saturday by Judge Thomas Quinn in a civil ceremony in Watsonville. The groom is president of Rossi Brothers, Inc., an agribusiness that includes a wholesale nursery concern, and the bride is a vice president there.

April handed the newspaper back to Joanna. 'I guess they deserve each other.'

'Oh,' Joanna said mildly, 'I think they'll be very good for each other. They're both very aggressive and upwardly mobile. I hope Connie is happy with him, and I mean it. They do seem suited for each other. Just like Christina and Woody.'

April looked at her. 'Have you heard from her?' she asked.

Joanna nodded, then she smiled mischievously. 'She called this morning. I shouldn't gloat,' she said with amusement in her voice, 'because I know that Christina is in pain, but I can't help myself.' She paused for dramatic effect.

'What?' April asked. 'Oh, tell me, Joanna, before I explode.'

'My dear sister and Woody were married in Montecito,' she said.

'No!' April said.

'Yes,' Joanna said, laughing. 'And guess what?'

'What?' April asked.

'He's already fooling around on her,' Joanna replied. 'How do you like that for poetic justice?'

'It's a miserable state of affairs,' April said, 'but I can't say that it ruins my day.'

'Nor mine,' Joanna said. 'I've certainly told her how I feel about her carrying on with Peter Rossi – and Woody, for that matter – and I've forgiven her. But not before I gave her a piece of my mind.' She paused and looked at April. 'I think forgiveness is important,' she continued, 'because we can't carry around resentments. They only eat us up. The way I look at it now is that Christina will always be family, but not my family of choice. That's you and Josh.'

She reached over and took April's hand. 'Listen to me, April,' she said.

April nodded.

'I looked and looked,' she said, 'hoping to find the perfect partner for Josh when I'm gone. I suppose I was trying to play God.' Her violet eyes gleamed with happiness.

April felt lightheaded suddenly, as if none of this were real, as if Joanna couldn't possibly be uttering these words so calmly and clearly, but she listened without interrupting.

'Then fate brought you from out of the blue,' she continued. 'And you've made me so very happy. And Josh. Now I hope you'll both – you and Josh – honor my memory by going on living. Living life to the fullest.' She paused, a beatific smile on her lips. 'I won't say anything more. I think you . . . know what I mean.'

April didn't know what to say, but with tears in her eyes, she leaned over and kissed Joanna and hugged her tenderly.

'Now then,' Joanna said. 'I'm going to my room for a nap, and I'll be down later to inspect your work.' She rose to her feet and placed a hand on April's head, stroking it lightly. 'So get busy on our crazy grotto.'

She turned away, and April watched her leave the room, almost overwhelmed with emotion.

An hour later, glad that Joanna was asleep, April borrowed Randy's cell phone and stepped outside the grotto to make a call. She'd gotten the number from the telephone book when Joanna had gone upstairs to nap. She punched it into the cell phone now, and waited for an answer.

JUDITH GOULD

'Rossi Brothers, Inc.,' a woman answered on the third ring.

'Connie Rossi, please,' April said.

'Who may I say is calling?' the woman asked.

'April Woodward,' April said, hoping that using her name wouldn't end the call then and there.

'Just a moment, please.'

April waited patiently to see what would happen, then suddenly she heard Connie, unmistakably.

'April,' she said, her voice full of confidence, perhaps even cockiness. 'What do you want?'

'I just want to tell you that if Josh has any more trouble at the nursery,' April said, 'I'll go straight to the police. I'll gladly tell them that I saw you having sex with the night watchman to gain access to the lab and greenhouses, and I'll get Miguel to verify it. Not only that but Josh will tell them what you told him in the kitchen before you left here.'

Then she crossed her fingers and lied. 'Christina will also testify that Rossi pumped her for information about the nursery business.'

For a moment there was no response, then Connie said nastily, 'It's your word against mine.'

'No,' April said. 'It's my word, *plus* Miguel's word, *plus* Josh's word, *plus* Christina's.'

April crossed her fingers again. 'I think you should know, too, that we've already hired a lawyer in case anything else happens.' She took a breath. 'Finally, I'm very friendly with some newspaper people here, and you can be certain that there'll be a huge newspaper article

386

about the whole thing – including you and Miguel – if anything else happens. I think your wedding photo would look really great with the article.'

She could hear Connie sigh heavily.

'So I suggest you convince your husband that he'd better lay off,' she said. 'You understand?'

'Yeah,' Connie said slowly. 'I understand. But I don't think you need to worry about trouble. Nobody wants that small-time operation anymore.'

She slammed the receiver in April's ear.

April pushed the End button, then sat down and sighed in relief. She could only hope that her call would make a difference. There was no guarantee, but she thought that Connie, for whom appearances were very important – especially since she was now the wife of Mr Peter Rossi, a rich Anglo – would do everything in her considerable powers to persuade Peter Rossi to back off.

She got up and went back to the grotto, returning Randy's cell phone to him. Then she got busy, working away, determined to finish this grotto, for herself, for Josh, and for Joanna.

Joanna looked down toward the grotto from her bedroom window. She couldn't see what was happening, of course, but she could picture it in her mind's eye. She smiled to herself happily. It would soon be finished, and it would be beautiful. A fantasy fulfilled. For herself. For April and Josh.

She turned and picked up her handbag, then walked

downstairs to the entrance hall. She took a quick glance around at the polished surfaces, the gleaming beauty that her father had started and that she and Josh had nourished. She slipped out the front door and rushed to her little Mercedes convertible. She put on her sunglasses, backed out of the garage, turned around in the courtyard, and glanced at the gracious, vine-laden house. Then she drove out between the stone pillars, past the open gates, looking straight ahead.

April looked at her watch.

Almost quitting time, she thought, *and Joanna still hasn't been down. I wonder what's up? Maybe . . . maybe she's slept through this afternoon. She was so lively and talkative at lunch that maybe she was worn out.*

'You about ready to leave, Randy?' she asked.

'I'm already cleaning up, April,' he replied tiredly. 'You've been so lost in thought you didn't even notice. Me, I can't do another ounce of work today. I'm bushed.'

'Well,' she said, 'get a good night's rest because there'll be more of the same tomorrow.' She smiled. 'I really appreciate the overtime.'

'And I really appreciate the opportunity,' he said, 'not to mention the money.'

They both laughed.

Randy finished laying out his tools for tomorrow, then picked up his jacket. 'See you in the morning,' he said.

When he was gone, she took off her smock, and

brushed off her clothes vigorously. Then she took her tools to the pool house bathroom and washed them, then dried them off. She brushed her hair and washed her face and hands as best she could, deciding that she'd go check on Joanna before leaving.

She walked up to the house and saw that Elizabeth was in the kitchen. 'Where's Joanna?' she asked.

'I don't know,' Elizabeth replied. 'I haven't seen her since lunch.'

'Thanks,' April said. 'I'm going to check on her.' She walked to the entrance hall, then climbed the stairs to the second floor and quietly tiptoed down the hallway to Joanna and Josh's bedroom.

The door was slightly ajar, so April pushed on it silently, peeking in. The bed was empty.

She must be in the bathroom, April thought. She stepped into the bedroom and called out. 'Joanna?'

There was no response. 'Joanna?' she called again, louder this time.

She saw that the bathroom door was wide open, and she walked in. No Joanna. She left the bedroom, walking back downstairs. She searched the first-floor rooms, but there was no sign of her.

What the devil? April wondered.

She went into the kitchen again. 'Are you sure you haven't seen her since lunch?' she asked Elizabeth.

'No,' Elizabeth replied. 'Why? Is something wrong?'

'She's not here,' April said worriedly. 'Or at least I can't find her.'

She heard a car in the courtyard and rushed to the

entrance hall, thinking that it might be Joanna. She swung open the front door and dashed outside. Josh was hopping out of his Land Cruiser.

'Where's Joanna?' he asked.

'I don't know,' April said. 'I was just looking for her.'

'You don't know?' he cried in alarm. 'Her Mercedes is gone.'

'What?' April exclaimed. 'Oh, Josh, I don't know what to think. We had lunch together, then she went up to rest. She said she was coming down to the grotto, but she didn't. I just came up to check on her, and couldn't find her.' She paused, looking about her wildly, as if Joanna might appear, walking in out of thin air. 'I didn't even think to look for her car.'

'What about Elizabeth?' he asked, putting an arm around her shoulders. 'Did she hear her leave? Or did Joanna leave a message?'

April shook her head. 'No,' she said. 'Elizabeth told me she hadn't seen her since lunch.' She looked up at him worriedly. 'Where – where do you think she's gone? What on earth could she be doing?'

With his arm across her shoulders, they walked together to the house, then on into the kitchen. Josh questioned Elizabeth again but received the same answers. Then he poured two glasses of wine.

'Here,' he said, handing her one, 'let's sit down in the library and think this through.'

In the library, they sat down on the big leather Chesterfield, sipping their wine.

'How was she at lunch?' Josh asked.

'Extraordinary,' April replied. 'That's the best way to put it. She was brilliant, as if nothing in the world were wrong. More alert and funny and chatty and . . .' Her voice trailed off and tears came into her eyes, but she quickly brushed them away.

Josh set his glass down and put his arms around April. Then his lips chastely brushed her forehead. 'Please don't cry,' he said. 'I couldn't stand to see you cry.'

April felt his arms around her and then his lips against hers, and her heart leapt in her throat despite the awfulness of the situation. She put her arms around him and hugged him to her, for a moment at least keeping guilt at bay.

They sat like that for a long time, then hesitantly parted. 'I didn't mean to . . .'

'Don't worry about it, Josh,' April said. 'I'm as guilty as you are. I . . . I . . . oh, let's not think about it right now. We've got to find Joanna.'

He nodded, but he was already staring at the floor thoughtfully, as if in another world. April could see that his mind was working feverishly.

At last he looked up at her. 'I know where she is,' he said quietly. 'She has to be.'

'Where?' April asked.

'Will you come with me?' he asked.

She nodded. 'Of course I will.'

He jumped to his feet. 'Grab a jacket and let's go,' he said, making tracks toward the entrance hall.

They were out in his Land Cruiser and on the road in a minute.

The sun had set before they reached the exit off the freeway that led to the lonely strip of beach at Pajaro, just north of Moss Landing, but the moon was full, washing the landscape in an eerie silver glow. Storm clouds had gathered earlier, threatening rain, but so far they hadn't fulfilled their promise.

As they raced west, headed toward the Pacific Ocean, they passed between perfectly flat acres of Brussels sprouts, strawberries, broccoli, and artichokes. There were no other cars on this lonely stretch, and Josh sped relentlessly ahead, his eyes fixed on the empty road, rigid in his seat.

April didn't ask any questions because she didn't want to intrude on his silence, but now she knew where they were going, although she had never been there before.

The old beach house, she thought. *It makes perfect sense.*

She knew that the ocean and the old house held great significance for Joanna. It was also here that she had come all alone, to suffer, to try to come to grips with her mortality, and to lick her wounds like a dying animal. As much as she could understand Joanna's love for this place, a chill went up April's spine at the thought of Joanna being here alone, of possibly . . . coming here to . . . die.

Josh swerved the big Land Cruiser off the pavement onto a track made of crushed shells and sand. It was very narrow, and vegetation crowded in on both sides, as if wanting to reclaim it. April saw a rusty old metal gate ahead, wide open. From the end of the gate dangled a much newer-looking chain of heavy links.

Josh slowed down and reached across and took her hand in his, squeezing it gently. She looked over at him and, sensing her gaze, he glanced at her.

'She's here,' he said. 'She must be, with the gate open.'

He drove slowly past the gate and around a slight bend in the road. He heaved a sigh and braked with a jerk. Straight ahead, the chrome of Joanna's Mercedes reflected his headlights.

He looked at April. 'Do you want to wait out here?' he asked, his voice almost expressionless.

April shook her head. 'No,' she said, 'I'm coming with you.'

He leaned over and kissed her cheek, chastely and tenderly. 'Thanks,' he said.

They got out of the Land Cruiser, and Josh came around to her side. Together, they started walking through the sand toward the house. They could see a dim light burning somewhere within.

Suddenly a flash of lightning rent the night sky and then a clap of thunder, so loud and ominous that April almost cried aloud. A torrential deluge instantly followed, soaking them both to the skin before they could reach the porch at the back of the house.

When they reached its protection, Josh looked down at her. 'Okay?' he asked.

April nodded. 'Fine,' she said.

He held his keys out, ready to unlock the back door, but they saw that it was open. He pulled the screen door wide, letting April go in ahead of him, then closed it and the inner door, too.

Straight ahead, even in the virtual darkness, April could see all the way to the front of the house with its huge window that gave onto the Pacific. Overhead, the storm raged loudly against the roof and skylights.

Josh took her by both arms and looked down at her. 'You can wait here,' he said. 'She must be there . . . in the front bedroom. That's where the light's coming from.'

April looked up into his eyes. 'No,' she said. 'I want to be with you.'

He hugged her a moment, and then together they walked to the front bedroom. The door was open, and they could see Joanna on the bed. She appeared to be sleeping peacefully, a beatific expression on her face. She was slightly propped up on pillows so that she could see out the floor-to-ceiling window that faced the ocean.

The light they had seen came from a single lamp at the bedside, and in its pool of light was a bag with shells spilling out. No doubt, April thought, the treasures she'd found on her last walk on the beach.

Together they walked to the bed and gazed down upon her. She was not breathing. They stared at her helplessly, their eyes beginning to tear.

She looks alive and as beautiful as she always did, April thought. *Only asleep.*

Josh leaned down close, taking one of Joanna's hands

in his. Then he put his head down on her chest, listening for a heartbeat that he already knew wasn't there.

April stood watching, fully understanding his gesture, despite its futility.

Josh sat down on the bed and took Joanna's lifeless body in his arms, cradling her, rocking her gently, weeping silently, his body heaving. As the storm continued to rage, April's tears began to flow freely, and she didn't think she'd ever before felt such a sense of loss or such agonizing pain. She wondered if a pain this great, this soul-wrenching, would ever completely go away.

At long last, Josh gently laid Joanna back down. He leaned over and kissed her tenderly, then looked up at April.

She had seen sorrow and anguish on his face before but never like this, never of this intensity, she thought. Reaching down, she offered him her hand, and he took it, rising to his feet. Together they stood looking down at her, saying good-bye.

The End as the Beginning
Winter 2000–2001

Despite their grief, the rain-chilled days of winter passed swiftly for April and Josh. Now, though spring's rebirth was only faintly discernible, April could sense its impending arrival. She stood alone in the spectacular fantasy of the grotto, surveying the months of effort she had put in. The work, she reflected, had been awesome, painstaking, but it was Joanna's initial vision that was responsible for this exquisite creation. Without her vision, April reflected, none of it would have been possible.

Josh hadn't once ventured down to the grotto since Joanna's death, even though April had finished. It had simply been too difficult for him emotionally. April had dealt with her own sorrow by struggling to complete the grotto – and it had been a struggle – wanting to see the vision that she and Joanna had shared fully realized. She had also lent a hand at the nursery so that Josh could devote himself to hybridizing – creating the all-important new orchids that the future of the business depended upon.

Now, months later, the two of them had overcome their grief enough to consider a christening of the grotto. Tonight, she and Josh would celebrate Joanna's legacy at last.

April looked around the room with wonder, despite the fact that she had spent the better part of her time here for months. Every surface was covered with shells or pebbles. On the ceiling was the resplendent sky with many of its constellations, and on the walls were now fantastic 'paintings' of rare orchids, executed entirely in colorful shells.

In niches, set on neoclassical plinths, were plaster busts of men and women, once merely famous, now bizarre and fantastic creatures from another world, entirely encrusted with shells. The windows and doors were surrounded with garlands of shells that emulated the intricate and brilliant carvings of Grinling Gibbons.

In the center of the room was a small fountain, a simple birdbath-type affair set in a small circular pool. April had used pebbles here, in many shapes and sizes and textures, to give the effect of mosaics. She had done the same with the floor, creating a mosaic of sea creatures, some of them entwined in 'kelp' that resembled garlands of orchids. Two chandeliers, which hung on either side of the fountain, were encrusted with shells, and beneath them were silver-leafed Venetian tables and chairs, all carved in a shell motif. Each table held crystal hurricane candle holders, which April now lit.

On one of the tables she had placed a silver wine cooler, in which rested a bottle of Louis Roderer Cristal champagne. Two crystal champagne flutes, Russian antiques that April treasured, stood waiting to be filled.

Finally, she turned her attention to a central wall panel that until today had been covered with a large canvas drop cloth. She smiled to herself. She'd told no one what was behind the canvas.

It was a surprise that she had secretly worked out for several weeks. April looked at it with pride and satisfaction: a shimmering pearl-white orchid made almost entirely of abalone. Below it, its name was spelled out in a mosaic of sea-smoothed pebbles: *Phalaenopsis* Joanna. On one of the Venetian tables was an example of the orchid itself. A hybrid that Josh had secretly bred and named for Joanna, it was of the purest white and, like its shell counterpart, seemed to shimmer when the light struck it.

He had let April in on his secret, but she had saved her rendering of the orchid as a special surprise for him. She could hardly wait to see the look on Josh's face when he saw the shell mural of the orchid for the first time.

She stood back and surveyed the scene once more.

'Oh, yes,' she said aloud, 'we can finally have that champagne tonight. To celebrate the grotto's completion.'

It was, she decided, more a work of art than mere craftsmanship. She looked from individual shell to individual shell: *Laliotis ruber, Lischkea imperialis, Spondylas princeps,* and *Wrightianus, Babelomurex spinosus, Ocinebra erinaceus,* the provocatively named *Purpura patual.*

My Lord, she thought, I've learned so much doing this. Not just about the shells themselves, but about design and execution. And possibilities. Oh, yes, she thought, most important of all about possibilities. Joanna had helped her to see the infinite creative potential in these humble, if beautiful, materials.

She switched off the chandeliers and started out of the grotto, on her way to get Josh, but turned once more and peered into the room. *And friendship and love,* she reflected. *I've learned more about friendship and love than I ever thought possible.*

April went into the grotto first and made certain the candles were still burning, then turned on the chandeliers and dimmed them to a romantic glow. She turned on the fountain, which began its singsong tinkle and splash. The effect of the whole was enchantingly breathtaking. Satisfied that everything was perfect, she stepped back outside to tell Josh that he could come in now.

'You sure it's finally ready?' he teased, hesitating to cross the threshold.

'Finito,' April said with a smile.

'Then let's christen it!' he said, stepping into the room.

His blue eyes swept around the room slowly, taking in its many splendors, and as they did, an expression of awe began to replace the amusement that had been on his face.

April watched the transformation with a growing sense of pride and accomplishment. Yet at the same time she was unnerved by his silence, a silence that stretched on and on as he continued to survey the scene. She desperately wanted him to be as pleased as she knew Joanna would have been, and she needn't have worried.

Finally his eyes came to rest on her. For a moment he was distracted by the beautiful Hermès scarf she was wearing. It was the one with the seashell motif that Joanna had given her. Then those handsome blue eyes gazed directly into hers.

'Well,' he said, 'you've done exactly what she wanted. Only more.' He paused for a moment, then smiled. 'It's exquisite, April, and I love it.'

April breathed a sigh of relief, and Josh, hearing it, put his arms around her and hugged tightly. 'You couldn't possibly think that I wouldn't be crazy about it, could you?'

'I hoped,' April said.

He laughed, then chucked her under her chin and kissed her lips. 'Now,' he said, 'let's have that champagne.'

He uncorked the Cristal, filled the two flutes, and handed one to April.

'I want to propose a toast,' he said.

April held her glass aloft, next to his.

'To life,' he said. 'And to our future,' he added.

'And to our future,' April echoed as she clinked glasses with him.

Unbidden, her heart surged in her chest, and despite the anguish of the last few months, she felt an excitement, a need and desire, that propelled her forward to *him*.

Josh put down his glass, and April followed suit. He put his hands on her shoulders and looked down into her eyes. She gazed up at him, an expectant look on her face.

On his handsome features, she could clearly see the toll that the last few months had taken. She had seen it in the mirror. Nevertheless, the bone weariness that had dwelled in his eyes for so long was disappearing, and the immeasurable sadness had slowly begun to ebb.

The grief that had enveloped them both was gradually being replaced by a renewed interest in life, in each other, and in love.

She stroked his lean, tanned face with a slender finger. He took her hand, squeezing it gently in his own. She hadn't wanted to disturb his quietude, to interrupt the thoughts that she knew must be coursing through his mind, as they were through her own.

'This is exactly how she would have wanted it,' he said simply, extending an arm as if to encompass the grotto. Then his eyes looked deeply into hers again, and he stroked her cheek tenderly. 'And so is this.' A hint of a smile spread across his lips. 'This is all part of her legacy. The grotto . . . and our love.'

April nodded and returned his smile, holding his gaze. His sunbleached hair had fallen into his eyes, and she reached up and pushed it away, then tenderly kissed his cheek.

'Yes,' she said softly. 'It's all part of Joanna's legacy. It's a new world, a new life, and her love for you – and me – paved the way for it.'

He embraced her, tightly enfolding her in his powerful arms, and together they began a celebration of their new life, of their love for one another.